THE VOICES WERE BACK!

Greg was *positive* he had heard them last night. Even now, they seemed to be lurking. He imagined pairs of eyes gazing at him from behind. Closing his eyes, he pressed his knuckles against the sides of his head.

Please! . . . Don't let them start again! . . . Please make them stop!

This wasn't the first time Greg had heard voices. Only recently he'd begun to connect them to his robberies. He pounded the sides of his head, but nothing seemed to stop the voices.

He cried out loud when he saw a small, distorted face peering in at him. The stray cat's narrow yellow eyes watched him with a steady glare, and it did not run off when he opened the window. Greg's hand closed like a vise around the cat's scrawny neck. It started hissing and clawing the air.

"You think you can trick me?"

He shook the cat violently, then started applying a slow, steady pressure to the cat's neck. It's eyes bulged and it's tongue stuck out as it feebly struggled to stay alive.

"Did you bring the cops here?"

Greg snapped the cat's neck.

HORROR FROM HAUTALA

SHADES OF NIGHT   (0-8217-5097-6, $4.99)
Stalked by a madman, Lara DeSalvo is unaware that she is
most in danger in the one place she thinks she is safe—
home.

TWILIGHT TIME   (0-8217-4713-4, $4.99)
Jeff Wagner comes home for his sister's funeral and uncov-
ers long-buried memories of childhood sexual abuse and
murder.

DARK SILENCE   (0-8217-3923-9, $5.99)
Dianne Fraser fights for her family—and her sanity—
against the evil forces that haunt an abandoned mill.

COLD WHISPER   (0-8217-3464-4, $5.95)
Tully can make Sarah's wishes come true, but Sarah lives
in terror because Tully doesn't understand that some wishes
aren't meant to come true.

LITTLE BROTHERS   (0-8217-4020-2, $4.50)
Kip saw the "little brothers" kill his mother five years ago.
Now they have returned, and this time there will be no es-
cape.

MOONBOG   (0-8217-3356-7, $4.95)
Someone—or some*thing*—is killing the children in the little
town of Holland, Maine.

IMPULSE

Rick Hautala

Pinnacle Books
Kensington Publishing Corp.

http://www.pinnaclebooks.com

PINNACLE BOOKS are published by

Kensington Publishing Corp.
850 Third Avenue
New York, NY 10022

Pinnacle and the P logo Reg. U.S. Pat. & TM Off.

First Printing: November, 1996

Printed in the United States of America
10 9 8 7 6 5 4 3 2 1

To my sister, Louise, and her family—Bob, Devin, and Brian

"May you always have a strong wind at your backs and a following sea. . . ."

Acknowledgments

Too many people help in too many ways, and I generally miss thanking too many of them in print, but this time around I want to thank a few people who are always there at the other end of the phone line and the lifeline.

First of all, thanks to Jimmy Vines, my agent, for his faith and support and enthusiasm.

Also, I want to thank Tom and Elizabeth McDonald, by any standards, friends solid and true.

I also want to thank the *other* "Tom and Elizabeth"—the Monteleones—as well as my brother Bob, Peter Straub, Charlie Grant, Jim and Bonnie Moore, all of the folks at White Wolf, Jill Morgan, Chet "Anthony N." Williamson, Bill Relling, Rich and Kara Chizmar, Doug Winter, Chelsea Quinn Yarbro, Matt, Anne Costello (of course!), Mike Kimball, Chris and Davene Fahy, Roman Ranieri, Joe Lansdale, and *mi amigo* Steve Bissette. It's people like you that make this crazy business . . . well, at least tolerable.

And, of course, I want to thank Bonnie, Aaron, Jesse, and Matti, and my parents for love, faith, and trust.

"There is advantage in the wisdom won from pain."

—Aeschylus (*The Eumenides*)

Part One
The Monster Hunter

"If we do not change our direction, we are likely to end up where we are headed."

—A Chinese Proverb

Chapter 1
Holdup

"Where's your brother?"

Angie Ross tried hard not to yell, but she was scowling as she entered the house and slammed the kitchen door shut behind her.

The weather outside was miserable, and she couldn't stop her teeth from chattering as she stamped her feet on the rug to remove the chunks of snow that clung to her boots. Brandy, her sixteen-year-old daughter, scowled right back at her as she cradled the telephone against her shoulder, cupped her hand over the receiver, and smiled at her mother.

"Hi, Mom. How was the meet—"

"Why are you on the phone?" Angie snapped, abruptly cutting off Brandy's greeting. "You told me that you had tons of homework to do."

With a casual yet defiant flip of her head, Brandy indicated the living room doorway and said, "JJ's playing Nintendo— like always, and I already finished my homework. What's the big sweat?"

Letting her shoulders slump, Angie took a calming breath and rubbed her forehead with one gloved hand. The leather was cold, almost numbing to the touch. A jab of pain stabbed her sinuses just above her eyes. She knew that she was overreacting because of what had happened at the school board meeting tonight, but still . . .

She glanced at the clock on the kitchen wall and saw that it was almost eleven-thirty.

"It's a school night, in case you didn't remember. You *both* should have been in bed *hours* ago."

She peeled off her gloves, tossed them onto the counter, then shrugged out of her heavy coat and hung it on one of the pegs beside the door. The snow that had fallen from her boots was already melting into the rug. She muttered a curse when she kicked off her boots and stepped into one of the ice cold puddles.

Brandy, who was perched with her stocking feet up on the counter and leaning back against the cupboard, whispered something into the receiver and then switched it off before hopping down to the floor.

"I had to talk to Jeff," she said with a high whine twisting her voice. "And I'm not gonna just sit there watching him play those stupid games."

She replaced the radio phone on its base, all the while eying her mother, trying to gauge her wrath.

"You're *not* supposed to *be* on the phone after ten o'clock," Angie snapped. "You know the rules."

Brandy turned and started walking away, muttering something under her breath that Angie didn't quite catch. After peeling off her wet socks, Angie followed her daughter into the living room where John Junior—or JJ as everyone called him—was frantically scooping up the games he had spread out across the carpet.

"And *you,* young man!" Angie said, wagging a finger at him.

"I . . . I didn't know what time it was," JJ said, shifting away from his mother to be out of striking range.

"Is your homework done?"

"Yeah . . . well, mostly," JJ replied.

Brandy stood in the hallway by the stairs, watching all of this. Angie turned and glared at her again.

"It's your *sister's* fault for not paying attention to what's going on around here. There are going to be consequences," she said, slapping her hand for emphasis.

"I knew *exactly* what was going on," Brandy shouted, her body stiffening defiantly. "Jeeze, Mom. He's twelve years old. It's not like he needs a friggin' babysitter or anything."

"Watch your mouth," Angie said sharply, but even as she did, she knew that it wasn't really the kids she was angry at. It was the asinine majority vote of the Bedford Heights school board tonight that had essentially killed the Gifted and Talent Program for next year . . . and with one stroke, put her out of a job come June.

Angie fought to keep her voice under control. She didn't like to spank her kids, especially now that they were so old, but sometimes—like now, when they pushed her limits—she was sorely tempted to.

"You're *not* supposed to be on the phone after ten o'clock! How many times do I have to tell you that?"

"At least I was downstairs," Brandy said. She still had that irritating whine in her voice that made Angie want to slap her. "I could have been up in my—"

"You're grounded from the phone tomorrow, young lady," Angie said, slicing the air with a quick chop of her hand. "And if you give me any more mouth, it'll be for the rest of the week! Do you understand?"

"Yeah, but I was just—"

"Did your father call?" Angie said, cutting her off again.

Brandy thought for a moment, then shook her head.

"Nope."

"Are you sure? I hope you answered the Call Waiting if it beeped?"

"Of *course* I did."

"I'm sure." Angie's frown deepened. "You wouldn't want to miss any calls from your friends, would you? Dad didn't call and say when he'd be home?"

Brandy was gnawing at her lower lip as she shook her head. JJ, meanwhile, had finished collecting his games and shoved them onto the bottom shelf where he kept them. He snapped off the TV and stood in a nervous hunch, still keeping an arm's length away from his mother.

"Both of you go upstairs right now and brush your teeth and get into bed," Angie said, forcing herself to take it down a notch. "I've had one *helluva* day."

Without another word, both kids turned and scurried upstairs. Angie stood at the foot of the stairs, gripping the banister tightly as she listened as one of them—probably JJ—went into the bathroom and hurriedly brushed his teeth.

"'Night, Mom," he called out.

"G'night, JJ. Tuck in now . . . Love you. Love you, too, Brandy."

"Uh-huh," was all Brandy could manage.

"Thanks for covering for me," Angie said, but this time Brandy didn't respond.

Angie waited at the foot of the stairs until the upstairs hall light winked out, and she heard the kids' bedroom doors shut. Through the floor, she could hear their bedsprings squeak as they climbed into their beds. Then, with a heavy sigh that seemed to originate deep inside her, she walked out into the kitchen. Without any hesitation or deliberation, she took a glass from the cupboard and the bottle of whiskey from below the sink, and poured herself an inch or two. She usually didn't drink, but tonight—Jesus, she *more* than needed it!

She wondered how John would react when she told him she was out of a job.

The thought left her with a cold tightening in her gut. She sighed and tilted her head back to take a sip, gasping and closing her eyes as the warm liquor exploded on her tongue. She swallowed, and when it hit her stomach, a thin tendril of warmth spread up to her throat. When she looked at the clock again and saw that it was now well past eleven-thirty, the tension inside her strengthened.

Where the hell is John?

He should have been home by now. He was scheduled to get off duty at eight o'clock.

She went to the kitchen door, wincing as she stepped into the melting snow again, and looked out at the thick night. She could see pencil-thin lines of falling snow around the halo of light cast by the streetlight down by the road.

She shivered and took another sip of whiskey.

It wasn't the snow that worried her, nor was it the icy driving conditions.

It was John's line of work.

And come June, unless she found something else, they were going to have to get by on just his salary as a New York City detective.

"Damn it," she muttered.

Her face was close enough to the window to fog the glass. The way her reflection was distorted made it look like her eyes were filling up with tears.

Greg Newman was feeling wired long before he entered the little convenience store between Casey's Pub and the abandoned warehouse of Scott's Electrical Parts Company on West Forty-seventh Street. The bright fluorescent lights hurt his eyes, and for just a moment, he imagined that both of his eyeballs were being stung by invisible wasps. He'd been stung by wasps before, so he could imagine what that would feel like.

Maybe that's what made him lose it the way he did sometimes, he thought, smiling thinly. Those damned bright lights!

Or maybe it was the man behind the counter.

The skinny little Asian-looking guy—Greg didn't even try to guess his nationality—eyed him suspiciously the moment he walked in. The door closed behind him, cutting off the cold blast of air and wind-blown snow.

Greg didn't like to think about things too much. All he knew was that the little man sure as hell *looked* like a foreigner, so what was he doing taking a job away from a *real* American?

If that was the case, then it really didn't matter what happened to him, did it?

Walking boldly up to the counter, Greg smiled and said, "Cold enough, ain't it?"

Greg was wearing gloves, and when he rubbed his hands to

warm them, they made a wet, slapping sound that sounded a bit like he had punched someone in the face.

The man nodded a greeting but said nothing.

Greg saw the man shift away from the counter. He figured the guy had a gun or some kind of protection stashed there, and he didn't like the looks of Greg, and was getting ready to defend himself if he had to.

Greg didn't care because *he* didn't much like the looks of this skinny little foreign guy, either. Here it was, the middle of January, and he's at work wearing nothing but a white T-shirt and faded jeans that were full of holes. The man didn't even know how to dress properly for a New York City winter!

Still smiling, Greg leaned forward with both fists knuckled against the counter. The baseball bat he was carrying nestled inside the lining of his coat hit the counter with a muffled thump.

"Gimme a couple of them lottery tickets, why don't 'cha?" Greg said, hoping the man hadn't heard the noise.

Narrowing his gaze, the man looked at Greg but didn't move.

"Do you even understand English?" Greg said. "I want-e - to buy-e a Lottery ticket-e. Comprendo? . . . Capace?"

"Yeah. Sure thing," the man said in flawless English.

For another beat, he regarded Greg coolly. Then, dropping his guard just a notch, he moved over to the Lottery display and unlocked it. Greg was still all smiles as he watched the man move with such careful deliberation. He was young, and Greg thought he looked strong, especially for his size. His arm muscles rippled in the bright store light. Greg figured he must work out at the gym with all those other greasy, muscle-bound buddies of his.

The instant the man's hands were away from the counter, Greg reached inside his coat and whipped out the baseball bat. Brandishing it above his head, he said casually, "Now you just keep-e your hands right there on top of that case, you dig-e?"

The man stiffened.

His arm muscles stood out like steel cables beneath his dark skin. A gleam of understanding lit his liquid brown eyes, but other than that, the man didn't react. He leaned forward and placed both hands on the display.

"I don't want any trouble," the man said, his voice low and sounding almost resigned, as if this had happened to him more times than he cared to recall. "There's not much more than fifty bucks in the register."

Greg didn't like the way this guy didn't seem very afraid.

Who the hell did he think he was?

He should be shitting his pants because Greg was all set to bash his fucking head in.

"It's fifty bucks I didn't have before I came in here," Greg said as he reached over the counter and started pressing keys on the register, trying to get it to open. After poking most of the keys a few times, he slammed the top of the machine with the baseball bat hard enough to make it ring. Still it didn't open.

"How the fuck do you open this?"

The man still didn't react. He seemed to be almost smiling as he regarded Greg coolly.

"Are you laughing at me? *Are you?*" Greg shouted. Spittle flew from his lips.

The man's expression remained neutral.

"Don't you be laughing at me, asshole! Why the fuck don't you go back to Cambodia or wherever the hell you came from?"

"I was born in Queens," the man replied.

Greg's face flushed as he jabbed the tip of the bat at the man.

"Queens, huh? Well I don't give a flying fuck! You open that goddamned register right *now,* or you're gonna be one sorry mother-fucker from Queens!"

The man raised his hands above his head and took a sliding step closer to the register. Greg backed off a step, keeping the baseball bat poised, ready to swing if the man made a move.

"I mean it, mister, I don't want any trouble," the man said as he lowered one hand to the machine.

"You take it nice and easy, mother-fucker, and you won't get hurt," Greg said.

His voice was low and steady, and didn't reveal how nervous

he really was. He didn't like it when things went wrong like this. He didn't like complications. He wanted to grab the money and get the hell out of here, not stand here chatting all night with some grease-ball.

Greg was ready for the man to try something, but still, he was surprised at how fast he moved.

As his left hand was reaching slowly toward the cash register, he suddenly dropped down below the edge of the counter and grabbed for something on the lower shelf. He was already coming up with a small pistol in his hand by the time Greg could react. With a loud shout, Greg swung the bat around in a whistling arc that connected with the side of the man's head. The impact made a hollow *thump* that sounded like he'd smashed a watermelon.

"Fuck you, you don't!" Greg shouted. His hands vibrated from the sudden impact.

The man slammed back against the display of medications on the shelf behind him. Bottles of cough syrup and liquid Tylenol exploded. Green and maroon liquid splashed onto the wall and floor, mixing with the dark red blood that had sprayed across the display.

The man moaned once, very softly, as he clutched the side of his head with both hands and slumped to the floor, his legs splayed wide. Streamers of blood that glistened brightly in the fluorescent light poured from his nostrils and left ear. The blood seeped between his fingers and stained his clean, white T-shirt. His left eye was bulging from the socket, and the white of his eye rapidly changed to bright red.

For a trembling moment, the man looked up at Greg with a glazed look as he focused past Greg on something in the middle distance. His lips moved as he tried to say something, but bloody foam issued out of his mouth and dripped onto his chest. He coughed once, then with a sigh slumped back against the smashed display. His eyes were wide open, unblinking and staring.

A charge of adrenalin was making Greg's body hum like a frayed high-powered cable as he stood back and looked down at what he had done.

The sense of release, of pure, ultimate satisfaction was incredible. His heart was slamming heavily in his chest, pushing against his ribs like a caged animal seeking release. He felt weak in the knees, and his hands were trembling out of control as he took a deep breath, held it for a few seconds, and then let it out slowly. It was a long time before his pulse began to slow down enough for him to realize where he was and what had just happened . . . What he had done!

He looked in amazement at his hands, which still gripped the handle of the baseball bat. Droplets of blood dotted the back of his gloves like strawberry freckles.

Ever so slowly, Greg relaxed his neck and shoulder muscles, groaning as he eased his grip on the bat.

There was no denying how great he felt.

Jesus, better than great!

He felt fucking *invincible!*

"Teach you to give me shit," he whispered.

Greg couldn't stop the sharp bray of laughter that burst out of him, but he was pissed when he realized that the man was already dead. All along he'd been planning to kill the foreign little son of a bitch, but he wished now that he'd had a little more time to taunt the asshole before he checked out, but what the hell? At least he had the money.

After glancing over his shoulder to make sure no one out on the street had seen what was going on, Greg leaped over the counter. Straddling the dead man's legs, he slammed the side of the register as hard as he could with the bat. The drawer made a *ka-ching* sound as it popped open.

"You lying sack of shit," Greg muttered when he saw the thick stack of twenties piled up in the cash slot. He stuffed the bills including the ones into his pants pocket, then pulled out the cash drawer and threw it onto the floor as he looked to see if there were any fifties or hundreds hidden underneath. He found two one-hundred dollar bills and smiled as he folded them into his pocket before slamming the drawer shut.

"'Bout time someone punched your green card, don't you think?" he said as he looked at the dead man on the floor.

Without a pulse or blood pressure, the blood had stopped

flowing. The man was sitting in a wide puddle of blood, and it looked like he had pissed his pants before he died.

Whistling a happy little tune, Greg wiped the smear of blood off the baseball bat and stuck it back into the lining of his coat. Walking casually around the counter, he headed for the front door but just as he about to leave, a small, elderly woman, her face muffled in her coat collar and scarf, came to the door. She glanced quickly at Greg, obviously not yet aware of what had just happened here.

Greg smiled widely and nodded at her.

He figured she wouldn't be able to identify him later, but just in case, he held the door open for her and waited until she had passed him before pulling the bat out of his coat. He turned around quickly, raised the bat over his head, and brought it down hard, like a chopping ax onto the woman's head.

There was a satisfying *crack,* and the old woman dropped to the floor as if someone had suddenly yanked her legs out from under her.

"Bad timing, bitch," Greg muttered.

He was just straightening up, getting ready to leave, when he saw the flicker of blue and red lights coming down the street.

"Shit," he whispered, glancing up and down the street to see if anyone was watching him. This late at night, the street was mostly deserted. Either the asshole at the counter had set off a silent alarm, or else someone had seen what was going on and called the cops.

Patting his pants pocket to make sure he still had the wad of cash, Greg left the store, turning left and heading away from the store and the approaching police cruiser as fast as he could go without drawing attention to himself. The winding sound of the cruiser's siren filled the night.

"There's plenty of teaching jobs up here. Why don't you consider moving up here? You've been saying for years how you want to get out of the city."

"We're not *in* the city," Angie said.

She grunted and took a tiny sip of whiskey. Even a small

amount was strong enough to make her sniff and almost choke. It was late, almost midnight, and John still wasn't home, so she had decided to call her brother, Rob, who lived in Bolton, Maine. Rob was a few years older and still, no matter how old she got—especially after their parents died—she considered him the second person she had to talk to whenever she had a problem or an important decision to make.

"You know what I mean," Rob said.

"Yeah, but it's not that simple," Angie replied. "John's still got his job."

"I thought you were pushing him to take early retirement." Rob's voice was low, prodding. "With his credentials, I'm sure he could get a job on the local police force. And I'm positive we could find something for you. In fact, I heard just last week that one of the teachers at Canal School, the elementary school, is pregnant. That'll mean a permanent substitute position when she goes on maternity leave."

"Oh, sure . . . It sounds great, but *you* try convincing John that we should move to Maine."

"Uh—no thanks," Rob said.

He laughed softly, but Angie detected the tightness in his laugh. As much as John and Rob maintained that they "liked" each other as family, they didn't have an awful lot in common. Rob saw John as pretty much a hard-ass kind of guy, made even more callous from years of working as a New York City detective, and Angie was sure, although he never said as much, that her husband felt at least a little bit awkward around Rob because he was gay.

"I'm just so *pissed* about what the school board did!" Angie said, feeling angry all over again. "The superintendent said he'd try to find another place for me within the system, but it's like—I can't *stand* the way they're cutting back on things like the Gifted and Talented Program! The things kids need most!"

"Welcome to the nineties," Rob said. "But seriously, Sis. Why not talk to him about it again?"

Angie opened her mouth and almost said something, but caught herself. Blinking her eyes rapidly, she took a deep breath as she focused on the dark rectangle of the living room window and the halo of falling snow she could see beyond it.

"I . . . I really *need* a job," she said, as much to herself as to Rob.

"Do you mean because you're gonna do it? You're thinking of leaving him?"

Hearing it said so directly hit Angie like a metal spike being driven through her stomach.

"No. I mean—well, I don't know *what* I'm going to do," she stammered, shifting her eyes toward the stairway to make sure Brandy or JJ weren't lurking there, listening to her conversation.

"You've been saying for a couple of years now that you're not really happy with the marriage, and that you want out."

Angie genuinely appreciated the concern she heard in her brother's voice, but still . . .

"I know," she said, her voice rasping hoarsely, "but it's . . . more complicated than that."

"You don't think it wouldn't drive the point home if you told him that you were moving to Maine, and that he could come or not if he chose?"

"It's not that easy."

"I *know* it's not that easy, Sis. Believe me. But it can't be any easier living the way you do."

"Yeah," Angie replied weakly.

She blinked her eyes rapidly, trying to stem the tears she could feel building up and getting ready to spill.

How many nights have there been like this over the last twenty years? she wondered.

How many times have I sat home alone, watching and waiting and worried as all hell that something bad's happened to him?

How many late nights have I had to sit here alone and wondering if my husband's been shot or beaten up or stabbed?

How long do I have to worry that I'm going to have to raise my children without their father who's been killed in the line of duty?

And how many more nights of this can I take?

"Hey, I just want what's best for you, Sis," Rob said mildly.

"You know that. If that means bailing out of the marriage and moving up here, then that's what it will take."

"Yeah, but I don't *want* to bail out," Angie said, cringing at the hard rasp in her voice. "I still love him, Rob. I really do. It's just that—that after being married as long as we have been, and the stress of his job and all, and now losing my teaching job, it's . . . the pressure's building up. I don't know what to do!"

"So why not come up for a visit?" Rob suggested. "Sounds to me like you could use a little time off. It's been—what? Five years at least since you've come up and visited me and Craig."

Angie didn't have the heart to tell him that the primary reason they never came up north to visit was because John felt so uncomfortable about Rob's living arrangements.

"I—I'll have to think about it," she said.

"Well you just hang in there, Sweetie. You know Craig and I are pulling for you."

"I know . . . Thanks," Angie said.

She tried to stop the tears but couldn't. Thin, warm streams ran down her cheeks.

"And stop worrying so damned much," Rob said emphatically. "You're a terrific person and a great teacher. I'm sure you'll find another job—something even better, probably!"

Angie tried to speak, but her voice choked off.

"So you get your little fanny to bed now," Rob said, "and I'll give you a buzz tomorrow night to see how things are going, okay?"

"Okay. Thanks," Angie said, hearing the edge in her voice.

She paused and licked her lips as she wiped the tears with the heel of her hand.

"I love you, Rob," she said softly.

"I love you, too, Sis," Rob said, and then he cut the connection, leaving Angie with a loud, droning buzz in her ear before she switched off the radio phone.

Outside, the snow was still falling.

Angie noticed that her glass was empty, but she didn't remember finishing her drink. She was feeling too wrung out even to get up and walk all the way to the kitchen for another one, so instead she just sat there on the couch in the darkness, watching the snow streak past the streetlight across the street.

And she waited . . . as she had waited far too many times for far too many years.

Chapter 2
Flight

Greg could feel the baseball bat banging against his leg inside his coat as he ran down the sidewalk past the boarded-over front of the electrical supply building. The snow was still falling, but the air was warming, so it melted as soon as it hit the pavement. The sidewalk was a slushy mess that splashed beneath his feet as he ran, soaking his pants and overcoat.

This could have turned out better, Greg thought when he glanced over his shoulder and saw the cruiser's flashing lights bearing down on him.

Without thinking, he ducked into the nearest alleyway just as the cruiser squealed to a stop in front of the convenience store. The blaring sound of the siren cut off, fading away like a dying shriek, but the emergency bar lights stayed on, flashing like summer lightning across the street and surrounding buildings.

The mouth of the alleyway was pitch black, but Greg could see that it dead-ended a little more than a hundred feet back. He couldn't be sure, but it looked like there was a large dumpster and heaps of trash blocking his way. The ground was littered with sodden trash.

"Mother *fucker,*" Greg muttered. He ran about halfway

down the alleyway and then stopped. He was feeling winded and had to lean forward with his hands braced on his knees as he tried to catch his breath.

When he looked back toward the mouth of the alleyway, he could still see the flashing police lights reflecting off the brick walls and the wet street. The shadows in the alley danced and weaved sickeningly as Greg looked around frantically for somewhere to go, somewhere to hide, but then—suddenly— he froze.

A hint of motion in the darkness down on one side of the alley drew his attention.

Icy tension filled him as he crouched behind the dumpster and stared into the engulfing darkness. He was positive that he had seen . . . something . . . something large enough to be a person—maybe several people—hunched in the doorway of the abandoned supply building.

The surrounding shadows seemed to intensify, growing deeper and denser with every pulse of light. Greg could easily imagine faces materializing out of the darkness and staring at him with blank, unblinking eyes, like that Oriental guy he'd just wasted. He listened to the soft hiss of falling snow and the strong gusts of wind whistling in the alleyway. He could almost imagine that below that he heard voices, whispering to him from the shadows.

"Man, I gotta get the fuck out of here," he whispered, hearing the high tremor in his voice.

He was sure it wouldn't take the cops long to notice his footprints in the slush and follow him down here.

He had to think of something.

Fast!

He had just decided to ditch the baseball bat in the dumpster and walk out of here as bold as could be when he saw another cop car pull up with a squeal of tires on the wet pavement. This one stopped at the mouth of the alleyway so its headlights were angled into it. The sudden brightness illuminated everything on one side of the alleyway in stark detail.

Peeking around the edge of the dumpster, Greg watched as a figure, that looked solid black against the glaring lights behind it got out of the cruiser and started moving slowly down the alleyway. He could see that it was a patrolman, and that he had his revolver drawn and at ready.

"Shit! Fuck!" Greg muttered as he punched the sides of his head with his gloved fists.

Suddenly, a high-powered flashlight winked on, and a strong, narrow beam of light swept back and forth across the alleyway. The oval of light rippled like glowing water across the uneven brick work of the building. The piles of trash stood out like jagged mountains.

Crouching low, Greg gripped the baseball bat so tightly it hurt the palms of his hand. Very faintly, below the scuff of approaching footsteps, he could hear the static and buzz of voices over the police radio. Every sharp *click* of shoe leather on the wet pavement set Greg's teeth on edge. He cringed against the dumpster, watching and waiting as the yellow light got closer.

"I know you're down here! Come on out with your hands up!"

The cop's voice was deep and echoed oddly in the narrow recesses of the alley. It sounded much too close to Greg as he looked around, fully expecting to see other faces materializing from out of the darkness behind him.

"What you got there, Pete?" another voice called out.

Greg guessed that this was the cop's partner, who was waiting in the cruiser behind the harsh glare of lights.

"I thought I saw someone run down here," Pete replied. "How's the guy and the lady in the store doing?"

"They're ten-seven," the partner shouted. "I've already called for backup and the ME."

Greg watched and listened as the cop's footsteps and beam of light drew steadily closer. He didn't know what ten-seven meant, but he hoped to God it meant that foreign little son of a bitch was dead meat. Greg was hoping against hope that the cop wouldn't notice his footprints or his steaming breath rising up from behind the dumpster. As he got closer, step by step, Greg shifted around the side of the dumpster. A few more steps, and the cop would be right beside him. Greg had been holding his breath so long he was starting to get dizzy. It was just a matter of seconds before either this cop or his partner saw him.

The policeman waiting back at the cruiser started talking into the radio microphone, but he was too far away for Greg to make out what he was saying. Gripping the baseball bat so tightly his wrists and forearms throbbed, Greg coiled up inside himself and waited for just the right moment.

The cop was still swinging his flashlight back and forth, scanning the building at the back of the alley. He was close enough to Greg so he could hear the soft rasp of his breathing. His breath misted in the air like smoke. He sounded like he'd had too many donuts in his lifetime.

The cop was just turning to start back toward his partner when Greg pushed off and, raising the bat high above his head, brought it down on the cop from behind.

The cop didn't cry out or make any other sound as he wheeled around and reflexively raised the hand holding the flashlight to protect his face. With his other hand, he tried to bring his gun up, but he wasn't nearly fast enough.

The bat came down in a whistling arc that knocked his upraised arm aside, shattering the bones in his forearm before ending with a dull *thump* that caved in his forehead. The cop's finger reflexively squeezed the trigger of his gun, and there was a sudden, bright flash and *bang*. Greg heard the bullet zing off the dumpster a few inches above his head.

"Bitch!" he muttered as he pulled back and swung again, connecting with the side of the cop's head. The impact sent an electric shudder up Greg's arms all the way to his neck.

With a stunned, stupid expression on his face, the cop went suddenly limp and then dropped silently to the ground. His flashlight fell from his lifeless hand and winked out when it hit the pavement and then rolled away into a pile of wet trash.

Just to make sure the cop was going to stay down, Greg spread his feet wide and took a third, solid swing at the back of his head. He smiled wickedly when he heard the wet crackle of splintering skull. A thick, wet mass seeped out of the back of the cop's head. His body twitched a little, but he never made another sound.

Stepping quickly over the fallen man, Greg waved the bloody baseball above his head as he charged toward the cop in the cruiser who glanced up and saw him coming. Throwing aside the radio mike, he scrambled to get out of the cruiser but, like his partner, he wasn't quite fast enough. He was reaching around to unholster his service revolver when the baseball bat caught him squarely in the jaw. He grunted as the impact knocked him backwards across the front seat.

It was a glancing blow, and the swing was strong enough to carry Greg halfway around. He almost lost his balance but couldn't help but laugh when he saw dark blood gushing from the cop's mouth. The windshield and dashboard were marked by a wide swatch of blood that looked like wet spray paint. Greg swung again, but he miscalculated the angle and hit the side window of the cruiser, shattering it into a spray of diamonds.

"You *son* of a *bitch!*" Greg wailed in frustration.

Just as he was positioning himself to take another swing at the cop, who now lay unconscious across the front seat, Greg saw more flashing blue lights coming down the street.

"Fuckin' -a!" he muttered.

Grunting viciously, he jabbed the tip of the bat like a pool cue into the cop's face one last time, hitting him hard enough to break the man's front teeth, top and bottom. Greg was aware of several people moving toward the alleyway from both directions, so he turned and ran the only way he could go.

Back into the alley.

John Ross and his partner, Frank O'Connell, had been only a few blocks away from the scene, just past the Port Authority and heading back to the precinct house, when the call came over the radio. Frank slapped the blue bubble light onto the dashboard, and John, who was driving, laid on the horn and ran a couple of red lights to get over onto eighth and then head uptown to the address the dispatcher had given them. Even before they pulled to a full stop beside the parked cruiser, they could see that they were too late.

John jammed the shift into *park*. A quick glance around showed him just how bad it was.

The patrolman's cruiser door was hanging open with the cop's legs dangling out onto the street. One shoe had flipped off his foot. John could see that the cop wasn't moving. The dome light of the cruiser was on, casting a pallid glow across the man's face. His skin was sheet white beneath the wide streaks of blood that ran from his nose and his smashed mouth. A small crowd had gathered but was keeping a respectful distance.

Frank grabbed the radio mike and switched it on.

"This is Unit Fourteen. Ten-seventy-four. We've got at least one officer down and need assistance. Request backup and an ambulance at West Forty-Seventh between Eighth and Ninth. Over."

John glanced at his partner as he grabbed his emergency flashlight, opened his door, and stepped out into the night.

A gust of icy wind and snow hit him full in the face, making him shiver. He pulled his jacket collar up around his neck, but that didn't help much. When he peered down the alleyway, a deeper chill gripped him. The headlights from the cruiser were angled obliquely into the alleyway, but there was enough light to see the body of the other fallen police officer. The crowd pulled back out of John's way as he approached the cruiser and looked inside.

"Anyone see anything?" John asked, turning to face the crowd. Mostly what he saw were the typically distinterested expressions of native New Yorkers. It was going to take more than a beat-to-shit cop or two to get this crowd excited.

"I seen a guy—a white guy run down 'dere," said a thin black kid who was hopping nervously from one foot to the other as he pointed down the alleyway. The boy's black leather jacket looked entirely too thin for a cold night like this, and his eyes had that wired look of someone who was speeding his ass off.

"White guy, huh?" John said suspiciously.

"Swear to God it was," the skinny kid said. The lights reflected in his dark eyes, making them look like large, wet marbles.

John turned and shined his flashlight down into the alleyway. The falling snow made pencil-thin white lines, across the darkness.

"Aw'right. All of you. Move along. Show's over," John said, waving his hand to disperse them. "Go someplace and get warm."

Most of the crowd left, content to be on their way, but a few onlookers, including the skinny kid with the thin leather jacket, simply walked to the opposite side of the street and kept watching. This was, after all, prime New York street theater.

Off in the distance, John could hear more sirens approaching. He figured it was the ambulance. Drawing his service revolver and holding it at ready, he started down the alleyway, following the weaving oval of his flashlight. The further he went, the more an unaccountable nervousness—something he wasn't at all used to—took hold of him.

Something wasn't right here.

He had been a detective in Manhattan for almost twenty years, and a beat cop for six years before that. During all that time, he had been in more than his share of dangerous situations. This wasn't the first time he felt a cold twinge of nervousness as he entered a situation with far too many unknowns, but right now—for some reason—this felt . . . different.

More intense.

Maybe he was still upset about the argument he'd had with Angie this morning before he left for work. He knew he should have called home earlier and told her that he pulled a double shift, but he tried to clear all of that from his mind as he focused on what he was doing. A cop who didn't give total attention to the situation at hand was a cop who was going to wind up in a flag-draped coffin.

"Jesus," John whispered when he saw the mangled face of the police officer. His breath appeared as a puffy ball of mist before the icy wind whisked it away.

The cop's face was hardly recognizable as human. The skin around his mouth was peeled back and bloody, exposing his teeth all the way to the gums. His eyes were bulging from his head like a frog that had been stepped on. Snow had fallen onto his face and had started to melt. It looked like he was bathed with sweat.

Looking back at Frank, who had gotten out of the car and was leaning over the other downed policeman, John called out, "It don't look so good down here. How's your man?"

Frank glanced up at him, his expression flat and matter of fact in the ambient light.

"If he ain't dead, he's sure as shit's gonna wish he was."

Just then the ambulance pulled up.

As soon as Greg saw the third police car coming, he ducked into the doorway of the electrical supply building and huddled in the darkness, shivering. He was convinced that the door was locked, that he was trapped. Unless something went his way *real* goddamned soon, his number was up tonight. Cops didn't like people who beat up on other cops. He'd be lucky not the have a little "resisting arrest" accident before he got down to the station.

A cold tightening filled his gut as he watched the cop get out of the car and start down the alleyway. Nearly desperate with fear, Greg reached for the door latch in the darkness and pushed down. It clicked hollowly and almost turned but then fetched up.

Closing his eyes and saying a silent prayer, he sucked in his breath and held it until it began to hurt. Then, gritting his teeth and sputtering a curse under his breath, he rammed his shoulder against the metal door as hard as he could.

The door reverberated loudly, like a Caribbean steel drum, but the first blow didn't do anything except knock the wind out of him.

On the second try, though, a rusted bolt or whatever was

holding the door shut on the inside gave way. Greg heard a faint *ping* sound as a piece of metal fell to the concrete floor inside. As he leaned forward, applying steady pressure, the door swung open slowly with a low, metal groan.

Without even a backward glance over his shoulder, Greg entered the darkened hallway and then eased the door shut behind him. He fumbled with the door but couldn't find any way to lock it. His ears were still ringing as he started down the pitch black corridor, but he had taken no more than a dozen steps before he tripped over something and pitched forward. Even before he hit to floor, a booming voice shattered the silence of the building.

"What the fuck're you doing here, asshole?"

John shivered again, stronger, when he heard a loud, resounding metallic boom. He sucked in a breath and held it as he continued cautiously down the alleyway, all the while sweeping his flashlight beam back and forth. His revolver was raised in front of him, and he paused every other step or so to scan the area.

Someone was down here.

Someone dangerous and crazy enough to beat on a couple of cops, a store owner, and an old lady with a baseball bat.

The shadows surrounding him were thick, almost solid. Several times John thought he caught a hint of motion off to one side in the corner of his eye, but when he turned and shined his light in that direction, he saw nothing. The tension filled him with a sparkling energy. He couldn't stop wondering why he felt so damned jumpy.

When he saw the footprints in the slush leading down a short flight of steps to a sheltered metal door, he paused and took another deep breath. For a few seconds, he just stood there, staring at the door so long his vision began to shimmer and shift.

He went this way, whispered the small voice inside his head. Over the years, he had learned to trust that voice.

Angling himself to one side to make as narrow a target as possible, John crept down the three steps to the metal door. He was surprised to find that the door wasn't locked. He couldn't deny the rush of adrenalin that roared through him when he gently pushed the door open and stepped into the darkness of the building.

Chapter 3
Pursuit

Greg was panting so hard his chest and back hurt. He knew that, at thirty-four years old, he shouldn't be this winded after running such a short distance, but he told himself that it was the cold and the excitement that were exhausting him. He couldn't stop thinking about how unbelievably *great* it had felt to beat the living shit out of those cops!

As he tried to catch his breath, he looked around but couldn't see a thing in the close darkness. He had no idea where the person who had spoken to him might be. He could hear a dull shuffling sound that must be the man dragging himself up off the floor, but he had no idea how close the man was to him.

"You holing up in here, or what?" Greg asked, trying to inject a level of casualness into his voice that he didn't really feel. He was still much too wired.

"No," the man replied gruffly, "I'm having a fucking private birthday party with all my wonderful rodent friends."

"Hey, chill out. I didn't know you were in here, all right?" Greg replied.

From the direction of his voice, he figured the man was a few paces off to his right. He gripped the bat, getting ready to swing at him.

"You got a bottle on yah, pal?" the man asked.

Now that he was starting to calm down, Greg realized that the man was either drunk or stoned. He still couldn't see him, but he caught a whiff of him as he moved closer. The reek of musty clothes, sour body odor, and a strong trace of cheap whiskey made Greg's stomach do a cold flip.

Greg glanced back along the dark hallway toward the metal door, convinced that, any second now, it was going to burst open, and the police were going to come charging in with guns blazing.

"Uh—no," Greg said, trying to think of something, fast. "I ain't got a bottle, but I . . . Look, buddy, I'll give you twenty bucks if you do a little favor for me."

"If you ain't got a bottle, fuck you and your fuckin' favors," the man rasped.

He started to laugh but ended up having a coughing jag that ended only when he hawkered deep in his chest and spat. Greg heard the gob of spit hit the wall or floor with a sickening *plop*.

"Look, man, I'm serious," Greg said, finding it difficult to keep the edge of nervousness out of his voice. In all the years of robbing stores and mugging people—even the couple of times he killed someone, usually just for the hell of it—he had never before come this close to being caught. It made him at least start to question his abilities and judgment. Maybe he was getting too old for this shit.

"There's this guy I owe some money, see, and he's pretty pissed at me right now. He was chasing me. I think he saw me come in here."

"You think I give a rat's ass?"

"Look, I said I'll give you twenty bucks if you stay here and slow him down if he comes this way, okay?"

Greg was almost laughing out loud at the brilliance of his idea.

"You don't have to do a damned thing," he said. "I don't want you fighting with him or anything. Just slow him down a couple of minutes until I get my ass out the back door."

"Back door's locked," the man said. "You probably ought to use one of the windows."

"Fine . . . fine, I'll use a window, then."

Greg dug the wad of bills from his pants pocket, pretty sure he had folded them so the twenties were on the outside. He made a point of crinkling the paper loudly as he peeled off the top bill. The sound reminded him of a crackling fire.

"Here's twenty bucks, bud," he said. "You can buy five—shit—maybe even ten bottles with this."

The man didn't reply right away. Greg was wondering why he was wasting time with this creep. He should just beat the shit out of him and be on his way. Before he decided what he was going to do, a loud scratching sound filled the darkness. A flame from a wooden match erupted with a sputter. The sudden brightness left traces of blue light trailing across Greg's vision, but he forced a smile as he held the bill out to the man.

Greg could see that the man's face was ravaged by age and alcohol, making him look at least sixty years old. Greg knew that living on the street aged a person much faster than usual. For all he knew, this guy could be in his twenties or thirties.

The man's hand trembled with the palsy of an alcoholic as he held the burning match up with one hand and reached out for the bill with the other. He snatched it away from Greg before he could stop him. Holding the bill up close to his face, he inspected it and then started laughing so hard he broke into another coughing fit.

"This here's a hunnert dollar bill!" he said between coughs.

Before the match burned out, Greg saw his mistake, but it was too late. The man shoved the bill deep into the pocket of his ragged woolen overcoat and, at the same time, flipped the wooden match away, plunging the corridor back into darkness.

Sudden, blind fury filled Greg. He gripped the baseball bat and was getting ready to whack the bastard a good one, but just then he heard the scrape of footsteps on the stairway outside.

"Shit! That's the guy who's after my ass," Greg said. "Okay, keep the fuckin' money. I don't give a shit about it. Just slow the bastard down so I can get away, okay?"

"Sure thing, mack," the old man said, but the way he said it made Greg think he didn't have the foggiest idea as to what he was supposed to do.

"Here," Greg said. "Take this, too."

Although he could only guess where the man was standing, he held the baseball bat out to him.

"Just in case you have to defend yourself."

"Hey! No fucking way! I don't need no gun or nothing," the man said, sounding suspicious. The scuff of the old man's feet echoed loudly as he backed away.

"It's just a baseball bat," Greg said, shoving it at the man until he felt him take it. "Thanks, man. I really owe you."

"My fuckin' pleasure."

Greg's vision was still filled with zigzag afterimages from the brightness of the match as he turned and started feeling his way down the corridor. The floor was uneven and littered with debris that tripped him up, but he trailed his left hand along the corridor wall to help him keep oriented.

He was walking away as fast as he dared, but he made an effort to keep as silent as possible in case another goddamned cop was lurking in the dark, lying in ambush for him.

He had trouble judging distances in the dark, but after a while he reached a wall and realized that the corridor branched off to the left and right. He had to think for a second or two to get his bearings, and even then he wasn't sure he was heading in the right direction when he turned to the right. He picked up his pace a little when he heard the heavy metal door slam open. The sound rolled like thunder in the narrow confines of the corridor.

He picked up his pace when he heard the dull echo of voices behind him and of someone who was shouting.

John's heart was racing when he kicked open the metal door and entered the dark building. The smell that assailed him was instantly nauseating, but at least he was out of the wind and snow. He flattened himself against the wall, his gun ready in one hand, his flashlight in the other.

The tension he'd been feeling heightened as he started inching down the corridor. He couldn't stop thinking that he had made a big mistake not waiting for backup. The man's tracks coming down the steps were fresh and unmistakable. He might not be the man who had robbed the convenience store, but even if he wasn't the perp, whoever was down here, John's "cop sense" told him that he'd be as dangerous as a cornered rat.

"I know you're in here, so why not come out with your hands up?" John called out.

His voice echoed weirdly in the narrow corridor, but after the sound had faded away, the silence was broken only by the sound of his rapid breathing.

"You're just making it tougher on yourself!"

Still pressed flat against the wall, John brought his light around and shined it down the hallway. He saw crumbling plaster walls and exposed lathing. The floor was littered with trash. The ceiling was a patchwork of water stains and rot. The further he went into the building, the stronger the stench became.

The coiling tension inside John kept rising with every step. He knew that anyone savage enough to bludgeon at least four people for a few hundred dollars from a cash register would fight like a pit bull. He cast a quick glance back toward the door to see if Frank was coming up behind him yet, but there was no sign of his partner.

John shivered violently in the damp air of the building. Unaccountably, he thought about Angie and, for a flashing instant, was filled with regret because of the argument they'd had that morning.

Jesus, focus! Focus! he commanded himself, but he still wasn't ready when a man suddenly appeared in the center of the flashlight beam.

"Hold it right there," John shouted, swinging around and taking a solid stance with his gun aimed straight at the man's chest.

The man looked to be fifty or sixty years old. His frayed, gray overcoat was torn at the hem and dragged at his feet, almost tripping him. His hair was a grizzled mess that hung to his shoulders. The man had his hands raised halfway, but John could see that he was holding something—a baseball bat in his right hand. Even at a distance of more than twenty feet, he could see the dark splotches of blood and matted hair on the wooden bat.

"I don't want no trouble here, bub," the old man said shakily. His voice was deep and slurred, and sounded like he'd been drinking all day and half the night.

No surprise there, John thought, but even if this guy was drunk, he knew that he had to keep his guard up. Drunk guys could be even more dangerous if they were too drunk to feel any pain.

"Put the bat down and lie face-down on the floor, now. Do it!" John commanded, but the old man kept walking toward him as if he hadn't heard or didn't understand him.

"I mean it!" John shouted, bracing his gun hand to steady his aim. "Get down on the floor *now,* asshole!"

But the old man kept walking toward him, all the while shaking his head as though absolutely bewildered. The bat was swinging from side to side in his hand and hitting the plaster wall with every other step.

"I said *now!*" John shouted.

The old man lowered his hands and gripped the neck of the bat with both hands. John could see the muscles and tendons in his hands tense.

"This is *my* place! You don't come in here and start calling me names, asshole!" the man said. "Now *you* get the fuck out of here!"

He took two more steps forward. As he did, he raised the bat to his shoulder as though preparing to take a swing.

John didn't hesitate. Years of training and experience told him that this man wasn't listening to him. He dropped to a crouch, took careful aim, and fired twice.

The explosion of the gun in such close quarters hurt John's ears. He watched cooly as the man jerked back with each hit. The bat dropped from his hands and clattered across the floor. The old man almost tripped over it as he staggered backwards. Two bloody holes had appeared in the center of his chest. Blood was seeping like an ink stain into the frayed wool of his coat. The man kept backing up until his knees finally gave away, and he flopped backwards onto the floor. His head hit hard enough to bounce once, but John knew that it didn't matter. The old geezer was dead before he hit the floor.

"John?"

The sudden shout behind him made John freeze. For a second, He didn't recognize Frank's voice. he turned around slowly as though dazed and watched as a beam of light cut the darkness, moving steadily closer.

"Yeah, I'm okay," John called out, "but I had to drop him. He was coming at me and wouldn't stop."

Frank came up beside John, and the two of them shined their flashlights onto the fallen man. His eyes were wide open and staring up at the water-stained ceiling. A line of blood was running from the corner of his mouth to the floor. He looked suddenly much smaller and not nearly as threatening as he had moments before.

"By the looks of it, I'd say you got the prick we were after," Frank said with a chuckle. He leaned forward and shined his flashlight on the two bleeding holes in the dead man's chest. "Nice shooting."

"I'm lucky he didn't have a gun. How are the guys doing out there?" John asked, nodding his head back toward the doorway.

"One of 'em—the cop in the alley—is ten-seven," Frank replied, his voice all business. "The other one . . . I dunno. The meat wagon hauled him off to Bellevue."

John tried to smile at his partner, but he was feeling suddenly exhausted. The letdown after such tension made every muscle in his body feel unstrung. He took a shuddering breath as he holstered his revolver and wiped the sweat from his brow.

"Well, let's get the M E down here," he said. "He's got some more work to do."

Greg was clambering out through one of the broken windows at the rear of the building when he heard the two shots go off. The sound startled him so that he lost his grip on the sill and fell about six feet to the litter-strewn alley. As he stood up and brushed himself off, he couldn't help but smile.

This might turn out better than he could have planned.

If the cops just nailed the old wino, it was going to keep them off his ass at least long enough so he could find his way out of here and get back home to Brooklyn.

He looked up at the snow as it fell, swirling like purple fireflies in the ambient glow of the city. He stuck his tongue out and let a few snowflakes land on it with a cooling touch.

"Better than I could have planned," he whispered, snickering as he started down the alley behind the building. He crossed over to Forty-Eighth Street and soon enough blended in with the other pedestrians. He was far enough away so he couldn't hear or see any of the commotion over on Forty-Seventh.

It had been close there for a while, he thought, but he wasn't worried. Even if the cops found his tracks out behind the building, he'd already lost them. Fifteen minutes from now, he be on the subway heading out of Manhattan.

All in all, it had been a pretty good night, even though he was still pissed that he'd given away a hundred dollars.

Then again, the best thing that could have happened probably *did* happen. If the cops shot and killed the damned fool, hopefully it was before he said anything about Greg. And even if the old bastard was still alive, he was so drunk he'd probably never be able to ID him, so either way—that was it.

He'd gotten away.

Greg figured it was probably the best hundred dollars he'd ever spent.

The sudden ringing of the telephone ripped Angie out of the thin sleep she had fallen into. She squealed and jumped as she sat up and grabbed the phone before it could ring a second time. She didn't want it to wake up the kids.

"'lo," she said, her voice so dry and scratchy it sounded like an old woman's.

"Angie?"

Even through her panic, she immediately recognized her husband's voice. A strong wave of relief swept through her.

"Jesus, John! What time is it?"

She smacked her lips and rubbed her eyes vigorously as she tried to focus on the dial of her wristwatch, but the light in the living room was too bright. It hurt her eyes and made them water.

"A little after two," John said softly.

"In the morning?" she asked, still confused.

"Yeah. Were you asleep?"

There was a short pause, and in that time Angie imagined dozens of terrible things that could have happened to him tonight.

"Yeah. Where are you?"

"The hospital," John said. "Don't worry. I'm all right, but—we had a some trouble with a robbery tonight."

"Frank's all right, isn't he?"

Although Angie didn't particularly like Frank O'Connell, she and John saw Frank and his second wife, Betty, socially. She knew how close her husband was with his partner.

"Oh, yeah. Frank's fine. He's back at the station working up the report. Some guy robbed a store and beat on four people including a couple of cops. Bastard used a baseball bat. Three of 'em are dead, and the other cop—I don't think you know him. Guy named Alan Prills. He got hurt pretty bad, too. Concussion and broken skull. I just stopped by on my way home to check on him."

Angie sighed as a wave of relief swept through her.

"Good Lord," was all she could say. At least her husband was alright, but she couldn't stop thinking that two police officers' clocks had run out tonight.

When was John's going to run out?

It seemed to be just a matter of time.

"I knew you'd be waiting up, worrying about me," John said. "Let me guess. You were sitting on the couch when you fell asleep. The reading light is on, and you have the TV on with the volume turned all the way down. Too late for Letterman. You probably had the remote control in your hand, too."

"Sounds like you know exactly what my nights are like when you pull night duty," Angie said.

She couldn't deny the rush of anger she felt, just knowing that he knew what she went through and acted as though she was supposed to accept it just because he did.

She heard him clear his throat.

"You sure you're okay?" Angie asked thickly. She could sense that there was something more he wanted to say.

"Yeah . . . really . . . I am. I just want to say . . . you know, sorry . . . about this morning—"

"Don't say it," Angie said, cutting him off before he could stumble through the rest of his apology. "We'll talk about it when you get home."

"Yeah, but I want you to know that I—I'm really sorry, Ange, okay?" John said.

Angie blinked her eyes rapidly, hoping she could stop the flood of tears that was building up inside her eyes.

"Please. Don't, John. I mean it."

Her voice was low and steady, but she knew that it could break any second now.

She wasn't sure why she wanted him to drop it.

Maybe it was because, after more than twenty years of this, she had heard it all too many times before.

Maybe, especially after talking with Rob earlier tonight, she was feeling that—finally—the situation was now beyond words.

Or maybe—just maybe—she wanted her husband to apologize to her in person after she delivered her own bad news, that after this school year, she was out of a job.

"You don't have to wait up for me," John said. "I still won't be home for another hour or two."

"Wake me up when you get home, okay? Tomorrow's— no, today's Saturday. I don't have to work."

"Are you sure you don't want to just sleep? You sound pretty beat."

"No. Wake me up. I want to see you when you get here. We've got a lot to talk about."

John started to say something but then fell silent. Angie heard him make a soft kissing sound into the receiver and then whisper "Bye" before hanging up.

The connection broke, leaving her with the droning, buzzing sound of the dial tone in her ear. By the time she found the base of the phone and got the phone hung up, tears were streaming down her face.

Chapter 4
Dead Voices

Early morning sunlight angled across the Ross' front lawn, making the fresh snow cover glow with an almost preternatural light. The two small, bare maple trees that lined either side of the front walk cast long shadows that looked like skeletal hands, clawing their way up to the front door. A noisy flock of chickadees had gathered at the bird feeder JJ had put outside the kitchen window last year as part of a school nature project. The ground below the feeder was strewn with cracked seed casings and bird droppings.

Breakfast was over, and Angie was seated at the table across from John. The kids had already taken off for the morning. JJ had gone over to his friend Arno's house to play the new Sega CD games he'd gotten for Christmas, while Brandy had simply left the house without bothering to tell her parents where she was going, who she was with, or when she'd be back. Angie had told her that she had on too much makeup, and that wearing such a skimpy outfit on such a cold morning made her look cheap, but Brandy left without changing her clothes.

Angie cradled her coffee mug in her hands, but the warmth didn't come close to penetrating the chill that gripped her heart.

John was leaning back in his chair, his thumbs hooked

through his belt loops. A paper napkin, twisted into a tight knot, lay on the table beside his empty breakfast plate, which was smeared with egg yolk. It was a little past eight o'clock. He didn't have to be to work until noon.

John's face was a network of shadowed lines as he looked at Angie, but she thought—even when he was looking straight at her—that he was focused on something else . . . something far away.

"I . . . I just can't explain it," he said, shaking his head thoughtfully. "I mean—I've been in situations worse than that too many times to count, but last night, when I went into that building, it was like . . . like I had this . . . this weird feeling, like . . ."

His voice trailed off, and he shook his head.

"Like what?" Angie said, prodding.

John sighed deeply, his face drawn and pale from worry and lack of sleep. He had gotten home a little after three-thirty that morning. Angie had stayed awake after his phone call, and they had talked for over an hour before finally going to bed. John hadn't taken Angie's news about her job nearly as badly as she thought he might. His only comment was that he was sure the superintendent would find something else for her within the school system.

"You felt like *what?*" Angie repeated, pressing him.

"Like I . . . I don't know," John said with a shrug. He leaned forward and gulped down the last of his coffee, wincing at the taste.

"You want more?"

John shook his head slowly as though he hardly heard her.

"I had the feeling that this guy I was chasing was going to get the drop on me," he said, still sounding shaky. "That I might not make it out of there alive."

"Do you think maybe your subconscious was trying to tell you something?" Angie suggested. She knew it wasn't fair to press too hard on this point, but she couldn't help it.

"You mean that it might be time for me to retire?"

John arched one eyebrow. The sneer that raised one side of

his mouth told Angie all she need to know about his opinion on that.

"You are eligible for early retirement, so why not take the pension and bail out now? You could always get into some other line of work."

"It's not that simple," John said, nailing her with a hard look.

Angie shrugged, trying her best to appear casual.

"Nothing's *ever* that simple. I'm not saying it is."

"Angie, I've always been a cop. My *father* was a cop, and ever since I can remember, *I* wanted to be a cop. It's not what I do; it's what I *am.*"

Angie tensed but was ready for this.

"But you're so much more than that," she replied smoothly as she reached out with one hand and gripped his fisted hand, which rested on the edge of the table. His hand was cold to the touch, and Angie couldn't help but think that twenty years as a New York City detective had turned her husband's heart just as cold and hard as his fist.

"You want to know the problem with you?" she continued. "I think you invest way up too much of your identity in what you do." She squeezed his unyielding hand tighter. "You're also a father and a husband, you know? And even after twenty-three years of marriage, you're still one hell of a good lover."

John gave her a quick half-smile, but Angie could tell that it was forced. He wasn't going to give an inch of ground on this issue.

"You know what people always say when someone loses their job?" she asked. "They always say, 'Just you wait and see. This is probably the best thing that ever happened to you.' I even said that to Rob when he lost his teaching job in Fort Lauderdale. I know it sounds like a platitude, but maybe it's true. Maybe this is *exactly* the opportunity we've been waiting for. Maybe this is our chance to make a really big change in all of our lives."

"Ange, com'on . . ."

"You saw how Brandy was dressed this morning," Angie

said. "My God! She had on so much makeup she looked like a damned streetwalker."

"That's just the style these days."

"Bull!" Angie said, slapping her hand against the table hard enough to make the dishes and cups jump. "You've been grousing for years about how the City's getting crazier every year. Even here in Bedford Heights—we're not protected from it anymore. Things are getting *really* scary out there in the world, and I think we can find a place to live that's a little more . . . sane."

The whole time she was talking, John just sat there, shaking his head slowly from side to side. Angie wasn't sure if he was trying to deny what she was saying, or if he was agreeing with her and shaking his head with disgust.

But it didn't matter.

The bottom line was, even though she hadn't dared mention it to him yet, she was more determined than ever to leave New York whether he came with her or not. If he was so damned tied to his job that it was the only way he could identify himself, then maybe he wasn't the man she loved . . .

Not anymore.

The only hesitation she had was because she didn't want to hit him with an ultimatum when he was feeling so vulnerable about what had happened last night.

But then again, she thought, cringing inwardly, *when is it a good time to tell your husband that you want to leave him?*

"So you tell me," she said, fighting for control of her voice. "Is this the kind of world you want your kids to grow up in? You know kids in Brandy's class are using drugs. Her friend Rachel smokes cigarettes, and I'll bet Brandy has tried it, too. I'll bet kids JJ's age—maybe even JJ have tried pot."

Squeezing his hand so tightly it hurt, she leaned forward across the kitchen table, pleading with her eyes.

"I didn't make the world the way it is," John replied evenly.

For just an instant, his focus snapped onto her. Angie felt excruciatingly uncomfortable. She couldn't stand it when he looked at her with that cold gleam in his eyes, like she was a suspect or something.

"I didn't say you did," she said softly, "and I'm not saying that you're not doing everything you can to try to make it better. All I'm saying is maybe . . . just maybe we should consider moving someplace else . . . someplace a little less . . . crazy."

John snorted and shook his head firmly as he pulled his hand away from her and leaned back in his chair.

"Bedford Heights is a great little town," he said. "Believe me, we don't have the same problems the City does."

His eyes shifted to the kitchen window, but he seemed not to notice the flock of birds making such a racket outside. The bright sunlight reflecting off the snow made his pupils contract to the size of BBs.

"If not for us, then how about for the kids?" Angie asked. "Think about it. Is this the kind of situation you want Brandy and JJ growing up in?"

He looked at her hard again.

"Com'on, Ange. You were born and raised in Brooklyn. You always told me that moving out here was your dream."

"Yeah, well dreams change." She resisted the urge to add— *and so can love.* "I was talking to Rob last night, before you called—"

John sniffed, his expression hardening into a crooked smirk. He started to say something, but Angie cut him off quickly.

"Don't say it," she cautioned him. "Don't even *think* it!"

Anger and nervousness flared inside her. She took a sip of her coffee before continuing.

"He invited us up to Maine to visit. Just to take a look around. He says there's probably going to be a permanent substitute job in the third grade next year, and he could put in a good word for me. I don't see why you couldn't apply at some of the local police departments. They'd probably *love* to hire someone with your experience."

John snorted and smiled crookedly. "Yeah—unless they think I'll bring some of the big, bad City up there with me."

"You wouldn't even have to work," Angie said. "I'll bet we could get by on my teaching salary and your pension."

"How big do you think that pension is?" John asked with a laugh.

Angie shook her head angrily. She didn't like being toyed with like this. She fought the impulse to get up and start pacing the floor, and just sat there, wishing to God that she could think of *something* to say that would sway him. She didn't want to have to play her divorce trump card because, as much as she hated the tension there seemed to be between them all the time now, she knew that—underneath it all—she did still love him.

At least she thought she did.

"Look, Ange. I don't think it's really fair for you to hit me with this right now, okay? I know how upset you are about your job being cut, and I'm upset about it, too, but I'm more upset about what happened last night—"

Words suddenly failed him. He chuckled dryly, closed his eyes and, pressing his fingers against his closed eyelids, shook his head.

"You're afraid you might have lost your edge, aren't you?" Angie said.

A heavy sigh was his only response.

"That's what I'm picking up from you. You're afraid you didn't have it last night, that for the first time in your life, you were in over your head, and that scared the shit out of you, didn't it?"

John just kept shaking his head. Opening his eyes slowly, he fixed her with a cold, steady gaze.

"It wasn't that," he said, his voice deep and resonant. "It was . . . something else."

"You were nervous and scared." Angie was trying hard not to shout at him. "Jesus, you can admit it to me. I'm your wife, for God's sake! The way I see it, maybe for the first time in your life you went after someone, and you had to deal with the genuine fear that you might be killed doing your job. And you were terrified!"

John kept shaking his head.

"You think I don't know what that feels like?" Angie asked. "I worry about you like that every single night you're on duty!"

"You were just upset because we'd had that argument earlier," John said.

For a moment, she could see the fear lurking in his eyes, but then the curtain came down, and he got that blank, masklike expression she always thought of as his "cop face." She could imagine how effective it was when interviewing a suspect, but she couldn't stand it when he used it on her.

"You were afraid that you were going to die. You realized last night that you're getting older, and that your reflexes and senses aren't quite as keen as they used to be."

John sniffed. "Don't go throwing the age thing in my face. I may be losing a little hair and getting a little soft in the middle, but I'm not ready to retire yet."

"I'm not asking you to retire," Angie said, finding it almost impossible to keep the pleading tone out of her voice. "I just want you to consider changing jobs—like I'm going to have to. Who knows? It might even save our marriage."

John jerked back in his chair, looking genuinely surprised. His mouth dropped open as if he were about to say something, but words failed him. He was still floundering for a response when the phone rang. The sharp electronic buzz made Angie jump as if a cold fist had hit her in the stomach. Like most cops' spouses, her conditioned response when the phone rang was to think: *Something's happened!*

John grunted as he heaved himself up from his chair and went to the counter to grab the receiver. He got it after the second ring. Angie leaned forward across the table, watching his facial reactions closely. She knew that it was bad news when his expression dropped for a second, then quickly hardened.

Please don't let it be something with one of the kids! Angie thought, suddenly aware that both children were out of the house.

John didn't say much over the phone. He just listened and nodded once or twice. After a few moments, he said, "Okay. Thanks for calling," and then placed the portable phone back on its base.

His shoulders dropped as he turned to face Angie. She could see the muscles in his jaw tensing as he ground his teeth. His lips were pressed into a pale, tight line. His eyes narrowed as though he were in pain.

"What is it?" Angie asked, hearing the worry in her voice.

"That was Frank," John said. "He wanted to let me know that Alan Prills—the other cop who got hurt last night—"

John heaved a heavy sigh as he leaned back with both hands braced against the counter and looked down, unfocused, at the floor.

"He died—?" Angie asked.

John couldn't speak. He simply nodded.

Angie gasped and covered her mouth with one hand. Her first thought was to wonder if Officer Prills had a family. Her second thought was to be thankful that it hadn't been John.

How much longer can I live with this?

The thought rolled like a peal of thunder through her mind as she watched John start pacing back and forth across the kitchen floor. His bare feet squeaked on the linoleum. His face was flushed bright red as he clenched his fist and smacked it repeatedly into his open hand.

"Jesus! *Jesus!*" he muttered, keeping time with his striding steps.

Angie could see the anger raging inside him, and all she could think was how, over the years, she had almost gotten used to his anger, as if that were the only proper response when things went wrong.

"I could have *done* something to *stop* it!" Frank said, his voice a low growl. "I *could* have!"

Angie took a shuddering breath. She started to tell him that— no, he *couldn't* have stopped it, that all three of the men and that old lady, too, were dead before he even got there; but words failed her. She knew that she couldn't reason with him when he was like this.

She wished she had the strength to go over to him and give him a hug to let him know that she still loved and cared for him, that she was glad *he* wasn't the one who had died last night as she had feared. She wished to God that he could see that this was *exactly* the reason she wanted him to consider retiring now and moving away from New York.

But she also knew that she had said it all before.

Too many times.

Maybe she was just going to have to accept the fact that he wasn't going to hear her . . . or that he didn't *want* to hear her.

The cacophony of noise from the precinct squad room cut down to a reasonable level when John closed the door to his boss' office. Lieutenant Charlie Boyle was leaning back in his chair with his feet propped up on his paper-covered desk. He looked up at Frank and John, smiling as he took a sip of coffee from a styrofoam cup. He nodded for the men to sit down as he took another moment to glance at the papers in his hand. John guessed it was the report Frank had typed up and turned in earlier this morning.

"Good piece of work out there last night," Boyle said as he scaled the paperwork onto his desk. "We tied that creep's MO in with a couple of other robberies. We make him good for possibly twenty jobs over the last five years. This isn't the first time he's killed someone with a baseball bat, either."

Frank nodded, accepting the compliment, but John couldn't deny the cold stirring he felt deep in his gut. Something about this case still felt all wrong.

"We went back out there earlier this afternoon and checked around a bit," John said. "The lab guys say it looks like someone else was in that building with him, but they couldn't lift any usable footprints."

"Your point being?" Boyle asked. One of his eyebrows shot up, looking like a dark comma against his pale forehead.

"There are footprints leading to the back of the building. Also some out back. And there's fresh evidence someone climbed out one of those windows. The lab boys found some threads from a coat that didn't match the stiff's overcoat. Also some smudges that indicate whoever was there was wearing gloves. Probably leather."

"Maybe it was OJ," Boyle said, but he was the only one who laughed. "They also say there's only one set of prints on that bat. The stiff had a hundred dollar bill in his pocket. Looks to me like you got your man. If there was anyone else there with him, and—hey, maybe it was a buddy of his, many even an accomplice, but the only witness you turned up says he saw one man—a white guy—running from the store. The description fits our stiff.''

''You know damned right well the 'brothers' will say it was whitey no matter what,'' John said testily.

''You got a name on that witness, Frank?''

''Ahh—yeah,'' Frank said, nodding. ''Name's Clarence Jones. Lives over on Forty-fourth Street above a record store. Calls himself 'Spike.' We were going to swing by later today and question him some more.''

''I'm not sure I'd take that crack-head's word for it,'' John snapped. ''The boy was wired last night. He could have seen anything.''

Boyle raised his hands, spreading his fingers as though completely helpless.

''You take what you can get,'' he said, sounding as if he just about cared. ''I'm banking that the stiff was our man, and John—you put him out of commission good. Did you turn in a 'Use of Deadly Force' report yet?''

John shook his head tightly.

''I'll have it for you before the end of the day, Lieutenant,'' he said.

''We'll have to have a review, of course, but the shoot looks clean.'' Boyle squinted at him. ''The only problem I can see is, once the autopsy's done, if the stiff's blood alcohol's was as high as you think it might have been, there might be some question as to why you didn't subdue him instead of shoot. He *did* have just a baseball bat, not a gun.''

''He was coming at me in close quarters,'' John said evenly. ''I wasn't gonna stand there and take it. I gave him plenty of warning.''

''Hey!'' Boyle slapped his hands together again and rubbed them vigorously as though washing them clean. ''I'm not saying the shoot was bad. I'm just— Look, sooner or later we're all gonna retire. I'd just hate to see some advocate for the homeless or some other bullshit liberal cause start a ruckus about police brutality or something that might jeopardize your pension. It's happened before.''

"Well, like you say—the shoot was good," John said, but even as he said it, the knot of worry in his stomach got bigger.

"I still feel a little hinky about this," he said. "Call it a 'gut feeling' if you want, but I'd like to keep the case open, at least until we get the autopsy report. This case is about a cop killer. We should canvas the area and see if anyone else saw anything. Maybe someone saw whoever that was leaving from behind the building.''

"Don't waste your time," Boyle said sharply.

"I just don't like this guy for it," John said emphatically.

"Suit yourself," Boyle said, but he didn't look at all like he meant it. "But it's not like you don't have other cases that need attention. You got a homeless wino stiff whose prints are all over the murder weapon. Unless or until someone starts working the same MO, I say the case is closed."

John started to protest but then felt Frank's hand tug at his elbow.

"You're still working the Monteleone case, aren't you?" Boyle asked.

Frank grunted "Uh-huh," and John nodded.

"Then I suggest you get to work on that. His secretary's already called a couple of times this morning. Far as I can see, you haven't done squat on that yet."

Frank and John nodded again as they turned to leave. John was still fuming as he opened the door, but he knew that it would be foolish to complain further. The last thing he heard Boyle say before the door swung shut behind him was, "And make sure you get that deadly force report on my desk, pronto!''

As he walked across the squad room back to his desk, for the first time that he could remember, John thought that maybe Angie was right.

Maybe he *was* due for a change . . . especially if it meant not having to deal with assholes like Boyle every day for the rest of his life.

* * *

Greg had been soaked to the skin, his overcoat twice as heavy as it usually was by the time he got back to his third-floor apartment on Myrtle Avenue in Brooklyn shortly after four o'clock that morning. The bad weather, not to mention the early hour, kept most people off the street, so he was pretty sure no one had seen him enter the building.

He'd been glad to see that his mother was asleep when he got home, but what did he expect? She was seventy-four years old and failing fast. Now, here it was, two o'clock the next afternoon—more than twelve hours after he had gotten away from that drunk asshole on Forty-seventh Street—and his mother was still asleep. He could hear her ragged snoring from behind her closed bedroom door, loud enough, it seemed, to vibrate the faded picture of Jesus on the kitchen wall.

Just to make sure that she wasn't faking it, Greg tiptoed over to her door and eased it open. Looking in, he saw her face, faintly illuminated by the glow of the night-light on the table beside her bed. Her dry, aged skin looked death-pale and was cracked by dark wrinkles. Her mouth hung open, looking like a dark, bloodless wound in the center of her face. Her false teeth were in a glass of water beside the light.

If Greg didn't know any better, he might have thought she was dead.

The idea didn't bother him in the least.

His mother wasn't seriously ill. It was just old age dragging her down, inch by excruciating inch. It seemed to Greg like he'd been waiting more than half his life for the old lady to die. He was tired of her listening to her complain about all of her aches and pains, tired of waiting on her, of bringing her meals and medicine in bed and running errands for her, and particularly tired of hearing her go on about how Jesus had taken his father too early and would soon be taking her.

Greg *wanted* her to die, if only so he could collect the little bit of life insurance he had on her. After last night, he knew the cops would be looking for him, so he'd just as soon not have to knock off any more stores for a while. His job at the corner video store sure as shit wasn't going to pay the bills— especially his mother's medical bills if she *did* get seriously ill before finally checking out.

In the daylight, he noticed a few spots of blood on the front of his overcoat. They weren't too bad, though. He washed them out at the kitchen sink as best he could, but when they didn't come clean, he daubed them over with green enamel paint. Before breakfast, he decided to take a hot shower to get rid of the cramps and chills he still felt.

As usual, he hadn't slept very well.

All through the night and into the morning, he kept thinking that he could hear voices, whispering to him from the corners of his bedroom. Once or twice, he thought he even heard someone call him by name, but he didn't get out of bed to check it out.

It was probably someone talking in the next apartment or out on the street. If so, fine . . . let it be.

And if he was imagining things—then fine, let it go.

If it had been his mother calling him because she needed help—then fine, let her die.

The sky above Brooklyn was overcast, but as far as Greg could tell, it was no longer snowing or raining. Diffused gray light cast fuzzy shadows across the worn kitchen floor. Even though the apartment was as cold as an icebox, Greg wore only threadbare pajama bottoms as he sat down at the kitchen table and poured himself a heaping bowl of Rice Krinkles. He sprinkled a huge spoonful of sugar onto the mound of cereal, then added milk and mixed it up. When the cereal started to crackle and pop, he put one ear close to the bowl and imagined—just as he had since he was a little kid—that the cereal was talking to him in a language he didn't quite understand but would, if only he listened hard enough.

Just like the voices I was hearing last night, he thought with a sudden shiver.

His nipples were rock hard, and goosebumps spread up his arms. For no apparent reason, he was suddenly absolutely convinced that someone was standing close by, watching him. He glanced at his mother's door, half-expecting to see her peering out at him from the darkened room, but the door was tightly closed.

Heaving a sigh, Greg leaned forward, picked up his spoon, and scooped up some cereal, hoping that eating would help him get his mind off things, but he found that he couldn't raise the spoon to his mouth.

The voices are back!

He couldn't stop thinking that, and it terrified him.

He was *positive* he had heard them . . . or *almost* heard them last night.

And even now, they seemed to be lurking just at the edge of awareness, sputtering like the hiss of a candle flame as it burns out.

The sound of the crackling cereal gradually faded away. Greg's eyes widened with mounting fear as he scanned the tiny kitchen. In the weak afternoon light, the linoleum floor was as dull as dishwater. The walls, table, counter, cupboards, and appliances—everything looked old and grimy, almost unreal. The yellowed window shade that looked out over the fire escape and back alley was tore at the bottom. It hung down at an angle that allowed a small triangular view of the gray building across the alley.

Everywhere he looked, Greg expected to see someone staring back at him. He imagined pairs of eyes gazing at him from behind, shifting to one side or the other whenever he turned to look at them.

"Shit," he said in a trembling whisper.

His hand convulsed, and he dropped the spoon, knocking over his bowl and spilling Rice Krinkles across the table. A river of milk ran to the edge of the table and dripped onto the floor. It sounded like someone taking a piss behind him.

Greg clenched his fists so tightly the veins and tendons in his arms stood out in harsh relief. Closing his eyes, he pressed his knuckles against the sides of his head so hard swirling patterns of colors began to explode across his vision.

Please! . . . Don't let them start again! . . . Please make them stop!

He thumped the sides of his head a couple of times. The sound inside his skull was like heavy drumming far off in the distance. The colored patterns behind his closed eyes intensified. Bright, jagged lightning bolts of red and purple turned inward on each other. After a while, Greg imagined that he could see faces, drifting toward him from out of the darkness.

Make them stop! . . . Please! . . . Please make them stop!

This wasn't the first time Greg had heard voices. He couldn't remember when they had started. Only recently had he begun to connect them with his robberies. This was the third time, now, that he had heard faint whisperings after killing someone. If he ever dared to tell his mother about them, he was sure she would say it was his conscience tormenting him. He didn't believe in God, and he certainly didn't cling to Jesus the way his mother did. His only concern was that this might mean that he was losing his mind—going insane, just like his father had when Greg was three years old.

"No! . . . *No!* . . . It's not that! *It's not that!*"

He continued to pound the sides of his head as he stared at the irregular splotches of shifting light. Spikes of pain shot down his neck and shoulders, but nothing seemed to stop the voices once they started. They were still there, hissing in his head like spit on a hot stove.

When he opened his eyes and looked around, his vision was distorted by the bright afterimages. Everything in the kitchen seemed to be composed of tiny, vibrating balls of energy that left purple trailers across his vision whenever he turned his head.

Nothing looked real.

He cried out loud when he glanced toward the window and saw a small, distorted face peering in at him.

For a panicked instant, he thought it was a person. Narrow yellow eyes watched him with a steady stare. After a panicky moment, Greg realized that a stray cat was outside on the fire escape.

For several seconds, he was too frightened to do anything about it.

The cat's steady stare remained fixed on him. Only when the animal blinked did Greg realize that it had to be real.

I'm not imagining this!

Greg took a long, shuddering breath.

His body unfolded stiffly as he stood up from his chair. Taking his cereal bowl in one hand, he walked over to the window. The stray cat—a rail-thin gray tabby—cowered away from him, but it didn't run off as Greg unlocked the window and slid it up.

The sudden blast of cold air made his teeth chatter, but the sensation helped ground him. He realized all the more that he was awake—that this was real. He wasn't imagining it.

"Here kitty, kitty," he called softly as he leaned outside and placed the bowl on the rusty grill of the fire escape.

The cat looked at him suspiciously, but seeing the milk in the bowl quickly won out over caution. Skinny tail erect, the cat moved up to the bowl and began lapping up what was left of the milk.

"Yeah, there you go," Greg whispered, almost cooing. "How's that taste, huh?"

When he reached out to pat the cat, the cat quickly darted away. Greg pulled back inside the apartment until the cat once again felt brave enough to approach the bowl and continue eating.

"Yeah . . . 'S that good? You like that?"

Greg inched back out until the cat was within reach. He kept clicking his tongue and making soothing noises until he judged that the cat's defenses were down. Then, like lightning, he made a grab for it. His hand closed like a vise around the cat's scrawny neck. The animal started hissing and clawing the air as Greg pulled it back into the apartment. One claw caught his bare arm just above the elbow. Blood beaded up along the long gash which stung enough to make Greg wince. The pain only increased his fury.

"You think you can trick me, is that it, you little prick?"

He shook the cat violently as he held it at arm's length so the claws couldn't get near him again. The animal was surprisingly light, and for an instant, Greg wondered if it was real.

But it didn't matter.

He grunted softly as he started applying a slow, steady pressure to the cat's neck. The animal was making a pathetic, low howling noise that sounded almost human. Its eyes bulged from their sockets, glistening wetly. Its tongue stuck out as though it were trying to lick its milk-rimmed mouth clean.

"Oh, yeah. All along I knew you were out there," Greg said. "I knew that you were watching me. Did you really think I was *that* stupid?"

The cat's struggles gradually lessened as its oxygen-starved lungs collapsed. Its claws raked the air uselessly; its mouth gaped open, exposing needle-sharp, yellow-stained teeth.

"What I wanna know is, did you tell them where I live?"

Greg's voice was low and trembling with barely suppressed rage.

"Did you bring the cops here?"

After another minute or so, the cat shuddered and then hung limply in Greg's grip. With a savage grunt, Greg squeezed the creature's neck all the harder until he heard the satisfying *crack* of its spine breaking. A thin stream of urine dripped onto the floor as the animal's bladder released. Greg shook the body roughly, enjoying the way it felt so floppy in his hands. He reveled in his power to control life and death.

"I guess the joke's on you, huh?" he said as he walked over to the window and leaned outside. The cold air burned his lungs, almost taking his breath away.

"I know they're looking for me because I killed some cops this time, so they're not gonna stop 'till they find me."

He paused and stared at the dead animal in his hand, then laughed softly.

"You want to know the funny thing, though?"

His laughter grew louder and echoed back to him. He turned the dead animal around and stared straight into its bulging, sightless eyes. Bloody foam was dripping from the cat's open mouth and falling through the railing.

"They won't find *me* before I find *them!*"

With a quick flip of his wrist, he tossed the dead cat out over the fire escape railing. The body twisted and turned as it fell and then made a satisfyingly loud *plop* sound when it hit the pavement three stories down.

"So much for landing on all fours," Greg said, laughing even louder. His breath puffed in the cold air.

For a minute or so, Greg stared down at the dead cat, sprawled on the pavement. When he finally realized how cold he was, he pulled back inside, ran the window down, and locked it. Turning to the mess he'd made on the kitchen table and floor, he rubbed his hands vigorously together and said, "Now, then . . . Let's see about getting something to eat."

Chapter 5
The Hunt Begins

It was a little after nine o'clock, and the night was the coldest it had been so far this year. Greg's chattering teeth diced the streams of mist that blew out of his mouth like puffs of cigarette smoke whenever he exhaled. He was standing in a phone booth, hopping from one foot to the other and trying his best to stay warm as he punched the numbers of the police station house. Even with gloves on, his fingers felt so numb he wasn't sure he hit the right numbers.

The harsh blue glare of fluorescent light inside the phone booth hurt his eyes, making them water. He didn't like the idea that anyone passing by could see him so easily while he wasn't able to see them, so—in spite of the cold wind—he jammed the door open and braced it with his foot as he listened to the phone line click and buzz.

The desk sergeant answered on the third ring. Greg inhaled sharply. The sudden snap of cold air in his lungs made him start coughing, and it took him a second or two to regain control.

"Yeah, yeah," he said, still gasping. "Sorry 'bout that. Look, I'd like to talk to whoever's in charge of investigating those killings that happened over on West Forty-Seventh last night."

Greg had a thick wad of bubble gum stuffed into his cheek

to distort his voice, in case the police station could record him and later identify his voice with voice prints like they did with fingerprints.

"Hold on. I'll put you through," the desk sergeant said. "Your name?"

Greg blinked his eyes nervously and looked around. No way he was about to give this cop his name. Didn't cops get anonymous phone calls all the time?

"I don't wanna tell you my name," he said. A low tremor shook his voice. "I don't want any trouble from this, see? I just wanna talk to the detective in charge."

"I'll put you through," the desk sergeant said, sounding as if he could just about care.

For a while—too long a time, Greg thought; maybe long enough for them to trace the call—the line went dead.

Greg's nervousness spiked. He was just about to hang up when the phone at the other end of the line started ringing again. On the fourth ring, a tired-sounding man answered.

"Detective Ross. How can I help you?"

"This isn't *Eddie* Ross, is it?"

Greg made sure to distort his voice as much as possible.

"No," the man at the other end of the line said. "My name's John. What can I do for you?"

"Okay, John . . . John Ross," Greg said, feigning that he was a lot slower mentally than he really was. "Well, you see, I used to know a cop by the name of Eddie Ross. I was thinking maybe he got promoted or something, but he wasn't even in your precinct, anyways."

"What can I do for you, Mr—? I didn't catch your name."

The cop sounded impatient, and this irritated Greg.

"You're investigating what happened over on West Forty-Seventh last night, right?"

There was a slight hesitation at the other end of the line. Once again, Greg wondered if the police would try to trace his call. For all he knew, a cruiser might already be on its way over to pick him up. He knew that he had to talk fast.

"'S there something you want to tell me about it?" Detective *John* Ross said.

Greg could hear the edge of eagerness in the man's voice, even though he seemed to be trying hard to mask it. He made the instant judgment that he didn't like this Detective Ross. The other night, he had caught only a glimpse of him in the dark—certainly not enough so he could identify him if he ever saw him again—but he thought Ross sounded too gruff and mean for his liking.

For an instant, Greg pictured that the detective might look a lot like his dead father. Now that he thought about it, he even sounded a little bit like his old man. Greg could easily imagine that Ross could hit and punch just as hard as his father used to, too. Of course, Greg wasn't so little anymore, and he intended to hit back.

"Uhh—no. No, I don't know nothing about it," Greg said, adjusting the wad of gum in his mouth and purposely slurring his words.

A cold much more penetrating than the night air reached inside his coat and gripped him. He took a shallow breath and closed his eyes, imagining for a moment that he could hear other voices whispering to him from out the night. He opened his eyes and turned quickly to look down the street, but he didn't see anyone.

But I know they're out there, Greg thought, shivering as he looked around. *I just have to be a whole lot faster to catch 'em watching me.*

"Look here, pal," Detective Ross said. "I don't have all night. You got something to say, then say it."

Greg was positive now that he didn't like this man's tone of voice in the least. He sounded like an impatient, short-tempered son-of-a-bitch.

Just like dear old Dad . . .

Memories of slaps across the face too numerous to count and punches to the stomach and back as he tried to shield himself filled Greg with galling bitterness. His eyes misted with tears, but he told himself it had nothing to do with the memories of what he had suffered from that man. It was just the cold and his nervousness.

"I—I'm really sorry 'bout what happened is all," Greg said,

forgetting for a moment to disguise his voice. "The guy in the store 'dere . . . he was a—a pretty good friend of mine, you know? I mean, I didn't know his name or nothin', but I went in there all the time, and he was always friendly to me."

"Were you anywhere near the store last night when the robbery took place?" The detective's voice was hard, pressing.

"No, no," Greg said. "Like I said, I just heard about it and was just—you know, hoping that you guys had nailed the son of a bitch who done it. I didn't see nothing in the newspaper or TV about any arrest being made."

"I can't discuss this case with you over the phone," the detective said mildly. "If you have anything that might help with the investigation, why don't you drop by the station?"

"I don't want no trouble, Detective Ross. I was just curious is all. I heard someone else was shot. I hope to God it was that scumbag who beat up and killed my friend."

"Where did you hear about someone else being shot?" the detective asked sharply. His voice reminded Greg of how Daddy sounded whenever he was working up a good head of anger.

Greg also immediately registered the suspicious edge in the detective's voice and realized that he may have just blown it. He didn't know if there had been any mention about the situation in the news. If he'd killed either of those cops—and he was pretty sure both of them were dead—it would have been big news. He knew that the cops wouldn't rest until the found their "cop-killer."

Narrowing his eyes to tiny slits, Greg cast another furtive glance up and down the street, thoroughly expecting to see a police cruiser with its headlights off, creeping slowly up on him.

Although the street was deserted, Greg still couldn't dispel the feeling that someone nearby, someone he could see was watching every move he made.

A sudden shiver shook his shoulders.

"I—I can't talk about it right now," Greg said between chattering teeth. "I was just . . . you know, curious to see if you were making any progress on that case or not. That's all. Honest to God."

"We're still actively working the case," Detective Ross said. "If you have any information and want to—"

Before he heard any more, Greg slammed the phone down so hard it made a loud *clang*.

Shivering wildly, he shoved his nearly frozen hands deep into the pockets of his overcoat and left the phone booth. He didn't care that the door slammed shut behind him hard enough almost to break the glass.

As he walked up the street, heading back to the laundromat where he was washing his and his mother's clothes, he saw a police car at the intersection up ahead. The black and white took the turn and started down the street toward him, slowing down as it passed by. There were two cops in the cruiser. Greg could practically *feel* their eyes on him as they checked him over. Without a backward glance, he wheeled into the brightly-lit laundromat as if he hadn't even noticed them. When he looked up a few seconds later, the cruiser was gone. The steamy heat of the laundromat had condensed on the plate glass windows, and Greg could feel tiny beads of moisture dripping like sweat from his face.

That had been close . . . *too* close.

Over the next few days, Greg had a lot to think about and a lot to worry about.

He hardly remembered what had happened the morning after the robbery when he had strangled the stray cat that had appeared on the fire escape outside the kitchen window. When he did remember it, he didn't give it much thought except to wonder why such black, violent moods came over him like that.

He wondered about these dark impulses that gripped him from time to time and made him do things that he didn't even remember afterwards, not clearly, anyway. He knew it might have something to do with his fear of being caught, but he couldn't remember exactly what it was. Other than running a few errands, he called in sick to work and spent the next couple of days after the robbery in his apartment with the door locked

and bolted, terrified that the police were going to swoop down
on him at any second.

He checked the *Daily News* every day, and kept an eye on
the TV news for something about the incident, but it was buried
under headlines about more trouble in the Middle East. Maybe
he hadn't killed those cops after all. Killing a cop was always
big news, and the police didn't let up until they found their
cop killer.

So what was going on here?

This should have been big news.

The only conclusion Greg could draw was that they knew
exactly who he was and were lying in wait for him . . . wearing
him down before they pounced.

Greg was glad about one thing. He still had the money
from the robbery—minus the hundred dollars he'd given to
the bum—but after counting it and discovering that he only
had a couple of hundred dollars and change, he knew that it
wouldn't get him very far. He never once stopped to consider
that three or four human lives weren't worth a couple of hundred
bucks.

The one thing that *was* on his mind—night and day—was
that he had to find out more about this guy John Ross. Greg
wanted to know who he was, how much he knew about the
case, and—most importantly—where the son of a bitch lived.
He figured if he could find the cop's home, he just might be
able to get to him before he got to Greg.

Of course, that presented a whole host of problems.

For one, Greg didn't have a car.

With his pathetic income from the video store, he had never
been able to afford a car, especially living in Brooklyn. Even
if he could have afforded a car, he couldn't have afforded the
high insurance rates, and he sure didn't want to deal with the
hassle of having his car broken into or stripped for parts or
outright stolen. The bicycle he had bought a few years ago to
get to and from work had been stolen after only a week or two,
so like most New Yorkers, he got around on foot or by using
public transportation.

But if he was going to find out who this detective was and

where he lived, he was going to have to find some wheels. Lately, what with all the high tech security systems and the Club, it was much harder to steal cars now than it had been back when he was a kid. But not *everyone* could afford or bothered with such protection. Besides, Greg didn't need an expensive car. He'd be satisfied with a relic that wouldn't draw much attention and probably wouldn't even be reported stolen. Any wreck would do. He was mechanically inclined and fairly good at hot-wiring cars, so when the time came, he was sure he'd be able to steal what he needed.

Three days after the robbery on Forty-seventh Street, once he was beginning to feel confident that the SWAT team wasn't about to break down the apartment door and arrest him, Greg took the train from Brooklyn to midtown Manhattan and started casing the precinct house where he knew John worked. It turned out to be not very far from the convenience store on Forty-seventh Street. He noticed that the American flag was flying at half-mast and realized it was probably for the cops he had killed. Still, he hadn't seen anything in the newspaper about a funeral for any dead cops.

It was Tuesday, warm for a January afternoon. The sky above the City was bright blue and clear. A warming breeze was blowing in off the Hudson Rover carrying with it the promise of an early spring. The sidewalks were clean and dry except for the blowing litter.

Feeling a bit nostalgia, Greg decided to take a walk by the convenience store. His anger flared momentarily when he looked inside and saw another clerk behind the register, a foreign-looking man who looked so much like the man Greg had clubbed with his baseball bat the other night that, for a terrifying instant, Greg seriously wondered if he had imagined what had happened that night.

For a long time, he stood there on the sidewalk, staring in at the man. When the clerk finally noticed him and reacted like he was getting suspicious of him, Greg quickly walked away.

He considered going down into the alley and checking around the abandoned supply building, but he decided against that just in case the cops had the place under surveillance and were waiting for him to come back to it.

After all, didn't the criminal always comes back to the scene of the crime?

Greg knew he was foolish to be hanging around here, so he walked to the nearest train station and caught the next train back home to Brooklyn.

The next day, though, he was back hanging around outside the precinct house. After thinking about it for more than an hour, he finally worked up the courage to go into the station and ask the desk sergeant if he could speak with Detective Ross. He couldn't help but wonder if this was the same desk sergeant he had spoken to over the phone the other night, but he decided that it really didn't matter. Greg was nervous that the desk sergeant might recognize his voice from the phone, but if he did, he didn't let on as he instructed Greg to go up to the second floor and have a seat in the waiting area.

He sat on the worn, wooden bench for over an hour, listening to it squeak every time he shifted his body. Finally, a man walked over and introduced himself as Detective Ross.

"My name's Harry . . . Harry Miller," Greg said as he shook the detective's hand vigorously. He sized the man up quickly— medium height, heavy-set but not overly muscular with short, dark hair, blue eyes, and that weary, cynical scowl all cops seem to get after a few years on the job.

"What can I do for you?" Detective Ross said, all business.

"I had a bike stolen over on Fifty-second Street," Greg replied.

He'd made a point of slurring his voice because he wanted Ross to think that he wasn't the swiftest guy on the planet.

Ross scowled at him and nodded. If he was trying to look sympathetic, he was failing miserably. Greg could tell that, just beneath the surface, this detective was sneering with contempt at him and his silly complaint, but he told himself that it didn't matter.

"Was it a valuable bicycle?" Ross asked.

"Uh-huh. I paid over five hunnert dollars for it," Greg said, nodding eagerly and licking his lips. He tried to adopt the inflection of the man he'd killed in the abandoned building that night but didn't think he quite caught it.

"Did you fill out a stolen property complaint at the front desk?" Ross asked.

Still feigning stupidity, Greg stared at him blankly and shook his head as though totally mystified.

"You have to fill out a stolen property report," Ross said, obviously trying hard to sound patient. "Someone will look into it when and if they have time."

It went without saying that, with more than two thousand murders a year in the Metropolitan area, a New York City detective was never going to find time to look for Greg's stolen bike.

"So what you're saying is, you can't help me, is that it?" Greg said.

He knew that he was pouring it on a little thick, but he was glad to see that Ross didn't seem to be catching on to him.

"I don't mean to disappoint you, Mr.—ah, Miller, but this isn't exactly a job for a detective." Ross' face was impassive. "Taking it to DMV is your best bet, but I'll be honest with you, the chances of you ever getting your bike back are pretty slim."

"The DMV?" Greg echoed, gnawing his lower lip as he shook his head.

"The Department of Motor Vehicles."

"But it don't have a motor," Greg said, squinting at Ross as he started digging his nose with his forefinger. He could see the disgust in Ross' expression.

"They have a division for stolen bikes," Ross said simply. "I'm sorry, but that's the best I can do for you."

"Yeah—well, okay, I guess," Greg said, shifting his feet and heading for the stairway. He considered starting a big scene about not being helped by the City but decided not to draw any more attention to himself.

As he walked down the creaking stairs to the first floor, Greg felt suddenly nervous that Ross *had* seen through his act. His heart was racing as he walked outside and started down the street as fast as he could go. He was satisfied that he had gotten what he had come here for—a good look at Detective Ross so he'd recognize him if he ever saw him again.

Because the detective had been at the station in the early afternoon, Greg figured Ross was on the day shift, probably from eight to four, at least for this week; so around four o'clock that afternoon, hoping to see Ross when he left the building, he came back and took a seat on a park bench under some trees across the street from the precinct house. A little after four-thirty, a late model, white, four-door Subaru with Detective Ross at the wheel pulled out of the parking lot behind the building and turned left onto the street.

Smiling to himself, Greg tracked the car until it was out of sight, then wrote the license plate number down on a matchbook cover and shoved it deep into his coat pocket. Satisfied, he got up from the park bench and walked back to the train station for the ride back to Brooklyn.

He was still feeling elated that night when he went to work at the video store. Even Fritz, the store manager who hardly ever said anything nice to him, commented on how he seemed so "up." After work, once Greg got back at the apartment, he went to bed and masturbated for the first time in weeks. That night, he slept better than he had since a long time before the robbery.

The next day was Thursday, Greg's day off. Around two o'clock in the afternoon, while strolling the streets near his apartment, he spotted a late model Ford that looked like it would suit his needs just fine. It didn't take long to hot-wire it, and by three forty-five, he was parked in front of the station house in Manhattan, waiting for Detective Ross to leave work.

An hour or so later, just when he was staring to get a little antsy, the white Subaru appeared with Ross at the wheel. Greg started up his car, shifted into gear, and pulled out into the stream of traffic. Keeping at least one or two cars between them, he followed Ross across town, heading west.

The white Subaru moved at a pretty good clip. Greg had to run a few red lights to keep up, but he wasn't worried about getting pinched. As the joke went, red traffic lights in New

York aren't real laws, just driving suggestions. Besides, he wasn't about to lose Ross so soon.

They drove over to West Side Highway and followed it north until it turned into Route 9-A. Greg was grateful that Ross didn't turn left onto the George Washington Bridge. He was never very keen about going over to New Jersey. They crossed the Spuyten Duyvil Bridge and followed 9-A north until it became the Saw Mill River Parkway.

Greg had a bit of trouble keeping up with Ross. The detective seemed to like to speed, and—no doubt—if he was ever stopped for speeding, all he would have to do was flash his police ID to get out of receiving a ticket. Greg knew that was how the system worked, and he knew that he would be in a world of shit if he was pulled over—especially if the car he was driving had been reported stolen.

Keeping the white car in sight wasn't easy, but Greg let Ross get several car lengths ahead of him and only sped up when he had to, to keep him in sight. He figured that today he'd see where Ross was heading, then drive back into Manhattan and dump the car. He'd get another car in a day or two, and pick up from here. It might take a while, but by leapfrogging like this, he would eventually find out where the detective lived.

And then he'd figure out the next step.

They drove for over an hour out of the city, heading deep into Westchester County—the "ritzy" area where the rich people who worked in the City lived. The further they went, the more Greg found himself feeling ill at ease. He preferred the anonymity of the crowded city and felt exposed the few times he had ever come out into the suburbs.

When he saw Ross' turn signal start flashing as he slowed for the turn at Exit thirty-nine, Greg sighed with relief.

BEDFORD HEIGHTS—MT. KISCO the green and white sign read.

"How the hell can a New York City cop afford a place out here?" Greg whispered, frowning to himself.

Still keeping back a safe distance, Greg followed the white Subaru to the traffic lights at the bottom of the exit ramp. At the intersection, he watched as Ross turned right onto a road marked Cedar Hollow Road. A small sign up ahead read: BED-

FORD HEIGHTS—3 MILES. Mount Kisco was four miles in the other direction.

Thinking that he had already taken enough chances for today, Greg turned left, did a quick U-turn at the gas station, and got back onto the Saw Mill River Parkway and headed back to Brooklyn.

It wasn't until he was driving back to the City that he realized how uptight he'd been feeling. He tried to take a deep breath, but his chest felt constrained, like it was encased in cement. His hand shook as he reached out and snapped on the radio, switching stations until he found something with a strong enough beat that wasn't rap music. Then he cranked the volume up so loud it rattled the cheap car speakers, rolled the driver's window down and, in spite of the steady blast of cold air, hung his arm out the window while slapping time on the roof of the car.

Tomorrow or the next day, he told himself, depending on how the weather was and how confident he was feeling, he would hot-wire another car in the afternoon and park somewhere along Cedar Hollow Road and wait until he saw Ross's white Subaru go by.

Greg was smiling so much it hurt his cheeks, but he had every right to be happy. In a day or two minimum, he would know exactly where Detective Ross lived. After that, he could take all the time he needed to figure out what he was going to *do* about it. He had a few ideas, but he wanted to check out Ross' house first. He needed to find out if the detective was married, and whether or not he had any kids. That would help him decide.

"Oh, yeah! Oh, yeah!" Greg shouted as he bopped in time with the music. He banged on the car roof until his hand was numb from the cold. Pulling his hand in, he rolled up the window, but as cold as he was, he was also feeling *damned* good!

"Oh, *yeah!*" he shouted, unable to contain a long bray of laughter. "This is going to be *some* fun . . ."

Chapter 6
Closing In

As it turned out, it took Greg more than a week to locate Detective Ross' house.

Four days later, on Monday, he stole a car some idiot had left running and double parked in front of a store. He drove out of the City as fast as he could but got stuck in the rush hour traffic, so it was a little after five-thirty and starting to get dark when he pulled over on the side of the road just off the Bedford Heights exit.

His patience started to wear thin as he waited more than fifteen minutes, but he didn't see the white Subaru. He couldn't decide if he had already missed Ross, or if the detective had gotten stuck in traffic and would be along any minute now.

Before Ross showed up, a Bedford Heights police cruiser with its red and blue bar lights flashing pulled up behind him. Greg jumped when the cop gave a quick chirp on the siren.

Looking all business, the patrolman got out of the cruiser and walked up to the driver's window. He didn't look at all friendly when he asked if Greg had a problem.

Greg told him that he was sure he'd flooded out the engine and was just waiting a few minutes before trying to start the car again. He tried not to show his relief when the cop didn't ask to see his license and registration.

Looking away from the cop, Greg made a show of turning the key in the ignition, glad that he hadn't hot-wired this car. The engine turned over and started running smoothly. Waving politely to the policeman and thanking him, Greg shifted into gear, muttering a curse under his breath as he drove off and headed back to Brooklyn.

The weather was lousy the next day, but Greg stole another car and drove to the precinct house, arriving a few minutes before four o'clock. He parked and got out to try to see if Ross' car was parked nearby, but he didn't see it. Rather than wait around and maybe be noticed, he decided to drive the same route he had taken every other day. This time, though, he drove more slowly, hoping that Ross would speed, as usual, and pass him at some point along the way.

This tactic didn't work the first two days he tried it, but on Thursday, Greg had just passed through the toll booth on the bridge when a white Subaru zipped past him. Greg sped up enough to catch the numbers on the license plate, smiling when he saw that it was Ross.

Like the first time he had tailed Ross, Greg got nervous trying to keep up with him. As they neared Exit 39, Greg started thinking that maybe he had been wrong the other day. Maybe Ross lived in another town further north and would drive past the exit this time. He let out a thin sigh of relief when Ross's turn light started to blink.

This time when he took the exit, Greg stayed right behind Ross, dropping back whenever the detective's car slowed down, speeding up whenever he sped up.

It was dark as they drove through downtown Bedford Heights. Greg couldn't stop looking at all the well-lit yuppie store fronts. This was a way of life he'd rarely seen and hardly imagined outside of his Brooklyn neighborhood. Everybody he saw walking along the sidewalks—adults and kids alike—were dressed in spiffy winter parkas with matching woolen hats, gloves or mittens. It all looked so quaint and homey it made Greg's stomach churn.

He followed Ross' car until the detective turned left onto a street marked Clinton Street. Even at night, Greg could see that both sides of the road were lined with large, gorgeous houses. Most of them were brightly-lit and cozy looking. These weren't the fanciest houses around. The real celebrities who lived in Westchester County—the movie and TV stars—had homes isolated from public view by tall shrubberies, long driveways, and high stone walls. But even this was a much higher standard of living than he would have ever experienced.

And how could a cop afford a home in a town like this? he wondered.

Greg decided that he couldn't . . . not unless he was on the take, like just about every other cop in the City.

As he followed Ross' car down Clinton Street, Greg began to get concerned that the rust bucket he was driving would be too noticeable in a fancy neighborhood like this, but he decided not to worry about it.

A mile and a half down the street, Ross' brake lights flashed as he slowed to turn into a driveway. Greg tapped his own brakes to slow down and glanced up at the house as he passed by, taking in as much detail as he could in the darkness.

It was two story house. Greg wasn't sure what style it was, but he had seen houses like this on TV. The top floor had an overhang above the first floor. The bottom story was ivy-covered brick, while the second story was either wood or stucco, painted white with dark trim. The outside lights on either side of the dark green front door lit up the black metal numbers *33*.

"Okay, thirty-three Clinton Street . . . thirty-three Clinton Street," Greg said, making it a chant so he wouldn't forget it.

The lights were on upstairs and down, making everything look so cozy it was sickening. With a house this big, Greg figured Ross had to have at least one kid. A childless couple would never need a house this large.

Greg's suspicion was confirmed when he eased past the house and saw a plastic snow sled and inflated Sno-tube in the driveway. He caught a only fleeting glimpse of Ross as he got out of the car and started up the steps to the side door.

"Okay . . . okay," Greg whispered to himself, trying hard to think what to do next.

Tension twisted like a snake inside his stomach. He was glad that he had found the place, and it hadn't been half as difficult as it could have been. The only close call had been with that town cop the other day.

Greg was positive that Ross hadn't noticed him or guessed that he was being followed, but he suddenly realized that he had been hyperventilating and was starting to get dizzy. Tiny bright spots of light drifted across his vision. A few houses down the street from Ross', Greg pulled over and leaned his head against the cold steering wheel. Closing his eyes, he took several slow, steady breaths, telling himself to calm down.

It was only when he looked up and glanced into the rearview mirror back at the house that he noticed the pile of trash bags that were stacked at the end of the front walkway.

That gave him an idea.

Chuckling to himself, he turned the car around in a neighbor's driveway and started back up Clinton Street. When he was in front of Ross' house, he turned off his headlights and coasted to a stop in front of the trash bags.

After checking up and down the street to make sure no one was around, he jumped out of the car and, moving quickly, ran around to the passenger's side, snapped open the door, and threw all three plastic bags into the car. They were cold to the touch and crinkled like cellophane in his hands. Keeping a wary eye on the house, he ran back around to the driver's side and got in, snapped on his headlights, and shifted into gear. He was laughing crazily as he drove away.

Greg was so excited he couldn't stop shaking as he headed back to Brooklyn. Instead of dumping the car off in Manhattan, as he had done with all the others he'd stolen, he drove straight to his apartment building in Brooklyn.

It was after eight o'clock when he got home, but the street wasn't busy, so he chanced leaving the car parked in front of his building while he carried the trash bags upstairs.

As expected, his mother was snoring away in her bedroom, so he didn't worry about her seeing what he was doing. She was hard of hearing, but Greg tiptoed into the kitchen just the same. He hoped she was a particularly sound sleeper tonight because he had no idea how he'd explain having three bags of someone else's trash in the apartment if she saw them.

Before he went through the trash bags, though, he wanted to ditch the stolen car. It wouldn't be very smart to leave it in front of his apartment building. He drove it over to Jackson Heights where he left it on the side of the road for anyone who might find it. He figured it'd be gone for a joyride in less than an hour. He walked back to his apartment, getting home a little after nine o'clock and set to work, going through the Ross' trash.

After about fifteen minutes of sifting through the trash, he found what he was looking for—a stack of torn-up check deposit receipts. On the top of them was John Ross' and his wife's name, Angela, along with their address and phone number.

"Angela ... Angela Ross," Greg whispered, feeling his smile spread across his face.

He read the address and phone number out loud several times, then sat back in his chair and laughed out loud, but it wasn't until late the next day, after work, that he decided to call. First he hit star six-seven, in case Detective Ross had a caller ID, then dialed the number. He was laughing so hard snot blew out of his nose when he heard the phone start ringing at the other end.

"Hold on a second, Rob. I have a call on the other line. It might be John."

Angie pulled the receiver away, pressed the *flash* button, then brought the receiver back to her ear. She glanced at her wristwatch, surprised to see that it was already well past nine o'clock, and John still wasn't home from work. The least he could do was call *before* he was late.

"Hello?" she said.

She was expecting to hear John's voice, but for a second or two, the caller didn't say anything. Angie tensed when she heard the low rattle of breathing as she waited. She was just about to hang up when a deep, muffled voice said, "Yeah, is—ah, John home?"

Angie had no idea why, but every alarm bell instantly went off in her head.

Whoever this was, she didn't like the sound of this man's voice.

She didn't like that he was calling when John was already overdue. Even the sound of his breathing set her nerves on edge.

"Umm—no. He's in the shower right now. Can I take a message?"

"Oh—I'm surprised he's home already," the man said. "I thought he'd still be at the station."

"May I ask who's calling?" Angie asked, hearing the hard edge in her voice. She didn't recognize this as anyone she knew, but there were lots of people John knew from work that she didn't know.

As she waited for the caller to answer, Angie got up off the couch and walked into the kitchen to glance at the number displayed on the Caller I.D. machine.

The message read *"Private."*

Whoever this was, he was smart enough—or cautious enough—to press star six-seven before dialing the number. Angie's sense of danger spiked.

"Why don't you give me your name and number, and I'll have him call you as soon as he's out of the shower," she said, hoping that the man didn't detect the tremor in her voice.

"Oh, that won't be necessary," the man on the phone said. "It's not all that important, anyway. I'll try to catch him at the station tomorrow. Sorry to bother you, Angela."

Nobody who knew her called her Angela, but before Angie could say anything, the man broke the connection. Feeling confused and worried, she was about to hang up when she heard the signal for call waiting beep again. She remembered that her brother was still on the other line. Shaking her head, she pressed the *flash* button again.

"Sorry about that," she said as she walked slowly back into

the living room and sat down on the couch. The seat was still warm from her sitting there.

"Anything important?" Rob asked.

Angie still felt off-balance. It bothered her that she couldn't figure out why the phone call had made her feel so apprehensive, but it just hadn't *sounded* right to her.

She considered telling Rob her worries but decided not to give him anything more to worry about. They'd been talking for over an hour, and in all that time he hadn't stopped pushing her—a little too hard at times, she thought—to divorce John if she had to and leave with the kids, if only for her own peace of mind.

"Nope . . . wrong number," she said, cringing at the tightness she heard in her voice. "Anyway, you were saying—?"

Rob took a deep breath, then let it out slowly.

"I was saying what I've probably already said too many times already. I just want you to know that I support you in whatever you choose to do, all right? No matter what! And if you *ever* need a place to stay—either you alone, or you and the kids—you know my door's always open, right?"

"Com'on, Rob. You know I'd never impose on you and Craig like that."

"Umm, *excuse* me?" Rob said. "I don't think it constitutes *imposing* if you're invited. And I mean it, Sis. Any time you want to drive up to Maine and visit, you can stay with us as long as you want. It's no imposition at all, believe me."

"I appreciate that, Rob. I really do," Angie said. Emotion choked her voice. She couldn't pinpoint why, but the sentiment touched her so deeply that tears started to fill her eyes.

"Hey," Rob said. "If we can't help each other out, what good are we, huh?"

"I know . . . I know, but—" Angie stopped herself, then sighed softly. "Look, I should let you go. John should be home any minute now, and we're supposed to go out for supper."

"Without the kids, I hope," Rob said.

"Yeah. They're staying with their friends overnight. I'll give you a call in a couple of days, 'kay?"

"No, let me call you next time so it'll be on my dime. I'll give you a buzz Saturday or Sunday, all right?"

"Sure," Angie said. "'Bye for now. Oh, and—hey, thanks for listening."

"Think nothing of it," Rob replied. "You hang in there, kiddo, you hear me?"

"Yeah, I hear you," Angie said, and then she heard Rob hang up.

For the longest time, she just sat there on the couch, staring at the dark rectangle of the living room window. Her nervousness about that strange phone call passed, and it wasn't long before she was getting angry wondering when the hell John would get home!

The night air was so cold it burned John's lungs as he ran the short distance from the car to the side door of the house.

He knew he was late, and he was pretty sure Angie was going to be upset with him; but he was hoping that what he intended to tell her tonight would make a big difference. The only question was: When would he tell her?

Angie was standing in the kitchen, scowling with her arms folded across her chest as he threw the door open and came inside.

"Hey," he said as he stomped his feet to remove the snow that clung to his shoes. "It's cold as a bugger out there."

"What took you so long?" Angie asked.

John could see the fire in her eyes, and for a moment he considered telling her his news right then and there, but he held back because he really wanted to surprise her.

"Can I have a minute to change?" John asked as he shrugged off his coat and hung it up on one of the hooks by the door.

Angie shrugged as if she could just about care.

"I got tired of waiting, so I ate a little something an hour or so ago," she said.

"I just want to change my shirt," John said, pulling at the armpits as though they really smelled. "I won't take time for a shower."

Angie pursed her lips and shook her head.

"You know," she said, "if it's going to be a problem for you, we can go always out some other night."

"No, no," John said with a curt shake of his head. "I want to go tonight. Really. I'm sorry I was late. I got hung up with some paperwork at the station, and for some reason, the traffic on the parkway tonight was bumper to bumper. I'll just be a second, I promise."

Angie just stayed where she was, her arms folded across her chest as John walked out in to the hallway. He started unbuttoning his shirt as he dashed upstairs thinking how uncannily quiet the house seemed with both kids gone. He grabbed a clean shirt from his closet, jammed his arms into the sleeves, and was shoving the shirttails under his belt as he started back downstairs.

"See?" he said when he entered the kitchen again.

Angie hadn't moved. She just regarded him with a steady stare and shook her head.

Once again, John thought that it might be best if he told her now what he had decided. Instead, he grabbed Angie's coat from the peg by the door and held it out to help her put it on.

When she stepped close and turned her back to him, John was filled with a sudden urge to grab her right there, turn her around, and start kissing and hugging her, but he could tell by her tense posture that she wouldn't be receptive to any romantic overtures.

Not yet, anyway, he thought. *Maybe later, once I tell her what I've decided.*

"The kids are all set?" he asked once he had his own coat on and they were moving toward the door.

Angie nodded as she opened the door and stepped outside. She gasped in the sudden cold of the night.

"They're all set. And I called the restaurant to tell them we'd be a bit late." She wasn't even trying to mask the hostility in her voice.

Making sure the house door locked behind them, John walked with her down to the car. He was shivering from the cold, but—thankfully—the engine was still warm from his drive home, so it didn't take long for the heater to fill the car with warmth.

They didn't say much to each other on the drive to *Le Bistro,* the restaurant on Croton Lake Road just outside of Katonah. It was one of the fanciest restaurants in the Bedford Heights area, and Angie's favorite place to eat. Because it was a little on the expensive side, they usually only went there for special occasions. John found the elegant red and black decor a bit too much for his taste, but he hoped that coming here tonight would put Angie in a better mood.

John stopped the car under the scalloped red awning and left the car running so the valet could drive off and park it. The doorman opened the car door for Angie and then hurried to open the heavy oak door to the restaurant for both of them. As they entered, their feet whispered on the plush carpeting. John helped her off with her coat and then gave it to the coat check. He gave his name to the maître d', who promptly led them to a small table at the back of the room.

The main dining room was filled, but once they were seated, John felt comfortable and private. The waiter came and asked if they'd like a cocktail. John asked for his usual—a beer, while Angie ordered a Manhattan, straight up with a twist. Once their drinks were delivered, they settled back.

John took a moment to study Angie in the soft glow of candlelight. He thought about how much he loved her, how much she really meant to him, and how he didn't like the icy tension there seemed to be between them all the time lately. He wanted it to disappear so they could feel about each other the way they had back when they had first met and fallen in love.

"You know," he said, leaning forward and reaching across the table to grasp her hand with both of his. "I've been thinking."

He gave her hand a tight squeeze.

"About what?" Angie asked, looking skeptical when he didn't immediately proceed.

"About what you said . . . About me being on the Job."

Angie's eyes narrowed. In the candlelight, John could see her cheeks flush as she opened her mouth expectantly.

"What do you mean?" she asked warily.

"I mean about what you've been saying, about wanting me to put in for early retirement."

"Yeah . . .?"

"And I've been thinking it's not such a bad idea."

"You don't mean it!" Angie said, loud enough so the people at the next table turned and looked at her.

John nodded.

"Yeah, I do. You know, after going to the funerals for those two cops who were killed that night, and thinking how I could just as easily have been one of them, or that if I had reacted a little quicker or something, I might have been able to—to catch that guy before he killed all of them—"

His throat suddenly closed off. Letting go of Angie's hand, he picked up his beer and took a gulp. He was happy to see Angie smiling at him in a way he hadn't seen her smile in a very long time.

"It's just that . . . I think maybe you're right," he said.

"Maybe?" Angie arched one eyebrow. "What's with the *maybe?*"

"No. I know I've had enough of the Job."

For just an instant, John thought his voice sounded like someone else's talking.

"And I know you have, too."

Angie rolled her eyes as she nodded agreement. Then she looked at him intently, not breaking eye contact with him for even a second.

"I . . . I can't believe you're really saying this," she whispered. "What's the catch?"

John smiled and shook his head.

"No catch," he said. "I mean, you know how much I love my work. I always have." He swallowed hard, and his throat made a funny gulping sound. "But when I realized what a toll it's taken on you and the kids." He sighed and shrugged. "I just decided that . . . enough was enough."

Angie slid her hand out from his grasp and leaned back in

her chair. Covering her mouth with both hands, she just kept shaking her head from side to side and looking at him like she couldn't believe what she was hearing. There was a distant glazed look in her eyes that might have been just the candlelight, but John didn't think so.

"So tell me," he said, beaming a smile at her. "What should we do? I mean, where do you want to retire to?"

"Gee, I . . . I don't know," Angie said. She sounded genuinely flabbergasted but was looking happier than she had looked in months . . . maybe years.

"Well, as of June, thanks to the budget cuts, you won't have a job, either. My pension's not going to carry us too far. but it should cover us for a while—at least until you and I can find something else to do. Besides, we have a few more years until the kids start college."

He grabbed her hand again and squeezed it tightly.

"The difference is, we can both find something we really *want* to do, not something we *have* to do."

He was trying to talk practically, but he could see that Angie was barely listening to him. She pulled away and dropped her hands into her lap. The smile that spread slowly across her face made him think of morning sunlight, spreading across the lawn. Without warning, she sprang out of her chair and came over to his side of the table. John turned to her as she wrapped her arms around him and started kissing him repeatedly.

"I . . . I just can't *believe* you," she said, squealing with delight between kisses as she hugged him as close as she could. The embrace almost smothered him.

After a few seconds, he eased her back and kissed her long and hard on the mouth. He could feel himself getting an erection as her tongue darted playfully into his mouth.

"Hey, hey," he said, backing her off a little. "This is a classy place, remember? We don't want to get thrown out of here."

Angie looked at him with a warm, genuine expression and said, "I don't care."

"No, no," John said, waving her off. "I came here to get a fancy-ass meal, and that's exactly what I'm going to get.

After that we can go home and . . . with the kids both gone for the night, you never know . . ."

Angie smiled at him and nodded.

"That's right," she said in a heated whisper. "You never know what might happen."

Chapter 7
Death and Burial

Greg was driving another stolen car that night, this one a late model Buick, something a little fancier than the others he'd stolen the last few times. He'd gone uptown Manhattan to get it because he didn't want whatever car he was driving to stand out in a ritzy place like Bedford Heights. As always, he wore leather gloves so he wouldn't leave any fingerprints for the cops to find after he dumped the car.

It was fairly late, almost nine thirty, when he saw John and his wife, Angela, leave the house.

At first Greg considered making sure they were gone and then breaking into the house. He was sure he could have some fun—especially if the kids were there with a babysitter; but even if no one was home, he was thinking he'd go through the house and ransack it, maybe even find some money or jewelry lying around to pay for his aggravation.

But then he remembered that the important thing was to get John Ross because he *knew* that John Ross was after him.

Over the last few days, the TV and newspapers had covered the funerals of the two cops he had killed that night on West Forty-seventh. There had been an official statement from the commissioner's office that the investigation was closed. The cops were satisfied that they had shot and killed the culprit.

But Greg knew better.

He knew that John Ross and the rest of the New York City police force was after him.

It only made sense to strike first.

Keeping a safe distance back, Greg followed them out of town to the Katonah town line, where they stopped at a restaurant. There was a huge carved wooden sign out front that read: LE BISTRO. It was obvious to Greg that this was the kind of fancy-pants place he would never be able to afford, the kind of place he would only see on TV or in the movies. He had to wonder again how someone living on a New York City detective's salary could afford to eat in a place like this and was all the more certain that Ross had to be on the take.

Greg wasn't sure what—if anything—he was going to do tonight, but just in case, he had brought along a gun—the fully loaded .38 special he'd found in the glove compartment of one of the cars he'd stolen last week. It was a perfect weapon for him because it was small, easy to handle, and he knew, after he used it, that it could never be traced back to him.

He barely slowed down as he drove past the entrance to the restaurant, glancing over just in time to see John as he got out of the car. He saw the valet, wearing a fancy red cap and coat, hustle around the side of the car and slide in behind the steering wheel. Satisfied that John and Angela were going to be inside for a while, Greg drove a short way down the road, rounded a curve, and did a quick U-turn.

As he approached the restaurant again, his pulse was pounding so hard in his head that he had to pull over to the side of the road about a hundred yards away from the restaurant's parking lot. Closing his eyes, he leaned his head against the cold steering wheel and slowly counted to one hundred. Gradually, the painful pulsing behind his eyes began to subside, but it didn't go away entirely.

"Just take it easy," he whispered, trying his best to calm himself. He kept staring into the darkness behind his closed eyes, mesmerized by the swirling patterns of light that shifted across his vision.

Suddenly he jumped and, gasping for breath, opened his eyes. For just a second, the darkness behind his eyes had coalesced into what looked like several faces, looming at him. The soft scraping of several voices, whispering, filled his ears.

"*Jesus,*" Greg whispered. His heart gave a single, solid punch against his ribs that he was afraid might signal a heart attack.

Spinning around quickly, he looked into the dark back seat, expecting to see those same faces materializing behind him, but the back seat was empty. Even so, Greg didn't feel any better. His heart was racing high and fast, and he was panting like he'd just run a couple of miles. Shivering, he wiped the sweat from his forehead with the back of his glove.

Finally he decided that, racing heartbeat or not, he didn't want to be seen sitting here on the side of the road in a stolen car. This one was worth enough so the owner had no doubt reported it stolen. Shifting the car into gear, Greg pulled back onto the road and slowly approached *Le Bistro*.

He still didn't have any idea what he was going to do. All he could think of at this point was to wait in the parking lot until John and his wife came out.

Maybe by then he'd have thought of something.

He noticed an Exxon station directly across the street from the restaurant. The lot was filled with late model cars that had been left overnight for repairs. Greg pulled into the gas station's parking lot and stopped his car, making sure to angle it so he could drive out without having to back up or turn around. He killed the engine and headlights, and then, for the next half hour or so, just sat there shivering in the darkness as he kept a watchful eye on the brightly lit front door of the restaurant.

His eye kept being drawn to the valet, who took the patrons' cars after they had parked under the awning and drove them into the lot where he parked them. Later, when the diners came back out, the valet would retrieve the cars while the patrons waited for him at the front door. As soon as he drove up, the doorman would open the door on the passenger's side while the valet would hold the driver's door open.

The valet was a young man—probably a smart-ass college kid, Greg figured, while the doorman looked a bit older, maybe in his thirties. Neither one of them looked particularly strong. Greg was positive he could beat up either one of them in a fight, but not both at once. Then again, his gun was an equalizer.

It was then that Greg got an idea.

Leaving the keys in the ignition, he slipped the .38 into his right coat pocket and got out of the car. The night wind bit through his jacket, making him shiver.

He hoped that, if anyone noticed him walking along the road, they would think he was just someone out for a late night stroll. He walked until the restaurant was out of sight and then, after checking to make sure no one was around, crossed the street and doubled back.

He kept to the shadows as best he could as he approached the restaurant parking lot. After scanning the area, he vaulted over the low split rail fence and ducked down behind the first row of cars. He took a few seconds to catch his breath, then, crouching low, moved up the line between the parked cars until he found the Ross' white Subaru.

I hope to Christ I don't freeze my ass off before they come back out, he thought as he hunkered down behind the car on the passenger's side. He didn't want the valet to see him—at least, not until it was too late.

Greg kept checking the luminous dial of his watch, watching as the minutes dragged slowly by. He cringed in the frigid darkness and had to skitter out of sight once or twice when the valet came and got someone else's car. The one time the valet came close to where Greg was hiding, Greg held his breath, hoping that the young man wouldn't notice the steam of his breath rising from behind the car where he was hiding.

Finally, after almost an hour of waiting in the cold, the valet came over to John's car and opened the driver's door.

Greg reacted so fast he surprised even himself.

He stood up so quickly the blood rushed from his head, making him momentarily dizzy, but he ignored it as charged around the back of the car and launched himself at the valet. The young man was just about to slide into the car behind the steering wheel when Greg hit him low and hard. At the same time, he punched the young man as hard as he could on the side of the head.

The valet staggered but didn't fall.

Shouting loudly, he twisted around and tried to defend himself, but Greg struck fast, punching the man repeatedly in the face. The valet made a tiny moaning sound as he crumpled to the ground. Greg stood back, panting heavily from the sudden exertion, then dragged the man around to the front of the car and dumped him.

He knew that the man had seen his face and that as soon as he regained consciousness he would probably be able to identify him. There was no other option that he could see, so he took the revolver from his coat pocket, pressed it up close to the unconscious man's chest, and pulled the trigger, once.

The gun snapped like a firecracker going off. The young man's body snapped backwards. His legs kicked straight out, and then he lay still. His left leg kept twitching as blood seeped from the hole in his chest and pooled on the frozen asphalt. The man's punctured lung made a high wheezing sound as air escaped through the hole.

"Asshole," Greg muttered as he grabbed the man's hat and placed it on his head, low over his eyes. He could see that the valet's fancy coat was too small for him. Besides, it was splattered with blood. He didn't want to get any blood stains on him if he could help it.

After picking up the car keys from where they had fallen on the ground, Greg plopped himself down in the driver's seat. His hand shook as he turned the ignition, and the car roared to life.

Icy tension filled Greg as he shifted into gear and slowly drove around to the front of the restaurant. He had studied the valet's parking pattern, so he knew what to do so he wouldn't raise any suspicions with the doorman. His racing pulse skipped a beat when he pulled to a stop underneath the bright red awning. Glancing out the side window, he saw John and his wife, huddled against the cold, waiting in the doorway.

Squeezing the handle of the gun, which he had stuffed into his left coat pocket to keep it out of sight, Greg looked straight ahead when the doorman came forward and opened the passenger's door for Angela. In the side mirror, he saw John coming around to the back of the car. Greg's grip on the revolver was so tight his wrist and hand had gone numb.

He knew that he had to time it just right. Holding his breath, he stepped out of the car before John could block him. As he turned to the left and looked at John, Greg felt oddly dissociated, as though everything had slowed down.

For a single, crystal instant that seemed frozen in time, Greg's gaze met John's. He was positive that he saw a spark of recognition in the detective's eyes, but this was quickly replaced by a look of stunned surprise when Greg pulled the gun out of his pocket and aimed it straight at him.

All of Greg's senses were heightened to an almost frightening degree by the rush of adrenalin coursing through his body. He felt oddly detached, like an observer who was watching everything as it happened in slow motion, like in a dream.

Greg thought he heard the man say something, but even sounds were sludgy and terribly distorted. He steadied his aim as if he had hours to do it, and then squeezed the trigger three times in rapid succession.

He heard John cry out as he grabbed at his chest with both hands. A large fantail splash of blood shot out from the man's chest. Greg could smell the hot, metallic aroma of fresh blood as it splattered everywhere, sounding like a heavy rain on a tin roof. The smell of cordite stung his nose.

John staggered back and coughed once, sharply. A bloody spray shot from his mouth and nose. His eyes held a weird glow that Greg found absolutely terrifying. They seemed to hang, suspended in the night, as they riveted Greg.

Turning around slowly, Greg looked into the car at Angela, who was cowering against the passenger's door. He heard her scream once, sharply, as she tried to grasp what had just happened. She scrambled to open her door with one hand while shielding her face with the other.

Greg had the distinct impression that the air had somehow solidified. He felt like he was fighting against a powerful, invisible tide as he struggled to turn the gun around and aim it at her.

He wasn't sure how many shots he had left, but just as he was about to pull the trigger, something slammed into him. He heard John shout something unintelligible as his weight knocked him off balance.

The revolver went off twice, and the windshield of the car exploded into a thousand diamond-shaped shards.

"Cocksucker!" Greg heard someone shout.

It must have been John because the voice ended in a strangled, bubbly gasp as the impact slammed Greg against the car. He stepped back and tried to shake John off and aim again at Angela, but when he squeezed the trigger, the hammer fell on an empty cartridge. Greg pulled the trigger three or four more quick shots, but each time, nothing happened.

His first impulse was to throw the gun away, but he checked himself and, gripping the revolver tightly, turned and ran across the street to where he had parked his car. His footsteps clicked loudly on the pavement, and beyond that he could hear voices shouting from the restaurant.

Greg stumbled as he swung open the door and jumped into the driver's seat. His breath was burning in his lungs as he cranked the ignition, and the car roared to life. He took off with a squealing of tires that sent up a trail of smoke and filled the car with the choking smell of burned rubber.

As he drove away, he glanced into his rearview mirror but didn't see anyone pursuing him. Slowing the car to just above the speed limit, he tried to calm himself as he drove through town until he found the entrance ramp onto Route 684 south. He felt a slight measure of relief as he blended into the traffic heading back to the city. He expected to be pulled over by the cops, but throughout the drive back to the city, he only saw two cop cars—one on his side of the road and one heading north. Neither one of them pursued him. While crossing the

Whitestone Bridge, he opened the window and slowed down enough to pitch the revolver over the railing and into the dark, shifting waters of the East River. He chuckled, wondering how many murder weapons were corroding on the muddy bottom of the river.

Even after he ditched the car in a vacant lot near Shea Stadium and caught the train back to his neighborhood, Greg was shaking with fear and excitement. He wiped off most of John's blood that had splattered him, but still, there was enough on him to make the few passengers on the train look at him funny and shift away from him.

Once he was walking down the street toward his building, he couldn't help but start laughing. He had no idea if the cops were after him, but he felt great that he had gotten the detective. He was positive the man was dead. He had seen it in his eyes.

The only thing that spoiled his pleasure was knowing that Ross' wife was alive and that she had seen his face—maybe not clearly in the darkened car, but probably enough so she could identify him.

Greg's mother was sitting up in bed when he got home. She called to him, demanding that he make her a cup of tea, but the first thing Greg did was go into the bathroom, grab his razor, lather up, and shave off his mustache. If Angela Ross had seen him, then he was going to have to change his looks as much as possible.

As soon as Angie realized that the man was out of bullets and had run off, she started screaming. Scrambling over the broken windshield glass to get out of the car on the driver's side, she went to John, who was lying on the ground on his back. A thick, dark puddle of blood was spreading out beneath him. It seemed to be pinning him down to the asphalt like glue.

John shivered and looked up at Angie with a glazed expression as she bend over him. When he tried to speak, the only sound that came out was a thick gurgle that ended with a high, whistling gasp.

"No . . . don't even try," she whispered as tears fell from her eyes. "Take it easy. Help's on the way."

Razor-sharp agony filled her as she stared long and hard into her husband's eyes. She could see that he was having trouble focusing on her. His eyes kept rolling back, exposing the dull, bloodshot whites.

"Jesus Christ!" she shouted when she realized the doorman and one or two other bystanders were standing there, stunned into inaction. "Somebody call an ambulance! Can't you see that he's dying!"

"Yeah . . . I—I'll—" the doorman said, shaking his head as though coming to. He turned and darted back into the restaurant.

Drawn by the commotion, a few patrons had come outside. They stood in a semicircle a short distance away from the car, watching Angie as she knelt on the ground and cradled John's head in her lap. She leaned close to him and kept whispering reassuringly as she rubbed his cheeks and forehead. She could tell from the dimming light in his eyes that he wasn't going to make it. Hot tears ran down her cheeks as she stared into her husband's eyes and tried to accept the fact that he was dying.

"I love you, honey . . . I love you, honey," she kept saying as she rocked him gently back and forth.

All she could think was, *if he's going to die right here in my arms, that's the last thing I want him to hear.*

"I love you, honey . . . I love you, honey . . ."

The doorman came back outside followed by the maître d' and a few other restaurant personnel. The maître d' came up to Angie and whispered to her that an ambulance was on its way, but Angie knew that it was too late.

Her senses were shutting down. The night seemed to have gone perfectly still. She glanced over at the spectators who had gathered, but she couldn't hear a single sound that they made. They looked like they were standing behind an inches-thick plate glass window, a wax museum exhibit, gawking at her.

She felt absolutely numb. A cold dread filled her as she thought that none of these people could even begin to fathom her misery right now.

She let out a long, low groan that broke into a wracking sob when John shuddered once and then sagged in her arms. He let out a final, whistling gasp and then lay still, his eyes wide and staring up at the night sky. Seconds later, she heard the distant wail of the approaching ambulance.

Deep, painful sobs wrenched her body as she slumped forward and buried her face into the crook of John's neck. As much as she hated to think it, the only thought that kept circling through her mind was that this was it—her secret, most terrible nightmare had come true.

No matter how much she and John had hoped and dreamed and planned that things would be otherwise, *this* was the only way she had ever imagined that he would leave the Job. In the cold, dark vacuum of her mind, she was already trying to figure out how she was ever going to tell Brandy and JJ that their father was dead. She vaguely knew that she was in shock and couldn't yet begin to think about what they were going to do or how they were going to get through this.

Angie had imagined the day of John's funeral for so long and in so many different ways that, when it finally came, she had the distinct impression that—somehow—she had already lived through it and was now just remembering it.

Both Brandy and JJ had been devastated by the loss of their father. Brandy retreated into herself, spending much of her time alone in her room. She barely talked to Angie whenever she tried to comfort her. She even stopped taking phone calls from her friends. Late at night, Angie could hear her sobbing in her bedroom, but every time she knocked on the door and asked to come in, Brandy would tell her to leave her alone.

JJ, on the other hand, reacted with hostility. He had been close to his father, had admired him and often bragged to his friends about his dad being a detective. His primary reaction to his father's death was one of anger—anger that something like this could happen, anger that his father had deserted him, and anger at the unknown person who had done this to him. Whereas Brandy kept her feelings to herself, JJ didn't hesitate

to lash out at anyone and everyone who tried to talk to him—
especially his mother.

Angie knew that something like this was too terrible to expect
him to accept, much less get over quickly. She knew from
losing both of her parents when she was quite young that grief
takes a long time to heal—if it ever does.

Angie had always had a close relationship with JJ. Even
though he was twelve years old, he was still her "little baby."
So far, he hadn't started in with the preadolescent rebellion
that Brandy had engaged in when she was his age. There was
never a good time to lose a parent, but Angie couldn't help
but think that twelve years old was possibly the worse, especially for a son to lose his father. She was worried that this
would leave JJ permanently psychologically scarred. She could
understand his anger because that's a lot of what she had felt
when she lost her mother at about the same age.

But she consoled herself that she and JJ would reconnect
once his anger passed and he started to process his grief. She
decided, with both of the children, to back off and give them
space to grieve in their own ways. Anger was part of that. Late
at night, when she heard JJ crying in his room, she would go
to him and lie down with him. After drying his eyes, she would
hug and kiss him until he finally settled, but she couldn't help
but feel the awful gulf there was between them.

In many ways, worrying about how the children were dealing
with their father's death made it a somewhat easier for Angie
to handle her own grief. She had plenty of support from friends,
people from work, and members of St. Anne's, the Catholic
church she attended. She appreciated it when several wives of
John's friends and fellow policemen offered to bring the family
a hot meal every night for the next couple of weeks.

Angie felt like she was suspended in limbo. Most of the
time, she kept the depths of her grief to herself, but it was
hard—especially at night. She found it almost impossible to
sleep because she couldn't get used to lying in their queen-
sized bed alone. So much seemed to be happening around her
that was out of her control. It was a comfort to know that she

had friends she could rely on to help get her through the next few days and weeks.

The morning of John's funeral at Ashland Cemetery in Bedford Heights was sunny but very cold. The temperature never got above twenty degrees. Powerful gusts of arctic wind blew up the sloping cemetery hillside, scooping the thin blanket of snow between the tombstones into sharp-edged, scalloped drifts.

Angie was wearing a heavy black coat, gloves, and veiled hat. She felt brittle from grief as much as from the cold as she stood by the grave side with JJ on her left and Brandy on her right. The morning after the shooting, Rob and his friend Craig had driven down from Maine and were staying at the house. They stood directly behind Angie. Throughout the burial, she could feel her brother's hand on her shoulder, squeezing and patting her.

The wind whistled with a high, hissing sound through the thin black veil that covered her face. Cold tears slid like glycerin down her cheeks. She couldn't stop sniffing and repeatedly had to reach underneath her veil to dab her eyes with a tissue.

Already the funeral service at St. Anne's Church was a blur to her, and she barely registered what the priest was saying now as he read from the *Bible* and recited a prayer for John's soul. She had her hands resting on each of the children's shoulders, and couldn't force herself to look away from the dark, polished coffin they had all selected for John.

I can't believe he's in there, she kept thinking, even though earlier this morning she had stood beside the coffin at the funeral and had given John's cold, pale lips a final kiss just before the funeral director closed and fastened the heavy oak lid.

Dozens of members of the police department including the Commissioner turned out in dress uniform for the funeral. John was given a policeman's funeral with full honors. Angie and the children watched as the policemen formed ranks beside the coffin, cocked and aimed their rifles, and fired a salute. At the

sound of the guns going off, Angie broke down and started
crying uncontrollably because the sound reminded her so much
of the sound the handgun had made outside the restaurant that
horrible night that already seemed like a lifetime ago.

After the salute, a trumpeter played taps, and then the priest
recited another prayer for John's soul and sprinkled the coffin
lid with a handful of frozen earth. As Mrs. Crosby from the
church choir sang *"Amazing Grace,"* her voice sweet and high
in the cold air, Angie and the children huddled together, hugging
each other tightly and crying.

They waited until everyone else had left the grave site before
turning to leave. With every step she took back toward the
waiting limousine, Angie's legs felt stiff as though they were
frozen solid. She couldn't stop sobbing and had to lean on Rob
for support.

Okay, so that's what the little assholes look like, Greg thought
as he cut across the cemetery and walked toward the assembled
mourners on the snowy hillside. The wind was cold and made
his eyes water, so he couldn't make out Angela's face very
well beneath the black veil she was wearing. But he had gotten
a pretty good look at her that night outside of *Le Bistro,* and
now he got a good look at the two children.

The boy looked thin and pale, probably from crying. He had
short, light colored hair, bright blue eyes, and looked to be
maybe ten or eleven years old. The girl was a little older—
maybe fifteen or sixteen, Greg guessed. What little he could
see of her face and the contours of her body beneath the winter
coat she was wearing looked pretty damned tasty. He felt himself getting an erection as he looked at her and thought about
what he'd like to do to her.

It had taken a bit of effort to find out when and where Ross'
funeral would be, but Greg had come out to Ashland Cemetery
well prepared. He had stolen a car to drive out here but had
left it parked a mile or so from the cemetery and had walked
the rest of the way, in spite of the cold.

As soon as he entered the cemetery, he grabbed a fresh-looking floral display from one of the graves and carried it with him as he walked around, looking for the mourners. Pretending to be visiting the grave of a relative or friend, he moved as close to the funeral service as he dared before kneeling down on the snowy ground in front of a gray granite tombstone. Folding his hands prayerfully and bowing his head, he only chanced to glance every now and then at Angela and her children.

At first Greg was unnerved when he saw the uniformed policemen line up beside the grave, each of them bearing a rifle. Greg couldn't help but think that they knew who he was and were here to get him. He tensed, ready to turn and run as he watched the policemen raise their rifles and fire several times in salute. The echoes of their shots rolled across the quiet cemetery like peals of thunder.

Greg finally realized that neither the cops nor the mourners were paying the least bit of attention to him, but he knew that— even though John Ross was dead—it wasn't over.

Not by a long shot!

The cops hated it when one of their own was shot, and Greg was positive that the investigation into who had killed Detective Ross and why was going to be intense. And the worst of it was that he knew Ross' wife had seen him that night and could probably identify him.

That was the only worry that had plagued him during the three days and nights since the shooting.

He knew he was going to have to do something in order to silence Angela Ross before she could finger him, and that meant he was probably going to have to do something to her children, too.

Greg saw no sense in leaving any loose ends.

Pretending that he had finished paying his respects, he stood up and brushed the wet snow off his knees. He considered how much curiosity he could show about the ongoing funeral without being *too* noticeable.

Could he move a bit closer without raising anyone's suspicion, or was it time to leave now?

He desperately wanted to get at least close enough so he'd

be able to see the children's faces clearly. He wanted to be able to recognize them if—no, not if . . . *when* he saw them again!

Take it easy, he cautioned himself. *No sense pushing your luck.*

Besides, there were too many cops here for his liking. He knew that he was going to have to lay low for a while before he figured out what to do next.

Before leaving the cemetery, though, he focused his attention once more on Ross' wife. He didn't feel the slightest twinge of remorse for what he had done to her husband or for the grief he had caused her and her family. He didn't doubt in the least that Ross would have done the exact same thing to him if their situations had been reversed.

It was just like in the jungle—kill or be killed.

Greg snickered softly to himself, watching as the misty puffs of his breath rose into the cold air and were whisked away by the wind.

For now, he was content. It wasn't as though he felt like he was being driven to do what he knew he was going to have to do next.

Hell, no!

He was going to enjoy it.

The only frustrating thing about it, in fact, was knowing that it was going to take a little more time than he would have liked. He would have to wait and see how close the cops got to him before he could make his next move.

But at least, for now, he knew what his targets looked like.

That was a start.

Chapter 8
I.A.

"I know how hard all of this has been for you, Mrs. Ross. I appreciate you coming down here today."

Detective Roy Allen, a detective from Internal Affairs, said this with a low, almost apologetic note in his voice, but Angie didn't think he was sincere. She looked at him as if to say: *What the hell else did you expect me to do?*

She didn't like sitting here in this man's office almost as much as she didn't like his brusque, icy demeanor. Detective Allen had cold, pale blue eyes, and was the kind of cop who favored a short crewcut and narrow tie, like someone stuck in the fifties even though he looked young enough not to have been born until the late sixties. Everything about Allen's desk and office was neat and orderly with an almost military precision.

"First off, the investigating detectives don't think that your husband's murder was a bungled holdup."

"They're absolutely sure of that?" Angie asked, arching her eyebrows. Her voice caught in her throat, and she could feel her eyes stinging as they began to fill with tears at just the thought of John.

Detective Allen's face remained absolutely impassive as he nodded curtly.

"No one's going to commit a robbery in a public place like that where there are so many potential witnesses," he said flatly. "Remember, he tried to shoot you, too."

Angie nodded as she recalled the terrible grip of fear she had experienced when she saw the man turn and aim the gun at her.

"As a matter of routine," Detective Allen went on, "we're checking through all of your husband's cases for the last several years. We need to see if this MO matches up with anything else he might have worked on. But I need you to tell me if *you* know of anyone who might have had a revenge motive against your husband."

Angie shivered as she shrugged. Over the last several years, if just for her own sanity, she had made it a point not to get involved with anything to do with John's work.

"Why can't you just trace the ballistics of the . . . the bullets or something?" she asked.

As soon as she said it, she vividly pictured the bleeding wounds in John's chest as he lay dying in her arms. A single tear spilled from her eye and rolled down her cheek. She sniffed and dabbed at it with the tissue she was clutching.

Once again, Detective Allen grimly shook his head.

"That's not as easy as most people think," he said. "The bullets we recovered were all severely damaged. Besides, we would need to find the gun in the possession of a suspect in order to match them. Chances are the gun the perp used was stolen and is long since gone."

He leaned back in his chair, squinting as he rubbed his cheek with one hand. It was his attempt to look casual, Angie guessed.

"I figure that gun's in a catch basin somewhere or at the bottom of the Hudson River," he said.

As much as she didn't like it, Angie found herself getting angrier by the second. She couldn't stand the way this man spoke with such a droning monotone and such seeming detachment about her dead husband. After a week of grieving over John's death and trying to help her children cope with the loss of their father, this man's approach seemed to be almost a parody of the detached, emotionless cop. She was tempted to get up and slap him across the face if only it would make him begin to grasp the depth of her loss.

"Like any cop," she said sourly "I'm sure my husband had plenty of enemies."

"Oh, I do, too," Detective Allen said, "but there was someone who was pissed off enough to kill your husband—and you, too, for that matter. That's a pretty big stretch, when you go gunning for a detective. It takes a special kind of wacko."

Angie's eyes hurt. She leaned forward and covered them, fighting back the powerful wash of emotion that swept over her. The funeral had been more than a week ago, and still the numbing hollowness of loss had her in an unrelenting grip.

"'S far as I can see, your husband's record is pretty clean," Detective Allen said. "He was either a very honest cop, or else he was very good and no one ever caught him on the take. I know you're planning a trip, but I'd like you to stay home for a few weeks, until we can clear up this investigation."

Angie bristled at this.

"Do you have a note pad or something handy?" she asked, nailing Detective Allen with a harsh glance.

She was happy to see that Detective Allen was momentarily flustered by her request. He shifted in his seat, scowling, and then nodded as he took a pen from his shirt pocket and flipped open a leather-bound note pad.

"Right here," he said.

"I want you to write this down. Memorize it if you have to," Angie said, trying to control the tremor in her voice. "My husband was a good man—an honest cop and a *damned* good person! You got that? You can screw around all you want, pretending that you're just doing your job by checking into his background for something he might have done wrong, but the truth is, you're just trying to cover up the fact that you and the rest of this department don't have the faintest idea where to start to find the man who killed him!"

Angie was seething with rage as she stood up. Clenching her fists, she leaned toward the detective across his orderly desk.

"Did you get all of that?" she asked. "I want you to write

it down, word for word, so you won't forget it! My husband wasn't a crooked cop! He may have had his faults, but he *wasn't* crooked!''

"Please, Mrs. Ross. Try to calm down,'' Detective Allen said, his voice still sounding flat and detached.

"No, I *won't* calm down!'' Angie yelled as she slammed her fist down hard on his desk. "Do you have any idea what I'm going through? I've lost my husband! My kids have lost their father! I'm not going to sit here and listen to you tarnish my husband's memory with your snide little innuendoes about his being crooked. I know that you want me to stay here in New York for the next few weeks while you investigate, but unless you arrest me or get a restraining order or whatever, you can't make me stay! I'm going to visit with my brother for a week. Can you understand that my children and I are trying to put the pieces of our life back together?''

"Certainly I can appreciate that,'' Detective Allen said cooly. "And I can assure you that I meant no disrespect to your husband's memory. I simply asked if you would stay in the area for a few more days until we clear this.''

"You don't need me around to do your job,'' Angie said. She was so mad her whole body was trembling uncontrollably. "I'll be back in a week. You can talk to me then if you have to!''

With that, she turned and strode out of the office. As she walked outside to her car, she was so upset and her vision was so blurred with tears that she could hardly see. She fumbled to unlock the car door and then practically collapsed into the front seat.

As soon as she was alone, the emotions she'd been trying so hard to control burst out of her, and she cried uncontrollably for more than fifteen minutes before she finally calmed down enough to start the car drive away.

When she got home, she glanced at herself in the hallway mirror, shocked to see how pale and worn she looked. It was like looking at someone else—someone who was old and tired and had lived her entire life in pain.

Bracing herself, she went upstairs and started packing her

suitcase. When she was done, she packed a bag for each of the children. Then she went downstairs and called the school to tell them that the kids wouldn't be coming back to class next week. The secretary, who knew all about what had happened at *Le Bistro,* offered Angie her sympathies and told her that it would be no problem.

When the kids got home from school, she told them that tomorrow morning, bright and early, they were taking off for Maine for a visit with Uncle Rob. She could tell by their reactions that neither one of them was thrilled by the idea, but neither one of them gave her much grief about it, either.

"Greggie . . . Oh, Greggie honey . . . Can you come in here?"

The voice, wafting like drifting smoke in the darkness, gently tugged Greg out of a deep sleep. He snorted and rolled over, tensing as he opened his eyes and looked up at the ceiling. He wondered if he had really heard a voice, or if he had dreamed it.

Then it came again.

"Gregory dear . . ."

"Jesus *Christ!*" he muttered as he sat up and glanced at his alarm clock. It was a little after three o'clock in the morning. He'd been asleep for only a couple of hours and having fitful dreams he couldn't remember any of the details, but they left him feeling drained and disoriented.

Flopping back onto the bed, he closed his eyes and pressed his fists against his eyelids so hard flashes of bright light shot across his vision.

Please . . . Please make her go away . . . he thought as every muscle in his body vibrated with tension.

"Greggie . . . I need a drink of water," his mother called out in a deep, rasping voice that sounded like someone was strangling her.

"I put a full glass of water on your nightstand before I went to bed," Greg said. "Just like I always do."

"I think I might have spilled it," his mother said.

What's the fucking mystery? You either spilled it or you didn't, Greg thought but didn't say.

"Could you please get me another one?" his mother called out. There was a tone of absolute helplessness in her voice that infuriated him.

Why the hell can't you get your skinny ass out of bed and get it yourself?

Greg wanted to shout this at her, but he knew that she couldn't get out of bed. His mother hadn't been out of bed in months, and he knew that she might never get out of bed again. She was slowly dying in her bed, and all he wished for was that she would hurry up and get it over with.

"Yeah, yeah . . . Just a minute," he called out.

He tossed the covers aside, shivering as a cold draft washed over him. A sharp chill jabbed up the back of his legs when he stepped onto the cold floor, stood up, and stretched his arms over his head. He heard something in his back or neck crackle.

Grunting and rubbing his face with the flats of his hands, he trudged into the kitchen and turned on the overhead light. Opening the cupboard, he took down a clean glass, went to the sink, and filled it with water. He didn't bother to run the water until it was cold. Chances were, his mother would take one tiny sip and put it back on her nightstand, anyway.

Squinting from the bright light, he stumbled across to her closed bedroom door. Just before he opened it, he cleared his throat roughly to raise a thick ball of phlegm. As he rolled it back and forth on his tongue, he brought the glass of water up to his mouth and spit into it. Chuckling softly to himself, he swirled the glass around, watching the glob of yellowish spit that floated in the water.

"Here yah go, Ma," he said cheerily as he opened the door and stepped into her room. "Anything else I can get for you while I'm up?"

The next day, in the silent gray of a February morning, Angie and the kids left for Maine. After discussing whether to take the fastest route or the more scenic route, they decided that the important thing was to get there, so Angie headed up Route 684. At the Connecticut state line, she got onto Route 84, heading toward Danbury and Hartford.

For the first time since she could remember, Brandy and JJ didn't fight and argue the whole way. In fact, they hardly spoke unless spoken to. If it hadn't been for the circumstances, Angie would have considered this a relief.

Brandy was still acting sullen and much quieter than usual. She sat in the front seat with her Walkman headphones on, listening to music as she stared out the window at the passing landscape. JJ was in the back seat. The constant *beep-beeping* of his Gameboy was getting on her nerves but for once she decided not to hassle him about it.

"I hope we don't have to stay too long," Brandy said, removing her headphones. "I don't want to miss too much school."

"Now *that's* a switch," Angie said, chuckling dryly as she glanced at her. "Is it the schoolwork, or Ted you'll miss more?"

"Cut it out, Mom . . ."

The landscape was glazed white with snow, but close to the highway, everything was muddy brown. The road was clear and dry, though, and the sky was bright blue without a cloud in sight.

The further she drove away from Bedford Heights, the more Angie felt relief from the heavy pressure that had been crushing her. It was still much too painful and uncomfortable to be in the house. Day and night, everywhere she turned, she expected to see or hear John. It was like his ghost haunted every room.

She felt even more uncomfortable because there was little progress in the investigation into the shooting. She lost count of how many times she was interviewed by one or more investigating detectives. Thankfully, no one was as hard to take as Detective Roy Allen.

Around nine o'clock, they stopped for a quick meal at the Roy Rogers in Sturbridge, Massachusetts. They were still only serving from the breakfast menu, but Angie was glad to see that both of the kids ordered and ate a decent amount of food.

While they were eating and once they were back on the road,

Angie tried a few times to get them excited about their visit to Maine. Rob lived in a little town called Bolton, just outside the city of Augusta. She tried to talk it up a bit, but neither one of the kids seemed to get excited about anything.

Throughout the drive, Angie sensed a tension in the car that she wished to God she could dispel. She knew that it had everything to do with John's death, but she was still filled with so much grief that she found it difficult to talk much about it with the kids. They were making progress, though. They were seeing a therapist, and over the last few days, they had talked about their feelings and cried together. Angie knew that it would take time . . . a lot of time.

The drive went much faster than Angie had expected. They pulled into Rob's driveway a little after noon. It was a workday for Rob, but he had taken the day off to be there when they arrived. He greeted them with big hugs in the driveway.

Rob's house, which he shared with his lover Craig, was small but neat. The first thing Angie noticed upon entering was the sharp smell of wood smoke. A fire was blazing in the kitchen wood stove, making the house almost as hot as a sauna. It quickly removed the chill they had gotten, walking the short distance from the car to the house.

They made a quick trip back outside to get their luggage, and then Rob showed them where they would be sleeping. After that, Brandy and JJ settled in the paneled den to watch a movie on cable while Angie and Rob sat at the table in the kitchen.

"So, you're hanging in there okay, huh?" Rob asked as he poured boiling water to make them each a cup of spearmint tea.

Angie shrugged and looked at her brother. There was so much she wanted to tell him and so much she wasn't sure she could.

"The kids seem a lot better than when we were down for the funeral," Rob said. He sat at the table opposite Angie and looked at her with a warm, sympathetic expression.

"Yeah. Brandy's coping all right, but I'm a little worried

about JJ," she said. She cupped her hands around her tea cup, hoping the warmth and aroma would soothe her.

"How about you?" Rob asked, his expression darkening.

Angie shifted in her chair and found that she couldn't maintain eye contact with him for very long. A long, uncomfortable silence followed, broken only by the crackle of the wood fire in the stove and the distant sound of the TV coming from the den.

"Have you thought any more about what we talked about?" Rob asked.

For a moment, Angie couldn't think what he meant. Then she remembered how he had been pushing her to move up to Maine and shrugged again as she took a tentative sip of her tea. It was much too hot to gulp.

"I hate to keep pressuring you like this, but it would seem to me, since we're all the family we have left, that it might not be a bad idea to be a little closer geographically."

Angie nodded but still couldn't say anything more than, "I don't know . . ."

"I've been checking around, and I'm pretty sure I could get you an interview for that permanent substitute teaching job at the elementary school. Beverly Grant's the woman who's taking a leave of absence next year. I can't guarantee anything, but I know the principal pretty well."

Angie let out a long sigh. Looking down at her folded hands, she was almost overwhelmed with emotion.

"I don't know," she muttered, shaking her head. "I just don't know . . ."

"I don't want to pressure you," Rob said, "but if I'm going to put in a good word for you, I'm going to have to do it pretty soon."

Blinking her eyes rapidly to keep the tears at bay, Angie looked past her brother to the kitchen window, which looked out over a wide expanse of a snow-covered field that was bordered in the distance by a line of dark pine trees. A flurry of motion caught her attention, and she tracked the three crows as they flew from the woods across the field. Faintly, she could hear their ragged cawing.

There certainly weren't any views like this where she lived, she thought, but it was more than that—much more.

"It'd be quite a change," she said after a long moment. "For all of us." She looked back at Rob and forced a smile. "All for the better."

"Maybe." Angie shrugged. "The kids and I are pretty well entrenched in Bedford Heights, you know? We've got friends and connections there with school and doctors . . ."

"Sometimes a major change like that is good," Rob said, his voice soft. "I mean, the memories of living in that house and that town have all got to be pretty painful."

Angie nodded her agreement. "You don't know the half of it."

Squeezing her hands tightly together to stop them from trembling, she leaned across the table and looked intently at her brother.

"It's been really rough . . . especially with the police still investigating the shooting."

"I can imagine," Rob said as he slouched back in his chair and rested the cup of tea on the bulge of his belly. "They still haven't found a suspect, huh?"

Angie bit down her lower lip and shook her head.

"Nothing. And the worst of it is, now they're digging into all of John's past cases,trying to come up with something. So far, all they've done is turn over the shit."

"What do you mean, *shit?*"

Rob leveled a steady gaze at her, making Angie cringe and wish to God that she hadn't brought it up.

"Oh—nothing," she said, but she could tell by Rob's expression that he knew it wasn't nothing. She squirmed in her chair. "You know . . ." She was unable to look her brother straight in the eyes. He made her feel like they were little kids again, and he was the big brother in control of everything.

"No, I *don't* know," Rob said levelly. Still trying to look casual, he took a quick sip of his tea, but he eyed her like a hawk.

"The usual stuff," Angie said haltingly. "IA—Internal Affairs—is always trying to find shit on the other cops."

"Even dead ones? Why would they do that?" Rob asked. He sounded all innocence, but Angie knew better.

"To justify their job, I suppose," she said. "In case you hadn't heard, there *are* dirty cops—cops who take bribes and stuff—especially in a big city."

Rob nodded thoughtfully, and the silence in the room lengthened. A faint burst of laughter came from the den, and Angie smiled wistfully when she realized how long it had been since she had heard either Brandy or JJ laugh out loud like that.

"So . . . was John a dirty cop?" Rob asked after a moment.

The question sounded casual, but Angie practically withered beneath her brother's steady stare. A rush of heat made the back of her neck prickle. As she looked at Rob, tears filled her eyes.

"I'm surprised that you'd even ask that question," she said, her voice threatening to break on every syllable. "You knew John. He was a good man."

All the while, Rob looked at her, nodding.

"I never questioned that," he said. "I know how much you loved him, in spite of the problems you two had. I know you considered him a good husband—"

"And father," Angie said quickly.

"Yes, and father," Rob echoed. "But that doesn't answer my question. Was he on the take?"

Angie let out a long sigh and, fluttering her eyes, looked out the window again at the snow-covered field. The sight made her shiver deep inside.

"He—" she said, then cut herself off, feeling suddenly dizzy as she looked at her older brother. He was watching her with total sympathy and understanding in his expression.

"Ange," he said softly as he leaned forward. "We're family, remember? You can tell me anything—I mean *anything*— and it's safe with me."

Angie shuddered as she took a deep breath, closed her eyes for a moment, and tried to picture John's face clearly in her mind. It terrified her when she couldn't get a perfectly clear image of him. Opening her eyes, she looked at Rob and slowly nodded.

"Yeah," she said, her voice sounding like she'd been gargling with Drayno.

"Are you serious?" Rob said, looking with her with absolute astonishment.

Angie grit her teeth and nodded.

"He didn't do it much," she said. "Honest. But early on, right after we first got married, he was involved with a drug bust and—well, some evidence, a briefcase with forty thousand dollars in it, kind of disappeared."

"You're shitting me!" Rob said, a smile twitching at the corners of his mouth.

Angie shook her head. "He did it just that once, that I know of. But like I said, we were just married, and we really wanted to get a down payment on a house."

"Jesus . . ." Rob said, whistling between his teeth as he sat back in his chair. The grin spread across his face, and he started to chuckle softly.

"I always wondered how you guys could afford that house in Bedford Heights," he said.

"I didn't like it, even at the time," Angie said. "When he told me what he'd done, I told him that I though he should return it. Evidence has a way of disappearing and then reappearing. I told him he should return the briefcase, but—"

"But he didn't."

Angie nodded. "Yeah, we kept it. You have to remember how much money forty thousand dollars was twenty years ago. That'd be like a hundred thousand or more today, and we really wanted to buy that house."

"I'm glad I've never been faced with a temptation like that," Rob said. "I don't know what I'd do."

"Yeah, but that's the problem now," Angie said. Once again, her eyes started stinging, and she was afraid that she was going to start crying. "If John ever mentioned it to anybody, or if someone else knows anything about it—"

"What can they do?" Rob asked with a shrug. "There's no proof he took it, no way they can trace the money. And there must be a statute of limitations. I don't think you have anything to worry about."

"I do if he was skimming money after that and didn't tell me," Angie said shakily. "And even if he didn't, I don't want the kids—"

Her voice choked off before she could say more. With a loud sob, she leaned forward and buried her face in her hands. Her voice was distorted when she said, "I don't want this to come out and have my kids thinking that their father was a . . . a crook."

She heard Rob get up from his chair and come over to her. She felt his hand as he patted her shoulder. The touch reminded her of the way he had comforted her during the funeral, and it broke her heart all the more.

Squeezing her eyes tightly shut and staring into the darkness behind her eyelids, she saw a clear image of her dead husband's face. It looked impossibly distant, and even as she watched it, it seemed to be retreating further away from her, dissolving into a smear of shifting patterns of light as it faded back into the darkness . . .

And then was gone . . .

Chapter 9
Decisions

Angie fell in love with the house the instant she saw it.

It was early Saturday afternoon. She was driving with Rob, Craig, and the kids out along Taylor Hill Road, heading back to Bolton from the mall in Augusta, where they had done a little shopping.

Looking for—much less *finding*— a house that she might be interested in was about the last thing on her mind. They had driven out this way instead of taking the main road home because Rob said there was some nice scenery along the way.

But when Angie saw the house with a Century 21 FOR SALE sign out front, she quickly pulled over to the side of the road and stopped the car.

"What is it" Rob asked, looking at her with sudden concern in his eyes.

"That house," Angie said, pointing at it. Everyone in the car turned to look. Angie wasn't sure what the style of the house was. It reminded her of the kind of large cottage a very rich family might have as a summer home on a lake. It was two stories tall, and was painted light yellow with green trim and shutters. The green paint had faded and had taken on the look of tarnished copper.

On one side of the house, on the left when viewed from the road, there was a large sun porch that had been winterized with large windows that looked out over the snow-covered lawn. A low stone wall that might be hip-high without the snow ran the full length of the front of the property. The driveway ran between two tall stone pillars and curved around to the front door and to the right of the house where there was a parking area in front of a separate two car garage.

The house sat well back from the road. The yard was edged on three sides by a dense pine forest. To the left, Angie caught a glimpse through the trees of the neighboring house, more than a hundred yards away. The ground was bare in spots underneath the pines. Chickadees and sparrows darted among the branches, chirping as they gathered seeds.

In spite of JJ's protests that he wanted to get back to Uncle Rob's so he could watch TV, Angie opened her door and stepped out. The sudden burst of cold air almost took her breath away.

The thin coating of snow on the driveway crunched underfoot as she started down to the house. She heard the other car doors open and bang shut but didn't bother to turn to see who had gotten out and who had stayed behind. She had fallen instantly in love with this house and its setting. It reminded her of something—some place she had seen before but couldn't quite remember.

"This isn't very far from town, is it?" she asked when she turned and saw both Rob and Craig close behind her.

They both shook their heads. "Two miles—three tops," Craig said, glancing at Rob for confirmation.

"Actually, the elementary school is even closer," Rob added. He pointed down the street in the direction they were heading. "It's just around the corner to the right there, maybe a half mile or so down Pine View Road."

"Really," Angie said, stroking her chin thoughtfully.

This was all very interesting, but she couldn't tear her gaze away from the house. It looked like there had to be at least three bedrooms upstairs. While not quite as large as their house back in Bedford Heights, it certainly looked big enough for her family.

Especially now that there's only three of us, Angie thought with a sudden twinge.

The cold vacuum of her loss filled her, but she immediately shook her head and focused on the house.

Obviously, the previous owners had kept the house well-maintained. What she could see of the snow-covered grounds looked well-tended with low yew hedges and gardens lining the front of the house as well as up by the stone wall. Even now, unoccupied as it was, someone had plowed the driveway and cleared the front and side steps of snow.

"It *is* kinda cool," Brandy said, nodding admiringly.

Angie turned, surprised to see that her daughter had tagged along with them. She looked at her and asked, "You really think so?"

"Umm," Brandy said with a simple shrug, obviously trying to act as if she wasn't really all *that* impressed; but Angie could tell that she liked the house.

"Can you imagine living here?" she asked.

Again, Brandy shrugged. "I dunno," she said. "I mean, it's so far away from . . . from *everything.*"

"Yeah—well, it's not New York, that's for sure," Angie replied, thinking that might have more pluses than minuses. Still mesmerized by the house, she walked slowly around to the backyard. The snow was deeper out back, but Rob, Craig, and Brandy all trudged through it with her.

From the back, the house looked a lot larger than it did from the front. Angie realized that it was because the yard sloped gradually down into the deeper woods, making the house stand much taller. A wide deck stretched almost the whole length of the back. Behind the garage at the edge of the lawn was a small tool shed painted the same colors as the house.

Angie paused for a moment and, closing her eyes, took a deep breath and listened. The cold wind whistled through the snow-laden branches of the pines. Usually a sound like that made her shiver, but this time she found it comforting.

"It's so . . . peaceful out here," she said dreamily.

"You know, I've noticed this house before," Rob said softly. "It's been on the market for quite a while. Over a year now."

"Really?" Angie frowned. "Do you think there's something wrong with it?"

Rob shrugged and shook his head.

"What you think they want for it?" Angie asked, but even as she said it, she knew that she was just daydreaming. The house and yard seemed so idyllic that the thought of actually buying this place was more than tempting, but she knew that it was unrealistic even to consider uprooting her family and moving to Maine.

She couldn't do something like that . . .

Could she?

"Couldn't hurt to call the broker and ask to see it," Rob suggested as though reading her mind.

Angie looked at him and thought for a moment that's exactly what she should do, but then she sighed and shook her head.

"It's nice to fantasize about," she said, more to herself than to anyone else.

"I think you should consider it," Rob said, looking at her earnestly.

"Don't be ridiculous."

Taking Rob's hand, she started back around to the front of the house. Once out front, she walked up the steps to the front door and tried the doorknob. Of course, it was locked.

Pressing her face against the cold glass of the side lights, she looked into the foyer. She couldn't see much through the gauzy curtain, just a short hallway leading into the kitchen straight ahead and what looked like the living room off to the left. There was a stairway on the right that led upstairs. The walls were painted a light, textured beige, and the floor was polished hardwood that reflected the daylight with a warm glow.

"How's it look?" Rob asked, stepping up beside her and peering in.

Without taking her face away from the window, Angie shifted to one side and said, "Just what you'd expect. *Really* nice."

She turned and, with a deep sigh, looked back at the road.

Brandy was standing in the driveway, hopping from one foot to the other and looking very cold as she waited with Craig. JJ was still in the car, his head down, no doubt busy playing Gameboy.

"I'll bet there's not much traffic out here," Angie said, still talking to herself as much as to her brother.

Rob shrugged. "I think everybody pretty much uses Route 9, the main road into town. It's more direct if you're going to Augusta. That's pretty much where everyone goes for anything."

Angie walked down the steps and over to the glassed-in sun porch. The snow in the yard was deep enough to go over the tops of her boots, but she ignored the cold as she stood on tiptoes and looked inside.

What she could see appealed to her. It was a spacious and homey-looking room with dark carpeted floor, wood paneled walls, and a large brick fireplace on one wall. Built-in bookcases lined the wall between the doors that led into the living room and, Angie guessed, either the dining room or kitchen. She instantly imagined how comfortable this room would be with a plush couch and an easy chair or two.

"I don't know," she said softly as she shook her head.

She was dying to get inside the house and have a look around, but after another few seconds, she turned and started back to the road. Halfway to the car, she stopped and turned around to look at the house again.

If anything, her first impression was even stronger.

The house looked like something that had been torn out of her secret dreams and placed right in front of her in broad daylight.

It was difficult if not impossible for her to imagine starting life over in a house like this; but as soon as she thought about it, she felt the deeper pain of trying to figure out how she was going to live her life without John in the first place. She couldn't stop thinking that it might be better for her and for the kids to make a radical change like this.

How hard was it going to be for *all* of them to stay in a house where, every single day, they were reminded in a thousand little ways of what they had all lost?

She knew she could afford to move anywhere she liked. John's pension along with the money from his life insurance and the sale of their house in Bedford Heights—if they sold it—would carry them a long way even if she didn't get the teaching job Rob had told her about.

And if she *did* get that job, it might not be so bad to live closer to her brother so they could see each other more than the two or three times a year that they got together. Like Rob had said, they were all the family either one of them had left.

The car horn suddenly honked, drawing her attention. Angie saw JJ waving for them to hurry up. Reluctantly, she started back to the car with the others. She was the last to get into the car, and as she started up and drove away, she couldn't help but stare in the rearview mirror at the house. Just before it disappeared from sight behind a screen of trees, she came to a decision—

I'm going to go for it!

Even then, she knew that, over the next few weeks and months, she would be plagued by doubts and questions, but she wanted a change—she and the kids *needed* a change, and just maybe something this extreme was what it was going to take.

"I think I'm gonna sleep on it," she said to Rob as they drove through town, heading back to his house. "Do you remember the real estate agent's name that was on the sign?"

"Sure. It's Ed Lewis," Rob said. "I know him from working on the school board."

"Sleep on what?" JJ piped in from the back seat.

Angie glanced at him in the rearview mirror, shook her head, and smiled. "We'll talk about it later, bud," she said. "Don't worry. We won't make *any* decisions unless *all* of us agree to it."

"So what do you think?" JJ asked, looking anxiously at Brandy, who was sitting in the front seat of the car.

It was Tuesday morning, and—finally—they were heading back home to Bedford Heights. After being on the road for less than an hour, they had stopped at the Burger King on I-95 in Falmouth so Angie could use the bathroom.

Throughout the week-long visit with Uncle Rob, JJ and Brandy hadn't had much opportunity to talk. Not that they talked to each other often any more, anyway. Now that Brandy was a teenager, she tried her best to ignore her younger brother as much as possible.

Following their father's death, though, they had spent a lot more time talking and crying together because, beneath it all, they still felt a close bond with each other. JJ figured that they would have talked more during the visit, but it seemed as though they spent the entire time with the adults, and they slept in separate rooms at night. The only time they had been alone was yesterday morning, when their mother had gone to the local school office to talk with the principal about a possible job opening. After that, they had all driven out to the house on Taylor Hill Road where they met Ed Lewis, the real estate agent, and had a hour long tour of the house.

"You mean about moving to Maine?" Brandy asked.

"Uh-huh," JJ said, nodding tightly. He was gripping the back of the car seat so tightly his knuckles had gone white.

"I dunno," Brandy said with a shrug, keeping her eyes straight ahead.

"What do you mean, you don't know?" JJ snapped. "Don't you think it will *totally* suck?"

"Umm . . . probably," Brandy said. "I mean, I'm not nuts about the idea of leaving all my friends behind and all that, but you have to admit that house is pretty cool."

"You want to have to make all new friends in a whole new school?" JJ asked.

"Not really," Brandy said.

"Well me neither," JJ said with a huff. "But can she do that?"

"Do what?"

"Make us move here, even if we don't want to?" JJ asked in near desperation. "I mean, all week long, Uncle Rob was *really* pushing her to go for that job, and she finally did it. Now she won't even talk to us about it. Every time I ask her what we're gonna do, all she says is, 'Don't worry. We'll see.' She keeps saying that we won't make any major decision unless we all agree to it, but I'm telling you right now, if she moves to Maine, I'm not gonna come."

"Of course you are, you idiot. You *have* to," Brandy said. "Don't be so friggin' *dumb!*"

"She can't make me! What if I can live with Arno . . . or with Devon Costello's family," JJ said edgily.

"I doubt they'd want to have a retard like you around," Brandy said coolly.

"Well I just don't wanna move here. God, it—it's in the middle of nowhere. There's *nothing* to do!"

"There's always the mall," Brandy suggested.

"Screw the mall!" JJ snapped.

"You never do anything, anyway, except play your stupid video games," Brandy said.

He couldn't help but wonder why she was being so contrary with him and finally decided that it was because, no matter what he said, she felt obliged to contradict it. If he'd been in favor of moving to Maine, she no doubt would be the one putting up the stink.

"But that mall sucked compared to what's back home," JJ said. "It didn't have *anything!* And those kids we saw there— God! They looked so . . . dweeby!"

"You should fit right in, then," Brandy said, turning and smirking at him. Before JJ could respond, she reached over the back of the car seat and punched him, hard, on the arm.

"And stop kicking the back of my seat!"

"Hey!"

JJ swung back at her, but Brandy pulled back, and he missed.

"Cut it out!" Brandy shouted, irritated by the idea that he would even *try* to hit her back. After all these years, he should *know* better!

"Here comes Mom," JJ said. "I'm gonna tell."

"Tell her what? That you're a twit?"

"Hey, what's up," Angie said as she opened the car door

and sat down. The sudden burst of cold air made both of the kids shiver.

"JJ says he doesn't want to move to Maine," Brandy said, using the high, whiny, baby-sounding voice she used to irritate her brother.

Angie frowned as she started up the car and began to drive. She didn't say a word to either of them as she sped up to merge with the flow of traffic on the Interstate. Once they were moving a little over the speed limit, she glanced at JJ in the rearview.

"Is that what you've decided?" she asked. "That you don't even want to consider it?"

JJ shrugged and wiped his eyes, not wanting her to see that he'd been close to crying.

"I dunno," he muttered, turning to stare out the side window.

"Look," Angie said, shifting her gaze back and forth between the rearview and the road ahead. "Nothing's been decided, all right? When we get home, we'll talk about it."

"But you already applied for that job," JJ said sullenly.

"So? There's no guarantee I'll get it. You know, it never hurts in life to keep your options open."

"Well, how about *this* option?" JJ said quickly. "If you move to Maine, I'll stay in Bedford Heights?"

Angie sniffed with laughter. "And just where would you live?"

"With one of my friends' families," JJ replied.

"Oh, honey," Angie said.

She took one hand off the steering wheel and reached into the back seat to pat him on the knee. JJ jerked away from her touch like it was a bee sting.

"If we're going to move, the whole family will stick together," she said. "I know this is a lot for you to think about . . . especially after losing your dad."

JJ crossed his arms and kept staring out his window at the passing snow-covered landscape. The glare off the snow along the roadside hurt his eyes, making them water.

"I just want to keep *all* of our options open. That's all," his mother said softly.

"Well I'll only *consider* doing it on one condition," JJ said.

"What's that?" Angie and Brandy said in unison.

"That I can get a dog," JJ said harshly. "I'll only move to Maine if I can have a dog. I've always wanted one, and you've always said I couldn't because a dog needs to be out in the country where he'd have lots of space to run."

Biting her lower lip, Angie nodded.

"Well," JJ said. "That house we looked at yesterday sure had a big enough yard, and there's all those woods out behind it."

Angie snickered softly as she shook her head.

"All right," she said, holding her hand out behind her back for JJ to shake. "It's a deal. If we move to Maine, you can get a dog."

"Cool," JJ said as he shook his mother's hand firmly, and for the rest of the drive home, he didn't feel quite so bad.

The days after John Ross' funeral weren't so bad for Greg, at least not at first, but the nights were tough. He had quite a great deal of difficulty sleeping. Night after night, he lost count of how many times he woke up, convinced that there were people in his bedroom. Although from time to time he thought he caught a glimpse of one or more of them in the deepest shadows, he could always hear them, shifting about the room, unseen in the dark.

Usually when he woke up like this, Greg was too terrified to move. He would lie there in bed, his heart beating rapidly in his ears as he stared, wide-eyed, into the darkness.

Not wanting—or daring—to go to sleep, he would spend many hours a night just sitting in the darkened living room, channel surfing. Late at night, almost everything seemed to be advertisements for exercise equipment.

With no more than a few hours of sleep each night, he found it increasingly difficult, sometimes almost impossible to drag himself to the work at the video store. His job performance, which had never been exemplary, got steadily worse until the last week of February, when his boss gave him a stern warning either to shape up—fast—or be fired. Greg would have quit right then, but he needed his meager income, so he did his best to disguise how frazzled he was.

The problem was, things back home weren't getting any better. They were worse, in fact.

In the coldest weeks of February, his mother's health steadily declined. Whereas she used to try to get out of bed at least once a day to go to the bathroom, she now stayed in her bed all the time. She complained that the apartment was too cold, no matter how high Greg put the thermostat. Thankfully, she was capable of using a bed pan, but Greg resented whenever she crapped herself and he had to clean up after her and change her bed sheets. He considered hiring a homecare nurse to help a couple of days a week, but he didn't have enough money, and recent cuts in federal aid made it just about impossible for him to get it.

Worst of all was his ever deepening anxiety that the police knew *exactly* who he was, where he lived, and what he had done, and that it was just a matter of time before they arrested him.

He knew they were out there, watching him all the time, but he almost never got a really good look at them. He had no doubt that his apartment was under surveillance. Late at night, he was sure someone was in one of the windows in the abandoned building across the street with high-powered, infrared binoculars, spying on him because whenever he sat in the kitchen and looked out the window, he could see pairs of dark, glowing red eyes, shifting back and forth from one window to the other. Sometimes, he even thought he could hear them whispering to each other . . . or else he was hearing the voices of the unseen people who were in his bedroom.

Greg had no idea why the police hadn't arrested him right away. He figured they were toying with him, trying to wear him down, make him jumpy and nervous. He didn't like leaving the apartment, even to go to work or to buy the few groceries he could afford, but it was even worse staying home and listening to his mother complaints and demands. Some days, he wished the cops would hurry up and arrest him if only to end the grinding pressure he was living under. If he went to prison, at least he would get away from his dying mother!

He knew that she was dying, and the truth was, he couldn't wait for that to happen. He wanted to be free of her nagging voice and the shit smell that filled the apartment, day and night.

Greg was getting so desperate that there were times when he actually considered turning himself in. Before he did that, though, there was one little piece of unfinished business he wanted to wrap up.

He had to get to John Ross' wife and kill her. It was as simple as that. What upset him most was knowing that she should have died that night at the restaurant as well. And she would have, except for her damned fool husband who knocked his aim off when he turned the gun on her.

So many times during the weeks that followed Ross' funeral, Greg had considered stealing another car and driving out to Bedford Heights, but he knew that the police would have her and the house under surveillance. It sure as hell didn't make any sense to walk into their trap.

Let *them* come to get *him* if they were going to!

Before that, though, Mrs. John Ross was a loose end, and Greg didn't like loose ends.

So while he waited with steadily mounting fear that he was going to be arrested any day now, Greg started planning what he was going to do about Angela. And while he was at it, he started thinking about what he would do about her two children. After all, without a mother or father, they might as well be dead, too.

It was a wintry day in early March, and school had been canceled, so the kids and Angie were all home. Brandy begged to go over to her friend Liz's house, but Angie thought it was too far to walk in the storm, and she absolutely wasn't going to drive anywhere.

"Why don't you get some homework done?" Angie said for the umpteenth time.

Brandy scowled and, biting her lower lip, shook her head.

She turned and was walking away when the phone rang. Moving much faster than Angie, she grabbed the receiver and said, "Hello." A moment later, her expression dropped and she handed the phone to her mother, saying, "It's for you."

Brandy gave no indication of whom it might be, so Angie felt unaccountably nervous as she took the phone from her and pressed it to her ear.

"Yes?" she said.

"Mrs. Ross. This is Arnold Meecham calling."

"Oh, Mr. Meecham," Angie said, suddenly flustered. "How are you? Is it snowing up there in Maine yet?"

"Sunny and bright," Meecham replied, "but a bit colder than I prefer. I guess the snow's on its way, though." He paused for a second, and in that moment, Angie's heart started racing. She swallowed loud enough to hear herself in the receiver.

"Well, we've had a chance to look over your application and credentials, and I'm pleased to inform you that we would like to offer you a job here in Bolton, starting in September."

"Really," Angie said, feeling suddenly dizzy. Her throat felt like it had closed off entirely. "Well, I . . . I don't know what to say."

She glanced over at Brandy, who was standing in the doorway, watching and listening to her. Feeling suddenly nervous under her daughter's scrutiny, Angie shooed her away with a quick wave of the hand.

"You don't have to give me an answer right now," Meecham said. "There's no real hurry. I realize that you have a lot of other things to consider before you can make a decision. I just wanted to let you know as soon as I could that we'd be very pleased to add someone with your background and experience to our staff."

"Why, thank you . . . Thank you very much, Mr. Meecham."

"Please. Call me Arnold," Meecham said.

"I do want to take some time to consider this and discuss it with my children," Angie said. "This will as much be their decision as mine, but I— Thank you. I think I can tell you right now that I— Yes, I most definitely am interested. I'll give you a call in a day or two to let you know for sure."

"Like I said, there's no real hurry here," Meecham said. "We'll be hiring you as a permanent substitute for the entire school year starting in September. That way, we don't have to advertise and all that. If things work out—and I see no reason why they wouldn't—then you'll obviously be the front runner should that or any other position open up within the school system."

"I—I understand," Angie said. "Thank you again. I'll talk this over with my family and, like I said, be back to you in a few days."

"Fine then," Meecham said. "I have a call on the other line. Look, if there's anything you need to discuss, feel free to call me anytime. You have my number?"

"Yes, I do. Thank you. Thanks for calling. 'Bye."

After she heard Meecham hang up, Angie replaced the phone on its base. She had no idea how she felt. It was a curious mixture of elation and apprehension and too many other emotions to try to untangle. She was trembling inside as she looked over at Brandy, who was still standing in the doorway, her arms folded across her chest. She was frowning.

"Don't tell me," Brandy said flatly. "They just offered you the job in Maine."

Angie ran her teeth over her lower lip as she nodded.

"Uh-huh. If I want it," she said. "What do you think?"

Brandy looked away, focusing for a moment on the white blur of falling snow outside the living room window. She suddenly shivered and hugged herself before turning back at her mother.

"I don't think it really matters *what* I think," Brandy said at last. "Not in the long run, anyway, because you're going to do what you're going to do no matter what I say."

"That's not true," Angie protested. She took a step closer to Brandy but stopped when she realized that her daughter didn't need a hug right now.

"We have plenty of time to think about it and discuss it before I tell them whether or not I'll take the job. Where's JJ?"

"Where else? Up in his bedroom, playing his stupid video games."

Angie didn't miss the sudden hostility in Brandy's voice.

"Would you call him down?" she said. "I think we all better sit down and talk this over right now so no one's nose gets bent out of shape."

Brandy regarded her for another long moment or two, then turned and, cupping her hands to her mouth, shouted as loud as she could up the stairwell, *"Hey! Dweeb! Get your fat butt down here!"*

"Thanks," Angie said, smiling at her.

"Think nothing of it," Brandy said.

Angie had no doubt what she wanted to do. Now it was just a matter of convincing the kids that moving to Maine was the best thing for all of them.

Part Two
The Burden of Regret

"I was misled by my fear."
—Sophocles (*Oedipus Rex*)

Part Two
The Murder of Regina

Chapter 10
Moving In

While neither Brandy nor JJ seemed particularly thrilled by the prospect of moving to Maine, after a week or so of talking about it, they did finally, reluctantly agree. After that, although it took Angie more than a month of almost constant work to line things up, everything seemed to happen much too fast.

Still consumed with grief over John's death, Angie found it extremely difficult at times to function. Too many times a day—every day—she would break down and start crying, and the nights alone in bed were worse. Detective Holden kept in touch once or twice a week, but he never pushed her too hard to answer anything. That was just as well because Angie was also consumed with guilt about the money John had stolen from the crime scene years ago. She prayed that had been the only time he had done it, mostly because she didn't want his name and memory tarnished by an investigation that might reveal he was a dirty cop. Holden didn't have any answers for her, either. The investigating detectives had made no progress in trying to find out who murdered John.

Once the family had reached a decision, the first thing Angie did was resign from her special education teaching job, effective immediately. Realizing that she was resigning because she had recently lost her husband, the principal, superintendent, and school board accepted her resignation without question. Edith Marshall, the principal at Angie's school, told her that she would give her a glowing recommendation for any job she applied to in the future.

Angie was going to miss her students most of all, but she consoled herself with the thought that she would have a whole new class to get to know next fall. Until then, she and her children could use the time to be together, to grieve and try to heal their wounds. Still, there were many nights when Angie could hear either Brandy or JJ, sometimes both, sobbing quietly in their bedrooms.

She had to keep telling herself that she was doing the best she could to help them heal, but her own pain was still so deep that she was never convinced she was doing a very good job of it.

The next and possibly biggest step of all was putting the house on Clinton Street up for sale. Angie had more than a few tearful nights herself, thinking that it was a major mistake even to *consider* selling the house—their home. Other than a few years in an apartment when they were first married, she and John had lived here their entire married lives. Because both of her parents had died when she was young, this had really been the only home Angie had even known. She knew she was going to miss it terribly once she was gone. She tried—as she had for so many years—to forget that they had been able to afford this house in the first place only because of the money John had stolen from that drug bust.

But living in this house had become an almost constant torture for Angie.

Without John, she felt as though she was trying to live someone else's life. Certainly the life she had known and thought was so stable had ended that night outside *Le Bistro*. She had no idea what part—if any—of that past life was really hers anymore. As the weeks went by, and the weather began to warm up with the promise of an early spring, she began to think more and more that her only *real* life was the life she and the kids were going to make for themselves in Maine.

Everything else was just . . . memories.

The most exciting aspect of it all was when she called Ed Lewis, the real estate broker in Bolton, and made an offer on the house on Taylor Hill Road. The asking price was quite a bit higher than she had wanted to pay, but the owners were anxious to sell the property, which had been on the market for well over a year. Offers and counter offers went back and forth a few times, but they eventually settled on a figure that everyone found acceptable. Angie had Ed Lewis fax her the contracts, which she took to her lawyer to look over, sign, and fax back the next day.

By the second week of April, Angie not only had a job and owned the house in Maine, but a young professional couple with three children had made an offer on the Bedford Heights house. The price wasn't what Angie had hoped to get, but she and John had enough equity in the property so she would walk away with a nice profit when—and if—the deal finally fell into place.

By the last week of April, during school vacation for Brandy and JJ, Angie hired some young men who ran a local moving company to help her pack up their belongings. She was ruthless as she sorted through the junk they had accumulated over the years. A local landscaper loaded up his pickup truck and carted off everything she no longer wanted. Over three days, the man made five separate trips to the landfill. Each time, his truck was loaded to the top.

On Monday afternoon, the movers came and packed the van with furniture and boxes. Early Tuesday morning, they were set to go.

The sun was shining brightly, and the day was warm, almost springlike when Angie and the kids, leading the van, headed out. The runoff from melting snow made large puddles on the roads, and Angie had to use her windshield washer almost constantly to keep her windshield clean. The movers had directions to the house in Maine, but Angie made sure to keep them within view in her rearview mirror as much as possible.

"This is exciting, isn't it?" Angie said several times.

She kept trying to get a conversation going, but neither

Brandy nor JJ seemed particularly talkative throughout the drive north. All the way through Connecticut, Brandy kept her Walkman headphones on, and JJ kept his nose glued to Gameboy.

By the time they crossed the state line into Massachusetts, dense, gray clouds were closing in from the west. As they drove east on the Mass Turnpike, large flakes of snow started to fall. Before long, they were in the midst of a full scale snow squall.

"Snow—? In April—?" Brandy said, incredulous.

She frowned as she stared at the falling snow, pencil-thin, white lines that looked like tracer bullets aimed straight at the car. When the wind gusted, and the snow swirled, Angie found it difficult to drive.

"Well, I know for a fact that this past winter, we had more snow in Bedford Heights than they had in Maine."

"In the southern part of Maine, maybe," Brandy said, and then sighed heavily.

Because of the weather, Angie drove much slower than she normally would have. Traffic slowed almost to a crawl on Route 290 through Worcester and on Interstate 495 through Lowell and into New Hampshire. She found it difficult to keep the moving van in sight throughout the whole trip. Smaller cars kept zipping between them, cutting them off. By the time they crossed the Kittery bridge into Maine, they were already three hours behind schedule. At this rate, Angie thought, they'd be unloading the van in the dark.

They took Interstate 95 north to Augusta, then headed west on Route 202. The closer they got to Bolton, the more Angie felt a dizzying mixture of excitement and apprehension. Maybe it was just from driving in the snow for so long that was getting to her, but she started to worry that she had built up such elaborate fantasies about the house on Taylor Hill Road that she and the kids were sure to be disappointed when they saw it again.

A little before four in the afternoon, with heavy snow swirling around them, they drove through downtown Bolton. Angie's heart was racing fast when they drove through town and then turned off outer Main Street onto Taylor Hill Road. Every twist and turn in the road was bringing them closer to what she hoped was going to be the best thing they had ever done as a family.

She couldn't help but let out a low whimper when, up ahead, through the curtain of falling snow, she saw the stone pillars that marked the turn into the driveway. Her hands inside her gloves were slick with sweat. Every muscle in her body tightened as she slowed down and flicked on her turn signal to warn the men in the van behind her that the turn was coming up. She shook her head to convince herself she wasn't dreaming when she pulled into the driveway of their new home.

Seeing the house again nearly took Angie's breath away. She was far from disappointed. If anything, it was even better than she remembered it. A fresh blanket of snow several inches thick covered everything, making the house and yard look cozy and quaint.

Turning in her seat, Angie looked at Brandy first, then JJ. Both of them had pale, pinched expressions as they stared out at their new home, looking as nervous as Angie felt.

"Well, here we are," she said in a tight voice.

Both of the kids grunted as they looked at the house through the falling snow.

Although she wanted to present a happy, excited face, Angie knew that she couldn't. Like it or not, there was no turning back.

Their life in New York was over.

This was their new house. She knew it would take a long time before it really felt like home, but this was where they were going to start new lives for themselves ... without a husband or a father.

None of them said anything as they opened the car doors and stepped out into the full-scale blizzard. Clouds the color of soot shifted overhead as the sky rapidly darkened with evening. Above the high whistle of the wind came the steady *beep-beep-*

beep sound of the moving van's warning buzzer as the driver backed the truck as close as he could get it to the front door.

"I can't tell you how happy we are that someone's finally moving in next door."

Angie tried to smile warmly as she regarded Ellen Harding, her new neighbor. She and her husband, Doug, had seen the activity next door and, in spite of the blizzard, had come over to introduce themselves. The best news Angie had heard so far was that they had a twelve year old son named Sammy. Hopefully, JJ and Sammy would hit it off right away and become friends.

"We're happy to be here, too," Angie said, looking around nervously.

She felt a bit irritated that the Hardings didn't seem to realize that now wasn't exactly the best time for her to socialize. Ellen invited them over to her house to warm up, but Angie said she was more concerned about overseeing the movers as they unloaded the van. JJ and Brandy were already upstairs, arguing over who got which bedroom, so she didn't ask if either of them wanted to go over to the Harding's house. After finally realizing they were in the way, they went back home with a promise to bring over some coffee and hot cocoa later.

Neither one of the movers said much as they worked, but they grunted and swore a lot as they off-loaded everything as fast as they could. In a little more than an hour, they had more than half the furniture and boxes in the appropriate rooms. The movers said they planned to drive back to New York tonight in spite of the storm, so Angie told them not to bother arranging anything. She wanted to wash the walls and woodwork first, anyway.

The front door had to be left open most of the time, and Angie could hear the furnace running constantly down in the basement. Hot water banged like hammers in the pipes throughout the house, but cold drafts swirled upstairs and down. The real estate agent had assured her that there was a full tank of fuel oil, but Angie worried that it was going to be used up

before the movers were finished. She didn't relish the thought
of spending their first night here huddled under blankets and
sleeping bags.

The movers were also making quite a mess of the floors,
tracking in clumps of muddy snow that fell from their boots
and immediately began to melt. There wasn't much Angie could
do about that except get a towel from one of the boxes marked
BATHROOM and keep wiping up after them as best she could.
The last thing she wanted was water stains on her hardwood
floors and carpets.

As night fell, the snow still hadn't let up. It haloed in the
blue glow of the streetlights that lined the road. Looking from
the front door, Angie could hardly see the stone wall out front.
It was lost under a sloping drift. She was exhausted, and all
she could do was hope that the movers would be done soon
so she and the kids could make their beds and try to settle
down for the night. She wondered if there was a snow shovel
in the garage or cellar because that was one thing she had
forgotten to bring along. John would have thought of that detail.

Finally, a little after six o'clock, the movers carried in the
last few things. Angie thanked them and offered to pay for
them to spend the night in a motel, but they were intent not to
let something like a little snow slow them down. They got back
into the truck and took off. The last Angie saw of them was
the red glow of their taillights before the storm swallowed
them.

Angie and the kids had already carried in their suitcases and
the few bags of groceries they had packed separately in the
car.

"Well," she said, turning to Brandy and JJ, who watched
her from the foot of the stairs as she closed and locked the
front door behind them.

"Gee, I don't know, Mom," Brandy said, shaking her head
as she looked around and shivered.

"Now Brandy says *she* wants the room you said *I* could
have," JJ said.

Before Angie could respond, Brandy gave her brother a

punch on the shoulder that made him yelp. He turned quickly and faced her, his fists clenched.

"You said we'd decide after the movers left," Brandy said, backing out of striking distance, her face flushed even though the house was still chilly from having the door open all evening.

"You two just cut it out!" Angie snapped.

Dizzy with exhaustion and close to tears, she closed her eyes and leaned her head back against the door. Next to the day of John's funeral, this had been one of the longest days of her life. All she wanted to do now was grab something quick to eat and then flop a few mattresses onto the floor, unroll their sleeping bags, and get some much needed sleep. They could deal with everything else in the morning. She was about to say this when the front doorbell rang with a deep *gong* sound.

"Hey, *c-o-o-ol* doorbell," JJ said as Angie pulled the curtain aside and looked out through the sidelight.

She was expecting to see that the movers had come back, maybe to take her up on her offer of a motel room. Instead, she saw Ellen and Doug Harding, huddled against the snow on the doorstep. She wasn't sure if she had an ounce of energy left for visiting, but she could see that—just as they had promised—Doug was holding two large thermos bottles. Ellen held a plate of sandwiches covered with plastic wrap, a bag of potato chips, and some paper plates and napkins.

"Welcome to your new home," Ellen said, smiling as Angie opened the door to let them in.

"We figured you'd be too bushed to make supper, so we brought over a little something," Doug said.

Angie smiled and nodded. Her first thought was that maybe this country friendliness was going a little too far, but she was grateful that she didn't have to do anything else tonight except, maybe, chew and swallow.

"You didn't have to," she said, hearing the weary drag of her voice.

"But we wanted to," Ellen said, smiling as she and Doug kicked their snowy boots off on the rug.

"Let's go into the kitchen," Angie said. "I think we can clear out enough space around the table for us."

Angie was so tired she hadn't realized how hungry she was. The sandwiches—tuna fish and bologna—and coffee tasted like something from a gourmet restaurant. JJ and Brandy wolfed down two sandwiches each and drank all of the cocoa, then went up to their respective bedroom to begin unpacking. Angie settled the argument about which room they would get by giving Brandy, the oldest, first choice. She seemed to have mellowed and told JJ that he could have the room he wanted.

The Hardings stayed for about an hour. Sitting around the kitchen table, they kept telling Angie what a wonderful house she had bought and how much they were all going to enjoy living in Bolton. Angie didn't reveal much about her own background. She was too exhausted to even try to explain why there was no Mr. Ross present. She figured, if Ellen and Doug didn't already know through some kind of community gossip line, then she could tell them about it another time. Right now, all she wanted to do was finish eating and get some sleep.

Around seven-thirty, the Hardings left. Angie told the kids that tomorrow was going to be a big day, and she wanted them in bed and asleep right away. For some reason, the phone wasn't going to be switched over for another day or two, so Angie couldn't call Rob to let them know how the move had gone. She considered driving over to his house to say hello but decided against it. There wasn't much protest from either of the kids, and by eight o'clock, the house was dark, and everyone was in bed.

Now that he had the bedroom he had fought with Brandy to get, JJ wasn't so sure that he wanted it. The room was about the same size as the room he'd had back home in Bedford Heights, but this one had two windows that looked out over the road. The glow of the streetlights out front shined through the bare branches of the trees and cast jagged shadows across the wall.

JJ would have drawn the window shades, but he was already settled inside his sleeping bag and didn't want to get up.

Outside, the wind howled. It found a few gaps in the windows where it whistled with a low, hollow moan. Long into the night, the radiator kept banging. JJ imagined that it was someone down in the cellar, hammering on the pipes.

He didn't want to admit it to himself, but he was scared. Not terrified, the way he used to be when he was a stupid little kid, but it felt . . . odd to be in this strange bedroom and to keep reminding himself that from now on, *this* was *his* room.

He kept looking over at the closet door, half-expecting to see it open a crack . . . and a pair of eyes, glowing dull red, staring back at him.

Trembling inside, he pulled the sleeping bag up to his chin and tried to close his eyes, but he didn't dare to.

Outside, the snow was still falling. He could see and hear it, pattering lightly against his windows. When the town snow plow passed by, the sound of its plow blade scraping on the asphalt set his teeth on edge. He lay there in bed, thinking he just might get some sleep if *only* the wind would stop whistling and the radiators would stop banging and the closet door would stop looking like it was inching slowly open . . .

He looked over at the clock on his desk and saw that it was already quarter to eleven. As tired as he was, he was beginning to wonder if he would ever fall asleep.

"Mom," he called out.

The sound of his own voice in the darkness surprised him.

"Hey . . . Mom?"

He knew that her bedroom was just down the hall, but it seemed so far away, not like back home in Bedford Heights. He tensed as he listened for her reply, but none came. A gust of wind rattled his windows, sending a chill tingling deep inside his belly. A dull pressure was building up steadily in his bladder, but he knew that he wouldn't dare get out of bed to go to the bathroom.

Not yet.

"*Hey, Mom!*" he called out.

He had to keep telling himself that he wasn't *really* afraid; he just wanted to make sure she could hear him.

His eyes were wide open as he looked around the strange

room, wondering who used to sleep here, and if the house might be haunted.

No, that was a foolish thought!

There were no such things as ghosts and haunted houses. It was just people's imaginations, getting carried away. He'd done that to himself plenty of times, back when he was a little kid, but not anymore.

His hands were clammy with sweat as he inched the sleeping bag down and tried to find the courage to get out of bed. He was sure that the bare wooden floor was going to be cold as ice when he stepped on it, so he kept his feet under the covers.

"Mom!" he shouted again, a little louder this time.

He waited, and after a moment heard a soft groan from the next room. He told himself that it was either Brandy or his mother, waking up because of his shout.

"Mom . . . Can you come in here?" he called out.

"What is it?"

JJ heaved a sigh of relief when he recognized his mother's voice. It sounded muffled through the walls and closed doors, but he was happy to know that she was awake.

"I . . . just wanted to talk to you," he said, trying hard to keep the edge out of his voice.

"Aww, honey . . . Can't you just go to sleep?" his mother said.

JJ could hear the tiredness and irritation in her voice, but he really did want to talk to her. He just wanted to see her, and then he'd be all right.

"I—"

A sudden, powerful gust of wind slammed into the side of the house, making the roof timbers snap loudly. A cold spike of fear shot through JJ. He wanted to call out to his mother again, but his voice failed. From somewhere in the house, he heard a faint clicking sound, then the soft scuffing of feet on the wooden floor. Panic filled him as he listened to the doorknob to his bedroom click and turn. His eyes were bulging from his head as he watched the door open slowly, and a shadow darker than the night filled the doorway.

"What is it, honey," his mother said softly.

JJ let out his breath when he saw his mother moving toward him. The bedsprings creaked when she sat on the edge of his bed. He sighed heavily before speaking.

"I—I'm not sure," he said, hearing the tremor in his voice. "It's just so . . ." His voice faded away.

"So *quiet?*" his mother finished for him.

JJ grunted as he nodded.

"Yeah . . . I guess," he said after swallowing hard. "This house doesn't make the same noises our old house did."

"You'll get used to it," his mother said. She took his hand and patted it gently. "It's going to seem different for a few nights, but wait and see. You'll be used to it in no time."

"I guess so," JJ said.

He wanted to tell her some of his other concerns, but he knew that now wasn't the right time. He was a lot more nervous than he had let on to her about starting school in a new town and having to make all new friends. In fact, he was worried sick about it.

"The storm's kinda freaky, too," he said.

"An old house like this is going to make a lot of noises when the wind's blowing," his mother said.

Her grip on his hand tightened for a moment. JJ thought it might be a good idea if he slept in her room, at least for the first night, but he was ashamed to ask.

"Are you gonna be all right?" his mother asked.

"Sure," JJ replied bravely, not really feeling it. "I was just—I woke up and wasn't sure where I was, that's all."

"I can leave the hall light on and have your door open a crack if you'd like," his mother suggested.

JJ shook his head and said, "Sure." He wanted to say more, but he was feeling tense, he couldn't think of what to say. Part of what had him worried was that the house and storm bothered him, and he was nervous about starting school in a couple of days, but it seemed to be more than that—deeper.

"I . . . I still miss Dad . . . a lot," he finally said.

As soon as the words were out of his mouth, a hot rush of emotion choked him. He sat up suddenly in bed and wrapped his arms around his mother, pulling her close. When he inhaled,

he smelled the faint trace of soap from the shower she had
taken just before bed. It was a smell he had always associated
with her, and it made him feel more secure.

"We *all* miss Dad," his mother said softly as she hugged
him and ran her hands up and down his back. "If you have to
talk about it, even if you have to cry about it sometimes, you
just go ahead and do it."

When he heard her sniff and felt her body twitch, he knew
that she was crying, too. He got mad at himself for upsetting
her, but the tangle of emotions inside him was so strong he
wasn't able to stop the tears that flowed from his eyes and ran
down his face.

He lost track of how long he and his mother sat hugging
and crying together in the darkness. At some point, he drifted
off to a deep, dreamless sleep. When morning came, he saw
that his mother had left without him realizing it. He got out of
bed, ran to the window, and looked out at the clear, bright blue
sky. The sunlight was blinding, reflecting off the blanket of
fresh-fallen snow that covered everything.

Maybe it's gonna be a good day, he thought as he turned to
go downstairs.

Chapter 11
The Hand of Darkness

Brandy didn't share the enthusiasm she heard in her mother's voice when, a little past eight o'clock the next morning, she called her downstairs for breakfast. Because there was nothing else for her to do, Brandy was sure that she was going to get stuck unpacking and cleaning all day. It was almost enough to make her wish she knew some of the local kids her age, so she could take off for the day and go hang around the mall or something.

It wasn't that Brandy didn't like their new house. In fact, although she would never admit it to her mother or JJ, she wasn't feeling too bad about moving away from Bedford Heights. Maine seemed pretty much out of it and, of course, she already missed many of her old friends—especially Alita and Tabby—but ever since her father's murder, she had felt detached and isolated from everyone. She had broken up with Jeff a while ago and didn't miss him in the least.

She felt lonely, and judging by the mood she was in pretty much all of the time lately, being alone was probably the best thing for her, at least for right now.

Many times throughout the next few days, she found herself wishing that she could talk to her mother about what she was thinking and feeling, but ultimately she decided that it didn't matter.

She knew that it was up to *her* to sort out how she felt about things and what she was going to do about it.

She wasn't too thrilled about starting at a new high school on Monday, but that was still a few days away. Until then, she would just have to deal with things as they happened.

The house felt cold to her as she rolled out of bed. She was shivering so much her teeth were chattering as she slipped on her bathrobe, then trudged downstairs to the dining room. The smell of bacon and fresh-brewed coffee drew her on. A tight sadness gripped her heart because the smell reminded her so much of mornings back home, in Bedford Heights.

Back when her father was still alive . . .

Brandy blinked back the tears forming in her eyes as she walked into the dining room and sat down. Her mother was looking bright and chipper, as if she had been up for hours. She smiled as she served Brandy a plate of over-easy eggs with bacon, toast and jelly, and orange juice.

"Thanks, Mom," she said huskily as her mother walked back out into the kitchen and started cleaning up.

The dining room was arranged pretty much the way it had been back home. Brandy would have felt even more comfortable if there hadn't been stacks of boxes surrounding her while she ate.

JJ, still wearing pajamas, sat across from her at the table. He was almost finished with breakfast, and was messily sopping up egg yolk with his toast.

"Happy with your room, twerp?" Brandy asked, scowling at him just on general principle.

"Best bedroom in the house," JJ said, smirking at her, showing dark crumbs of toast that were stuck between his front teeth. He looked like he had inhaled a mouthful of soot.

"Wasn't that you I heard crying like a little baby last night?" Brandy asked in a teasingly, sing-song voice.

JJ tensed and started to protest but then looked down at his plate. Brandy knew immediately that she shouldn't have pushed him on that. She was having enough trouble herself, trying to get used to the idea that their father wasn't going to be with them anymore. Every now and then, she could almost convince herself that he was just late getting home from work, but then it would hit her.

He was dead . . . Really dead!

"Don't you two get started," her mother said when she walked back into the dining room carrying a mug of coffee. "We have a lot to do today, and I don't want to hear any more—"

The sudden ringing of the doorbell interrupted her. Brandy looked over at her mother and frowned. "Is that the front or the back door?"

"I'm not sure," Angie said with a shrug as she got up and went to check the front door first. "It's probably Uncle Rob dropping by to see how we're doing."

"Maybe it's the Hardings again," Brandy said, her frown deepening.

"God, I hope they don't turn out to pests," Angie muttered."

"Maybe *they're* the reason the last family that lived here moved out," JJ suggested with a dry chuckle, but nobody else laughed.

Brandy listened as her mother walked down the hall and unlocked the front door. This was followed by a soft buzzing of voices and light laughter.

"Hey, JJ. Come here," Angie called out from the foyer. "There's someone here to see you."

Curious as to who it might be, Brandy got up from the table the same time JJ did and followed a few steps behind him to the front door. Over his shoulder, she saw a small, freckle-faced boy, all wrapped up in a bright-red winter coat with a woolen hat, mittens and scarf. With the sun behind him, his breath was a frosty mist around his head.

"JJ, this is Sammy Harding from next door. Sammy, this is John. Everyone calls him JJ."

Turning to JJ, she said, "Sammy came over to see if you wanted to go out and play for a while."

Brandy couldn't see the expression on JJ's face, but she guessed that he wasn't too thrilled by the idea.

"There's a really cool sliding hill not far from here," Sammy said, his blue eyes sparkling brightly.

"Sounds like fun," Angie said, "but I'm not sure I know where your sled is."

"That's okay," Sammy said. "I brought an extra Sno-Tube, just in case."

"Oh, how thoughtful," Angie said with a smile.

Brandy thought that her mother was acting odd—too friendly to be real. She knew she was putting it on for Sammy.

"The hill's over behind the school," Sammy said. "Just through the woods out behind the house."

Brandy thought Sammy's voice sounded a bit too low for someone his age and size. Maybe it was from the cold. If they stood there much longer with the door wide open, the whole house was going to be an icebox.

"You can go. You don't have to unpack the stuff in your bedroom right away," Angie said.

Turning to face JJ so Sammy couldn't see her, she indicated with a hard look that she thought he damned well better decide to say *yes*.

"Mom . . . It's really cold out," JJ said, wrapping his arms around himself and shivering. "Maybe Sammy can come inside and play for a while. We could get my new computer hooked up in my room."

Angie shook her head firmly, cutting him off.

"You can do that later. I have a lot to do today, but first I was thinking about driving over to see Uncle Rob. If you're going to stay inside, I expect you to be working. Maybe later today you guys can set up the computer . . . after you get some fresh air."

"But Mom . . ."

"My mom's always saying that to me, too," Sammy said to JJ with a knowing half-smile.

JJ hesitated for a moment, then slowly nodded and said, "Yeah . . . well, I guess so . . ."

Angie hugged herself from the cold, her teeth were chattering as she turned to Sammy. "Why don't you come inside to wait so I can shut the door?"

"Thanks," Sammy said, his smile widening.

He stomped his feet hard to knock off as much snow as he could before stepping inside and closing the door behind him. When he took off his woolen hat, Brandy saw that he had bright red hair to match his freckles. She thought he looked kind of cute, in a little kid sort of way.

"I think the box with the gloves and mittens is in the pantry, by the back door," Angie said to JJ. "I'll see if I can find something for you. If you're done breakfast, go upstairs and get dressed."

Still looking reluctant and resentful about being forced into making friends so quickly with his new neighbor, JJ started slowly up the stairs to his room.

"You're sure it's all safe for you guys to be playing over by the school?" Angie asked.

"Come *on*, Mom," Brandy said. "This isn't New York City, for crying out loud!"

"I know," Angie said. "It's just that I . . . wanted to be sure everything was okay."

"I take the path through the woods to school every day," Sammy said with a casual shrug. "I figured we might as well start trampling down the snow now."

"Good point," Angie said. She smiled and nodded, then went to the foot of the stairs and called up to JJ. "Come on! Don't keep Sammy waiting!"

Brandy was more than a little resentful that JJ was going to get out of working this morning, but she would just as soon stay home, anyway. She heaved a sigh as she walked back into the dining room to finish breakfast. The eggs were stone cold and rubbery from the door being left open.

Over the next two days, Angie and Brandy worked long, hard hours, unpacking and arranging everything in their new home. Rob was on vacation that week, so he came over on Wednesday and Thursday and helped Angie move the heavier furniture around until she was satisfied with the arrangement. Angie planned to buy a new sofa and chair set for the sun porch, which she had designated the family reading room. The TV was consigned to the living room.

On Thursday, the first delivery of their mail forwarded from their old address in New York arrived. Angie felt a sharp pang of regret when she saw their old street address crossed out, but all in all, she tried to convince herself that she was happy with their decision.

Several times each day, Brandy complained that she didn't think it was fair the way JJ got to spend most of his time hanging out with Sammy while she had to put stuff away and scrub floors and walls; but Angie told her that she was glad to see that the boys were hitting it off so well. The only incentive JJ had to finish unpacking the boxes in his room was so he could set up his new computer and play the new CD-ROM games he'd gotten. Angie wasn't happy that he and Sammy spent more time playing games inside than they did outside; but the weather was still unseasonably cold for April, so she decided not to make too much of an issue about it. Once or twice a day she encouraged Brandy to go downtown and try to meet some of the local kids who might be hanging around, but she refused.

On Thursday evening, the Hardings dropped by with a casserole and a loaf of homemade French bread that Ellen had baked for them. Angie was grateful because, even though she now had everything in the kitchen unpacked, she was too tired at the end of the day to do much more than heat up a can of soup. The family had been surviving on soup, cold sandwiches, and take-out pizza and sub sandwiches which Rob had brought over on Wednesday evening with Craig.

The only time Angie bothered to clean herself up was on Friday morning when she went to the school administrative offices to register Brandy and JJ. After that, they visited the area high school, which was much bigger than either Angie or Brandy had expected. The high school principal, Chet Newley, gave them a tour of the school so Brandy wouldn't be completely lost on her first day.

Late Friday afternoon, JJ and Angie walked the path through

the woods to the elementary school. Mostly, Angie wanted to check it out to make sure it was safe for them.

At the school, Arnold Meecham, the man who had hired Angie for next year, introduced them to Mrs. Judkins, JJ's sixth grade teacher. Angie still couldn't quite believe that she would be teaching in this school in September, but right now, that seemed like such a long time away. She had plenty to do to make their new home comfortable, first.

They all worked hard on Saturday, and by Sunday afternoon, most of the boxes were unpacked, flattened, and waiting to go out with the trash, or else stored away in closets or the attic or cellar to be unpacked later. There was still lots of cleaning to do, but Angie told herself that she would have plenty of time to finish that once the kids went back to school on Monday. On Sunday evening, when Rob called and invited her and the kids out for supper at the *Campbell Inn,* his favorite restaurant, she gladly accepted. She didn't think she even had the strength to open a can of soup tonight.

When they arrived at the restaurant, Angie realized with a slight shock that, other than Burger King or Roy Rogers along the highway, she hadn't been out to eat in a restaurant since the night John was shot. She found it disconcerting how the horror of that night still seemed so immediate and real while, at the same time, it seemed so far away, as if it had happened to someone else in another lifetime. She felt tense and jittery throughout the meal, but she didn't think Rob, Craig, or the kids picked up on it.

Later that night, after both Brandy and JJ were in bed, Angie found it difficult to settle down. Dark thoughts and gnawing worries stirred like sharks deep inside her and kept her from drifting off to sleep.

As she lay on her left side in bed, staring at the cold, gray light that filtered through the bedroom windows, she couldn't help but listen to the rapid flutter of her pulse in her ear against the pillow. She wasn't sure exactly when she started thinking about it, but after a while she realized that she was dwelling on something that she hadn't thought about in years.

Back when she was a junior in high school, living in Weathersfield, Connecticut, with her father and Rob after their mother had died, something horrible had happened. A twelve year old boy named Gary Moulton—the younger brother of Lisa Moulton, one of Angie's best friends—had been playing with one of his father's many guns. He later claimed that he didn't know the gun was loaded, but when it went off, his ten year old brother, Roy, was struck by a bullet and killed.

Gary had tearfully insisted that it had been an accident, but there were many people around town who never believed him. His parents were grief-stricken and, as far as Angie knew, never recovered from their loss. It had been years since she had wondered about how—and if—Gary had ever recovered from his tragic mistake. She knew that the loss had turned her friend, Lisa, into a sour, depressed person, but she had lost touch with her shortly after the incident when Lisa got pregnant and dropped out of school during their senior year.

Angie suddenly realized that what might have triggered all of this was thinking that she, too, was trying hard to cope with a senseless, tragic loss, something from which she might never recover. True, losing a child had to be even more difficult than losing a spouse, but Angie was sure that John's death—his *murder*—had scarred her for the rest of her life. She only hoped that she could work through or around it and that—eventually—the kids would get over it and not let their father's death ruin their lives.

Staring into the hazy darkness that filled her bedroom, Angie realized something else that was bothering her. She suddenly sat up in bed, her body tingling as if an electrical current had passed through it.

Against her better judgment, she had a gun in the house.

Taking a deep breath, she tossed the covers aside. In spite of the chill that raced up her legs when her feet touched the wooden floor, she walked over to her desk, which was placed under the window that looked out over the back yard. Her heart was racing high and fast as she pulled out the chair and sat down. The soft, blue glow of moonlight was shining over the snow-covered lawn and edging the jagged, black pointed tops of the pine trees. The sight, while pleasant, sent another, deeper chill through Angie.

For several seconds, she just sat there, drumming her fingers on the felt ink blotter. She wasn't sure why she was even doing this, but she fished the small key from the cup on top of her desk and, bending down, unlocked the bottom drawer and slid it open. Reaching into the back of the drawer, underneath a stack of old papers, she felt around until her fingers curled around the hard, textured hand grip of the gun.

A low whimper from deep in her throat escaped her as she slowly withdrew the gun and raised it so she could see its dark silhouette against the ambient light of the night sky. The gun felt surprisingly heavy in her hand. It looked and felt dangerous. Of course John, being a policeman, had owned several guns, but as part of her cleaning out their old lives, Angie had sold most of them to a local gun collector in Katonah.

All except for this one—John's service revolver.

She had no idea why, but she hadn't been able to part with it. Maybe it was because this .38 was a symbol of what, next to his family, had been the single most important thing in John's life.

She hated the idea of having a gun in the house—in fact, she detested guns and what they could do to people—but she told herself that this gun would be safe as long as she kept it and the half-empty box of bullets locked up in the bottom drawer of her desk. As far as she knew, neither one of the kids knew she had it. This wasn't an issue . . . except for her.

Still, she dreaded that either one of them—especially JJ—might find it. She cringed at the memory of what had happened to the Moultons. Many times since John had died, she had considered getting rid of this gun, but she convinced herself that keeping it was important, not only as a reminder of her dead husband, but also as possible protection, now that she was living in a strange town where she didn't know very many people. It struck her as odd that she would feel more threatened living out in the country than she ever had living so close to New York City, but that's how she felt.

Angie sighed as she hefted the gun, being careful to keep

her finger off the trigger even though she knew the gun wasn't loaded. She had checked it yesterday afternoon when she unpacked it and hid it in her desk.

"We're safer here than we ever were before," she whispered as she looked out across the backyard again. The view made her shiver when she saw the branches sway gently in a gust of wind.

Her hand felt weak and shaky from holding the weight of the gun. She leaned forward and placed it gently back inside the drawer, putting it as far back as she could and then covering it with a stack of papers. She slid the drawer shut, making sure to lock it, then dropped the key back into the cup.

Moving slowly and feeling as though she were walking in a dream, she went back to her bed and lay down. The sheets were still warm from her body heat as she pulled the covers up to her chin. She felt cozy, but still, sleep didn't come for a long time because she couldn't stop thinking about what had happened to Gary and Roy Moulton . . . and to her husband . . .

You're going to have to find her and kill her.
The voice, speaking as clearly as if someone was standing right there beside his bed, woke up Greg instantly. He made a funny gagging sound in the back of his throat as he sucked in a breath sharply and opened his eyes. Without lifting his head from his pillow, he looked around the small, cluttered bedroom.

Everything looked just the way it should.

The window shades didn't quite block out the city lights, so in the diffused light, he could see the dark bulk of his bureau, the desk and chair on the opposite wall, the pile of dirty clothes at the foot of the bed, and the dark wedge of the half-opened closet door. The pictures hanging on the wall were nothing more than dark, featureless rectangles.

Just like every night this past winter, the apartment was uncomfortably cold. Even huddled under three blankets, Greg shivered as if the windows had been left wide open.

As his mind gradually cleared, Greg realized that it was

impossible for anyone to have been in the apartment. Last night, like every other night, he had made sure to double-lock the door. Still, he couldn't get rid of the feeling that *someone* was here. When he looked into the darkest corner over by the closet door, especially out of the corner of his eye, he was sure that he caught a glimpse of dark motion shifting against the wall.

"Who . . . who's there?" he whispered, his voice sounding like a raw, tearing sound in the night.

He was tensed as he listened for a reply, but all he heard was his own rapid breathing and the faint rumble of his mother's snoring from the next room. Out on the street, a car passed by, its engine sputtering and bucking as it backfired.

Clutching the bed covers tightly with both hands, Greg slowly eased himself up into a sitting position. The bedsprings creaked like old floorboards. A cold draft of air swirled over him, making him shiver again. When he tried to swallow, his throat closed off with a click.

"Who . . . Who am I . . . going to have to kill?" he asked, addressing the darkness around him.

You know who, replied a voice that seemed to come at him from several directions at once.

Greg's eyes widened with mounting terror. No matter where he looked, the darkness at the fringes of his vision shifted with subtle motion.

"No, I . . . I don't know who," Greg said shakily. "Tell me."

You had your chance, but you let her get away.

"I didn't let *anyone* get away," Greg said sharply as a sudden surge of anger filled him like fire.

Oh, but you did, the voice said mildly, almost taunting. *And I think you're too chickenshit to do anything about it.*

"Tha—that's not true," Greg whispered, wishing he believed it. "I ain't chickenshit."

He shifted around on the bed, hearing the dry rustle of sheets. The fear that was growing stronger inside him was like a ball of ice lodged in the center of his chest.

Oh yes it is, hissed the voice. *You panicked and ran. How long has it been since you even went out to her house?*

"There are cops watching that house," Greg said.

No. The truth of the matter is, you're a fucking coward who doesn't know how to finish what he's started!

Realization suddenly hit Greg when he recognized the voice.

It was his father's voice!

Tension held him like a tightening vise.

"You can't talk to me that way!" Greg said, his voice trembling wildly. "I'm through with you! Do you hear me? Through! You're dead, so please . . . *please!* just leave me alone!"

No, I won't leave you alone . . . not until you finish what you set out to do, the voice said.

Greg clenched his fists. Moaning deep in his throat, he started rocking back and forth, all the while punching the sides of his head as if that would make the voice stop. He wished he dared turn on the light, but he was afraid of what he might see. Everywhere he looked, he saw weaving, menacing shadows reaching out for him as if the darkness had hands.

Was it possible?

Could his dead father really here in his room, talking to him?

"Go away! Jesus Christ! Leave me alone!" Greg wailed in a high, wavering voice.

Fear and anger choked him as he watched the darkness in his bedroom swirl and condense. Off to either side, he thought he caught fleeting glimpses of figures closing in on him, but when he turned to look, they were gone.

"Just tell me what you want me to do!" Greg cried out, but he already knew the answer.

Panting heavily and covering his face with his hands, he stared into the darkness behind his eyelids. It pulsed in time with his rapid heartbeat. He whispered so softly that he had no idea if he was speaking, or if it was someone else.

". . . I'm going to have to find her and kill her . . ."

Chapter 12

First Impressions

Monday morning finally felt like an April morning was supposed to feel. The sky was a clear, vibrant blue, and the sun was strong and warm on Angie's face when she opened the front door and leaned outside to take a deep breath.

Even this early in the morning, the day was warm enough so the snow from last weekend's surprise blizzard was melting rapidly. Water gurgled like a fast-running brook as it ran into the gutters off the roof and dripped from the down spout at the end of the house. The air had a sharp freshness to it that stung Angie's nose.

"You know what, JJ?" Angie said as she looked out over the front lawn. The top row of rocks on the stone wall were glistening in the sun. "I'll bet the path through the woods is going to be a mess. I could give you and Sammy a ride, if you'd like."

"Naw . . . we'd just as soon walk," JJ said as he came into the entryway and hefted his backpack, now that he had his coat and boots on.

"Don't you mean 'no thanks, Mom?' " Angie said, turning and nailing him with a hard look.

"Oh. Right . . . No thanks, Mom," JJ said with just a trace of sarcasm in his voice.

"So what's up with you today?" Angie asked. "Did you get up on the wrong side of the bed or something?"

"Nothing's up with me," JJ said, apparently unphased by her reaction.

"All I meant was, it's no problem for me to drive you. I have to go in town, anyway, to do some shopping."

"I said *no!*" JJ snapped, scowling darkly. The angry gleam in his eyes stopped her cold, and for just an instant, she saw in him the same hostility she used to see every now and then in John. It frightened her. As much as she loved and missed her husband, she had always acknowledged that there was a barely repressed streak of violence in him that had always made her nervous, even though she realized it had to be one of the attributes that made him such a good detective.

But she didn't like seeing the same hardness developing in her son.

Then again, she reminded herself, JJ was just as much John's son as he was hers. She thought the same silent prayer that had been in her mind a lot over the last few months, that John's death wasn't going to scar JJ's personality and turn him into a bitter, hostile person.

"Are you going to walk over to Sammy's and meet him?" Angie asked, making an effort to keep her voice mild.

JJ shook his head. "He said he'd come by and pick me up. What time is it, anyway?"

There was still an edge in his voice that Angie didn't like. She glanced over her shoulder at the clock on the mantel in the living room and said, "A little after seven-thirty."

"I'd better go get him," JJ said as he pushed past her and walked down the steps into the sunshine. "See yah later," he called out without bothering to look back.

Angie had been hoping that he would walk up to the road to keep his feet dry, but he cut diagonally across the lawn, walking through the sloppiest muddy sections seemingly on purpose.

A wave of sadness washed over her as she watched him leave. She acknowledged that he was growing up fast, but he still looked so small and defenseless. She was having trouble not seeing him still as her little baby boy.

He's trying too hard to grow up too fast, she thought.

From personal experience, she knew that processing the loss of a parent was one of the most difficult, agonizing things a kid ever had to face. The younger they were at the time, the harder it seemed to be, and the more scars it seemed to leave.

Tears misted Angie's vision, and she almost called out to him but then caught herself.

If there was one thing she had learned about raising children—and it seemed all the more important now that JJ was almost a teenager—it was to choose her battles and not let the little things bug her. She knew, no matter what she said, that he was going to get his feet wet and muddy in the woods today.

Wiping her eyes, she forced herself to smile as she waited for him to turn around so she could wave to him one last time, but he disappeared over the crest of the hill without a backward glance.

Long after he was gone, Angie stayed on the front steps, trying to enjoy the beautiful morning, but instead she felt an immense sadness. The more she thought about it, the more she realized that JJ was probably so snappy with her because he was nervous about starting school today not knowing anyone except Sammy. The night before, she had offered to take him to school today if he wanted her to, but JJ had insisted that he was a big kid and could handle it by himself. Angie told herself that she had to accept that maybe here in Maine she didn't have to be quite as protective and worried as she had been when they lived in New York.

Besides, like it or not, he *was* growing up—and away from her.

The scuffing sound of footsteps behind her drew her attention. Angie smiled wanly as she turned and saw Brandy standing in the foyer.

"And just what do you think you're doing?" Angie asked when she saw how Brandy was dressed. She was wearing a short dress and a sheer white blouse that was practically see-through and had applied much more makeup than she usually wore. Her lips were a bright, blushing red, and her eyes were shadowed with a dark blue that made her look like she hadn't slept for the last couple of nights.

"I don't wanna be late for the bus," Brandy replied, shrugging and sounding all innocence as she grabbed a lightweight jacket from the closet. "Didn't they say it would come by the house around quarter of eight?"

"Yeah, but . . ."

Angie crossed her arms over her chest and shook her head. She didn't want to say anything that would hurt Brandy's feelings, but her first impression was that she had dressed like this purposely trying to look cheap. It was discomforting to realize just how fast both of her children were growing up.

"Don't you think you're—ah, overdoing it just a tad with the makeup?"

Brandy looked at her with an mixture of defiance and hurt in her expression. Her eyes looked scared, and her lower lip started to tremble slightly, but it was obvious that she had no idea what—if anything—she could say in her own defense.

"I don't want to sound mean," Angie continued, "but I'd prefer it if you took some of that makeup off. You don't want to make the wrong impression on your first day, do you?"

Brandy still looked like she had no idea what to say or do. Hoping to make it easy for her, Angie said, "Just wipe a little of the lipstick off, and tone down the eye shadow a bit."

Brandy glanced at her wristwatch and said, "But I don't have time. The bus will be here any second."

"I'll watch for the bus. You take off some of that makeup."

She congratulated herself for not saying: *What would your father think?*

Angie opened the door and stepped back out onto the front steps, once again grateful for the blast of warm, clean-smelling air that rushed over her as she looked up at the road. A few seconds later, she heard Brandy coming up behind her.

Angie turned and looked.

"Much better," she said, even though she still thought the clothes Brandy had picked were a little too sexy for the first day in a new school. But it was too late to change unless she made an issue of it and ended up driving her to school.

Before she could even offer that option, a horn tooted, and she turned and saw the yellow school bus pulling to a stop at the top of the driveway. The red warning lights started blinking as the side door flapped open. Brandy grabbed her bookbag, kissed her mother on the cheek, and started up the walkway.

"Have a nice day," Angie called out, waving after her.

Just before she climbed onto the bus, Brandy turned and gave her a quick, nervous wave. Angie could see the trepidation in her, and she wished to God there was something she could say or do to make the day go well for her. But she was resigned that it was out of her hands. Besides, she had plenty to deal with of her own today. The first and most important one was getting the rest of the unpacking done.

I feel like a turd in the punchbowl . . .

That's what Brandy kept thinking all day long as she wandered around, trying to find her way around the high school. All of the teachers, and even a couple of the students, were helpful, but in general, she felt like a rat lost in a complicated maze. Everyone—especially the boys—were watching her like she was some kind curious insect specimen they had never seen before. Several of the girls, particularly the ones Brandy could tell were most popular, regarded her with barely concealed hostility, as if afraid that she posed a threat to their popularity or their boyfriends.

One thing she kept telling herself to make herself feel better was that it was obvious she was much more sophisticated and city-smart than most of the kids in this school. After all, she had been born and raised just outside of New York City. Most of the kids here were probably hicks whose idea of a big city was something like Augusta, Maine. They'd be lost and scared to death in a place like New York City. Throughout the day, Brandy couldn't help but feel superior to everyone else, even most of the teachers.

She kept thinking back to how she and her friends had treated

Lois Tilton, the "new kid" at her school freshman year. While never being outright mean to her, they had been slow to allow her into their circle of friends.

She could understand how terrible and awkward Lois must have felt that first year or so, and Brandy wished to God that she didn't have to go through with this, now. But she knew it was going to take a while to replace the close friends she had left behind in Bedford Heights. As the day progressed, she started missing her home town more and more.

What she really wanted was for just one or two of these kids to say something nice to her.

That didn't happen until after English Literature, her last class of the day, but not in the way that she expected.

Actually, she had noticed one boy in particular earlier in the day during lunch. He'd been sitting a few tables away from where she sat—alone. He'd been joking around with several of his friends, and Brandy had noticed how one or two of the girls watched him with such obvious interest. It was sickening the way they kept laughing at anything he said, no matter if it was funny or not.

Not that Brandy blamed them.

She didn't know his name, and she didn't know anyone to ask about him. Chances were, she would never find out, anyway. He was tall and *really* good looking, with long blond hair, blue eyes, and a face that even this early in the spring was tanned. Brandy guessed he was a skier. He looked "cool" in the true sense of the word in that the clothes he wore seemed to suit him, and the way he conducted himself came across as totally natural. She had no doubt he already had a girlfriend.

Later that day, Brandy just about died when she saw that this boy sat beside her in English class. She blushed when the teacher—Mr. Driscoll—introduced her to the class and asked her to stand up and tell them a little bit about herself. Without mentioning that her father had been shot and killed last winter, she stumbled through something about how her family had moved to Maine to get away from the pressures of living near the city, and then sat down. She was red-faced and felt like crying for most of the class, especially knowing that *he* had been watching her.

The class was studying *Macbeth,* which Brandy had read last fall, but not wanting to show off, she didn't volunteer to answer any of the simple questions Mr. Driscoll put to the class. She was having a hard enough time keeping herself from sneaking glances at the boy beside her, whom Mr. Driscoll referred to once or twice as "Mr. McDowell."

When class was over, all of the students rushed out of the room, leaving Brandy behind. She went up to Mr. Driscoll's desk to get a paperback copy of *Macbeth* and the weekly assignment sheet. After chatting with the teacher for a minute or two, she thanked him and left.

When she exited the room, she was surprised to see that "Mr. McDowell" and several other boys from the class were lingering a short distance down the corridor, obviously waiting for her to leave. One of the boys said something that Brandy didn't quite catch, but all of the boys except "Mr. McDowell" snickered.

Trembling inside, Brandy started down the hallway, heading back to her locker. As she passed the group of boys, one of them gave an off-key wolf whistle, and Brandy heard someone else whisper something. The only thing she caught sounded like *"easy lay."*

As soon as she was past the group of boys, "Mr. McDowell" said out loud, "You guys are animals. You should show a little more class."

Brandy turned to look at him. Not watching where she was going, she walked smack into the side of a locker, hitting it hard enough to knock her bookbag from her hand. It landed on the floor with a dull *thud* that echoed in the nearly empty hall and opened up, fanning papers across the floor.

"Spazoid," someone said, and the others all cackled with laughter as she knelt down to pick it up. While she was kneeling, thoroughly flustered, "Mr. McDowell" walked over quickly and helped her scoop up the papers.

"Here yah go," he said, smiling broadly as he handed them to her. "Oh. By the way, my name's Evan."

"Oh," Brandy said with a thin smile, "I thought it was 'Mr. McDowell'."

"Evan will do," he said, smiling back at her.

They stood looking at each other for an awkward moment, then Evan said, "So, do you have a name?"

"Brandy."

"Well, Brandy, do you mind if I walk you to your locker?"

Brandy was speechless. She felt her face blush as she nodded and looked up and down the crowded corridor. "The truth is," she said, "I'm not really sure which way to go."

"What's your number?"

"Three-eleven. I think it's . . . up those stairs?" She pointed to the flight of stairs to the right.

"Nope. The other way," Evan said, indicating the stairway behind them with a broad sweep of his hand.

"Oh," Brandy said, feeling stupid because her voice sounded so high and silly. Then again, Evan didn't seem to mind. Her heart was fluttering as they walked down the hall. Brandy couldn't stop imagining that she and Evan hadn't just met—that they were, in fact, already going steady.

"Do you know your bus number and where to get it?" Evan asked once they were at Brandy's locker, and she was busily shuffling books and papers around, stuffing them into her bookbag.

"Out by the front door where it let us off this morning, I'd guess."

Evan nodded as he leaned casually back against the row of lockers, his hands deep in his pockets. He didn't seem to be in much of a hurry to leave, and Brandy was hoping it was because he wanted to spend some more time talking to her as much as she wanted to talk to him.

"Well," she said, hefting her bookbag once she was packed and ready to go. It seemed to weigh a ton. "Thanks for the help."

"Hey, no problem," Evan replied with a wide smile.

Brandy smiled back at him, really liking the way he looked at her.

"I was heading that way, myself," Evan said casually. "Mind if I tag along?"

"Not at all," Brandy said, and for the first time since she moved to Maine, she thought the situation actually might not be hopeless.

"You ain't nothin' but a *pussy!*"

"Oh, *yeah?* Well I hear *you* suck *farts* out of dead *rats!*"

That got a reaction from the knot of kids gathered around JJ and the dark-haired boy he was faced off against.

"So, you think you're smart, huh, city-boy?" the dark-haired boy snarled. He stood more than a head taller than JJ and easily outweighed him by twenty or thirty pounds.

"I've only been here one day, and already a bunch of kids have told me you're nothing but a butt-sniffing *fart*-sucker!"

"Why you—"

His face livid with anger, the dark-haired boy lunged at JJ and took a wild swing. JJ dropped and ducked to one side before it connected, and the momentum of the swing brought the dark-haired boy all the way around. When his back was turned to JJ, he leaped forward and punched him as hard as he could between the shoulder blades.

The impact staggered the dark-haired boy, but it didn't drop him. His face was flushed with anger as he wheeled around. Keeping his fist low this time, he swung again and caught a glancing blow across JJ's chin.

JJ staggered backwards, seeing tiny white lights spin like sparklers across his vision. His knees buckled and almost gave out on him, but he shook his head to clear it and braced himself.

"Butt-sniffing fart-sucker!" he wailed, and the kids around him hooted with laughter.

Furious now, the dark-haired boy came at him fast. This time his fist caught JJ squarely on the nose, making his teeth click together in his head. His vision blurred and then darkened. He barely felt the impact when he toppled backwards and hit the ground, landing flat on his back. When he opened his eyes, he looked up to see the dark-haired boy bending over him with his fist raised. JJ's vision was distorted.

"You got anything else to say, wise-ass city boy?" the dark-haired boy growled.

JJ wanted to call him a *butt-sniffing fart-sucker* again, but he wasn't sure he was able to speak. A thick, sticky, warm taste was flooding the back of his throat. He didn't know that it was blood until he snorted and spit into the boy's face and saw the bright red saliva land on the boy's forehead.

"You fuckin' little weasel! Are you trying to give me AIDS or somethin'?" the dark-haired boy wailed, and then he dropped like a load of bricks onto JJ's chest.

JJ felt the first couple of punches, but after that everything blurred into one massive, flaming pain as the dark-haired boy pummeled him with both fists.

"I'll ... teach ... you ... to ... call ... me ... a ... fart ... sucker ..."

The words seemed to be coming from far, far away, rolling like distant thunder. But with each word, a sharp pain jarred JJ's head against the ground. The whole time, one small, clear corner of his mind was chanting—*This is it! I'm gonna die!* when—suddenly—the pressure bearing down on him lifted.

"All right you boys! Stop it right *now!*"

At first, all JJ knew was that this sounded like an adult. His ears were ringing terribly from the impact of the blows, so he wasn't even sure if it was a man or a woman. But it didn't matter, as long as the dark-haired boy—he didn't even know his name—was no longer punching him.

"He started it!" JJ heard the dark-haired boy shout.

"I don't care *who* started it! It's not right for you to be beating up on *anyone* half your size."

"But he called me a—"

"I'm not interested in what he called you, Billy. I want you to report to the principal's office this instant!"

The whole world looked like it was underwater as JJ opened his eyes and tried to focus on whoever it was who had just saved him from certain death. It was an adult—that's all he knew for sure before the darkness closed around him, and he slipped into a silent, dark place.

"I'm sure it's the move and all of the adjustments he's having to make that are bothering him," Arnold Meecham said mildly as he looked across his desk at Angie. "I can certainly appreciate the situation he's in."

He was smiling patiently at Angie, but all she could think was, if JJ continued to act like this at school where she was going to be working next year, it might even jeopardize her job.

"But I . . . I just can't understand it," she said. "I mean, we've never had any trouble like this with him before. He's always been such a mild-mannered, cooperative child."

Meecham shrugged. "Kids tend to get into scraps now and then," he said leaning forward and lowering his voice. "Being new here, I'm sure JJ feels like he has to stand up for himself. Look, between you and me, Billy Wilson has always been a discipline problem. He's in my office at least a couple of times a week for something or other, usually picking on someone half his size. I'm sure he picked the fight with JJ because he's the 'new kid.'"

Angie covered her mouth with one hand and shook her head tightly.

"Maybe," she said, still embarrassed that her boss had to have this kind of introduction to her son, "but I'm going to make it clear to him that he can't go around getting into fights just to prove himself."

"I'm certainly not saying I approve of it, you understand," Meecham said, "but you know and I know that kids are going to get into schoolyard scraps. And the bottom line is, you have to admire JJ's gumption for standing up to a kid who's so much bigger than he is."

Angie wanted to agree with him, but all she could think was—just as she had this morning when she saw him off to school—that the same violent streak she had seen and dreaded in her husband had been passed along to their son. She could try to *understand*, but she didn't have to *like* it.

"He's going to have one heck of a shiner," Meecham said. "I'd suggest you ice his eye tonight to keep the swelling down. The school nurse already looked at the cut on his upper lip. She doesn't think it needs stitches."

"Thank God," Angie said, her voice almost a whisper.

"I'm going to have to give both of them a few days detention, if only to make it fair," Meecham said, "but don't worry. I'll keep an eye on Billy Wilson and make sure he doesn't do anything like that again."

Angie nodded. "Thanks," she said, but all she could think about was what she was going to do to punish JJ when she got home. For starters, he was going to be grounded for a few days.

Chapter 13
Losing It

"Cannibal mountain," Greg whispered, snickering softly to himself as he ceremoniously cracked an egg on the edge of the table and then dumped its runny contents into the scooped-out center of the mound of raw hamburger he had piled up on his dinner plate.

Smacking his lips, he picked up a fork, broke open the yolk, and stirred everything together. The mixture made a wet sucking sound as he scooped up a huge forkful and stuffed it into his mouth. Bits of raw hamburger and uncooked egg white dribbled into his lap from the sides of his mouth as he chewed. After swallowing, he grabbed the can of beer from the table, ripped back the pull tab, tilted his head back, and took a long, noisy gulp. The beer bubbled in his throat as it washed the rest of the hamburger and egg down. Leaning back in his chair, he let loose a satisfied belch, wiped his mouth with the back of his hand, and then took another scoop.

Over the last several weeks, as winter passed slowly into spring, the days and nights had started to blend together for Greg. He seemed to be living in a curious twilight zone. Every now and then, he thought it might be because he was drinking a lot more than he usually did, but he excused that, telling himself that he had more than enough reasons to drink.

He had *lots* of problems!

The most immediate one—the one that he lived with, day and night—was lying in bed in the next room.

His mother.

Even though her bedroom door was closed, he could hear her labored breathing. He couldn't stop thinking about how sick to death he was of taking care of her, although that was little enough. He had no idea what was wrong with her, but he certainly didn't have the money to take her to a doctor. If she ended up in the hospital, they had no health insurance, so he'd lose what little money he had.

She was sick and dying, he knew that much, but he didn't care.

It seemed as though, no matter how much she ate, and over the last few months that had been steadily less every day, she was rapidly losing weight. Her arms and legs were nothing but pale, wrinkled skin and brittle bones. When he lifted her to change her bed sheets, which he did less frequently as the weeks went by, her body seemed as hollow and light as a bird's.

What he was going to do about her was one problem, but an even bigger, more pressing problem was Angela Ross and what he was going to do about *her!*

He'd saved all of the newspaper articles about her husband's death and funeral. He had read them so many times over the winter that the paper was yellowing and wrinkled, the newsprint fading to dull gray. But just about every night over supper, he enjoyed reading about the "unidentified gunman" who had shot and killed the New York City detective outside a restaurant in Katonah. The day after the shooting, the *Daily News* even ran a photograph of the car with its shattered windshield. Greg would have taken even greater pride in what he had done if he hadn't left it unfinished.

But he'd left a loose end . . . a witness.

Throughout the winter and on into spring, he had to live with the constant fear that Angela had identified him, and that it was just a matter of time before the police arrested and convicted him. The fact that they hadn't done that yet didn't ease his gnawing fear that his time was running out. He was positive that the police were just biding their time, waiting him out and hoping that, eventually, his nerves would crack.

And they were cracking, Goddamnit!

He had missed so many days of work at the video store that his asshole boss finally fired him. That happened sometime in March. Greg wasn't sure exactly when because it didn't really matter; but after he'd lost his pathetic income, he'd had to risk a few more burglaries just so he would have enough money to buy food and beer.

He took another long pull of the beer. Before long, he was enjoying the buzzing spin it gave his head.

Greg had hoped that alcohol would numb the constant dread he was living under, but it didn't seem to be helping . . . not much, anyway. There were still far too many nights when he would drink more than he should and then go out for a long walk. Sometimes, as he staggered down the streets not even sure of where he was going, he thought he saw faces watching him from the shadows. Every now and then, he thought he almost recognized the faces as those of the two policemen or the store clerk and old lady he had killed that January night. At other times, he thought he saw John Ross' face, nothing more than a ruined mess of splattered blood, torn and rotting flesh, and sharp bone fragments. Sometimes, he would only see a shifting shadow that reached for him with thin, dark arms.

And sometimes at night, the shadows would be in his room, whispering soft and terrible things to him.

Everything seemed to be closing in, and Greg knew that he wouldn't be able to take this kind of pressure much longer.

Leaning forward with his elbows on the kitchen table, he took another bite of raw hamburger and egg, but when he tried to swallow, it got caught in his throat. Standing up quickly, he ran over to the kitchen sink, making it just in time before he vomited. A sour, choking taste filled his throat as his stomach convulsed, and undigested egg and hamburger splashed into the sink and onto the counter.

"Jesus ... Oh, *Jesus* ..." he moaned, leaning forward and
rolling his head from side to side as he squeezed his eyes tightly
shut until the worst of the convulsions passed.

His eyes and throat were burning terribly as he turned on
the faucet, ran the water until it was cold, and then took several
gulps. When he splashed his face with water, chills wracked
his body; but after a while, he regained a measure of control.

Lurching back to the kitchen table, he thought he should try
to finish his supper, but his stomach clenched when he looked
at the half-finished meal. Moaning softly, he grabbed the beer
can and took another long drink, but even that didn't wash
away the terrible taste of vomit that filled his mouth.

"Fuck it! *Fuck it!*" he whispered in a low, cracked voice
that sounded like someone twice his age. "What I need is some
fresh air."

He grabbed his jacket from the stand beside the door, made
sure his keys were in his pocket, and—after draining the beer
can and tossing it at the trash—staggered out the door.

He was vaguely aware that the night was warm and pleasant.
He had no idea what time it was, but the streets seemed oddly
deserted.

Must be late, he thought.

A few passing cars swept him with their headlights, but he
didn't care. He figured he looked dangerous or crazy enough
so no one was going to mess with him. His feet dragged on
the pavement as he walked with no idea where he was going
or what he planned to do.

He just had to get away from it all!

"Fuck," he muttered. "I'm gonna have to kill her! ... That's
all there is to it!"

The few pedestrians he encountered crossed the street to
avoid him, moving swiftly and silently, like shadows. Sometimes Greg had trouble deciding if they were real or not. He
started to panic, thinking some of them might be the same
shadows that plagued his sleep. As he staggered down the
street, he waved his hands wildly and shouted for them to leave
him alone.

A small corner of his mind was aware that he was acting

like he was insane, but he no longer cared. A patrolman stopped him at an intersection in front of a liquor store and asked him his name and what he was doing out at this hour. Greg didn't remember what he told him, but apparently he was satisfied with his answer because he let him go on his way.

"Prob'bly scared the shit out of him," Greg muttered as he glanced up and down the street, trying to figure out where he was so he could head home. Somehow, he managed to find his way back to his apartment building. He was about to enter and go upstairs when the night suddenly ripped open all around him with a high, wailing scream of sirens.

Greg blocked his ears with both hands and crouched down with his eyes closed, but that didn't block out the sound.

Maybe it's inside my head, he thought as it wound higher and higher, drilling his nerves.

"No! *No!*" Greg shouted, as he pounded the sides of his head. "Make it stop! *Jesus Christ! Make it stop!*"

But the sound rose higher in the night, like screams of torment from the depths of hell.

Frantic with fear, Greg looked around until way in the distance, he saw flashing blue lights. He was panicking too badly to connect them to the siren sound as, all around him, the shadows of the building deepened, condensing as they writhed with terrifying energy.

For several seconds, Greg was paralyzed, rooted to the spot, unable to move or think as the sound drilled deeper into his head. No matter where he looked, the shadows slithered toward him, reaching . . . grabbing at him . . .

The night was alive with flashing light that stung his eyes. Everywhere he looked he saw a confusing kaleidoscope of light and shadows. Even when he closed his eyes, frightening shapes materialized out of the darkness behind his eyes. He wasn't aware that he was making any sound as he ran up the front stairs of the building and threw open the door.

His feet clomped heavily on floor. His heart was pounding a fast, steady beat that throbbed painfully inside his head. His hands were shaking so badly he almost dropped his key ring as he fumbled to unlock his apartment door. Grunting like an enraged beast, he slammed the door open with his shoulder so hard it hit the edge of the counter hard enough to vibrate. He wheeled around and kicked the door shut, then locked it. Panting heavily, and fearful of everything he saw no matter where he looked, he pressed his weight against the door and started to sob as he slid to the floor.

The wailing sound filled the night outside.

Or was it in his head?

Greg stared at the window that looked out over the alleyway, expecting to see dark silhouettes of policemen—or worse!— preparing to burst into his apartment to *get* him!

Clapping his hands over his ears and closing his eyes, he started rocking back and forth on the floor, sobbing so hard the pain wracked his chest and back. The darkness behind his eyelids swelled and opened up like a huge, gaping mouth. He felt suddenly weightless, unable to resist as he pitched forward ... tumbling ... into the swelling blackness that was colder and more terribly silent than anything he had ever experienced before in his life. The last shreds of consciousness slipped away from him.

"You're nothin' but a little mama's boy who has to have his mommy come to school to protect him."

"Oh, yeah? Screw you," JJ said mockingly as he looked around at the small group of kids who had gathered around him and Billy Wilson.

JJ's upper lip was bandaged, so when he spoke, his words were slightly distorted. He thought he sounded a little bit like Elmer Fudd, but he tried to ignore that. His left eye was swollen and still painful to the touch. The last thing he needed was a reprise of yesterday's encounter.

"Skrow you ... Skrow you, you wascally wittle wabbit," the dark-haired boy said, taunting him.

JJ grit his teeth and shook his head as though disgusted before turning and walking away. But Billy Wilson wasn't going to be satisfied so easily. He moved to block him.

"I ain't done with you yet, Ross," Billy said, scowling so he looked a lot like an angry pig.

JJ considered making a comment about that but decided he had to take the moral high ground and avoid another fight . . . even if it meant that *no one* except Sammy was going to be his friend.

"Get a life, why don't you?" JJ said, pulling away quickly. He was about to turn away again when Billy cocked back his fist and took a swing at him. Acting more on reflex that thought, JJ ducked under the punch as it came around and at the same time braced himself and kicked Billy's left leg, just above the knee.

Billy howled in pain as his leg buckled, and he went down hard. Seeing his advantage and not wanting to lose it, JJ darted forward. Clenching his fist tightly, he drove it straight into the center of Billy's face.

JJ had been in a few fights before, but he had never heard anyone cry out in pain the way Billy Wilson did. The sound was an odd blend of scream and heart-stopping fury. JJ staggered to get his balance, expecting Billy to get up and launch himself at him; but he was down, and he stayed down with both hands covering his face. After a heartbeat, a dark red ribbon of blood began to seep between his fingers. His eyes glazed over with a vacant stare as he looked around, unable to focus. JJ imagined tiny, chirping cartoon birds, circling Billy's head.

"All *right!*" someone shouted.

JJ wasn't sure who it was. He just stood there, staring blankly at his fallen foe.

"I can't believe you took Billy Wilson down," someone else cried out.

A cheer went up from the boys who had gathered. A short distance off, a small group of girls watched as well.

Billy's eyes were still unfocused, but he looked up at JJ with an expression of total shock and humiliation. He tried to get up but was too dazed to catch his balance.

"You dick! You busted my fuckin' nose!" Billy wailed. His voice was so distorted, he pronounced *s* as if it were *th*.

Still charged with adrenalin, JJ stepped up close to him,

looming above Billy. Shaking his fist close to the fallen boy's face, he said in a low, steady voice, "And from now on, I want you to leave me the fuck alone! Understand?"

Billy stared up at him as though he couldn't believe this was happening. A scrawny kid half his size had actually put him down! After a few moments, still looking groggy, he nodded and grunted.

"Mister Ross!"

The voice sounded so suddenly behind him it made JJ jump. He spun around and saw the principal, Mr. Meecham, standing nearby with his arms folded across his chest.

"But he—"

"I don't want to hear it," Mr. Meecham said, pointing angrily at JJ. "Apparently you don't learn the first time. I guess it's time we have a serious conference with your mother."

Angry that his moment of triumph had been so brief, JJ let his shoulders slump. Another cheer went up from the bystanders as he walked away, but JJ didn't look back. He knew that he was in big trouble now. The only bright spots were that now—maybe—Billy Wilson was going to leave him alone, and—maybe—some of the other kids would want to be his friend . . . when—and if—he ever got out of school detention and being grounded by his mother.

It was daylight when Greg awoke. He was sitting on the floor with his legs splayed and leaning against the door. The floor was cold and sent a spike of pain up his rump to the small of his back. When he opened his eyes, the daylight stabbed him like a lance. He moaned, but making even that soft a sound hurt inside his head.

"Jesus," Greg whispered, hearing how dry and cracked his voice sounded.

He licked his lips and swallowed dryly. The rotten taste in his mouth was so bad he thought he might vomit again, but after a while, the sensation passed and his stomach settled down.

He wanted to get up but knew that he couldn't move.

Not yet.

Every muscle, every joint and bone in his body felt frozen. Deep shudders ran through him when he tried to remember what had happened the night before, but his mind was a chaos of images and thoughts that didn't make sense, no matter how he tried to arrange them.

He had gone out for a walk, he knew that much, but after that . . . What? Something had happened . . . Or maybe something had happened before that.

He wasn't sure.

Moaning deep in his throat, he looked up at the clock on the kitchen wall and tried to make sense of it. The hands on the clock were blurred and shifted around as if the hour hand was sweeping faster than the second hand. After concentrating hard on it for what seemed like much too long, he saw that it was a little before eight o'clock.

"Morning . . . eight o'clock in the morning," he muttered, finally realizing through the haze of confusion that it couldn't be this bright at eight o'clock at night.

He tried to stand up but couldn't. The pain was too great. It felt like there was an steel rod running up his spine. He could hear the faint sounds of activity both inside and outside the apartment building and tried to focus on them, to see if he could determine what was going on, but nothing made sense.

All he knew was that he had to stand up but couldn't. Dark waves rolled with an audible rush through his mind, making it impossible for him to think or see clearly. He felt himself nodding out.

It was well past eleven when he came to next. The haze that filled his mind seemed thinner, and he was finally ready for the challenge of standing up. Bracing his hands against the door and wall, he pulled his legs underneath himself and slowly, painfully, pushed himself to his feet.

It was more difficult than climbing a mountain, but after a minute or two of struggling, Greg gained his feet. He was exhausted from the effort and couldn't stand without leaning against the wall for support, but he was glad to be up.

He wasn't sure when he first thought about his mother, but

after a long while he realized that he hadn't heard any sounds from her room. She would have expected breakfast long before now. Wouldn't she have called out to him, demanding attention?

"Mom," he called out. His voice was so faint and cracked, he knew she wouldn't hear him.

Keeping close to the wall for support, he edged over to her door. He leaned his head against the wall and listened. A sliver of fear cut through him when he realized that he couldn't hear her breathing. Usually, even when she wasn't snoring, he could hear the raw, watery gasp.

Shit, something's wrong, Greg thought as the fear twisting inside him blossomed into panic.

He didn't know if he had the strength to open the door, but he grasped the doorknob and started to turn it, his grip as weak as a baby's. He could barely feel the doorknob in his grasp, much less turn it, but—somehow—it clicked, and the door swung open with a high squeaking of old hinges.

"Mom?" Greg whispered.

Even at midday, the room was lost in shadow because his mother insisted on keeping the shades drawn. She hadn't seen real daylight in more than six months. But even in the diffused light of the room, Greg saw to his horror that his mother was dead. Her head was cocked back at an awkward angle. Her tongue, looking huge, dark, and swollen, hung from her mouth. Her unblinking eyes glistened wetly in the faint light. Greg knew that it was only a trick of the light or his imagination when he thought he saw her chest rise and fall.

"Jesus . . . Oh, Jesus," he muttered. His legs felt all rubbery, and he grabbed at the wall.

She's dead! . . . Jesus, she's DEAD!

His vision blurred with the warm sting of tears, but he didn't cry. The longer he stared at her, the paler and colder she looked and the more it struck him as . . . almost funny.

Yes, funny. After all these weeks and months of waiting, he had gotten what he had wanted!

She's dead! . . . Dead and gone!

"Yes . . . Yes," he whispered as he closed his eyes and rolled his head back and forth, grinding it hard against the wall.

The fog in his brain began to dissipate, and one clear thought struck him, filling him with fear.

What if I did it?

He took a deep breath, feeling a tight constriction in his chest. *Did I kill her?*

It doesn't matter, whispered another voice.

Suddenly filled with fear, Greg looked around the room, convinced that the voice hadn't been inside his head, that someone else in the room had spoken to him.

"But it . . . it *does* matter," Greg said as though defending himself against an unseen accuser. He stepped forward, his eyes wide as he looked around the gloomy room.

"It matters because if I . . . if I *killed* her, then I'll go to jail for it,"

He could hear the edge of panic in his voice, but there was nothing he could do to stop it. But as his mind filled with thoughts and fears, he realized something else.

Maybe that voice *was* right!

Maybe it *didn't* matter!

Now that his mother was dead, that left him with only one problem to solve; and now that she was dead, he was free to deal with Angela Ross.

He hadn't realized until this very moment that having to take care of his mother had been the only thing standing between him and Angela. Now that she was gone—and the voice was right: it really didn't matter if he had killed her himself—he was free. Maybe *this* would put an end to the voices inside his head that didn't sound like his own thoughts. And maybe he was finally free of the shadows he saw late at night . . . shadows that reached out and tried to grab him, tried to catch him and drag him down.

Before he did anything, though, he knew he would have to sober up. He was going to have to get a lot smarter about things than he had been up until now. The first step was to steal a car and drive out to Angela Ross' house. And then he'd kill her!

The soft sound of laughter filled the dark room. It took Greg a while to realize that he was the one laughing as he slowly sank to the floor.

* * *

"Look, JJ, I know you were just standing up for yourself," Angie said. "And that's usually a really good thing to do, but you have to realize that you *can't* go beating up on people."

JJ was seated at the kitchen table. The sky was darkening, and Angie had the overhead light on as she stood at the sink, preparing supper.

"I didn't beat up on him, Mom," JJ replied, sounding like he was getting exasperated. "You saw how big he is! He's almost twice my size! A jerk like that isn't going to back off, so when I saw my chance . . ." His voice trailed off as he shrugged. "I took it."

"That's exactly my point," Angie said, pointing at him.

She was feeling frustrated because JJ didn't seem to be getting it. She accepted the fact that he was growing away from her. That was a necessary part of growing up and being a preteen. But he seemed to be changing faster than she wanted him to, and she didn't like what she was seeing. If she didn't stop him now, it was only going to get worse later on. The anger and hostility seething inside him was unnerving. She had hoped that making friends with Sammy would help him adjust, but—as much as she wanted to deny it—the move to Maine just didn't seem to be working out for JJ . . . not yet, anyway.

"As far as I can see, you had a perfect chance to walk away when he fell down," she said.

She stopped cutting the green beans at the sink and, drying her hands on a dishtowel, came over to him. When she tried to put her hands on his shoulders, he pulled away from her.

"No I *didn't* have a chance to walk away!" JJ said, his voice almost breaking. "Not with all those kids standing there, watching. They would have laughed at me and started calling me chickenshit for the rest of my fuc—"

"Watch your mouth, young man!" Angie snapped, wagging a finger at him.

"Well . . . that's what *Billy* called *me*."

Angie saw the fire in his eyes, and it truly frightened her. With a cold, sinking sensation in her stomach, she realized that, before too long, JJ was going to be bigger and stronger than she was. Just because his father had been a hard-ass New York City detective didn't mean he had the right to go around getting into fights. If he was having problems and feeling hurt and angry about what had happened, the last thing she wanted him to think was that resorting to violence would solve anything.

"Fighting's *never* good," she said emphatically, struggling to keep her voice low as she knelt down in front of him. "Never! Do you understand me?"

For a long time, JJ didn't say anything. He just sat there, staring past her, focused on some middle distance. When he finally did speak, he had such a cool, detached tone of voice that Angie knew she wasn't getting through to him.

"It is when you win," he said so softly it might have been just to himself.

"No it *isn't!*" Angie snapped, feeling her anger flare. "Not *ever!*"

She cringed, realizing that over the years she'd had this same discussion, or some variation of it, too many times with John. She was desperate not to have someone else in her family who thought that quicker fists or the fastest gun always decided who was right. For the first time in her life, she found herself wishing that JJ wasn't John's son.

She started to say something, but just then the telephone rang. She stood up quickly and grabbed the phone.

"Hello."

"Hi, Mrs. Ross. Can I talk to JJ?"

Glancing over at JJ, Angie shook her head and said, "I'm sorry, Sammy, but he's grounded for the week, and that means from the phone, too."

JJ glared at her, his expression hard and filled with hostility.

"I'll tell him you called," she said and then switched off the phone before Sammy could protest.

"Supper won't be ready for another half hour or so," she said, turning to him. "Why don't you go back up to your room and get your homework done."

"I don't *have* any homework! I did it all in detention today!"

"Fine, then." Angie told herself not to rise to the bail. "Then you can go up to your room and do something else. I'll call you down when it's time to set the table."

JJ turned and stomped out of the kitchen. As he went, Angie heard him mutter under his breath, "Screw setting the table for supper!"

As he walked down the hallway, she heard him punch or kick the wall. The heavy thump reverberated like a drum through the house. Angie almost called him on it, but after checking and seeing that he hadn't made a hole in the wall, she decided to let it slide for now. He was being punished enough as it was.

She waited at the foot of the stairs until she heard him slam his bedroom door shut. There was so much more she wanted to say to him, but she chose not to go upstairs right now. Let him simmer for a while. He'd have to calm down, first.

Walking back into the kitchen, she looked up at the wall clock and saw that it was already past four o'clock.

"Damn," she whispered, glancing out the window. "And just where is *Brandy?*"

Back home in Bedford Heights, Brandy always came straight home from school, but for the last few days, she'd been late almost every afternoon. What irritated Angie most was that she hadn't called to tell her where she was and what she was doing.

Feeling absolutely drained, Angie walked over to the counter and, moving slowly as though her arms were made of lead, continued cutting beans. Every now and then she would have to stop and blink her eyes to hold back the rush of tears she could feel building up.

"*Please,*" she whispered, rolling her eyes back and looking at the ceiling. "*Please* don't let anything happen to her, too!"

She sniffed loudly and wiped her eyes with the back of her hand, but it didn't do any good. As she finished preparing supper, she couldn't stop thinking how, now that she was finally getting past the initial grief of losing her husband, she could see that raising two kids by herself with no support was going to be much tougher than she had ever imagined.

Twenty minutes later Brandy came home. Even though her

sadness, Angie noticed a gleam in her daughter's eye and a bounce in her step, but when she asked her where she'd been and what she'd been doing, Brandy's only response was, "Oh, nothing . . . Just hanging around."

Chapter 14
Tracking

Everything actually went much more smoothly than Greg had anticipated. After cleaning himself up and straightening up the apartment a little, he dialed 911 and told the dispatcher that he was sure that his mother was dead. He gave her the address and told her to send the police and an ambulance over right away.

At first, the dispatcher reacted to his call like it was an emergency, but Greg calmly explained that his mother was elderly and had been sick for a long time, and that she had apparently died in her sleep. Before the ambulance arrived, though, he forced himself to go into her room—one last time, he told himself—and check her over to make sure there wasn't any incriminating evidence that he might have killed her.

The truth was, he honestly couldn't remember if he had anything to do with her death or not. Over the last six months or more, there hadn't been a day or night that he hadn't considered using a knife or gun or baseball bat or *something* to kill her. Night after miserable night, as he sat in the small apartment living room, watching TV and drinking, he had toyed with the idea of cutting back on her medicine . . . or maybe overdosing her with something to make it look like an accident. Late at night, when the shadows shifted in his bedroom and whispered to him, he imagined that the low, hollow voices were urging him to go into his mother's bed room and kill her—strangle her ... or smother her with a pillow ... or do something—*anything* to get her out of his life. He had wanted her to die for so long that this felt like a gift from heaven.

And now—thank God!—it had happened!

Without having to do anything—at least as far as he could remember—he was *free* of her!

A half hour after his call, the medical examiner arrived. It didn't take him long to pronounce Estelle Newman dead of natural causes and order the ambulance crew to load her onto a stretcher and wheel her out of there.

For Greg, the hardest part about the whole thing had been acting like he was genuinely broken up by this. As long as he *hadn't* killed her—or as long as the police or medical examiner or someone else didn't find any evidence that he had—he was free and clear.

Arranging the funeral the next day went without a hitch. Greg's mother didn't have many friends—at least, not many friends who were still living—so the funeral was private, with just Greg, a minister that the funeral director put him in touch with, and the funeral director.

Greg had decided to have his mother cremated, so he picked out the cheapest coffin he could find. A few days later, when he received her ashes, he promptly brought them home and flushed them down the toilet. His only concern was that they might clog up the crappy plumbing in the apartment, but after three or four flushes, the toilet bowl was pretty much clean except for a thin gray film that lined the inside of the bowl.

Over the next few days, Greg was busy as he closed out his mother's bank account, collected the small amount of money from the life insurance policy he had on her, and cleaned out the accumulated junk from her bedroom. All of it—clothes, furniture, personal possessions—went out onto the sidewalk in front of the apartment building where street scavengers carried it off within a matter of hours.

There was more money in his mother's account than he had

expected. Even after paying for the funeral he was surprised
to realize that, counting the insurance money, he had nearly
eleven thousand dollars.

It was shaping up to be a good year after all.

In the first week of May, on a beautiful, warm Saturday
morning, Greg boosted a car from Manhattan and drove out to
Bedford Heights. It had been a long time since he'd been out
to have a look around. He wanted to see how Angela Ross was
doing and figured it was safe for him to check up on her. If
the cops were going to arrest him for killing her husband or
anything else, they certainly would have done it by now.

Driving into Bedford Heights was disorienting. Greg had
only seen the town a few times in the depths of winter. Back
then, the town had seemed small and rather desolate. Now, with
leaves on the trees, grass turning green, and flowers blooming
everywhere, it looked like something out of a TV show. Everyone walking around downtown looked handsome and healthy—
and rich! He passed several people he was sure were either
movie or TV stars, but he couldn't recall their names.

It was all too perfect, and by the time he took the turn onto
Clinton Street, Greg was fuming with anger. His anger went
over the top when he drove past the Ross' house and saw the
FOR SALE sign on the front lawn. Slapped across the bottom of
the sign was another smaller cardboard sign that read: UNDER
CONTRACT.

"No fuckin' way!" Greg shouted, banging the dashboard
hard enough to send a flash of pain up his wrist. A dull red
haze drifted across his vision as he looked up at the obviously
vacant house.

Fuming and sputtering obscenities, he drove down the street
past the house, and turned around in someone's driveway. When
he came back, he pulled to a stop in front of the Ross' house.

I should have come out here sooner! he thought. Now she
was gone, had slipped away!

Gripping the steering wheel tightly with both hands, he
leaned back, closed his eyes, and let out a long, agonized howl
as he shook the steering wheel hard enough almost to break it.

"You bitch!" he screamed. The pressure in his head made

his face flush and his eyes bulge. "You lousy, mother-fucking, rotten *bitch!*"

A wave of dizziness swept over him, and he almost passed out as he stared up at the house. The windows had no curtains, and the front lawn looked untended. The grass had been cut, but the garden by the front patio was thick with as many weeds as flowers. There were no toys in the yard, no cars parked in the driveway. No signs of life anywhere except for the small flock of birds, flitting around a feeder that hung from a tree.

"Fuck it! *Fuck it! FUCK IT!*" Greg shouted, all the while punching the car seat beside him.

When he glanced into the rearview mirror, he noticed a man on a bicycle riding up the street, moving toward him. Greg knew that he had to calm down and not make a scene, but his anger rose as he watched the man getting closer. He was well-dressed, wearing a light-weight, blue jogging suit with bright white sneakers, wrap-around shades, and a shiny black crash helmet. He leaned forward, pedalling hard. On the back of the bike, strapped into a safety seat, was a little kid, also wearing a helmet.

Greg sucked in his breath sharply, telling himself just to sit still, but he was so furious he *had* to do *something!*

He had to lash out!

Maybe he should stop this guy and ask him if he knew where Angela Ross had gone. They must be neighbors. He might know.

No, Greg thought.

What he had to do was wait and time it just right so when this rich asshole was beside the car, he could fling the car door open and knock him off his bike onto his sorry ass.

Yeah, *that* would show him!

But as he watched the man coming ever closer to the car, Greg realized that such a move would be foolish. There was a good chance if he did anything in a town like this, he'd get picked up by the police and taken to the station for questioning. Once he was there, the cops would realize soon enough that the car he was driving was stolen. After that, it probably wouldn't be all that difficult to trace things back. Before he knew it, he'd

be arrested for shooting John Ross and for killing those cops,
that old lady, and the convenience store clerk last January.

"This is your lucky day, asshole," Greg whispered harshly
as he turned his head to track the man as he and kid whisked
past the car. The gears of the bike made a high, fast clicking
sound that grated Greg's nerves, but he sat there at the wheel
as still as a statue.

Greg stared at their backs until they disappeared around the
bend in the road, then let out the breath he hadn't realized he
was holding. Boiling with rage, he sat there in front of the
house for another few minutes, wondering what—if anything—
he could do. Finally, he shifted into gear and drove away, still
muttering curses to himself.

On the drive back to Brooklyn, he had plenty of time to
calm down and think about what to do next. He decided that—
pain-in-the-ass though it was—it shouldn't be all *that* hard to
track Angela Ross.

He had enough money for the time being, and he had nothing
keeping him here, now that his mother was out of his life and
he was out of a job. Chances were he would lose the apartment
because it had been in his mother's name, and no doubt the
landlord would want to jack the rent up, anyway.

So what else did he have to do except find Angela Ross?

It might even be fun.

And then, once he *did* find her, he sure as hell was going to
make her pay!

"Oh, yeah," he whispered to himself, chuckling at the
thought. "She'll pay! . . ."

"What—? What do you mean, he's dead?"

The desk sergeant looked at Greg with expressionless eyes
that held that blank, "I-could-just-about-give-a-shit" look a
lot of city and federal employees seem to adopt just to get
through their daily grind.

"I mean he's dead. What, you don't read the papers or watch
the TV?"

"No, I . . . I just moved back home from—ah, L.A."

"Well, Detective Ross ain't here anymore," the desk sergeant growled, "so unless you got some pressing business, I'd suggest you move along."

Greg glanced over his shoulder at the squad room. It was buzzing with activity. Several people, all of them looking sad and defeated, sat on the bench across from the desk, but no one was waiting in line behind him. He knew that coming in here was risky. The cops *must* still be investigating Ross' murder but so far, this was the only thing he had thought to try.

"Shit," he muttered in a hoarse whisper which he wasn't even sure the desk sergeant heard. He sighed, looked down at the floor, and shook his head as though trying to absorb the sudden shock of this news.

"Ah, excuse me," he said, "but I been out of touch with—ah, with John for quite a while. Is—ah, are Angela and the kids still living in Bedford Heights?"

The desk sergeant stiffened as he looked up from the paperwork he was filling out and nailed Greg with barely concealed hostility. A rush of fear ran through him that he had pushed it too far this time and had raised the cop's suspicion.

"Look, bub," the desk sergeant said, "I ain't about to hand out information to any old yahoo who walks in off the street, claiming he's friends with John Ross, got it?"

Greg nodded his understanding, but this guy's reaction only stiffened his resolve.

"Yeah, but John and I were pretty good friends a long time ago. I'd just like to know if Angela is still at the house so I can go out and see her—tell her how sorry I am."

This, obviously, wore out the last shred of patience the desk sergeant had. He slammed his hand down hard on the desk and, craning his neck forward, snarled, "Look. I want you to move your butt out of here. *Now!* I ain't gonna give you any more information. Got it?"

"Sure . . . sure," Greg said, nodding as he backed away from the desk and waved his hands in front of him. Having been born and raised in Brooklyn, he knew he had to give the guy at least a little attitude before he left, so as he headed for the door, he shot back at him, "Thanks for nothing, asshole."

It was just loud enough for the desk sergeant to hear, but when Greg paused at the door and looked back at him, the cop was concentrating on whatever he'd been working on before. Greg made sure to slam the door open as hard as he could before he stepped outside.

The sun was warm on his face, but he was seething with rage as he walked away from the station house. His first impulse was to go back in there and deck that asshole at the desk, but he knew he couldn't do that.

He had to get busy.

The problem was, he had no idea where to start.

While people certainly could disappear, they always left some kind of "paper trail" unless they were *trying* to get lost. It was just going to be a matter of picking up Angela's paper trail and following it.

The next day, after sleeping on it, Greg got a better idea. He stole another car, this time from over in the Bronx, and drove out to Bedford Heights. He skipped driving past the house on Clinton Street, knowing that would only make him angry. He knew, if he got mad, he might blow what he was going to try to do. It took a bit of driving around, but after asking the pump jockey at the corner Sunoco station, he found what he was looking for—the Bedford Heights Post Office. The small, red brick building was just as quaint-looking as the rest of the town. Rows of bright red flowers—Greg had no idea what their name was—lined the short cement walkway that led up to the front door.

A knot of nervousness tightened in the pit of his stomach as he swung open the heavy wooden door and entered.

He shivered and took a deep breath of the faintly musty air. The strong smell of floor wax reminded him of his old grammar school. Unlike the post office in his neighborhood, this one had only two windows with no bars across them. There were no lines at either window, either, just a thin, balding old man who was trying to get the stamp vending machine to take his wrinkled dollar bill. It kept grinding and spitting it out, like in the *Pepsi* commercial.

Greg forced a smile onto his face as he walked up to the

rather plump woman with gray hair and too much makeup who was at the counter window nearest the front door.

"Good morning," she said, looking up at him all bright and cheery. The name badge on the breast pocket of her blue shirt said MARGE. Greg chuckled to himself, thinking there couldn't have been a more perfect name for her. He glanced at the clock on the wall behind her and saw that it was already a little past noon.

"It's afternoon now," he said with a tight smirk.

"Oh, so it is," Marge said, glancing at her wristwatch and smiling wide. Her whole face was a nest of wrinkles, especially around the eyes. "And how may I help you, sir?"

Greg took an instant dislike to this woman. Her voice was too high-pitched and nasally. It reminded him a little too much of his mother's voice. He cringed inwardly.

"Well," he said, hoping his nervousness didn't show in his voice. "I'm looking for a friend who used to live around here."

"And who might that be?" Marge asked.

It may have been Greg's imagination, but he thought her eyes narrowed as though she were suddenly suspicious of him.

"Angela Ross," Greg said quickly, surprised that he could even say the name out loud. He had thought her name and muttered it to himself hundreds of times over the last few months, and every time it filled him with a strong, violent surge of anger. He was surprised that he didn't just start shouting at the woman behind the counter.

"Oh, my. Wasn't that just horrible what happened to that family last winter?" Marge said, her frown deepening. "And such nice folks, too."

"Umm, yeah. Just terrible," Greg said, fighting the urge to break into a smile. "But you see—the problem is, John Ross still owes me some money—quite a bit of money, in fact, for some yard work I did for him a while back. I sent 'em a couple of bills, but they all came back to me, stamped 'non-deliverable' or whatever."

"Really?" Marge said, rubbing her ample cheek. "Now that's odd. They should have been forwarded like the rest of their mail. Are you sure you had the right address?"

"I think so," Greg said, frowning as he stuck his finger into his ear and wiggled it around. "Something—maybe 14 Clinton Street."

"That's it, all right. Do you happen to have one of the letters with you?" Marge asked. "I can make sure that it gets forwarded this time."

"If you just tell me where she's moved to, I can send it directly to her," Greg said. "Business has been slow, and I'm kinda in a hurry to get that money."

Even before Marge spoke, Greg could sense that—just like at the police station—this wasn't going to work.

"I'm sorry," Marge said, "but our policy is not to reveal customer's forwarding addresses. Confidentiality and all. You understand."

Greg clenched his jaw, wanting to shout at her that—*no,* he *didn't* understand, but he struggled to keep his steadily rising anger in check.

It took a moment or two to sink in, but eventually Greg realized that he had just stumbled across a way to find Angela Ross even if Marge wasn't going to cooperate. Like she had suggested, he could send Angela Ross another bill. What he could do was type up a phony bill for something or other and send it to her. The post office would forward it, and then Angela would either send him a check or a letter, claiming that she didn't owe him any money.

Either way, her return address would probably be on the envelope. And even if it wasn't, there would be a postmark that would probably be enough to go on.

"Oh, you know what?," he said, looking at Marge earnestly as he patted his pockets. "I didn't bring that with me. I knew I should've when I left this morning, but that's what I'll do. I'll send another one out in a couple of days. You're sure you can get it to her?"

"Absolutely," Marge said, nodding so deeply the flab under her neck squished out like a thick, fleshy collar.

"It'd be a lot quicker if you'd just give me the address so I can send it to her directly."

"I'm sorry," Marge said, shaking her head.

"All righty, then," Greg said, and he turned and walked away. The thing that bothered him most was that he was going to have to wait when, here he was, all set to get down to business. Sending a letter and waiting for her response could take a week or more, probably more like a month, and he'd waited long enough as it was.

"Shit," he muttered as he walked down to where he had parked the stolen car. He kicked at the red flowers a few times as he went, sending clots of dirt and petals flying.

By the time he was back in his car, he was so mad at Marge that he considered waiting around until she got off work and following her home. Maybe what she needed was a little visit to show her what happens to people who don't cooperate.

But then again, that would be getting him off track.

He had to stop fucking around and find Angela Ross! *She* was the problem!

As he started up the car and drove away, he glanced at the post office in the rearview mirror.

"Thank your luck stars, Margie-girl," he whispered, smiling at the wicked gleam he saw reflected in his eyes. "You have no fucking idea how close you just came to having me cancel your postage."

It wasn't a conscious decision, but before he left town, he turned right onto Clinton Street, figuring what the hell? He'd drive by the house once more. He gasped with surprise and pulled over to the side of the road when he saw the activity at the Ross house.

A huge yellow and red van marked TRI-STATE MOVERS was parked by the front door. Its wheels had made deep ruts across the front lawn. A metal ramp extended from the back of the truck, and three men—all of them wearing jeans and yellow and red T-shirts—were scurrying back and forth, unloading furniture and boxes. Standing on the small porch by the doorway was a young black woman who was overseeing the operation and keeping an eye on the two little girls who were playing around the truck at the same time. The woman was young and attractive. Her dark skin glistened like polished wood in the bright sunlight.

"You stay out of the way, now. You hear?" she shouted when one of the girls started clambering up onto the back edge of the truck.

One of the workers said something to the woman, but even with the window down, Greg didn't hear what it was.

Well, there goes the neighborhood, he thought, wondering if this was the first black family to move into quaint, upscale, lily-white Bedford Heights.

He sat there for several minutes with the car idling, all the while watching the new owners of the house moving in. After a few minutes, a tall, heavily-built black man came out onto the patio and stood beside the woman. When he smiled at her and put his arm around her shoulder, pulling her close, she reached up and gave him a quick kiss on the mouth.

They looked so damn happy, Greg thought, but he just sat there drumming his fingers on the steering wheel and staring at them. All the while, his anger and frustration raged like a hurricane. He knew what he should do was drive away from here right now, before anyone noticed him and called the cops, but he had an idea. If it worked, he wouldn't have to wait the weeks or months it might take to get a reply from Angela Ross.

He switched off the ignition and slumped down in the seat to think it through. Finally, he sat up, took a deep breath to calm himself, opened the car door, and got out. He was smiling and walking with a happy bounce in his step as he angled across the lawn toward the front door. As soon as the new owners of the house saw him coming, he let his smile widen and waved a greeting to them.

"Afternoon," he called out as cheerily as he could.

He glanced at the sky and saw that, indeed, it was a fine afternoon. Not a cloud in the sky. The men working to unload the van didn't look like they were enjoying the day. They were dripping with sweat as they hustled back and forth from the house to the van and back again. Greg found it rather amusing to see three white guys busting their humps for a black family.

"Afternoon," the man replied, but the slight scowl on his face indicated that he wasn't so sure this stranger's presence would keep it a nice afternoon.

"So, you're moving in today, I see," Greg said, still smiling as he approached the bottom of the steps. "Beautiful day for it."

He hadn't been invited up, so he stayed down on the ground, squinting as he looked up at the couple.

"Can I help you wif' something?" the man asked.

He shifted to one side as two of the movers went by, carrying a huge, overstuffed couch. The man's wife held the door open for them. They had just enough clearance to get it inside.

"Well, you see," Greg began, "I've been trying to get in touch with the previous owner of this house. I was wondering if you could help me out."

The man's scowl deepened as he folded his arms across his chest. His biceps bulged like slabs of meat inside the tight sleeves of his T-shirt. Greg can see that this man wasn't about to help him, but just then his wife spoke up.

"We've never met Mrs. Ross," she said in a low-pitched, pleasant-sounding voice. "Not in person, anyway. But we did talk to her over the phone back when we did the closing."

"This has nothing to do with your new house," Greg said, knowing he had to reassure the man. As soon as he said it, the man seemed to relax a bit. "I just need to get in touch with her about payment for some yard work I did for her last year."

"If she don't pay it, you ain't gonna be chargin' us for it, I hope," the man said.

"Oh, no . . . no. I just wanted her new address so I could send the bill to her."

The man didn't move a muscle, but after glancing quickly at her husband, his wife shook her head and said, "We don't have her address. We only dealt with her lawyer, some fellow up in Maine."

"In Maine, you say," Greg said.

He wasn't entirely sure where Maine was. He thought it might be an island off the coast of Canada. This time when he smiled, it was completely genuine. At last, he was making progress.

"Excuse me," he said, "but I didn't get your names."

"I don't see where that's any of your damn business," the

man said gruffly. "And I'm not so sure I likes you comin' 'round here, askin' all sorts of questions."

"Just one more," Greg said. It was an effort to not lose his temper, but he knew, if it came to a fight, this guy could easily break him in half. Greg wasn't looking for a fight . . . not unless he had a gun or his trusty baseball bat with him.

"I just need the address, if you have it."

"Like my wife says, we ain't got no address," the man said. He stepped back when the movers came back outside and tromped into the van.

"I think—what was the name of that town, honey?" the woman said as she grabbed her husband's arm and gave it a shake. "Bolton. Wasn't that it?"

The man scowled and shook his head, obviously not willing to offer anything.

"Yeah, that was it," the woman said, snapping her fingers. "Bolton, Maine's where she moved to."

"Are you sure of that?" Greg asked, hardly able to believe his fortune. He hadn't even planned on driving over here today, and here *exactly* what he needed had fallen into his lap.

"Look here, mister," the man said, his frown deepening. "We got a lot of work to do, gettin' settled in 'n all, so if you don't mind—"

"No, I don't mind at all," Greg said. "I appreciate your help."

He turned and started back to his car but halfway there, he looked back and called out, "I certainly hope you enjoy your new home."

The man gave him a hard stare, then looked away. His wife smiled and waved to Greg as he got into the car. He was grinning like a fool as he started up the car and drove away.

"How the hell are race relations ever going to improve if blacks and whites don't help each other out, huh?" Greg said as he watched the house recede in the rearview mirror. "Maybe I ought to go back there and mess with his black ass."

But even as he said it, he knew that he wouldn't do that.

Not yet, anyway.

Now that he had the name of a town in Maine where Angela

was living, he figured he'd take off as soon as he could get packed. He'd never been to Maine before, but what would he need besides a road map and a full tank of gas?

As he drove back to Brooklyn to ditch the car, he decided that it might make sense to buy a car that would be legally registered to him, rather than steal one for the trip. It wouldn't make sense to cross state lines driving a stolen vehicle.

Besides, what difference did it make?

He had enough money to buy something fairly decent and still have enough left over to live on for a while—at least until he found Angela Ross and took care of her. If everything went well in Maine, he could always resell the car and get most of his money back. After that . . . hell, he could do pretty much anything he liked. Maybe he would come back here and even things up with that arrogant black bastard. Although his wife had tried to help him, the man had it coming.

"But first things first," Greg said, followed by a dry chuckle. "First things first . . ."

Chapter 15
Blackie

It rained on Friday night, so on Saturday morning the path Sammy and JJ walked every day to school was slick with mud that glistened like a light brown ribbon, winding its way through the pine trees and thick brush.

"You're *sure* Billy Wilson won't be there?" JJ asked a bit nervously as he followed along the path a few paces behind Sammy.

Each boy was carrying his baseball glove. Sammy also had a short aluminum bat, which he used to beat the brush along the side of the path. JJ was bouncing a baseball from one hand to the other. Once upon a time, the ball had been bright white, but now it was scuffed with dirt and grass stains.

"Look, even if he *does* show up, he ain't gonna start anything," Sammy said over his shoulder.

"Yeah, easy for you to say," JJ said. "You're not the one he wants to kill."

He took a deep breath and told himself that he should be enjoying the morning. The smell of damp earth and growing things filled his nose. The air had a wonderful freshness to it, much cleaner than what he was used to back home in New York. All around him, the forest was alive with singing birds and chattering squirrels and chipmunks that scampered about in the branches overhead. It was a beautiful day, but JJ couldn't get rid of the cold fist of nervousness in his gut.

"I just got lucky that day," he said tightly. He heard the tremor in his voice and wondered if Sammy heard it, too. "*You* know and *I* know that Billy Wilson could pound the piss out of me anytime he wants to."

He reached up and touched his upper lip, which was still sore but healing fast. His swollen eye no longer hurt, but there was a bulging black line below it that looked like a wide pencil mark.

"Yeah, but he won't," Sammy said casually.

"What makes you so sure?"

"Because you made him look like a jerk, and he'd look like an even bigger jerk if he picked another fight with you. After school the other day, I told him that you have a black belt in karate and could have killed him if you wanted to."

"Shit, you didn't!"

"Uh-huh."

"Did he believe you?"

"It doesn't matter. I think he's more scared of you than you are of him."

"That's not possible," JJ said, more to himself than to Sammy. "You know, back home, the guys would think he was an even bigger jerk if he *didn't* pound the shit out of me just to even the score."

The path suddenly opened up into a wide playing field behind the elementary school. Even this early in the spring, the grass was high. Bright yellow clumps of dandelions speckled the field. As they walked out onto the field, Sammy suddenly stopped and looked around.

"Crap!" Sammy said, squinting as he shielded his eyes with his hand and looked all around. "No one's here yet."

"They all knew we were playing here today, right?"

"As far as I know," Sammy said, nibbling his lower lip and nodding.

"You're sure it was *this* field? Maybe they're over at the high school."

"I don't think so. We never play over there 'cause the high school team usually practices there Saturday mornings."

"Well . . . ?" JJ shrugged. "What do we do now?"

Sammy was still nibbling his lower lip as he shook his head.

"I dunno. I guess we can bat the ball around while we wait. After a while, if no one shows up, maybe we'll ride over to the high school and check it out."

JJ, who would just as soon go back home and play computer games, shook his head at the suggestion. Sammy walked a little further out onto the field, then turned and signaled for JJ to throw him the ball. JJ tossed it to him underhand. Sammy caught the ball, dropped his glove, then braced the bat on his shoulder with one hand and popped the ball into the air with the other. He quickly gripped the bat and swung.

There was a soft, satisfying *thunk* sound, and the ball went sailing into the sky.

"Nice one," JJ called out, watching the ball arc and then begin to drop.

Before the ball hit the ground, a sudden, loud rush of activity from the bushes behind them made both of them jump and turn around. JJ let out a surprised squeal when he saw something large and jet black charge out of the brush.

His first thought was that they were being attacked by a bear or something, but the animal rushed past them and ran to the ball. JJ was so surprised it took him a moment to recognize that it was a black Labrador Retriever, galloping across the field with its tongue lolling out one side of its mouth. The dog stopped short where the ball had landed and snapped it up, clamping it in its slobbery jaws.

"Hey!" Sammy yelled. "That's mine!"

Before he could take more than a few steps forward, the dog turned and trotted over to him. Panting heavily, he dropped the ball at Sammy's feet and then started prancing around and barking. The sound echoed hollowly from the surrounding woods.

The ball was covered with dog-slime, but Sammy picked it up and then positioned the bat on his shoulder again, tossed the ball up, and swung.

The bat made another loud *crack* sound, and ball went flying. Both boys started laughing when the dog spun around and took off after it like a shot. He was so fast he almost caught the ball before it hit the soggy playing field with a dull *thud*.

"Here, boy . . . Com'ere Blackie," Sammy called out, wedging the bat under his arm and clapping his hands together like he was applauding the performance.

The black Lab trotted back to him with an easy, loping gait and dropped the ball at his feet again.

"Nice boy," Sammy said, kneeling down and scruffing the dog's neck hard enough to make the dog's tags jingle like Christmas bells.

"Do you know him?" JJ asked, moving a little closer but still keeping a cautious distance. He'd been warned about approaching dogs he didn't know.

"I've never seen him before in my life," Sammy said, "but obviously someone's taught him a trick or two. Here you go, fella."

Sammy took the ball and batted it a third time.

"Go get it, Blackie," he shouted, but he didn't have to; the dog was instantly off after the ball again.

"Looks to me like we got ourselves a star outfielder," Sammy said, laughing as he walked over to the baseball diamond. "You want to pitch or bat first?"

"Bat, I guess," JJ said, still looking warily at the dog.

He wedged his glove into the metal mesh of the backstop, high enough so the dog wouldn't be able to grab it thinking it was a ball, then hefted the bat, which seemed surprisingly light. He stepped up to the plate as Sammy got ready on the pitcher's mound, carefully avoiding the shallow depressions where muddy water from last night's rain had collected.

"You ready," Sammy called out, winding his arm around like a windmill to loosen it up.

JJ nodded and dug his feet into the wet earth, being careful not to step directly in the puddle in the batter's box. He gripped the bat tightly and, squinting against the bright sun, waited for the first pitch.

Sammy wound up and delivered it, high and outside, but JJ

went for it anyway and caught it off the tip of the bat. The ball dribbled down the first base line and rolled foul, making a faint whispering sound as it plowed through the deep grass. The black dog was on it in a flash and scooped it up in his mouth.

"Here, boy. Bring it here, Blackie," Sammy called, tapping his knee with his glove.

The dog pranced over to him and dropped the ball so it rolled into the little puddle. Smiling widely, Sammy looked at JJ and said, "This is cool, huh?"

JJ nodded and, getting more serious, dug his feet in, getting ready for the next pitch.

It turned out that none of the other kids showed up for the game, but JJ and Sammy didn't mind. They spent the better part of an hour taking turns at bat and pitching while the Lab fielded the ball for them. Blackie never seemed to tire of the game, either.

"I wonder whose dog he is," JJ said.

He couldn't stop thinking about the deal he'd made with his mother, that he would agree to move to Maine as long as he could get a dog. True, Blackie was wearing dog tags, but there was no owner's name or address on them. JJ wondered what a nice dog like this was doing out without his master. If he was lost or a stray, JJ wanted to take him home when they left. Maybe his mother would let him keep him.

It was getting on time for lunch when the boys finally decided to pack it in and head back to JJ's house. Sammy's mother was visiting with JJ's mother, so they planned to have lunch together and then go shopping at the Augusta Mall that afternoon. With bats, ball, and gloves in hand, they started back across the field toward the path.

Blackie followed beside them until they entered the shaded cool of the woods. Then, with a single, sharp bark, he drew to a halt. Prancing about in circles as though trying to catch his own tail, the dog kept up a steady stream of barking that echoed shrilly.

"I think he still wants to play," Sammy said with a laugh.

JJ whistled between his teeth and called out, "Come on, boy. Come here, Blackie."

The dog stopped jumping around for a moment and stood absolutely still, so motionless he looked like a statue.

After a moment, Sammy shrugged and said, "Maybe he's afraid to come this way." He looked at JJ, and his expression shifted to a dark, scowl. "You know, I haven't told you about these woods, yet, have I?"

"What do you mean?" JJ asked.

The tight feeling instantly returned to his gut, and he couldn't help but turn and look down the dark, winding path. Even though it was midday, the shadows in the woods seemed somehow darker, threatening. A soft breeze that he couldn't feel on his face was fluttering the leaves high overhead. Still sweaty from playing so hard, JJ couldn't help but shiver as a chill raced like tickling fingertips up his back. Goosebumps broke out across his arms.

"These woods are supposed to be haunted," Sammy said using a deep, spooky-sounding voice.

JJ could tell by the humorous glint in his friend's eyes that he was goofing on him, but he also couldn't deny the creepy feeling that suddenly came over him.

"Maybe that dog's a lot smarter than both of us," Sammy said, nodding in the direction of the black Lab. "Maybe he *knows* something or can *see* something in the woods here that we *can't*." He turned and called out to the dog, "Is that it, Blackie? You can see ghosts?"

"Cut it out," JJ said. "You're making this up."

"No, I'm not," Sammy said, lowering his brows. "This kid named Frank Sheldon disappeared one summer, something like ten years ago or so. The whole town went looking for him. The hunt lasted for weeks, but he was never found until that fall, once school started. Some girls playing out behind here found him hanging from a tree. His skin and clothes were all rotted and peeling off, and they say his eyes had popped right out of his head and were hanging down on his cheeks, dangling on the ends of his optic nerves."

"Cut it out," JJ said as the chill gripped him tighter.

Sammy looked warily to the left, then to the right. JJ couldn't help but do the same.

"And you know . . ." Sammy was whispering now. "They say his ghost is still out here, haunting the woods. They say, if you come out here late at night, especially at midnight when there's a full moon, you can see him, still hanging from the tree where they found him."

"You're not scaring me, you know," JJ said, hoping that Sammy couldn't see how much the story was getting to him. Even if Sammy's story was true, JJ told himself he had nothing to worry about now, not in broad daylight.

"We're gonna be late for lunch if we don't get a move on," he said. He turned to look out over the field again and was surprised to see that Blackie was nowhere in sight. Momentarily confused, he looked at Sammy and said, "Did you see where he went?"

Sammy shook his head. "Maybe he was never even here . . . Maybe he's a ghost dog . . . Frank Sheldon's ghost dog!"

"Cut it out," JJ said, swatting Sammy on the arm hard enough to make him wince.

They started down the path, heading for home, but the deeper the woods got, the denser the shadows of the trees grew and the more JJ started to think that just maybe Sammy's story about Frank Sheldon's ghost might be true. It didn't matter, though, because he wasn't planning on ever coming out here at midnight, anyway, even if he was with someone else.

And as strange as Blackie's appearance and disappearance may have seemed, JJ was convinced that dog had been real. When he squeezed the baseball in his hand, he could still feel the sticky slobber from the dog's mouth.

By the time they got back to JJ's house, he had determined not to mention the dog to his mother, but the first thing Sammy did was blurt out about how there was this "really cool" black dog at the baseball field today. That got JJ a stern warning from his mother to be careful about approaching a dog or any other animal he didn't know.

"Ahh, you don't have to worry about Blackie," JJ told her. "He's a good dog. I think he's a stray, and if I see him again, I'm gonna bring him home."

"Like heck you are," his mother said, but JJ gave her a

harsh look and said, "You *promised* I could get a dog, and *that's* the one I want!"

"We'll talk about it later," his mother said.

JJ knew that this was her signal for him not to pester her in front of company, but it made him all the more determined that when and if he ever saw Blackie again, he was definitely going to bring him home.

While JJ and Sammy waited outside, Ellen and Angie cleaned up the kitchen after lunch. There wasn't all that much to do, but Angie appreciated the gesture. She was beginning to realize that, although Ellen could be a bit overbearing at times, she seemed to be genuinely interested in being friends. And because Angie didn't have anyone else to talk to—not even Rob, because he was so busy with his own life—Angie decided that she felt comfortable enough with Ellen to unload some of what was bothering her.

"Are you finding Sammy . . . I dunno, maybe a little bit harder to deal with lately?" she asked, not exactly sure how to broach the subject.

Ellen's eyes widened as she shook her head. "He hasn't been any trouble for you, has he?"

"Oh, no. Not at all. He behaves just fine. Perfect, in fact." Angie was embarrassed that Ellen had taken her the wrong way. "It's JJ I'm worried about."

Ellen considered for a moment, then shook her head.

"He seems fine to me," she said. "Maybe a little on the quiet side sometimes, but I think that's normal at his age."

"It's—I don't know. His attitude, I guess." Angie sighed as she leaned back with both hands on the edge of the counter. "Preadolescence is tough enough as it is. I've already dealt with it with Brandy, but sometimes—a *lot* of times lately, JJ's been . . . I dunno . . . kind of edgy and really snappy . . . especially with me. He even swore at me the other day."

She heaved another, deeper sigh.

"I thought, you know, that maybe it's just the move and all

that's bothering him . . . and, of course, losing his father this past winter—''

"Yeah, that's *got* to be tough," Ellen offered, nodding sympathetically. "Especially for a boy his age. They really need a man around at that age."

"You can say that again," Angie replied, but as she looked down at the floor, she felt a deep stirring of guilt.

"But you see," she continued, choosing to ignore the tiny voice inside her head that was telling her that she should probably keep all of this to herself. "Don't get me wrong. John was a good husband and a wonderful father, but I'm afraid that his job and the way he dealt with it may have—I can't quite put my finger on it, but I don't like the level or the acceptance of violence that John seemed to regard as a . . . as just a necessary part of his job. *The Job,* as he always called it, like it was in capital letters."

"Well, I can't imagine being a New York City detective would be very easy," Ellen said, smiling thinly. "I mean, dealing with murderers and drug dealers and hookers all the time. God!"

"It wasn't all *that* bad," Angie said, "but he was a really good detective. I just worry that the . . . the attitude toward violence may have affected JJ . . . in a bad way. He never used to get in fights back home in Bedford Heights. Here, he's already been in two that I know of in the last two days."

"Well, 'boys will be boys, no matter how long you fry them in fat,' as my mother used to say," Ellen said with a shrug.

"Does Sammy get into many—into *any* fights?" she asked. Ellen shook her head, *no.*

"Does your husband have any guns at the house?" Angie asked.

The sudden change of topic seemed to catch Ellen off guard. She did a quick double take, then looked at Angie with a crooked smile.

"Doug? Guns? Good Lord, no! Doug would *never* have a gun or even allow anyone else in his house to have one. Every fall, he rails against moose and deer hunting, saying we should just let nature thin the herd. Just wait. I'm surprised you haven't already heard his harangue about how deer hunters don't need to be armed with semiautomatic rifles unless or until the deer start shooting back."

"I've got one . . . a gun, I mean," Angie said, a little nervously.

Ellen looked at her as though she was neither surprised nor offended.

"It's John's gun, actually," Angie continued. "I don't even know why I keep it."

"Why not just get rid of it then?" Ellen said.

She made it sound so easy, but Angie knew it wasn't. She bit her lower lip and shook her head.

"I don't know," she said. "Maybe because it's John's, and I want to . . . I dunno, maybe keep a reminder of him."

Ellen sniffed with laughter. "You could do better than his gun, I would think." She suddenly stiffened. "I'm sorry. I didn't mean that the way it sounded."

"It's okay," Angie said, feeling suddenly embarrassed that she had brought this up in the first place. "I mean, I know I have lots of things to remember him by—the kids especially, but this gun was a part of his work, you know, and I . . ."

Her voice faded away, and she ended with a feeble shrug.

"Look, if it's bugging you that much, why not take it down to the police station and turn it in?"

"Umm . . . Maybe I'll do that."

Just then, the back door banged open, and JJ stuck his head inside.

"Hey! Are you guys coming or not?"

Angie bristled at the harsh tone of command in his voice, but she smiled and told him that they were coming now. Glancing at Ellen, she said softly, "We should get going so I'll be back in time to help Brandy. She's going to the dance at the high school, and I know she'll need me to help her get ready."

"Who's she going with?" Ellen asked.

"A boy named Evan . . . Evan McDowell."

"Oh, I know the McDowells. Evan's a nice boy," Ellen said with a smile.

Again, Angie nodded, but she couldn't stop thinking about what they had been discussing before JJ interrupted them.

"You know," she said, "it's probably me who's having the trouble adjusting."

"I don't blame you in the least," Ellen said softly. "As far as I can see, you're doing a terrific job with everything."

"Thanks," Angie said. She took a deep breath that made her shudder. "But you know—I don't think I'll *ever* get over what happened."

The heavy throb of the music from the gym made it all the way through the cement walls and into the boy's bathroom. The band—a local group called *Dead Eyes Emerson*— was pretty good, and Evan was having a lot of fun dancing with Brandy. He was feeling just fine as he walked into the boy's room, unzipped his fly, and stepped up to one of the urinals.

Standing beside him, just about finished with his business, was Mark Haskell. Evan and Mark were friends, although they weren't quite as tight as Evan was with Jeff Stuart or Conner Collins.

"How's it going?" Evan asked, just to be sociable as he leaned his head back and started to piss. Sweat was running down his forehead and the back of his neck, making him shiver.

Mark glanced over at Evan, smiled and nodded, then quickly looked away.

"*I* should ask *you* that," he said, followed by a faint chuckle.

Evan instantly bristled. When he looked over at Mark, he was focused straight ahead on the green cement wall, his eyes half closed as he relieved himself.

For the last few days he'd been taking a ribbing from all of his friends about how he had fallen so hard, so fast for Brandy. He'd been surprised when she actually accepted his last-minute invitation to the school dance. The May "Spring Fling Dance" was a big deal at Bolton High School. People usually arranged their dates well in advance. Some couples even wore tuxedos and gowns, and arrived in chauffeured limousines.

This year, though, Evan hadn't been interested in going

because he'd broken up with Julie Sikes, his girlfriend of almost two years, a couple of months ago, and he was enjoying not being pinned down to anyone. He hadn't asked anyone else because he hadn't planned on going . . . until Brandy showed up at school.

"I'm doin' all right, all right," Evan said, nodding. "Doin' all right."

"Christ, *I'll* say you are," Mark said, snickering.

Evan thought he heard a note of envy in Mark's voice. When he realized that Mark's smile looked more like a leering smirk, it irritated the hell out of him. He felt a little silly, feeling such a strong rush of anger at one of his friends while he was standing in front of a urinal, but he couldn't let the comment slide.

"What the hell do you mean by that?" he said, his voice low and controlled. He was trying to concentrate just on how good it felt to relieve his bladder; he didn't want any trouble, but he was getting tired of taking shit from his friends.

"You know what I mean," Mark said with a casual shrug as he zipped his pants and flushed. For a moment, the sound of rushing water masked the sound of the band in the gym. "That New York chick you're here with. She sure as shit looks like a fine piece of ass. You get any of that yet?"

Evan wasn't quite finished pissing, but he wheeled around and grabbed Mark by the throat so quickly that Mark didn't have a chance to react. Evan's hands shook as he gripped the boy by the throat and started to squeeze. He was vaguely aware of his warm urine now dripping down his leg, but he didn't care.

"I don't want you—or anyone else—talking about Brandy that way," he said, low and tight. "You got that?"

Evan's face was flushed, and he had to restrain himself from squeezing any harder. In the back of his mind, a tiny voice was whispering, *Be careful! . . . You could kill him!* But another voice inside his mind was telling him that he should if he says anything else like that about Brandy.

"I said, *you got that?*" Evan said, squeezing a little tighter with each word.

Mark's face was getting bright red, and his eyes were bugging out. When he didn't answer right away, Evan gave him a quick, hard shake that banged his head against the metal partition behind him.

"Hey . . . I . . . didn't . . . mean . . . nothin' . . . by it," Mark gasped.

Evan held his friend's throat for a heartbeat or two longer as they stared each other straight in the eyes. The heavy beat of the music from the gym seemed to keep time with Evan's racing pulse.

He knew he could do it.

He was telling himself that it would be easy.

All he needed to do was apply just a little more pressure, and he could cut off Mark's air. He would drop to the floor like the load of shit he was. And Evan was mad enough to do it—to Mark or anyone else who insulted Brandy.

After another moment, though, Evan snapped to and realized what he was doing. Panting heavily, he stepped back and released his grip. Mark gasped as he grabbed his throat and rubbed it.

"Jesus *Christ,* man," he said shakily, his voice sounding raw.

Evan turned to one side, reached down, and quickly zipped himself up. For another few seconds, both boys just stood there staring at each other, neither one of them knowing quite what to say until Mark started backing up toward the door. He kept a wary eye on Evan, looking like someone who was trying to walk away from a rattlesnake that was coiled and ready to strike.

"Fuck you, asshole," Mark said as he swung the door open and went outside.

"Fuck you, too," Evan shouted as the door whooshed shut.

His first impulse was to tell Mark that he was sorry for overreacting like that, but he was still too flushed with anger. The bottom line was, he was sick and tired of the way his friends talked about Brandy. Just because she had lived in New York, that didn't make her some kind of slut. In the back of his mind, Evan guessed it was because all of his friends were attracted to her, too, and were maybe a little jealous that he had made the first move.

But—hey, he told himself, those were the breaks. If you snooze, you lose.

He sighed as he closed his eyes and rubbed them hard enough to made spiral patterns of light appear in his vision. He could feel the adrenalin humming in his body. His legs felt shaky, as if they were about to collapse underneath him as he walked over to the sink and ran the water until it was ice cold. Leaning forward, he cupped his hands and scooped a handful of water into his face. The sudden cold made him shiver, but after a few seconds, he felt himself beginning to calm down. He stared at his reflection in the mirror, a little unnerved to see how crazed he looked. His lips were thin and pale, and his eyes were red-rimmed.

He heaved a deep sigh, but when he turned to leave, he noticed the wet stain on his pants leg. He grabbed a handful of paper towels from the dispenser and tried to dry it, but all that did was make more of a mess. Finally, he told himself not to worry. The gym was dark enough so probably no one would notice it, anyway.

As he squared his shoulders and walked out of the boy's room, he still felt a winding tension because he knew, if word hadn't already spread about what he had done to Mark, he wouldn't hesitate to beat the crap out of anyone who insulted Brandy. The last thing he wanted was for someone to be dissing his girl!

In a way, he was grateful to Mark for saying what he had. Until then, Evan hadn't realized just how serious he felt about Brandy. He found himself hoping that she felt just as serious about him. He was smiling and ready to boogie as he walked back into the gym and looked around for Brandy.

Chapter 16
Headin' North

Greg braced his hands on the edge of the bathroom sink and leaned forward to stare at the mirror, shocked by what he saw. A few months ago, before attending John Ross' funeral, he had shaved his mustache and had kept it off since then, but now that he had cut his hair and dyed it a few shades darker, he thought even his own mother wouldn't recognize him.

If she was alive, that is.

He couldn't help but laugh out loud, his face close enough to the mirror so his breath fogged the water-speckled glass.

His pulse was throbbing in his neck as he gazed long and hard into his own eyes. If he had wanted to spend the money, he supposed he could get a pair of those contact lenses that would change his eye color, too. With those, the only thing that would identify him as Greg Newman would be his fingerprints and his new driver's license.

He wished now that he had waited until after he cut his hair and changed its color before getting the license from Benny Capozza. Everyone in the neighborhood called Benny "The Scab" because of the dark mole as big as a half dollar on his left cheek that looked like a nasty scab about to flake off and start bleeding. Benny "The Scab" could get you pretty much anything you wanted. On the off chance that he couldn't get it, he always knew someone who could.

Greg's request had been easy. He wanted a New York State driver's license with his photograph and his real name and address on it. Benny knew better than to ask why he wanted it, and after Greg paid him the agreed upon amount—a bit more than Greg thought it should be—they parted ways.

Using the driver's license as identification because he didn't have any credit cards, Greg had gone out and bought a fairly nice car—a late model, white Pontiac, for which he paid cash. The car had low mileage and decent tires, but Greg wasn't going to be too picky because all he really needed it for was to get to Maine, find Angela Ross, then get back home to Brooklyn. Once that was done, he'd resell the car and maybe take a bus or train down to Florida. He'd decided that he'd dealt with his last New York City winter.

It was late on Monday morning during the last week of May when Greg threw a few suitcases into the car, filled the gas tank, bought a road map from the vending machine at the filling station, and took off. He would have gotten an earlier start, but the night before—like nearly every other night for the last several months—he hadn't slept well.

He had dreamed that his mother—at least he *thought* it was his mother; it was an old woman dressed in black—had come into his bedroom and sat at the foot of his bed for most of the night. The whole time, she was whispering things to him, but upon waking, he couldn't quite remember what they were. Still, he was filled with an uneasiness that even the warm, morning sunlight didn't relieve, so he was feeling tired and cranky as he drove north on Route 684, heading into Connecticut.

He was surprised to learn that Maine wasn't an island off the coast of Canada after all. That was Nova Scotia. Maine did border Canada, though, and once he was on his way, he started toying with the idea of going all the way up into Canada to check out Quebec City, or maybe Montreal or Toronto. He'd heard from his boss at the video store that there were some dynamite strip joints in Toronto.

That, of course, would have to wait until after he had taken care of Angela Ross. Besides, for all he knew, it might still be winter in Canada, and he'd had enough cold weather this past winter to last a lifetime.

The further north he drove, the worse the weather got. What had started out as a gorgeous, sunny day in Brooklyn rapidly deteriorated as a gray overcast ble   in from the west. By the time he crossed into Massachusetts, the clouds had lowered, and rain was falling

One thing Greg hadn   thought to check out on the car was the condition of the wiper blades. When he turned them on, they made a terrible scraping sound and left wide dirty streaks on the windshield. It was almost impossible for him to see the road, so he tried driving without the wipers, but that didn't work very well, either.

Just outside of Worcester, Massachusetts, he stopped for a late lunch at the Roy Rogers. He took his time eating because he'd just as soon wait to see if the rain was going to let up.

If anything, it got worse.

All of the cars and trucks passing by in either direction on the Mass. Pike had their headlights on. They left huge, gray fantails of spray in their wake. On the opposite side of the turnpike, the nearly gale force winds tossed the tall, dark pine trees back and forth. The sight made Greg shiver.

After waiting for over an hour, he finally decided to spring for a new set of wiper blades at the Mobile station next door before getting on his way. A little after three o'clock in the afternoon he was back on the road. As he drove, he kept telling himself not to worry, that he wasn't in any hurry, but he found as he drove that he was filled with a heightening agitation.

He knew it wasn't money that was bothering him. He had enough to last him easily through the summer and into the fall. He planned to take care of Angela quickly, then head down to Florida by July or August at the latest.

Another thing he hadn't thought to check out was the car's radio. It had worked just fine when the car was parked on the lot, but he hadn't turned it on while he was test driving. Obviously, there was a loose connection somewhere because, whenever he switched on the windshield wipers, the radio started pulsating with strong bursts of static that kept time with the sweep of the wipers. It was *damned* irritating, so for most of the drive he had to do without any music or Rush Limbaugh.

"Just as well," he told himself.

With every passing mile, the rain seemed to be coming down all the harder. Greg found himself hunched over the steering wheel, squinting to see the road ahead. He couldn't follow any other vehicles too closely because the spray from them only made the visibility that much worse. He was so mesmerized by the hissing of his tires on the wet road and the steady slapping of the wiper blades that he missed the turn onto Interstate 95 and found himself halfway to Salisbury Beach, in Massachusetts, before he realized his mistake and backtracked.

The countryside—what little he saw of it through the steady downpour—fascinated Greg. Other than in movies and on TV, he had never seen anything like it. There were long stretches of highway where there were absolutely no houses to be seen. Deep woods lined both sides of the highway, broken every now and then by stonewall-lined fields and huge farms. Several times, Greg caught a glimpse of what looked like cows or horses grazing in the fields in the rain. The animals were too far away for him to be sure what they were, but he couldn't get over the idea that people actually *lived* out here in the middle of nowhere. How could they stand it? It was almost creepy. Already, he found himself missing the close quarters of the city.

Another thing Greg noticed, something that really amazed him, was how friendly everyone was. It made him feel downright uncomfortable and a bit suspicious the way the collectors at the toll booths smiled and made some friendly comment about the weather or whatever when he stopped to pay. He was used to toll collectors around New York City whose idea of a friendly greeting was to look at you and scowl as they took your money. One person even called out to him: "Have a nice day!" as he drove away.

When the rain was the heaviest, the traffic slowed down to under fifty miles per hour, so the drive was taking a lot longer than Greg had hoped. It was already well past six o'clock when he stopped for something to eat at a Burger King along the Maine Turnpike. The name of the town was Kennebunk. He remembered that it had something to do with one of the recent presidents, but he couldn't remember which one.

He checked the map frequently and knew that in order to get to Bolton, he had to get onto Route 202 in Augusta and head west. He panicked for an instant, thinking maybe he'd heard that black woman wrong, and the town was Houlton, Maine, which was a lot further north. He sure as hell wasn't going to drive that far today! Because of all the slowdowns and delays, he realized that he probably wasn't going to get to Augusta until well after dark. He figured he'd have to spend the night in a motel somewhere around Augusta and start looking for Angela in the morning.

Night came on slowly, blending imperceptibly with the thick storm clouds. Without the radio to distract him, and after listening to the steady beat of the wipers for several hours, he was starting to get sleepy. The road became even more of a blur as his vision began to drift. He kept catching himself just before he'd fall asleep, jerking awake and gripping the steering wheel tightly. After a while he became aware of something else.

He realized with a mild shock that there was someone else in the car with him.

When the thought first hit him, he was so sleepy that he wasn't all that surprised. He didn't cry out and turn around to see who it was; he just gradually became convinced that there was another person—maybe more than one—in the car. He turned around and looked a few times, but caught only a glimpse every now and then out of the corner of his eye. Whoever it was, he or she seemed to shift to one side or the other before Greg could see them clearly. Whenever he looked directly into the rearview, he couldn't see anything except the misty spray he was leaving in his wake. It was only when he was looking straight ahead at the road that he would see . . . *Someone* . . .

He wasn't sure if it was a man or a woman, but after a while he accepted how ridiculous it was to think there could have been anyone in the car all the way from Brooklyn. He was spooking himself, remembering a movie about a car whose previous owner had died and now haunted the car.

"Jesus, don't be stupid!" he whispered to himself, even though the impression was still strong enough so that, from time to time, he actually imagined he could hear the person, shifting about in the back seat and muttering something to him.

"So . . ." Greg said, surprising himself with the sudden loudness of his voice. "What do you want with me, anyway?"

Are you going to kill her . . . like you did me?

The voice was so clear, Greg had no idea if he had actually heard it or if it was inside his head. He couldn't tell if it was a man or woman's voice, but he sniffed with laughter, convinced that he had imagined it even though the distinct impression that there was someone behind him wouldn't go away. He shivered and reached to turn up the heat in the car.

"Yeah," he replied, grunting and chuckling softly to himself. "I'll tell you what I'm gonna do. I'm gonna waste the bitch. You got a problem with that?"

He shuddered as he yawned and rubbed his eyes, which were starting to burn from eyestrain. In his peripheral vision, the roadside was a monotonous, gray blur of pine trees and red granite where the hillsides had been blasted away. The dotted white line on the road ahead began to blur and weave back and forth like zigzagging tracer bullets. That, along with the high, steady whine of the tires, was hypnotic.

No, I don't have any problem with that, the voice behind him whispered, *but I don't think you're up to it . . . In fact, I don't think you have the balls or the brains to do it!*

"Oh, yeah? Well fuck you!" Greg shouted.

He pounded the steering wheel so hard his hand ached, then had to jerk the car back into line when he realized that he was veering toward the side of the road. A car that was passing him on the left sped past with a long, trailing blast of its horn.

"Fuck you!" Greg yelled, jabbing his middle finger at the car and hoping the driver could see him in the rearview.

"And you! Stop fucking me up!" Greg said, his voice low as he glanced over his shoulder into the empty back seat. "You're fucking up my concentration!"

He thought he heard a faint sniff of laughter as he looked at his own reflection in the rearview mirror and for a moment was startled when he didn't recognize himself.

Only his wide, staring eyes looked familiar.

Then he remembered the haircut and the dye he had used. He could still see a faint ring of darkness at the edge of his scalp where the dye had stained his skin. He hoped it would go away after a few days.

"You're gonna get me killed, for Christ's sake, if you keep distracting me like that," he said, struggling to control his voice.

Well, we wouldn't want that, now, would we?

The voice was a deep, grating whisper.

Greg told himself that he must be imagining all of this, but no matter how hard he tried to stay focused on the road ahead, it kept disappearing into a gray haze. Several times, he was jerked violently back awake when he realized the car was drifting off to one side or the other.

"Fuck, man," he whispered as he glanced at his frightened eyes in the darkened rearview mirror. He cringed as he waited to hear the voice start in again, but the car was eerily silent except for the hissing of the tires, the slapping windshield wipers, and his own fast, ragged breathing.

"I'm beat . . . That's all it is," he whispered, and even as he said it, his eyes began to drift shut again.

The car shifted back and forth, and for a scary, timeless instant, he felt as though he were in freefall, spinning and falling into the hazy darkness that surrounded him. What brought him to was the sudden loud wail of a siren that filled the night.

"Shit," he muttered when he saw the flashing blue lights of a Maine State Police cruiser closing in on him from behind. He snapped on his right turn signal and slowed to a stop in the breakdown lane.

Cold sweat broke out over his forehead as he watched the trooper, wearing a yellow, ankle-length rain slicker, get out and approach the car. The blue emergency lights flashing behind him created an aura around his head that looked like a halo. Greg's hand was shaking as he rolled the side window down after the trooper tapped on it with the butt of his flashlight. A gust of wind blew rain into Greg's face as he looked up.

"I'm sorry, I—"

"License and registration please," the trooper said, all business.

The trooped looked too young to be a cop. He had a smooth, square jaw, and a cold, detached distance in his eyes. Greg leaned forward and fished his wallet from his back pocket. His hand was shaking slightly as he handed it to the statie, then snapped open the glove compartment and took out his car registration.

"New York, huh?" the trooper said as he ran the beam of his flashlight over the license and then shined it into Greg's eyes.

Greg winced and looked away, but not fast enough. The light left a smeared afterimage trailing across his vision.

"Your temporary plates are gonna run out in six days," the trooper said. "You planning on getting back to New York before then?"

"Absolutely, officer," Greg said, hoping that he didn't sound too nervous. "I'm just driving up for a few days to visit with some friends."

"Do you have any idea why I pulled you over?" the trooper asked tonelessly.

Greg could tell that this guy wasn't going to start chatting nice and friendly with him, the way the toll collectors on the pike had.

"I figure I was kind of drifting there on the road," Greg replied with a quick nod.

"Been driving very long?" the trooper asked.

Greg almost said *ever since I was a kid*, but then realized what he meant. He nodded again and said, "Six or seven hours, I guess. The weather's been slowing me down."

"Probably a good thing. Would you mind waiting while I call this in?" the trooper asked.

"Look, I ain't been drinking or nothing," Greg said tightly. He knew that this cop could give him plenty of trouble just for the way he'd been driving, but Greg was suddenly afraid that he knew a lot more than he was letting on. Was he going to arrest him now for shooting John Ross and killing those other cops last winter?

Greg considered taking off before the trooper got back to his cruiser, but he knew that his Pontiac wouldn't be able to outrun a police cruiser, especially in bad weather like this. He cringed as he watched the dark silhouette of the trooper in the rearview mirror as he sat behind his steering wheel. He wasn't worried about having any record of any driving offenses. Until a week ago, his driver's license didn't even exist. Unless this cop found out somehow that it was a forgery, he'd be out of here with, at worst, a ticket he would tear up.

It seemed to take much longer than necessary, but eventually the trooper walked back to Greg's car. When Greg rolled the window down again, another cold blast of rain hit him in the face.

"There's a rest area a few miles up ahead, Mr. Newman," the trooper said, nodding as he handed the license and registration back to Greg. "I'd suggest you pull over there and rest a while before you drive any further."

"Good idea . . . I will . . . Thank you, officer," Greg said, only now realizing how relieved he was that the cop hadn't pushed this any further.

He shifted into gear and drove away, making sure not to speed and to keep his car squarely in the center lane. Five miles up the road, he saw the sign for the rest area. The state trooper was still following along behind him, so Greg snapped on his turn signal and slowed down to under twenty miles per hour as he took the exit. The trooper sped on past him and was soon out of sight. At the first available parking slot, Greg braked to a stop and killed the engine.

"Mother-fucker," he muttered under his breath as he bunched his coat up to make a pillow against the driver's window. He shifted around in the seat but knew that he was never going to find a really comfortable position. As rain thumped heavily on the car roof, he closed his eyes and tried to sleep. As dark as it was and as lulling as the sound of the rain should have been, sleep didn't come easily.

And when it did come, the voices returned with it, and Greg's car was filled with people that Greg couldn't see . . .

"And just *where* have *you* been?"

Angie, wearing her bathrobe and slippers, was standing in the center of the kitchen floor with both hands on her hips, scowling at Brandy, who eased the door quietly shut behind her.

"Ahh . . . Just out," Brandy said in a high voice. She slipped off her dripping raincoat and hung it up on one of the pegs beside the door. Rain dripped from it and puddled on the floor.

"Do you have any idea what time it is?"

Brandy shrugged and shook her head as she bent over and untied her shoes.

"Not really," she said, her voice soft and restrained. She obviously knew that she was in deep trouble. When she raised her head and looked past her mother at the clock on the kitchen wall, her face barely registered her surprise.

"It's almost two o'clock in the morning!" Angie said, trying hard not to yell. "What the dickens do you think you're doing, staying out this late? And on a school night, no less! God, I was worried sick that something had—"

"I was just . . . Evan and I went to the movies."

Brandy kicked her shoes away and shrugged, looking all innocence.

"I *know* you went to the movies," Angie said, feeling a hot rush of anger. She clenched her fists and gritted her teeth so she wouldn't start shouting. "You left for the movies more than five hours ago."

"Yeah, well . . . after the movie we just . . . sorta hung out and . . . talked for a while."

"Talked?" Angie echoed, not believing her for an instant.

"Yeah . . . Talked."

Brandy stiffened her shoulders defensively as she took a few steps into the kitchen, but she was keeping a safe distance between her and her mother.

"I—we're just—you know, getting to know each other, and there was—we have a lot to talk about."

"Oh, I'll just bet," Angie said, shaking her head. "Look, do we need to have another mother to daughter talk?"

"No, Mom. We don't need another mother-daughter talk," Brandy said, scowling. Angie could see the defiant fire shimmering behind her daughter's eyes.

"We were just talking, Mom . . . Honest."

"Well, you'll be doing most of your talking to the walls of your bedroom for the next few nights. You're grounded for a week!"

"A week!" Brandy shouted. "That's not fair!"

Angie took a single step backwards when she saw her daughter clench and raise her fist.

"No, *I'll* tell you what's not fair!" Angie said, wagging a finger at her. It was still a struggle to keep her voice low, but she didn't want to wake up JJ. "It's not fair for *you* to stay out this late. Even if it *wasn't* a school night, this is too late. And it's not fair that you didn't even call me. I've been worried sick that you'd gone off the road in the rain or were . . . were—"

"Were what? Off screwing somewhere?" Brandy said, arcing her eyebrows.

That stopped Angie cold, but only for a moment. She had been too worried and too angry for too long to let Brandy get the upper hand. Maybe she'd been a little too careful, tiptoeing around both of her children because their father had died, but she knew that it was time to draw the line now.

"Yes," she said, nailing Brandy with a hard look. "To tell you the God's honest truth, that's *exactly* what I was worried about."

"Well don't be," Brandy said, crossing her arms defiantly and cocking her hip to one side. One corner of her mouth curled up into a snarl. "I'm not stupid, you know?"

"I didn't say you were stupid. I said I was worried that you might get careless."

As Angie studied at her daughter, a deep sense of loss and sadness swept through her. Her vision blurred, and her eyes filled with tears as she considered that, just as she had lost John, she was also losing Brandy and JJ. Both of her kids were growing up too fast. Before she knew it, they'd be leaving her to start lives of their own.

And *then* what would she do with herself?

The question left her feeling cold and hollow. Her grief and loss were much too recent for her even to consider finding another lover. The thought had barely crossed her mind, but she realized now more than ever that she might be looking to both of her children to fill the emptiness she felt because of losing her husband.

"I . . . just want you . . . to . . ."

Her voice choked off as tears began to spill from her eyes and run down her cheeks. She sniffed and wiped her face with the back of her hand. Brandy just stood there, looking at her for a terribly long and awkward moment. Then, without bothering even to say "good night," she walked past her and stomped up the stairs to her bedroom. It sounded like a gun going off upstairs when she slammed her bedroom door behind her.

Feeling tired and absolutely wrung out, Angie walked shakily over to the kitchen table, pulled out a chair, and sat down heavily. A low, vibrating groan that started somewhere deep inside her escaped her as she folded her hands on the table and slumped forward to cradle her head against her arms. Then she cried, so hard her chest and throat felt like they were on fire.

Greg awoke with a start and sat up so fast he wrenched his neck. Frantic with fear, he looked around, not at all sure where he was or what had awakened him. All he knew for sure was that he was so freezing cold. His teeth chattered wildly, and for one crazy instant, he thought he was back home in Brooklyn in the dumpy apartment he shared with his mother.

Then he remembered . . .

His mother was dead, and he had left Brooklyn yesterday morning.

Was it really only yesterday morning? Christ, it felt like ages ago!

But . . . no, he had driven to Maine because he was going to find someone . . .

Angela Ross . . .

Yes. That was it.

Although it was still dark outside, the rain had stopped. The streetlights lining the parking lot cast a soft blue glow over the entire area. Drops of rain fell from the trees and hit the car roof with irregular, loud *plops*.

The back of Greg's neck ached with a deep, pulsating pain. His body felt as though a mild electric shock was running through him as he slowly straightened up and turned to look carefully into the back seat.

He let out a breath that he didn't even know he'd been holding when he saw that the back seat was empty.

Of course it was empty.

He grunted and shook his head, having no idea what—or who—he expected to see back there, but a vague memory of someone—maybe several people, talking to him while he slept—or *tried* to sleep—flit through his mind. Even now, knowing that he was alone didn't relieve the hard knot of tension deep in his gut.

''Jesus . . . Fuck,'' he whispered as he stretched out his arm and glanced at his watch. It was a quarter past two. How could he have slept so long?

He snorted and wiped his face with both hands, then gripped the steering wheel tightly, but still he didn't feel awake enough to drive.

His stomach was empty and grumbling like distant thunder, and he had to go to the bathroom, bad. There were public restrooms a short walk across the parking lot, but since there were no other cars around, he decided that was too far to walk and got out of his car to urinate on the side of the road.

Feeling at least marginally better, he got back into the car and turned the key in the ignition, wanting to get the heater going as quickly as possible. It amazed him that, even at the end of May, nights in Maine were so cold . . . much colder than they were back home in Brooklyn.

For almost five minutes, Greg sat there, shivering wildly as he tried to wake himself up. He thought about what he should do next, but his mind was still too fogged. Turning on the dome light, he unfolded the road map and studied it for a several minutes. He guessed he was still at least an hour away from Augusta, and Bolton looked like another half hour to an hour west of that.

Still stiff in the joints, he folded up the map, shifted the car into gear, and backed out of his parking slot just as an eighteen wheeler roared into the rest area. A few seconds later, he was back on the road, listening to the high whining of his tires on the pavement. Without the wipers going, he tried the radio again, but he couldn't find anything worth listening to this late at night. Other than the cones of his headlights, there wasn't much of anything to see throughout the rest of the drive to Augusta.

He got off the highway at the first exit for Augusta. As he headed west on Route 202, he looked for a restaurant that would still be open this late. The only thing he found was a Denny's.

"Christ, it figures," he muttered as he pulled to a stop by the front door. "No one ever goes to Denny's. You just end up there."

He ordered a huge breakfast of eggs, toast, bacon, and home fries, and started feeling better after wolfing it all down along with three cups of black coffee. When he looked up at the clock and saw that it was after four in the morning, he swore softly under his breath. He'd been on the road almost twenty-four hours!

He started to get pissed at how long the trip was taking him, but then he reminded himself that he wasn't in any big hurry. If Angela Ross lived in Bolton or anywhere nearby, he'd take however long he needed to find her.

And when he did . . .

He started laughing. The waitress who had served him breakfast looked over at him like he was some kind of loony, but he didn't care. This was going to be a vacation for him, he told himself as he got up and walked over to the register to pay his bill.

This was going to be *fun!*

Chapter 17
A Slight Change of Plans

"Jesus Christ, that's her! That's *got* to be her!"

A powerful jolt slammed Greg's body the instant he saw the girl walking along the sidewalk. He pressed his foot down on the brake pedal, intending to stop the car right there in the middle of Main Street, but he immediately realized that he couldn't be so obvious. Instead, he slowed the car down and stared at her in the rearview mirror as he drove past.

He enjoyed watching the way she walked.

She was wearing a tight-fitting red tank top and jeans that emphasized how young and firm she was. He could feel himself getting an erection just looking at the way she held her head high, her smooth skin glowing like gold in the slanting afternoon sunlight. She was holding hands with a tall, blond boy who was wearing tattered jeans and a pale purple T-shirt with some rock and roll band's logo. The boy had a smug, arrogant look about him that Greg instantly disliked. He looked like the kind of kid who would fit in perfectly in a place like Bedford Heights.

Greg didn't think downtown Bolton amounted to very much, but then again—how could it? Stuck out here in the middle of nowhere, pretty much all it had to offer was a corner convenience store, a video rental store, a couple of pizza joints, a

Dunkin' Donuts, post office and town hall, Trustworthy hardware store, three gas stations, and a few other shabby-looking storefronts, many of which had white-washed windows and boards nailed across the doors.

That was it.

Augusta was the nearest thing that passed for a city, but Greg's first impression of Augusta had been that, if that's what folks who lived around here thought was a real city, they were all nuts.

He wondered why Angela Ross would have chosen a podunk little town like this, but he didn't dwell on it for long. If she was trying to make a clean break with her past life, then a hick town like Bolton was as good a place as any.

It was also the kind of place where someone driving a car with temporary New York license plates, skidding to a stop in the middle of Main Street, was going to get noticed. That's why late last night, after cruising Bolton's Main Street a few times, Greg had driven back to Augusta and stolen a set of plates from an abandoned car he found in a shopping mall parking lot.

He had no intention of spending another miserable night sleeping in his car, so he rented a hotel room on River Street, a seedy section of Augusta. He told the desk clerk—an overweight, middle-aged woman with blue hair and pasty complexion—that he'd be staying about a week. He figured it wouldn't take him any longer than that to find Angela Ross, but just in case, he wanted a place where he could stay as long as he needed and where no one would ask too many questions. This woman looked to him like someone who would rent to Jeffrey Dahmer, as long as he paid for the room up front.

The room wasn't much, but it was cheap, almost clean, and there was a working man's diner just down the street that served decent food.

Greg had only seen Angela Ross' daughter once before, on the day of her father's funeral, and not from very close up, so he couldn't be positive, but this girl looked so much like her mother—who Greg *had* seen up close—that he knew it *had* to be her.

A tingle of excitement filled him because this seemed to be coming together so easily. Yesterday morning, he had called directory assistance and asked the operator for Angela Ross' new phone number. The operator informed him that the number was unlisted, and that she wouldn't give it out. When Greg asked for the address, she flatly refused, telling him that it was company policy to protect the privacy of their customers.

Greg was furious and wished there was some way he could get even with this woman, but what could he do?

Seeing Angela's daughter on the street meant that he was close and getting closer. They had live somewhere nearby. All he had to do was keep out of sight and follow the girl home.

Greg drove a little way down the street, then pulled over into an empty parking space in front of a hardware store. The girl and boy were still coming toward him, taking their time, laughing and talking. Even with the passenger's side window down, Greg couldn't catch anything they said until they were right up close to his car.

As they passed by, he heard the girl complaining that she had to be home before supper, and that she wouldn't be able to get out later because she was still grounded. The boy said, "I've got an idea," but Greg missed what that idea was as they walked away from the car.

Watching the girl from behind, Greg became aware that he still had a rock solid erection. He focused his gaze on the nice, smooth bulge of her ass and dropped his right hand down to his lap and began to rub himself.

It felt good, and the more he thought about how good it felt, the more he started thinking that maybe he should change his plans a little.

After all, he wasn't in any hurry.

He had a place to stay, so why not stick around for at least a couple of weeks until he thought of a few things he could do to fuck with Angela Ross and her family?

For starters, picking up that young girl some night and fucking the shit out of her and then slitting her throat struck him as a good place to start. He might have even considered doing it today if it was a little closer to evening and that blond asshole wasn't hanging around.

Then again, a rape and murder in a town like this was going to get plenty of attention. This wasn't the kind of place like Brooklyn, where he could disappear into the crowd and where murders weren't big news. Here, the cops probably went all out to solve a crime because they didn't see real crimes like rape or murder very often. Greg decided that he wouldn't do *anything* until he learned where Angela lived; then he'd take it from there.

Snickering to himself, he watched the young couple round the corner and disappear from sight. He'd left the car running, and he considered driving up to the intersection to see where they were headed, but instead he switched off the ignition and got out of the car.

He was all smiles as he strolled into the hardware store and asked the rail-thin, balding man at the counter if they sold baseball bats. He figured a town like Bolton was too damned small to have its own sporting goods store, and he was right. The sales clerk directed him over to a display at the far corner of the store where there was a wire rack with several bats to choose from. There were both aluminum and real wood, but after checking them over, Greg selected a heavy Louisville Slugger that had a nice, narrow handle. He stepped back and hefted the bat, thinking how much he liked the clean, solid feel of a good piece of wood in his hands. It was so much better than a gun or a knife.

The Mickey Mantle of crime!

"Batter up," he whispered, chuckling softly as he checked for clearance and then cut the air a few times with full, vicious swings.

"Find what you need?"

The voice, speaking so suddenly behind him, made Greg jump. He turned and saw the balding sales clerk at the head of the aisle, watching him with a dark look of suspicion.

"Yeah," Greg said, smiling. "I think this'll do just fine. I like the feel of it. Good solid wood."

He took one last swing, enjoying the way the sales clerk cringed as though expecting him to knock something over.

"Don't you think it's a crime the way metal bats are taking over?" Greg said to the clerk as they walked over to the cash register.

The clerk smiled and nodded, but it was obvious that he had no opinion on the matter.

"I mean, when did we forget about tradition, huh?" Greg said, leaning close to the man and enjoying the clerk's discomfort.

Trying his best to ignore him, the clerk rang up the sale and took Greg's money without another word. Greg wondered if this guy was treating him with such thinly veiled hostility because it was so obvious that he wasn't from around here.

Was this how he treated all out-of-towners?

He made a mental note that, when and if he ever did use the baseball bat on Angela or either of her kids, he would have to come back here and nail this sales clerk, too. He wouldn't want anyone around who might be able to identify him later.

Slipping the bat under his arm, Greg took the sales receipt and walked out of the store, whistling a happy little tune and swinging the bat like he was stepping up to the plate. He opened the car door and slid the bat under the front seat before getting in. When he started the car, he laughed out loud as he considered the prospects that were open to him.

Angela's daughter and her boyfriend were long gone, and Greg was a little miffed at himself for not following them, but he was still whistling as he shifted the car into gear and pulled out onto Main Street.

What was the hurry?

He had plenty of money and a place to stay, so once he found out where Angela Ross was living, he could take all the time he wanted.

And as he drove out of town, heading back to his hotel room to take a shower, he thought that he might just as well stick around Bolton for a while, if only to see what might develop.

* * *

The moon was low in the sky, so its light wasn't nearly strong enough to see by, but JJ's binoculars made it a little easier for him to see what was going on out in the backyard. The rest he was filling in with his imagination.

He couldn't believe his luck.

He just been starting to drift off to sleep, so he almost hadn't heard his sister when she tiptoed out of her bedroom and, a few minutes later, met up with her boyfriend out in the backyard. A warm breeze was blowing through the open bathroom window, carrying their whispering voices, but he couldn't quite make out what they were saying. He thought for a second that his sister sounded upset, but then again—maybe she was just enjoying what Evan was doing to her.

And the bottom line was, it didn't matter.

The show—what he could see of it, anyway—was incredible! JJ was positive that Sammy would never believe him when he told him about it on the way to school tomorrow. Sammy would say he was lying and—short of trying to take pictures or calling him up right now and telling him to come over and see for himself—there wasn't much JJ could do to get the proof he needed. In fact, he was having a lot of trouble believing that he wasn't imagining all of this.

His best hope was that this was something Brandy and Evan were going to try to get away with on other nights. JJ was thinking that, maybe if he planned to have Sammy over for a sleep over some night or something, they might get lucky again.

If not . . . well, at least JJ was going to enjoy the show while it lasted.

"Don't . . . Please . . ." Brandy murmured. "Stop it right now." Lying flat on her back on the damp grass, she twisted to one side, trying to get away from Evan's groping hands. Her tank top was hiked up over her breasts, and for the last several minutes, Evan had been fumbling with the catch on her bra, trying to release it. All the while, he had his face buried between her breasts and was whispering things she couldn't make out as he nuzzled and licked her skin just above the edge of the sheer fabric.

"Aww, come on," Evan said, looking up at her. His eyes gleamed with near desperation in the faint moonlight as he shifted so he could kiss her full on the lips. His body was fairly vibrating as he held her close, squashing her breasts against his bare chest.

"You know how much I love you, don't you?"

"Yeah, it's not that—"

Brandy stopped talking because she didn't now what else to say. All the while, Evan kept nibbling at her neck and shoulder as she looked around to the darkened windows of the house. The night air was mild, but the ground was cool and damp. The chill that ran up her back made her nipples stiffen. It was well past midnight, and she had sneaked out of the house to meet Evan only after she was positive that her mother and brother were asleep. Now she was thinking that, if she had known Evan was going to try to push her so far, she probably wouldn't have met him. It wasn't that she didn't like the feelings his touch stirred in her.

Far from it!

She liked it a lot. But she also knew better than to go too far. Maybe it wasn't such a bad thing that her mother had grounded her for the week, she thought. If she had stayed in the house tonight and told Evan that she couldn't see him, none of this would be happening. She would have had more time to think things through.

Evan was so intent on feeling her up that he seemed absolutely unaware of how she was reacting. He shifted around and gripped her waist tightly with both hands, then moved his hands up her sides, trying to slide them underneath her bra.

Brandy grunted and twisted away from him again, but with his weight pressing her down into the grass, there wasn't much she could do. She made sure to keep her knees clamped together, no matter how much Evan tried to wedge them apart with his knees.

"I . . . I don't want to be doing this, Evan . . . Not now," she whispered. "Stop it!"

She could hear the high whine in her voice and hoped that he got the message that he was scaring her.

"Come on . . . Come on, Brandy," he whispered heatedly, his voice thick and low as he worked all the harder to get her bra off. He finally succeeded in flipping the bottom edge up, and Brandy felt her breasts fall free. Without any hesitation, Evan's hands were all over her again as he lowered his head. Tears filled her eyes, and a burning pain nearly choked her as he begin kissing and sucking her nipples, first one, then the other.

The conflict of desire and fear was too much to take. A small whimper escaped her. Clenching her fists tightly at her sides, she narrowed her eyes and stared up at the sprinkling of stars overhead until they blurred into a hazy, gray smear.

This is as far as I'm going to let him go, she insisted to herself; but even as she allowed him this first, small victory, she regretted it.

Why was it, she wondered, feeling a great sadness swell up inside her, that all boys—even the nice ones, like Evan— seemed to have one thing and *only* one thing on their minds?

Why couldn't he understand that she just wasn't ready to do stuff like this, that she didn't *have* to do stuff like this to prove that she loved him?

She was sure that she loved him, but over the last couple of years, there had been other boys that Brandy had thought she loved—Jeff especially, and she had found that, as soon as they got what they wanted from her, they started to lose interest.

It didn't make sense.

It was almost as if they were looking for a girl who would put out for them, but as soon as she did that, they'd start treating her like she was cheap.

Well, Brandy thought, her resolve stiffening, *she wasn't just a whore, cheap or otherwise!*

She liked Evan, and she wanted to spend as much time as

she could with him, but she didn't want to spend it *this* way! Jeff, her last boyfriend back in Bedford Heights, had told her he'd stop pushing her as long as she gave him a hand job and, just as soon as she had done that a few times, he started pushing her to suck on his penis.

Well, it wasn't going to be like that with Evan, she decided.

Evan moaned softly as he twisted from side to side, grinding his hips against her crotch. Brandy could feel the rock solid bulge of his erection, chafing against her belly. He rolled over onto one side and, taking her hand, tried to guide it down into the front of his pants, but she pushed him away violently and sat up.

"No!" she shouted and with a single, quick motion, she flipped her bra and tank top down. Her voice was loud enough to echo from the surrounding woods. She sniffed and wiped her eyes, hoping to God that he didn't see her crying.

Evan sat up quickly and lunged forward to hug her, but she pushed him away again.

"I said *no!* I don't want to do that, and I *mean* it!"

She wanted to scream but held herself back.

"Come on, Bran," Evan said, his voice low and urgent. "You know I don't want to do anything you don't want to do, but I . . . I thought you loved me."

Tears stung her eyes. She sniffed loudly and wiped her face again with the flats of her hands. Evan tried once again to hug her, but she kept him at bay, resisting the sudden urge to haul off and slap him across the face.

"I'm not sure what you think of me," she said, her throat catching with emotion, "but I've heard the way some of your friends talk about me—"

She wanted to say more but her voice cut off with a painful hitch, and she couldn't speak. The night was a dark, shimmering blur all around her.

"It's not like that," Evan said after an awkward moment of silence filled only by the sounds of insects in the grass. He touched her shoulder, caressing it lightly but not making any move to hug her.

"Honest, it isn't."

"Yeah . . . well, I just want you to know one thing." Brandy was so filled with emotion she still could hardly speak. She wondered if she could make sense out of the thoughts that careened through her mind. "I'm not that kind of girl, okay? Just because your friends—and maybe even you—joke about me being from the city and all, that doesn't mean I'm easy. That's not how it is."

"I know, I know," Evan whispered.

He moved his hand up and caressed her cheek, smearing her tears. This time when he shifted closer to her, she let him put his arm around her shoulder and pull her close. The torment of conflicting emotions was too much to bear. She let her breath out in a long, trembling sob as she leaned forward and pressed her face against his bare chest. His skin was slick with sweat. She inhaled deeply, enjoying the heady mixture of scents— cologne and body sweat. It was intoxicating, and as she considered just how much she liked Evan and wanted him to like her, she started thinking that maybe she should do it.

Maybe she should let him go all the way.

Tonight.

What harm would there be?

She took another deep breath and felt a powerful shudder run through her belly.

She wanted to do it.

Right now, she wanted to pull his pants down and touch him, maybe even take him in her mouth the way Jeff had wanted her to. She had seen people do it in the porno movie she and her friend Lisa had swiped from Lisa's older brother last summer.

But she couldn't.

She knew she wasn't ready for it.

Not now . . . She didn't want it to be that way with Evan.

"I . . . I like you . . . I mean a *lot*," she whispered. "But I . . . I don't want to . . . you know . . . *do* it."

"Never?" Evan asked with an edge in his voice.

"No, not never," Brandy said. "Just not now . . . not for a while."

"I understand," Evan said, and this time he sounded like

he really meant it. "Look, I'm sorry if I—you know, if I kind of lost control there." He snickered and shifted to adjust his pants. "You know how guys can get."

Brandy placed her forefinger across his lips to hush him. After a moment, she took her hand away and kissed him full on the mouth, her tongue playing between his lips and teeth, teasing. It didn't take long for Evan to respond. He held her close, prolonging the kiss and running his hands up and down her back.

When the kiss finally broke off, Brandy pulled back and then stood up. She straightened out her clothes as she glanced up at the house again.

"I'd better get in before my Mom catches us out here," she said, thinking she caught a hint of motion in one of the upstairs windows.

Evan grunted, and all Brandy could hear in that grunt was the depth of his disappointment that she had stopped him. She was a virgin, but she couldn't help but wonder if Evan had done it with anyone else before. She wanted to ask, but she wasn't sure she would still feel the same about him if she knew he had.

And what exactly did he mean by that remark that she knew how guys could be?

She decided that, for now, anyway, not knowing was best. Ending their time together with a good-night kiss and hug was the right thing to do.

"See you tomorrow at school, 'kay?" she whispered, bending down to give him a quick kiss on the cheek.

Before Evan could say or do anything, she turned and ran up to the porch. She glanced back at him as she eased the door open. He was still sitting on the lawn, his bare chest glowing like bone in the pale, blue moonlight.

"Love yah," she called out in a stage whisper.

He waved to her, but she didn't hear if he said anything as she went back inside and closed and locked the door. She hurried upstairs, surprised that she hadn't gotten caught. As she undressed for bed, she ran her hands over her breasts, still confused by how Evan's hands, grabbing and caressing her, had made her feel. She wanted to think that it had been thrilling and exciting, and in a lot of ways it was, but mostly it had scared her. She knew that going too far could cause problems she wasn't ready to face.

There were a couple of things she was sure of: She didn't like the idea of Evan thinking she was *that* kind of girl, and she sure as heck wasn't going to be forced into doing anything to prove how much she liked him!

"So what gives?"

"Huh?"

Evan had his locker door open and was stuffing the books he didn't need for homework tonight onto the top shelf.

"Did you fuck things up with Brandy already, or what?"

Evan felt his face flush. He slammed his locker shut and turned to face his friend, Jeff Stuart, scowling as he looked him squarely in the eyes.

"What do you mean by that?" Evan asked through clenched teeth.

Jeff instantly reacted to the danger he saw in Evan's stance. Raising both hands defensively, he took a quick step back and said, "Whoa! Easy there, pard'ner. I didn't mean nothing."

"Yeah, I'll bet you didn't," Evan said.

He wasn't going to let this slide, so he took a threatening step forward and flexed his hands, getting ready to grab Jeff by the shirt front the instant he said or did anything else wrong.

"Seriously. I mean it," Evan said, his voice a low rolling growl that seemed to come from somewhere deep in his belly. "What did you mean by that?"

"Not a fuckin' thing," Jeff said in a high, trembling voice. "It's just—" He shrugged, looking sheepish. "I saw you and Brandy together at lunch today, and it looked like there was . . . maybe a little bit of tension between you guys. That's all."

"You know," Evan said levelly, "I don't see where that's any of your goddamned business."

"I didn't say it was," Jeff replied, taking another step backwards. "I was just . . . commenting, you know?"

"Yeah? Well if I was you, I'd keep my ugly face out of other people's business. It's better for your health."

He raised a fist and, just like the other night at the dance when he thrashed Mark Haskell, could feel himself wanting to beat the shit out of Jeff.

"Good advice," Jeff said, nodding rapidly. "Look, I—uh, I've got track practice. Catch you later."

Evan folded his arms across his chest and just glared at Jeff as he turned and walked away as fast as he could without actually breaking into a run. His sneakers chirped like birds on the freshly polished linoleum.

Evan waited until Jeff was around the corner and out of sight before he relaxed his fists, but his body still felt wire-tight as he bent down and picked up his bookbag.

He had no idea why he was feeling so edgy.

It was true that he and Brandy had been a little bit distant with each other today. He hoped it wasn't because of what he had done—or *tried* to do—last night out behind her house. Since then he had realized all the more how much he really liked Brandy, and how he didn't want his own physical needs— much less his friends' gutter minds—screwing things up between them.

He felt a twinge of guilt because after she had gone back inside, he had walked off into the woods behind her house and jerked off. But that was just a natural physical need, he told himself. He couldn't help it that he was a horny teenaged boy, just as he couldn't help how being with her made him think about and want to do things with and to her.

But he had vowed *never* to do anything like that with her again if she didn't want to do.

That wasn't his style.

If his friends were going to be so crass as to suggest or even hint that he was getting laid, he'd vent some of that energy by pounding the living shit out of them!

Evan was trembling deep inside as he slung his bookbag over his shoulder and started down the hall. Brandy had told him at lunch today that she was still grounded and had to go straight home from school, so he figured he might just as well go home and get his homework done. He didn't really feel like hanging out with the guys tonight, so he'd probably watch a little TV and then maybe go to bed and jerk off again. He felt confused by a lot of things, but one thing he was sure of was that he felt things about Brandy that he had never felt about any of the other girls he had dated.

It was different with her, and this time *nothing* was going to screw things up.

Chapter 18
Play Ball

Over the next few days, Greg tried not to be too obvious as he drove past or parked out in front of Bolton Elementary and Eagle Lake High School. He found the addresses to both schools easily enough in the phone book, but it was another thing to spot either one of Angela's kids on their way to or from school.

He quickly learned that the high school let out at two fifteen, and the middle school got out at two forty-five. For three days in a row, he waited outside the high school until two-thirty, then drove over to the middle school and waited until sometime after three. In the rush of students, he never saw anyone who looked like either of Angela's kids.

It rained on Monday, so he decided to stay at the hotel that day, but on Tuesday afternoon, while he was parked out in front of the high school where several other parents were waiting in cars to pick up their kids, he saw the girl he'd seen downtown, the one who *had* to be Angela Ross' daughter. She came out the front doors of the school and got onto a bus.

Greg was relieved to see that her dip-shit boyfriend wasn't with her. He noted the number of the school bus she got onto— bus number eighteen—and waited until the red warning lights stopped flashing and it pulled away from the curb before starting his car and following it.

That first day, he followed the bus only a short distance down the street before turning off onto a side road. He didn't want the driver getting suspicious about someone following the bus all over town and figured that, over the next few days, he could wait somewhere along the bus route and follow it a little further each time until he saw where the girl got off at home.

Then he'd have to check to make sure Angela Ross and her family lived there before making his next move.

He still wasn't sure what he'd do after that, but he felt confident that he could improvise.

He finally got what he wanted on Friday afternoon when bus number eighteen turned onto a road called Taylor Hill Road. The bus made fewer stops this far from the center of town. The progress was excruciatingly slow, but Greg didn't pass the few times the bus driver slowed down and signalled to him that it was safe to go by. He wanted to wait for another stop or two before giving up for the week. If he didn't get what he wanted today, then he'd just have to pick up again on Monday.

The brakes on the bus squealed loudly as the bus slowed to a stop in front of a yellow house with green trim. The warning lights started flashing yellow, then changed to red once the bus had come to a complete stop, and the side door flapped opened.

Someone—a girl—stepped out.

Greg's heart gave a quick, hard thump in his chest when he saw that it was the one he was looking for. She checked the traffic both ways, looking straight at Greg's car for a moment, then started across the street. The bookbag she had slung over her right shoulder bounced heavily up and down as she dashed down the curved driveway to a nice-looking house.

The bus shifted into gear and then lurched forward with a blast of thick exhaust. Greg knew that he should drive off, but he took a few seconds to study the house.

It looked so perfect, with a low stone wall out front and well-tended gardens along the front of the house and by the stone wall. Greg could easily imagine Angela Ross choosing a house like this. It had more yard that her previous home, but other than that, it wouldn't have looked at all out of place in Bedford Heights.

"Bingo!" Greg whispered, cackling with joy as he drummed his hands on the steering wheel hard enough to make it vibrate.

Looking up the road, he watched as the school bus rounded the distant corner and then disappeared from sight. He was grinning widely as he shifted into gear and drove away. Once he was around the corner and out of sight from the house, he did a quick U-turn and drove slowly past the house again. He wanted to stop and check the place out carefully but didn't dare to now, in case someone happened to notice him.

He wasn't very far down the street when he saw two kids riding their bikes in the gravel strip along the edge of the road. Greg couldn't be sure with just a glance, but he thought one of them looked like the same boy he had seen at John Ross's funeral last spring.

"What the hell?" he muttered, as he watched the boys take a turn onto a side road and turned to follow them.

The boys sped down the street that Greg knew led to the elementary school. Judging by the baseball gloves and bat they were carrying, he guessed they going to play ball. Pulling over to the side of the road, he waited until they were out of sight, then continued to the school. When he pulled into the most-deserted parking lot, he made sure to park far enough away from the playing fields so no one would notice him or his car and connect it with anything—

. . . if anything happened . . .

Angie wasn't sure whether or not JJ heard her yell to him to be home before dark. For the last several nights—ever since he got off his grounding—he hadn't been home on time for supper. That bothered her more than it used to, and she knew exactly why. Since John had died, it seemed much more important to her to make sure the rest of the family was home for supper. She considered another day or two of grounding to drive home the importance of on time but decided not to deny his fun on such a beautiful spring afternoon.

As she stood by the front door and looked down the street where the boys had taken off on their bikes, she debated whether or not she should drive over to the school to remind him to be home before dark.

She had just stepped back inside the house and was closing the door when she noticed a car coming up the road. It caught her attention immediately simply because it was moving so much slower than most cars did on the road. Sunlight glinted off the windshield, making it impossible for her to see who was driving, but she was filled with a sudden unaccountable feeling of discomfort.

She saw the car's brake lights flicker once, and thought that maybe the driver was lost and looking for someone to ask directions; but her sense of alarm increased, and she decided not to let whoever this was know that she was watching.

"What the hell?" she muttered as she closed the door to a narrow slit and peered out to track the car.

"Did you say something?" Brandy called out from the kitchen where she saw working on her homework at the kitchen table.

"Uh . . . no. Nothing," Angie called back. She waited a few seconds until the car was out of sight, then asked, "What kind of car does Evan drive?"

"I'm not sure," Brandy replied. "It's a dark blue . . . something or other. Some kind of foreign car. Toyota, maybe."

"Umm."

"Why'd you want to know?"

Angie could hear the expectant edge in her daughter's voice and knew that Brandy was probably wondering—hoping— that Evan had stopped by the house to see her while she was grounded.

"Oh . . . no reason," Angie replied. She didn't know much about cars, but this one definitely was a large American-made car—a Buick or Pontiac, and it was white, not dark blue.

But why had she noticed it in the first place? she wondered.

What had there been about it—besides the fact that it was moving too slow for the road—that would draw her attention?

She wished she had caught a glimpse of the driver. Now she was more convinced than ever that she should drive over to the school to check on the boys. Just because they lived in Maine didn't mean they were perfectly safe. There were wackos in Maine just as well as there were wackos in New York City. It was just that, percentage-wise, there were *more* wackos in New York City than anywhere else, and they seemed to get the media attention.

As she walked back into the kitchen to check on the rolls she was baking for supper, she told herself to remind both kids—once again—that they had to be careful around town, especially because they were new here and didn't know everybody.

She knew she was probably just being over-protective, but the uneasy feeling wouldn't go away.

All of the major unpacking from the move was long since done, and they were settling into the house nicely. Over the last several days, the weather had been nice so she had worked outside on the gardens and lawn ... mostly to keep herself occupied, she realized. Now that the yard work was under control and the house didn't really need any painting or remodeling inside or out and she wouldn't start teaching until next September, she figured she had time on her hands ... time enough to worry. Maybe she should find something else to keep herself occupied so she wouldn't have time to worry.

The rolls were browning up fine, so while she waited for the timer to go off, she walked back to the front door and made sure that it was locked.

Just to be on the safe side, she told herself.

She jumped when the timer bell suddenly chimed, and Brandy called out, "They're done."

Greg chuckled to himself as he got out of the car and pocketed the car keys. Grunting softly, he reached under the car seat and grabbed the wooden baseball bat. Squinting into the sun, he propped the bat on his shoulder like a rifle and started out across the parking lot toward the ball field.

Long before he could see them, he heard the boys shouting to each other. They kept calling the name "Blackie," and as Greg got a little closer, he heard a dog barking excitedly.

He instantly froze.

He didn't like dogs. They always meant trouble, as far as he was concerned.

He hadn't noticed a dog running along with the boys when they left the house, and he wondered if the dog was with them or with someone else. Either way, he'd have to check things out a little more carefully before he tried to do anything.

He kept walking until the boys came into view. They were small, indistinct figures against the dark backdrop of the woods that backed the ball field. Greg didn't see the dog he'd heard barking, but that didn't mean he wasn't around.

Greg noticed the woods that surrounded the perimeter of the field on three sides. A dense undergrowth grew close to the backstop by home plate where the boys had left their bikes. A well-trodden path led off into the woods, so Greg decided it would be best if he remained out of sight until he decided what he was going to do. Using the baseball bat to beat the brush aside, he entered the woods.

The sun was getting low in the sky, but Greg knew it wouldn't be dark for another hour or so. As soon as he stepped into the dense shadows of the trees, the air temperature seemed to drop by several degrees. He couldn't help but shiver as he looked around.

He didn't like the way the trees seemed to press in on him. Even with fresh, green leaves on them, the branches looked like grasping hands, reaching out for him. He felt trapped, confined, and couldn't stop thinking about the dangers that might be lurking close by without him even knowing they were there until it was too late. The city was so much less threatening than the woods, he thought. At least in the city you generally could *see* trouble coming your way long before it actually got there. The woods held too many surprises.

Greg made his way slowly along the winding path. Narrow

paths branched off from the main one into the woods, but he stuck to the one that circled around behind the backstop. He wanted to get a good look at the boys and make sure, if he could, that one of them was Angela's son before he did anything.

With every few steps, though, Greg stopped short and looked around, convinced that he had heard something rustling behind him or had caught a glimpse of something—or someone— moving off to one side or the other. In the eerie silence, the dense shadows beneath the underbrush shifted like curling smoke. The wind hissed high overhead, making the branches sway with low, creaking sounds that reminded him of an old door, swinging back and forth on rusted hinges.

The nervous tension in the pit of his stomach got steadily tighter. Greg wondered why there weren't any birds or animals around. It was almost as though they had all been scared off by something.

You are going to kill him, aren't you?

The voice spoke so clear and loud inside his head that Greg was convinced he had heard it, not thought it. He quickly looked around, expecting to see someone standing nearby, but all he saw were shifting shadows beneath the trees. He smiled tightly and whispered softly. "You bet your ass I'm gonna kill him!"

Through the screen of foliage, he could hear the boys whooping it up and shouting to each other as they played. Every now and then he caught a glimpse of one or both of them. One of them was pitching to the other one, who stood at home plate, batting with an aluminum bat.

Greg hefted his own wooden bat and squeezed the narrow grip, enjoying the surge of power it gave him.

So go ahead! Use it to bash his fucking brains out, the voice inside Greg's head whispered.

He looked around carefully but didn't see any sign of the dog he was sure he had heard barking before. He wondered if the sound could have carried across the field from someplace else, or if the dog had run off.

Bending low, Greg crept closer to the edge of the ball field, convinced that he had seen the boy at bat before, at John Ross' funeral. He certainly had the same build and hair color as Angela Ross's son. It *had* to be him!

The fact that Angela's son had a friend with him didn't bother Greg any. Whoever he was, it was just that kid's bad luck that he was here today. Greg considered that it might be fun to nab both kids right now and kill them.

Why not?

What better way to get back at Angela Ross than to kill her son as well as her husband?

Maybe he'd torture both boys before killing them, make their pain linger for awhile before finally releasing them.

The sun was setting, and shadows gradually lengthened across the field, but Greg knew that he wouldn't be able to get out onto the field without either of the boys seeing him long before he got close enough to them. If the boys planned to stay here until it was dark, he might be able to get them then. He'd just have to wait.

Sighing with frustration, he hunkered down in the dense weeds that lined the edge of the field and watched the boys play. It had been a long time since he had decided that he *had* to kill Angela Ross. The last several weeks of trying to find her had been frustrating as all hell, and the last few days in Maine had filled him with a gnawing anxiety. After not doing *anything* for so long, he knew that he was going to have to do *something* soon!

So go get them now, whispered a voice, so close and real sounding that Greg was positive someone was standing nearby, talking to him. Or maybe someone—somehow—was reading his mind and sending him their thoughts.

"I will . . . I will," Greg whispered as he crouched in the bushes. He couldn't stop squeezing and rubbing the grip of the baseball bat as he watched the boys take turns pitching and hitting. Every now and then, one or both of them would stop and look around—sometimes looking directly at where Greg was hiding—and call out for "Blackie." Greg flattened himself on the ground, hoping that they hadn't seen him.

The ground was rough and cool in the shadows, and Greg began to think that it was ridiculous to lurk in the woods like

this. If that was John Ross' son, then he should *do* something—
now, like the voice inside his head was telling him.

Shifting up into a crouch, he scanned the field, looking to
see if anyone else was around. There didn't seem to be, but he
was positive that he wouldn't be able to get very close to either
of the boys. They'd see him coming and run off if he scared
them.

And then what would they do?

They'd tell their parents, and maybe their parents would tell
police, and before he knew it, all of his planning and trouble
would end in failure.

Greg wouldn't stand for that.

He finally decided that he'd have to wait until he saw a better
opportunity, one that was much more likely to succeed. He got
up from the ground, brushed himself off, and was just about
to turn to go back to his car when a loud, thrashing sound in
the brush behind him drew his attention.

He spun around quickly and dropped into a defensive crouch
as a huge black Labrador came bounding out of the underbrush,
heading straight for him.

The dog was barking wildly. The sound echoed from the
surrounding woods.

"What the fuck!" Greg shouted as he raised an arm to shield
himself, forgetting for a moment that he was holding a baseball
bat.

The dog came straight at him, its mouth hanging wide open,
exposing a set of wicked-looking teeth. Greg tensed and drew
the bat back, getting ready to strike, but before he could, the
dog drew to a sudden halt in front of him and started prancing
about, looking like all he wanted to do was play. All the while,
he kept barking so loudly it hurt Greg's ears.

"Go on! Get the fuck out of here!" Greg shouted, glancing
nervously over at the boys while threatening the dog with his
bat. They had seen what was going on and were walking toward
him.

"Hey, mister!"

"Cut it out, Blackie!"

"He won't hurt you!"

The boys' voices, high and piercing, filled the air. Greg was angry at himself for letting them catch him like this, but there was nothing he could do about it now.

"Call your damned dog off," he shouted.

The dog had stopped leaping about, but Greg didn't dare turn away from him. He held the baseball bat poised, ready to defend himself if he had to as he glanced over at the boys. Unable to disguise the slight tremor in his voice, he said, "Who's mutt is this?"

"Not ours," one of the boys said. Greg didn't see which one it was as he continued to eye the black Lab, who was now rolling around on the ground, thrashing the grass and digging up dirt with his wide, flat paws. He looked harmless enough, but Greg knew that it was just like dogs to act all playful until your back was turned, and then they'd go for you.

"What're you doing out here?" one of the boys—the one with freckles across his face—asked, eying Greg as suspiciously as Greg was eying the dog.

"I came out to see if anyone wanted to play a little ball," Greg said, thinking quickly.

"You coaching one of the little league teams?" the boy who looked like Angela Ross's son asked.

Greg was positive, now, that's who he was. He had the same dark hair, the same facial features, and the same piercing brown eyes as his mother had that night in the car outside *Le Bistro*. He thought he could also see a lingering trace of fear in this boy's eyes.

"No, but I was thinking about it," Greg replied, nodding.

"I've never seen you around town before," the other boy said, looking at Greg with obvious mistrust.

"Yeah, I just moved up here from Florida," Greg replied, squinting as he looked past the boys to the ball field. "Couldn't stand the summers down there. Too humid for my taste."

He knew that, the more he talked, the deeper he got into it, so he cautioned himself to be careful not to say any lies that might trip him up later. Both of these kids looked pretty sharp.

"What are your names?" Greg asked, turning back to the boys and smiling as friendly as could be. "My name's Sam."

"Hey, that's my name, too," one of the boys said. "My friends all call me Sammy."

"Well, I'm pleased to meet you, Sammy," Greg said, sticking out his hand so they could shake. This coincidence of names seemed to satisfy the boy at least enough so he lowered his guard a bit. Greg turned to the other boy and said, "And your name is—"

"John . . . John Ross," the boy said softly. "Everyone calls me JJ for short."

"JJ," Greg echoed, nodding.

"It stands for John Junior," JJ said, lowering his eyes and looking down at the ground.

"Oh, so your dad's name is John, too?" Greg tried to keep the excited edge out of his voice, but he could hardly contain himself. He hoped his expression didn't betray how thrilled he was to hear this.

Fucking-a! he thought, wanting to let out a wild whoop. *I've got him!*

"Yeah, but my dad . . . died."

"Sorry to hear that," Greg said, fighting hard to keep from laughing out loud. He scanned the field but still didn't see anyone else who might have noticed him talking to the boys.

"Well, Sammy and JJ . . . What do you say we pop a few?"

Sammy and JJ looked at each other, then shrugged.

"Why not?" Sammy said after a moment.

"I don't mind pitching if one of you wants to bat while the other one fields," Greg said.

"You should see Blackie fetch the ball," JJ said, suddenly more animated than he had been. "He catches it and brings it right back to you."

"Long as you don't mind a little dog drool," Sammy added, wrinkling his nose with mild disgust.

"You don't say," Greg said, nodding and stroking his chin as he looked at the Labrador who was now sitting still and looking straight at him. "That's some smart dog you got there."

At that moment, the dog didn't look at all intelligent. His mouth was hanging open, and a foamy gush of droll was dripping onto the ground at his paws. He had that faraway, stupid

look in his eyes that all dogs seem to get, like he was just
waiting for an idea what to do next.

"Well, let's see what you boys can do." Greg hefted his
bat and walked out onto the field. "You never know. You
might end up on my team if I decide to coach."

For a moment, the boys held back, but then they followed
Greg over to the diamond. Blackie seemed content to stay
where he was, panting in the shade, but he perked up and came
running as soon as JJ clapped his hands and whistled for him.

"Is this your dog, JJ?" Greg asked, warily watching Blackie
trot out onto the field. Now that he was moving, the dog seemed
full of intelligence and energy, and much bigger.

JJ lowered his eyes and shook his head. "Naw. My mom
promised me I could get a dog, but she's being kind of a
butthead about it."

"I see," Greg replied, nodding and trying hard to repress a
smile. "Well, moms can be like that from time to time. I know
my mom certainly was."

All Greg could think was that maybe today, if not today,
then sometime soon, he was going to do *something* to JJ just
to make his "butthead" mother suffer. In fact, if things went
the way he hoped, this boy, his older sister, *and* his mother
were *all* going to suffer in ways they couldn't begin to imagine.
He'd left witnesses before—both the night he robbed that store
on Forty-Seventh Street and the night he shot and killed John
Ross. He wasn't about to leave *any* loose ends again!

So it was just a matter of time—time and patience—before
he decided when and how to strike.

"So," Greg said, smiling as he strolled over to the pitcher's
mound. "JJ, why don't you bat first? Here. Lemme borrow
your glove. And Sammy, you take first base."

JJ reluctantly handed him his glove, then walked over to
home plate. As he was bending down to pick up the aluminum
bat from the grass, Greg whistled and, waving his hands, said,
"No, use my bat—the wooden one. Those metal bats are for
pussies."

JJ frowned as he walked back and took the bat from Greg.

"It's kinda heavy," he said as he stepped back and took a few practice cuts in the air with it.

"You'll get used to it," Greg said. "Believe me, I know a thing or two about baseball bats. You know, the major leagues won't let you use a metal bat."

JJ didn't look all that convinced as he walked back to home plate, scowling as he dug his feet into the dirt.

Greg punched the glove a few times, then rotated his pitching arm to loosen it up before he wound up and threw. His first pitch cut right across the plate. JJ grunted as he swung at it, but he struggled to bring the heavier bat around and missed it. The ball hit the ground behind him with a *thud* and rolled into the grass and weeds that grew at the edge of the backstop.

"Take a few more practice swings. You'll get used to it," Greg called out after JJ retrieved the ball and tossed it back to him. JJ shook his head, looking disgusted at himself for missing.

"I don't know if I like this," he said. "The handle's a lot thinner than I'm used to."

For the next few pitches, Greg tossed easy ones right across the plate, but JJ missed all but one of them. Sometimes he swung so hard he lost his footing and almost fell as he came around in a complete circle. Watching from the first base, Sammy started getting impatient and razzed JJ every time he missed.

"Screw you! You try it," JJ finally shouted in frustration. His face flushed with anger, he tossed the bat hard onto the ground.

"Hey! Watch it with my bat!" Greg yelled. He smiled with satisfaction when he saw JJ cringe and look back at him.

"Sorry," JJ said sheepishly.

Sammy gave his glove to Greg, and Greg tossed JJ's glove to him as the boys traded places.

On the first pitch, Sammy connected and sent the ball flying high over Greg's head.

"Whoa! Nice pop," Greg said, turning to watch the ball fly.

"Go get it, boy!" JJ yelled, and in a flash, Blackie, who had been lying down in the fringe of woods, leaped to his feet and took off. His collar and tags jingled merrily as he bounded across the field and scooped up the ball with a quick snap of his jaws.

"I ain't gonna have to fight him for it, am I?" Greg asked, nervously watching the dog as he trotted over to him.

"Just stand still and snap your fingers. He'll drop it right at your feet," JJ said, and that's exactly what Blackie did.

Greg smiled tightly as he picked up the ball, being careful to shake off the dog drool. For the next ten minutes or so, he pitched, and Sammy belted flies. Greg stopped as many as he could get to without having to run too hard and threw them to JJ on first base.

Greg had to admit that this was kind of fun, but the longer they played, the more his frustration grew. He didn't bust his ass driving all the way to Maine just to play baseball with a couple of kids. He had things to tend to, and crap like this was getting him nowhere.

Once JJ got back up to bat again, this time using the metal bat, Greg got an idea. He delivered a few easy pitches, many of which JJ blasted into the outfield for Blackie to retrieve. As Greg watched JJ dig in his heels and set himself at the plate ready for another, he wound up and purposely threw a fast ball straight at him.

The boy saw it coming, but not soon enough. He let out a short cry as he spun around and dropped to the ground. The ball caught him squarely between the shoulders.

"Aww, Jesus!" Greg shouted the instant he saw JJ go down. Blackie let out a sharp bark and came running. He was the first one to get to JJ, who was lying on the ground, rolling back and forth while moaning softly. The dog started licking JJ's face as Greg and Sammy leaned over him. Greg could see that the boy was hurt bad and trying not to cry, but tears filled his eyes.

"Jesus, I'm really sorry 'bout that," Greg said as he knelt down and rubbed JJ between the shoulders. "That ball kinda got away from me. Probably 'cause it's all wet from the dog's mouth."

Unable to speak, JJ looked up at him with a glazed expression of pain in his eyes. Greg was happy to see that the boy was hurt so badly, but he tried not to let it show.

This is just the beginning, kid-o, he told himself, remembering the voice he'd heard earlier, urging him to kill both boys.

"Can you get up?" Sammy asked, looking really worried as he glanced back and forth between Greg and JJ.

JJ tried to say something, but the only sound he could make was a low, watery gasp.

"Knocked the wind right out of you, huh?" Greg said. "Just stay still and try to relax. You'll be okay in a minute."

JJ winced and nodded, then lay on his side on the ground. Tears flowed from his eyes and slid down his face to his ear, which was pressed into the dirt. Whenever he tried to take a deep breath, his throat made a funny rattling sound.

"Jeeze, kid. I . . . I don't know what to say," Greg said, glancing at Sammy. "I've been hit like that once or twice when I was a kid. I know how it feels. You're lucky you didn't get it in the cookies."

"I'll . . . be . . . all right," JJ said, gasping.

After another moment or two, JJ took a deep breath and shifted around to sit up. He still didn't have the strength to stand, but he forced a smile and wiped his tears with both hands. He winced when he shifted his shoulders from side to side, trying to loosen up.

"Man, that *kills!"* he said hoarsely.

"Maybe I should give you a ride home so I can explain to your mom what happened, huh?" Greg said, hoping he was hiding his gathering excitement.

"Naw. We got our bikes," Sammy said.

Greg looked at him and could see that the caution was back in Sammy's eyes. He had obviously had it drilled into him not to take rides from strangers, no matter how nice they might seem.

"Maybe you could lock 'em up and come back for 'em later," Greg suggested. "I just don't want you going home hurt like this and getting your mom all pissed off at me."

"I'm . . . okay," JJ gasped, his voice sounding tighter than normal. "Once I catch my breath, I'll be all right."

"You sure?" Greg asked, hoping that wasn't the case. He desperately wished that there was some way he could lure both boys into his car, but he knew he'd only make Sammy more cautious if he pushed the issue too hard.

"It's getting late," Sammy said, glancing up at the darkening sky. "We should probably be getting on back, anyway."

Greg wanted to ask once more if he could give them a ride, but he decided to let it drop as he helped JJ to his feet. JJ looked unsteady, but he and Sammy walked over to the backstop where they had left their bikes.

"Thanks for letting me use your glove," Greg called out, waving as they started walking away. "And . . . sorry about hitting you."

"It's okay," JJ called back, smiling thinly.

Greg watched the boys walk their bikes across the field, telling himself that—for now, at least—he would have to be content to leave things as they were. No need raising any unnecessary suspicions. Beside, he should be happy because he was sure now that, against the odds, he had found them! If anything, JJ might even consider him a friend. If he could use that to gain the confidence of the whole family, this might work out even better than he could have planned.

Greg realized that he still had JJ's glove on his left hand. He didn't even know he'd kept it and now had no idea what to do about it. For a long time after the boys were out of sight, he just stood there beside home plate and stared out across the field.

He wasn't sure what to do next.

He couldn't stop thinking that maybe it hadn't been such a good idea to let JJ and his friend see him. Then again, it wasn't like he'd had a choice. If that damned black dog hadn't drawn attention to him, they would never have known he was there today.

Scowling angrily, Greg looked around for the black Lab but didn't see him. By now the sun was well below the trees, and a thick wall of gray shadows was reaching like a stain across the ball field.

Finally, Greg turned to walk back to his car, carrying JJ's

glove in one hand and the wooden bat in the other. Once he was past second base, he wheeled around and threw the glove back toward home plate, watching as it hit the ground and skidded in the dirt, raising a small cloud of dust before finally coming to a stop in the weeds by the backstop.

Before Greg turned and continued on his way, the black dog suddenly burst from out of the brush and, barking wildly, ran over to the glove and scooped it up in his mouth. Greg was filled with a slow-burning anger as he watched the dog adjust the glove so it was securely in his mouth, and then trot over to him.

The closer the dog got, the more Greg's anger rose. He tightened his grip on the bat and eyed the dog narrowly.

"What a clever little piece of shit you are," he said using a low, mellow voice. He found it amusing that the dog responded to the pleasant tone of his voice and not to what he said.

"Can't you see that I don't want that fucking thing, you fucking idiot?"

The dog started wagging his tail when he dropped the glove at Greg's feet. Saliva dripped from his mouth as he looked up as though expecting a reward.

"You really are a complete numb shit, aren't you?" Greg said, still using a pleasant, sing-song voice. "Yes, you are."

He reached down and scruffed the dog's neck, making his tags jingle. The rage burning inside him was getting stronger by the second as he gazed into the dog's liquid brown eyes.

If it wasn't for this idiot dog, he thought, *those boys never would have seen me!*

"Here you go, you numb shit," Greg said. He bent down, pick up the glove, and tossed it as far as he could toward the woods.

With a single, sharp bark, the dog wheeled around, its paws churning up huge clots of grass, and took off after it. He scooped up the glove and carried it back to Greg, but before he dropped it, Greg, who maintained a painfully tight grip on the baseball bat, brought the bat around fast and hard, hitting the dog squarely on the top of the head.

The dog let out a short, pained yelp and dropped to the ground. Its legs twitched for a moment as though it was still chasing after something and then lay still.

"Good doggie," Greg whispered. "Lie down. Play dead!"

Thick red blood seeped from the dog's nose and mouth, staining the black fur around its muzzle and turning the drool around its mouth to a bright pink. Both of the dog's eyes were bugging out of their sockets, the bloodshot whites glistening wetly in the dying daylight. Its tongue was hanging out as though he were trying to lick the ground.

"Sorry 'bout that," Greg said mildly as he straightened up and inspected his bat for damage. There was a large splotch of blood just above the burned-in trademark. "But you know? It was all your fault in the first place. If you'd just kept your fucking mouth shut—"

A thought suddenly occurred to Greg. Narrowing his eyes, he leaned forward and studied the dead dog carefully.

"Was it *you?*" Greg asked with a sudden, tight tremor in his voice.

The more he thought about it, the more convinced he became.

"It *was* you, wasn't it? *You're* the one I heard in the woods, telling me to kill them!"

Greg's eyes lost focus as he took a deep, shuddering breath and looked around. The shadows in the woods seemed to condense and reach out for him.

"Jesus," Greg whispered.

The dog lay absolutely still on the ground, but Greg had the distinct impression that it was still breathing. Tightening his grip, he raised the wooden bat above his head and brought it down in a swift chopping motion, like an executioner's ax. The bat hit the dog in the side just behind its front shoulder. The impact made a satisfying loud *thump* as the animal's ribs caved in. Something dark and liquid shot from the dog's mouth.

"You *bastard!*" Greg wailed as he brought the bat down again and again on the dog. "You lousy, rotten, fucking *bastard!*"

Blood fragments flew everywhere as Greg continued to pummel the dead animal. A hazy red cloud drifted across Greg's vision as he recalled the voice he had heard. A tiny corner of his mind was telling him that it was impossible for a dog to talk, much less urge him to kill anybody, but he was past all rational thought.

It wasn't long before the dog was nothing more than a mis-shapen, black mess of fur, blood, and shattered bone, hardly recognizable as having once been a living thing, but Greg didn't stop beating on the animal until exhaustion finally overtook him. Stepping back, he let his arms drop, realizing vaguely that he was bathed with sweat. His breathing came in hot, ragged gasps. Almost the entire length of the bat was stained red and stuck with matted clots of fur.

The dog was dead, Greg knew, but the animal's bulging eyes still stared up at him, mocking him as though they could see straight into his soul.

"Fuck you, too," Greg muttered as he wiped the sweat from his eyes. He was horrified when he looked at his hands and saw that they were splattered with blood.

For a single, dizzying instant, he got confused and thought that he was back in the convenience store on Forty-Seventh Street, that this wasn't a black dog but a jerk-off foreigner store clerk who didn't even have the decency to learn English even though he was living and working in America.

Grunting savagely, Greg gave the side of the dog one last, solid whack, then turned and walked back to his car without a backward glance. His insides were shaking terribly when he started up the car and drove away. For a single moment, he wondered if it was a dog he had just beaten to a pulp or JJ Ross.

His mind gradually cleared as he drove, and he realized that—as much as he would have liked it—it hadn't been the boy, but as he got onto Route 202, heading to Augusta, he vowed that very soon he *would* do the same thing—and worse!—to Angela and both of her kids!

"What do you mean? What man?" Angie asked, unable to keep the edge out of her voice.

As soon as JJ started telling her about what had happened at the baseball field, her internal alarm had gone off. She didn't like the sound of this one bit.

"I don't know who he is," JJ said, shaking his head. "Some guy named Sam."

"Sam . . . Sam *what?*"

JJ's face was pinched with pain as he shrugged. It was obvious his back still hurt.

"Either he didn't tell us his last name, or else I forgot it," JJ said. "He'd seemed all right. He said he might be one of the little league coaches this year."

"Is that so?" Angie said, stroking her chin. "Well, you listen to me, young man. I don't want you hanging around out there talking to just *anybody* who shows up, do you understand?"

JJ's scowl deepened as he shook his head.

"I know, Mom . . . Sheesh!"

"Sheesh, nothing! I mean it" Angie wagged her finger at him. "You can't just assume that everyone you meet around here is going to be friendly. How do you know this guy wasn't really trying to hurt you when he threw that bean ball?"

"It was an accident," JJ replied. "He's a little league coach, for crying out loud."

"You said he *might* be a coach," Angie snapped. "You don't know who he is. And I'm not sure I like the idea of grown men just showing up at the baseball field, looking for kids to play ball." She gnawed at her lower lip and frowned as she shook her head. "It doesn't seem right. Did Sammy know who he was?"

"The guy said he was new in town, that he just moved here from—uh, Florida, I think he said. Oh, damn!"

JJ's eyes widened, and he suddenly slapped his hands together.

"What?" Angie asked.

"My glove. I let that guy borrow my glove, and I never got it back from him." He glanced past his mother to the living room window. "It's still not dark. I gotta go out there and see if he left it."

"Oh, no you're not," Angie said, grabbing him by the shoulder before he could move. "You're not going anywhere."

"Dad gave me that glove," JJ said.

As soon as he said it, Angie saw the hurt in his eyes.

"I don't want you going over there alone, after dark," she said.

"Are you afraid the ghost of Frank Sheldon might get me?" JJ asked.

"Who?" Angie asked.

"Come on, Mom," JJ said as he pulled away from her. "God, you're treating me like I'm a baby or something."

"No I'm not. I just want to make sure it's safe for you and Sammy to be out there. That's all."

"It's safe," JJ said as he turned and started for the door. "Look, I'll get Sammy. We can ride our bikes over before it's all the way dark."

"You'll do no such thing," Angie said harshly. "Go get in the car. I'll be right out."

JJ started to protest but then caught himself and went outside while Angie hurried out to the kitchen to grab her car keys and purse. Brandy was still doing her homework at the kitchen table. The smell of fresh-baked rolls filled the room, but Angie was too worked up to enjoy the aroma. She almost said something to Brandy about not answering the phone or door while she was gone but quickly decided that would be overreacting.

"We'll be right back," she said as she hurried down the hallway and out the front door, making sure to lock the door behind her.

She didn't know why what JJ had told her filled her with such a sense of alarm, but after everything else they had been through over the last several months, she certainly wasn't going to ignore it.

JJ had run ahead of his mother, so he was the first to see the distorted lump lying on the ground just past second base. For the longest time, even when he was standing close to it, he wasn't sure what it was. Daylight was fading fast, and he had no reason to believe that this could possibly be Blackie. When he looked closely and saw the collar and the dog's tags, a fiery jolt shot through him, and he realized what he was looking at.

"Mom . . . ?" he said, his voice quavering until it twisted off. He looked over his shoulder and saw that she was still halfway across the field.

"You see it?" she called out, her voice faint with distance.

JJ couldn't speak or move as he watched her come closer. He could see the rising concern on her face.

"What is it, honey?"

JJ tried to speak, but it was as if the gears in his brain had locked up. The only sound he could make was make a funny little hitching gulp in his throat as he pointed at the thing on the ground—the thing that *couldn't* be Blackie but was. In the gathering darkness, the dog looked much smaller that he had when bounding across the field. His bulging eyes and exposed teeth gleamed wickedly in the dying light.

"My God! What is that?" his mother whispered, covering her mouth with both hands.

"Who . . . who could have done this?" JJ asked in a fragile voice. A deep tremor raced through his body.

"Was this here when you and Sammy were here?" his mother asked. She was standing behind him, and he could feel her hand on his shoulder, but he didn't respond to it.

"No, Mom. That's—that's . . . Blackie." JJ was surprised that he speak at all, but when he tried to say something more, it quickly dissolved into a high, winding wail.

"This is the dog you were telling me about?"

A hot, sour taste flooded the back of JJ's throat as he nodded. He wanted to look away, afraid that he was going to throw up, but he couldn't. He had the same dizzying sensation he'd felt last winter, when he had first looked into his father's open casket and realized that his father was truly dead.

And now Blackie!

No matter how long he stared down at the dog's motionless body, he couldn't believe that something like this could have happened.

"I'll bet *he* did it," JJ said, his voice shaking horribly as tears spilled from his eyes. "That son of a bitch killed him!"

His mother grabbed hold of him and pulled him close to her, but—just like at his father's funeral—it didn't make him feel any better. Rage and grief tore through him like a hurricane.

"You mean that man who was playing ball with you and Sammy?"

He could hear the nervous edge in his mother's voice, and that scared him all the more. Her voice sounded so far away, like she was still halfway across the field. JJ looked at her and sniffed back his tears.

"Uh-huh. I *know* he did it," JJ said, "and I think you're right. I think he might have hurt me on purpose when he threw that beanball at me."

Waves of dizziness crashed over him, threatening to pull him under, but he locked his knees so he wouldn't fall down. He clenched his fists and knuckled the sides of his head as if that would stop the tidal wave of grief and fear that was sweeping over him.

"That bastard killed Blackie, Mom! He *killed* him! On purpose!"

"You don't know that for sure," his mother said, hugging him tightly. "You don't know what happened."

"He used his baseball bat on him," JJ shouted, his face flushing as his anger spiked. "He beat him to death!"

And then, as much as he'd been trying to keep the tears at bay, the floodgates opened and with a long, wavering cry, he hugged his mother, holding her as close as he could as the grief he felt for losing his dog—and his father—poured out of him.

Part 3
Waiting in the Light

"Dreams are real while they last. Can we say more of life?"

—Havelock Ellis

Chapter 19
Getting to Work

That evening, once he got back to his hotel room, took a hot shower, and drank a few cold beers, Greg realized that he might have seriously blown it by killing that dog.

Not that the dog hadn't deserved it.

Far from it!

Greg had a clear memory of hearing a voice inside his head—a voice that didn't sound at all like the voice he usually heard there—telling him that he *had* to kill both of those boys. If that dog hadn't been communicating to him telepathically, then who *had* it been?

There was no easy answer to that question, but late that night, when he was trying to get to sleep, Greg had a disturbing dream.

He woke up—or *thought* he woke up—and found himself back in the apartment in Brooklyn. The room looked exactly like his bedroom back home. The faint yellow light seeping in through the shabby window shade was the same. Even the bed, with its narrow, lumpy mattress, felt the same. When he opened his eyes and sat up to look around, he saw an indistinct figure, sitting at the foot of his bed.

"Wha—? What the fuck are you doing here?" he asked in a high-pitched voice.

"Now, now, Gregory," came the soft reply. "You shouldn't be using that language."

Greg froze, instantly recognizing his mother's voice. Somehow in the darkness, in his half-dreaming, half-waking state, it almost made sense that she would be here.

"How did—what are you doing here?" he asked, his voice shaking so terribly he wasn't sure if he had spoken out loud or just thought it.

"I've come to check up on you, Gregory," his mother said softly. Her voice echoed with a hollow, distorted sound. "I wanted to see how you were doing."

Greg's eyes widened as he stared into the darkness, trying to see his mother's face, but the most he could make out was a thick, black silhouette—the shadow of a shadow that seemed to shift from one side to the other whenever he tried to look straight at it.

"I—I don't need you to . . . to be che-checking up on me," he said. "I'm doing just fine."

"Oh, are you?" asked his mother. "Are you really? Even after what you did today?"

"What do you mean, what I *did* today?" Greg said. "I didn't do anything!"

For just an instant, he caught a glimpse of his mother's eyes, hovering in the darkness a few feet above his bed. They shined with a dull glow, like headlights seen through a dense fog. Greg couldn't help but be reminded of how that black dog's eyes had looked after he'd smashed its head with the baseball bat—bloodshot and bulging from their sockets, glistening like wet marble . . .

"I—I didn't do nothing wrong," Greg said.

He hated the way his voice kept breaking off, but a small corner of his mind was telling him that none of this was real.

How could it be?

All he had to do to end this nightmare was open his eyes and wake up.

But even as he was thinking this, he couldn't stop staring at the solid shape with dim, glowing eyes that hovered before him in the darkness.

It seemed so real!

He couldn't be sure, but the silhouette certainly *looked* like his mother. The figure had the same narrow, slouched shoulders, the same wisps of thin, white hair that floated like a halo around her face. Greg could almost imagine that she was reaching out to him with bony hands. He cringed inwardly, remembering the crinkly feeling of her paper-thin skin.

"Go away, Ma," he said, trying to inject firmness into his voice. He waved a hand in front of him as if trying to fan away a cloud of smoke. "I . . . I don't want you here! Leave me the fuck alone!"

"Now, Gregory. What did I just say about using that kind of language?"

Cold, dark terror gripped Greg. He couldn't see his mother's hands, but he was convinced that she was reaching out for him from out of the darkness.

"I didn't do nothin' to hurt you, Ma," he said, his voice rising and threatening to break again. "I didn't do *nothin'* to *anybody* that they didn't deserve."

The bedsprings creaked as a heavy weight shifted on the mattress. Greg knew that he hadn't moved and was frozen with terror as he watched the dark shape shift closer to him. He wanted to scream but didn't have enough air in his lungs to make even the tiniest sound. He whimpered softly when a cold blast of fetid breath washed over his face.

"I mean it, Ma!" he shouted. "Leave me the fuck alone!" Chills raced like a flood of ice water up his back. "Please, Ma . . . please . . ."

Tears burned his eyes as he raised his hands to shield himself when the figure suddenly loomed closer. He let out a piercing scream when the shape darted at him and in a horrifying flash, a face materialized from the darkness.

It wasn't at all what he expected.

Instead of his mother's face, he saw the horribly mangled muzzle of a huge, black dog. Its bloodshot eyes bulged out from the dark wells of their sockets, and a thick, bloody foam

Rick Hautala

was dripping in thick, looping strings from its gaping jaws. Greg almost vomited as he inhaled the rotten stench of the creature's breath.

The creature's eyes rolled from side to side as though trying to focus on him, and when they did, a jolt of blinding fear seized Greg.

He recognized the eyes!

They were his mother's eyes!

As horrible as the face those eyes were in appeared to be, he knew that he would always be able to recognize the cold, distant glare of his mother's eyes.

With another, louder shout, he pushed himself backwards so hard his head slammed against the wall behind his bed. An explosion of white stars spiralled across his vision.

"Hey! Cut the shit in there!"

The voice sounded distant and muffled, and was followed by a heavy pounding on the wall. It took Greg a moment to realize that it was coming from the room next door.

Still whimpering in terror, he rolled out of bed and stumbled across the floor, feeling blindly for the wall light switch. When he found it and slapped it on, the room instantly filled with a blazing white light that hurt his eyes.

Greg bent over with both hands on his knees, panting heavily as he looked over at his bed. The brightness of the light still stung his eyes, blurring his vision, but he didn't dare even to blink. The sheets and blankets were a tangled mess on the floor. His pillow was jammed between the mattress and wall, but there was no one there.

"Jesus *Christ,*" he whispered heatedly into his cupped hands as he rubbed his face, his skin damp and cold to the touch.

Even though he knew that he was wide awake now, the dream still seemed vitally real. Every shadow in every corner of the room seemed charged with dangerous energy. He cringed inwardly, expecting when he looked to one side or the other to see the horribly mangled dog face leering at him. He couldn't believe that he was alone in the room.

"Jesus," he whispered as he straightened up and ran his fingers through his hair.

In a dim corner of his mind, he could hear his mother's voice chiding him for using foul language, but he ignored it. His legs felt like they were going to collapse under him as he walked shakily into the small bathroom and ran the water until it was cold. Bending over the sink, he splashed his face several times, blubbering and snorting and telling himself that he was awake—that it had only been a dream . . . a nightmare.

When he looked at himself in the mirror, his eyes looked back at him with a frantic insanity. He leaned so close to the mirror his breath fogged the glass as he whispered harshly, "It wasn't real! . . . Jesus, it *wasn't* real! . . . *She wasn't here!*"

Although he thought it might be a mistake to drive to Bolton first thing the next morning, Greg headed out after having breakfast at *Sally's,* the diner on the corner just down the street from the hotel.

The sun was warm and bright, and he drove with his window rolled down so he could enjoy the morning; but no matter what he tried to think about or do, there seemed always to be a cold, hard knot in the center of his chest that wouldn't go away. Below the whining sound of the tires on the road, he thought he could still hear his mother's voice, chiding him. As much as he tried to forget about it, he couldn't stop thinking about what he had seen in his room last night—that person he had *thought* was his mother, but who had that horribly deformed dog's face.

He was still feeling nervous when he drove down Taylor Hill Road. Glancing into his rearview to make sure nobody was following him, he started slowing down, knowing that Angela's house was around the next bend. When he was about a hundred yards away from the driveway, he saw a car—a white Subaru—pull out of the driveway and turn right.

"All right," he muttered when he caught a glimpse of Angela at the wheel. He didn't see anyone else with her.

Greg pulled over to the side of the road and stopped, waiting until Angela's car was out of sight. He was tempted to follow her, but it didn't make any sense to let her see him.

For a moment, he toyed with the idea of going to the house

and seeing if either or both of the kids were home, but he decided to follow Angela instead.

After all, she was the one he was after.

He stepped down on the gas and caught up with her as she took the turn onto Route 202, heading toward Augusta.

"So, where are we off to today?" Greg whispered, settling into his seat. A few miles down the road, he saw Angela's turn signal flash as she slowed to turn into the Mobile gas station.

Greg started to slow down, too, not quite sure what to do. For a moment, he considered pulling up to the pump beside her, just to get a good look at her. He felt confident that she wouldn't recognize him, now that he'd shaved his mustache, and cut and dyed his hair, but—again—he didn't see any point in pressing his luck. She might recognize his eyes, just as he had recognized his mother's eyes inside that mangled dog's head he had dreamed about last night.

As he drove past the gas station, Greg noticed two things. One was Angela Ross, wearing sunglasses and looking pretty fine as she sat in her car, waiting for the gas jockey to come out and start pumping. The other was a hand-lettered sign with black marker on yellowing cardboard in the window of the station that said: HELP WANTED.

Stepping down on the accelerator, Greg sped by and tapped on his horn a couple of times while waving to Angela out his window. In the rearview mirror, he caught a glimpse of her, looking up as he sped by. The confused expression on her face was priceless.

"Just keep wondering, babe," he whispered, chuckling to himself.

He didn't go very far down the road. Just around the corner where the road widened, he pulled over onto the dirt shoulder and shut off the engine. Keeping his eyes fixed on the rearview mirror, he sat there drumming his fingers on the steering wheel as he waited.

The road up ahead shimmered with heat. Insects buzzed in the weeds in the roadside ditch, their droning sound as maddening as the high, steady whine of a hundred tiny buzz saws. The trees on both sides of the road swayed gently in the warm breeze that was blowing up from the south. The air had a damp, rich smell, not at all like what Greg was used to back home in Brooklyn.

But he couldn't take much time to appreciate the sights and sounds of nature. As beautiful as this all was, the openness of the country still made him feel nervous, exposed.

Besides, he had to concentrate. He was waiting to see Angela drive by so he could follow her and find out where she was going. On a fine day like this, he guessed she might be heading to Augusta to do some shopping, maybe. It was a school day, so the kids wouldn't be home unless one of them was sick.

Maybe he would wait until she drove by and then go back to the house on Taylor Hill Road.

Greg started getting impatient when, after a full five minutes, Angela still hadn't driven past. He began to worry that she may have gone back to town. He knew he shouldn't have assumed that she'd keep going to Augusta.

He started up the car and was just getting ready to turn around and head back to Bolton when her car appeared in the rearview mirror, coming toward him. Heaving a sigh of relief, Greg reached for the shift, ready to follow her after she passed by. Before she was even beside him, though, another idea struck him. Leaning back and slouching low in the seat, he reminded himself that he wasn't in any hurry, that he could wait.

He peeked up over the edge of the dashboard and watched as her car sped by. She probably hadn't even noticed him or his car parked along the side of the road.

Greg grunted and narrowed his eyes as he sat up and watched her pull away. As soon as she was out of sight over the crest of the hill ahead, he shifted his car into gear. His tires spit out a shower of dirt and gravel as he stepped down on the accelerator and did a quick U-turn. He was humming to himself as he drove back to town.

As he approached the gas station, though, another idea hit him. Although he still had plenty of money, he knew that his resources weren't unlimited. He was a pretty good mechanic, so why not ask about the job opening? It might give him a good cover.

He checked himself in the mirror, raking his fingers through his hand before he pulled into the station and parked close to the pumps. A skinny, pimple-faced blond kid wearing a tattered MISFITS T-shirt and faded jeans sauntered over and asked what he wanted.

Greg glanced at his fuel gauge and saw that it was just under half full.

"Top it off with regular," he said.

Before the kid could start the job, Greg asked him, "Who do I talk to about that job opening?"

The kid squinted as he looked at him, then nodded toward the small office building. The garage had two large bay doors, but both of them were closed. Greg couldn't see cars in either one. A Coke machine stood by the front door, and faded and torn advertisements and posters were stapled to the side of the building and taped to the inside of the grimy windows. Greg stretched as he got out of his car, wondering how he had even noticed the HELP WANTED sign amongst all the trash.

His shoes scuffed the asphalt as he walked to the office, took a deep breath, and opened the door. The smell that hit him was like a slap in the face—a terrible combination of gasoline, cigarette smoke, body sweat, and a rotten, musty smell that he didn't even try to identify.

A heavyset man with short, dark hair, wearing what had once been a white T-shirt and faded bib overalls was seated behind the counter. A cigarette dangled from one corner of his mouth, and he squinted against the smoke as he looked up at Greg. The man was holding a fried egg sandwich in one hand that was stained black with oil and grease. He narrowed one eye as he studied Greg.

"What can I do for?" the man asked as Greg walked up to the counter.

"I saw your sign," Greg said, nodding in the direction of the window, "and was wondering if you're looking for a mechanic or just for someone to pump gas."

"What can you do?" the man behind the counter said. He looked about as interested in Greg as he was interested in discussing hang nail surgery. He made a loud gasping sound that was almost a burp as he twisted around and put his sandwich on the desk behind him, then heaved himself to his feet and walked over to the counter.

"I'm a pretty good mechanic," Greg said, "and I guess I can pump gas with the best of them." He smiled, hoping the man would catch his humor, but apparently he didn't. The man stroked the side of his face, leaving a long, black streak on his neck just below his left ear.

"You got a name?" the man asked, still squinting at him.

Greg panicked for an instant when he realized that he couldn't give this guy a phony name. All he had for ID was a driver's license and Social Security card with his real name.

"Greg ... Greg Newman," Greg said after a moment's hesitation. He stuck his hand out and shook hands with the man, ignoring the slick, greasy feel of the man's hand.

"I just moved here from New York City, and I'm looking for work."

"'S that so," the man said, nodding thoughtfully.

Greg noticed that the man hadn't told him his name, but he figured he wouldn't push the issue. People in the country seemed to have a whole different style than Greg was used to in the city.

"Well, mostly I need someone to pump gas evenings and weekends, especially on weekends," the man said. "You ain't opposed to working nights and weekends, are you?"

"Absolutely not," Greg said, nodding eagerly.

"Normally, I'd ask you to fill out an application—" The man glanced over his shoulder, then shook his head with disgust, "but I prob'bly couldn't find one in this pigsty, anyway."

Greg could see that the desk was piled high with old work orders, bills, car parts catalogs, and other assorted junk. The trash can beside the desk was overflowing with junk mail, and the oil-stained floor had an inch thick of litter, dust, and dirt. Greg wondered how the man dared to eat in such filth.

"If you want the job, I guess you got it," the man said, brushing his hands and making a dull clapping sound.

Greg was a bit taken aback by such a quick decision. For a moment, he thought he hadn't heard the man correctly.

"What?" he said, leaning forward.

"I said you've got the job if you want it," the man said. I've had that freakin' sign in the window going on a year, now, and you're the first person to ask about it. I swear to Christ, that's what's wrong with this country today. People don't know what it means to work for a living. They'd just as soon let the govern'mint hand them a check every goddamned month while they sit around on their sorry asses."

"Speaking of check," Greg said, "you didn't say what you're paying."

The man's eyes narrowed as he looked at Greg; then he nodded.

"Six fifty an hour's the best I can do for starters," he said, "and I'll be needing you tomorrow afternoon, if that's all right with you."

At this point Greg knew that he couldn't say no, and he was regretting his snap decision to come in here in the first place. But the truth was, he didn't want to drain what money he had left while he hung around, waiting for an opportunity to strike at Angela Ross. He might as well keep himself busy for the time being and earn a few bucks. He could always bug out of here at a moment's notice.

"Sure. Six fifty sounds good to me." Greg nodded and tried to look eager as, once again, he stuck his hand out so he could shake with the man.

"Six fifty it is, then," the man said, smiling and shaking hands hard enough so his heavy jowls jiggled. "Sorry. I can't afford any health benefits or anything. Be here at noon tomorrow."

Greg nodded and was about to turn to leave when he realized something.

"You know," he said, "I never got your name."

The man behind the counter smiled and said, "That's 'cause I never tole you." He smiled at Greg as though waiting for him to laugh, then said, "M'name's Larry Lee. Most folks call me Junior on account of my old man who used to run this place was named Larry, too."

Greg glanced again at the trash on the desk and floor and thought that maybe this paperwork was from back then.

"Well then, Junior," he said. "I'll see you tomorrow at noon, sharp."

Just then the door banged open, and the blond teenager walked up to Greg.

"That'll be twelve fifty," he said flatly.

Greg smiled as he fished his wallet from his back pocket and produced a twenty dollar bill. After the boy rang up the sale on the grease-stained, antiquated cash register and handed him back his change, Greg turned and started for the door.

"See you tomorrow, then," he said before he opened the door and stepped outside. All the while, he was thinking that, if it came right down to it and he really needed some money, he could always take what he needed from the register, like he used to at the video store.

As he got into his car and drove away, Greg still wasn't sure what to think about what had just happened. One thought that kept floating through his mind was that, if this was the gas station Angela Ross habitually used, then he might be seeing more of her over the next few days and weeks. That would be good.

Greg was tempted to go straight back to the hotel and clean himself up, but he figured he take another swing past Angela's house first, just to see if anything was happening. He drove slowly through town, not wanting to draw anyone's attention. By the time he got to the house on Taylor Hill Road, he had decided that he might just as well have a look around. You never knew what you might find until you tried.

He didn't want to leave his car parked out in front of the house where anyone passing by could see and possibly identity it, so he drove a half mile or so down the road and parked. After making sure all of the doors were locked, he pocketed the keys and started back towards the house.

The sun was warm on his shoulders, and this time, for some reason, he actually found the buzzing sounds of insects along the roadside almost relaxing. He stayed close to the woods that lined the side of the road so when he heard a car coming, he could duck into the brush before the driver saw him.

An electric tingle of excitement ran through him the instant the house came into view. Thinking that he didn't want to look too suspicious, just in case one of the kids was home or someone passing by saw him, he walked boldly down the driveway to the front door. If he met someone, he could always say that his car had broken down and he needed to call for a tow truck.

The instant he stepped into the shade of the roofed porch, another, stronger chill ran through him.

Shit, this is going to be fun, he told himself, but he couldn't deny feeling a tightening in his gut as he pressed the doorbell.

From somewhere in the house, there came a low *gong*. Stepping close to the sidelight, he looked inside and saw the rich wood tones of the floor in the foyer. Sunlight reflected off the kitchen floor with a bright blue glare.

Not bad, Greg thought, feeling a mild twinge of jealousy that he would never be able to afford a place like this . . . not that he would ever *want* a place like this!

He waited a few seconds, then rang the doorbell again. When no one came to the door, he glanced quickly over his shoulder to make sure no one was around, then knelt down and inspected the door knob and lock. Taking his plastic-encased driver's license from his wallet, he slid it between the door and the jamb, and wiggled it around.

"Come on, baby," he whispered. "Give it up, bitch . . . Give it up."

After a few passes, the card caught the bolt, and he applied pressure. The plastic bent so much he wondered if it was strong enough to do the trick, but he grunted with satisfaction when he heard the door lock click. It never failed to amaze him how most people thought they were so secure behind locked doors when, in fact, their locks were usually much too easy to spring.

Greg was smiling as he twisted the doorknob and pushed the door open.

"Fuckin' locks only keep out the honest people," he muttered as he stepped inside and eased the door shut behind him.

"Hello . . . ?" he called out. "Anybody home?

If anyone was home, he still figured he'd pretend he simply needed to use the phone, but he could tell by the dense silence in the house that he was alone.

Perfect! he thought as he walked from the foyer into the living room.

Sunlight filtered through the sheer living room curtains, illuminating the room with a soft, gauzy glow. He realized that he was holding his breath and let it out slowly. The air in the house had a sharp pine-scent that stung his nose, almost making him sneeze. He listened to the low, steady *ticktock* of the clock on the fireplace mantel.

Now that he was inside Angela Ross's house, Greg wasn't quite sure what to do. He figured he would look around a little and see if anything suggested itself. He certainly didn't want to burglarize the place. It wouldn't make sense to do anything that would put Angela on the alert, much less get the police involved. He'd just have a quick look around, upstairs and down, and then—unless he found something *really* interesting—leave.

In the kitchen, he opened all the cupboards but didn't find anything very exciting there—just the usual pots and pans, dishes, and cooking utensils and ingredients. One thing he couldn't resist doing was taking down a couple of the coffee cups and spitting into them. After rubbing the spit around the insides of the cups, he put them back in place.

Next he walked through the living room and into the den, but there wasn't much he could think to do other than unplug the VCR and then plug it back in so the digital clock was blinking twelve o'clock. He wasn't even consciously aware that he was whistling "Whistle While You Work" as he went up the stairs to check out the bedrooms.

The first room he came to obviously belonged to the boy. Greg checked out the computer and considered trying to do something to sabotage it, maybe run a magnet over it to screw up the hard drive, but he decided not to bother. He left the room and walked down the hall to the next bedroom.

This one belonged to Angela's daughter. Greg felt himself

getting the stirrings of an erection as he walked in and looked around at the frilly, cheap-looking decor. The bed was covered with a lacy bedspread and pillows. Stacked at the foot of the bed was a collection of stuffed animals. The walls were painted bright pink and decorated with posters of various rock bands, none of which Greg recognized.

Greg was still whistling as he walked over to the girl's bureau and ran the top drawer open. There he found a stack of her underwear, bras and panties. He smiled to himself as he took out a pair of panties so sheer they were almost see-through when he held them up to the light.

Just handling the girl's silky underwear made Greg's erection rock solid. He chuckled to himself as he slipped his hand into the undies and then slid his hand down inside his pants and grabbed himself. After stroking himself a few time, he considered jerking off into her panties and putting them back but decided not to . He balled the panties up, put them back in the drawer, and slammed it shut.

The next room he checked out was the bathroom. There, he unzipped his pants and pissed into the toilet, making sure to splash a little bit of urine onto the seat and floor. Next he took all three of their toothbrushes from the wall-mounted rack. After hawking up a mouthful of spit, he put each toothbrush, one at a time, into his mouth and brushed his teeth before replacing them in the same slots.

The last room he checked—the one he'd been waiting to see—was Angela's.

The bedroom was spacious, with walls painted a deep, almost emerald green. The bed was enormous. Greg guessed it was either queen-or king-sized. He pulled the bedspread down and leaned forward to sniff the pillow, inhaling the lingering scents of Angela's soap and perfume. His penis was still erect, and—as he had in the daughter's bedroom—he considered taking a pair of her underwear and masturbating into it, but then he got a better idea.

After peeling the bed covers all the way down, he undid his pants, dropped them to his ankles, and then, bracing himself with one hand, leaned over the bed. Closing his eyes, he began to stroke himself, all the while filling his mind with erotic images. After a minute or so, he could feel himself reaching climax. Grunting and thrusting his hips forward, he squeezed himself while stroking faster and faster until he suddenly shuddered with dizzying release. He sighed and opened his eyes, watching as his body convulsed, and thick gobs of creamy fluid shot across the sheets.

"Yeah . . . oh, yeah," he gasped, his voice sounding deep and raspy. "There you go, baby . . . That's all for you."

He pulled his pants back up and wiped his hands over the sperm-splattered sheets, rubbing until the liquid dissolved into a wide wet splotch, then pulled the bedspread back up and smoothed it out. He knew that his load would dry before long, and he couldn't help but laugh when he imagined tonight, when Angela Ross, without even suspecting it, slept on his dried cum.

There wasn't anything else he could think to do, and it was getting on time for lunch, so he wandered back downstairs and left by the front door. At first, he was going to make sure to lock the door behind him, but he decided to leave it unlocked just to give Angela one more thing to think about when she got home.

As he walked up the street back to where he had left his car, Greg was feeling pretty good. But as he unlocked the driver's door and slipped into the front seat, a subtle feeling of anger took hold of him. When he put the key into the ignition and turned it, he realized that he was gritting his teeth. He shifted the car into gear, aware that he was gripping the shift so tightly the palm of his hand ached.

"Jesus," he muttered as he tromped down, hard, on the accelerator.

The rear tires skidded in the dirt, raising a cloud of dust behind him. They spun out until they gained purchase on the asphalt, and the car took off with a long squeal of rubber. The back end fishtailed until Greg got control.

"Fuckin' god*damn* it!" he shouted, pounding his hand hard on the dashboard and glaring at his eyes in the rearview mirror.

As he sped down the road toward Route 202, he realized

that he was pissed because, no matter how funny he thought what he'd just done was, the fact of the matter was, he still hadn't come any closer to actually *doing* something to hurt Angela Ross. He could play all the mind games he wanted, but he knew he wasn't going to be really happy until he took care of her *and* her kids.

Then and *only* then would he be satisfied!

Chapter 20

Protection

"JJ . . . ? Brandy . . . ?"

Angie was frowning as she walked into the house after getting home from shopping a little after one o'clock. The front door was unlocked, so she assumed that one of the kids had come home early from school. She walked into the kitchen, but there was no one there. After putting the two bags of groceries she was carrying on the counter, she walked into the living room.

"Hey, guys . . . ?"

No one was in the living room, either.

"Anyone home?" she called out.

She stood in the middle of the living room floor and listened to the dense silence of the house. A soft glow of afternoon sunlight filtered through the lacy curtains, lighting up floating specks of dust that swirled in her passing. In spite of the warm day, a teasing shiver ran up her back.

She was *positive* she had locked the door on her way out this morning. After what had happened yesterday out on the baseball field, she had made a point of it. She had reported the incident to the police, but they told her that, without witnesses, they couldn't do much of anything, especially since it appeared as though the dog was a stray. No one in town had reported a missing dog that fit the black Labrador's description.

As she walked slowly back into the foyer, Angie tried to convince herself that one of the kids must have come home to pick up something they'd forgotten, and then not locked the door on the way out, but that didn't satisfy her. She couldn't explain it, but the house had a subtle feeling of having been . . . violated, somehow. All of Angie's senses were honed as though she could still detect the lingering presence of someone who had been here but shouldn't have been.

Was it a smell . . . or a sound . . . ?

Whatever it was, *something* made her feel alert, on guard as she tiptoed up the stairs.

Her hand slid lightly along the banister. With every step, the tingling sensation of alarm grew stronger inside her. She winced when a floorboard creaked underfoot.

Maybe Rob dropped by, she thought. That could be it. He had a key and maybe because he felt so comfortable in this town, he didn't think to lock the door on his way out. If he had entered by the front door, he might have left by the back door and not even thought to check the front.

Maybe, Angie thought . . . but she didn't think so.

There was a *feeling* about the house that made the hairs at the nape of her neck stir. She listened to her heart beating high and fast, a *whooshing* sound in her ears that was strong enough to affect her vision, making it pulsate.

But if the house had been broken into, why wasn't anything missing?

The TV and stereo system were still in the den, and nothing else looked out of place. Still, Angie couldn't deny the sensation that *someone* who didn't belong here had been in the house, and not long ago!

"Jesus," she whispered, as a sudden panic seized her. "The gun!"

Heedless of the possibility of danger, she ran down the hallway to her bedroom, where she threw open the door. She went to her desk and fished the key to her bottom drawer from the jar where she kept it. Her hands were shaking so badly she almost dropped the key as she tried to fit it into the lock and turn it. A raw, burning dryness gripped her throat like tightening fingers when she heard the lock *click*. She felt like she was going to scream as she ran the bottom drawer open and shifted aside the stack of papers she had piled on top the gun.

For a single, flickering instant, she didn't see it and was convinced that somebody *had* been in the house, had found the gun and taken it. Only after she grabbed a handful of files and tossed them onto the desktop did she see the gun, wedged against the side of the drawer.

"Shit," she whispered as she wiped her forehead with the back of her hand. The air went out of her lungs like they were deflating balloons, and she felt all weak and trembling inside as she sagged back in the chair.

After a few seconds, once she had begun to calm down, she leaned forward and picked up the gun. It felt heavy and oily in her grip, and she noticed that she didn't feel the least bit more secure holding it. Her vision blurred with tears as she hefted the gun, remembering that—not so long ago—it had belonged to her husband.

"God, I miss you, John," she said in a high, strangled whisper that twisted off into a wracking sob as tears fell from her eyes.

Still holding the gun in one hand, she leaned forward onto the desk and covered her face with the other hand as loss and grief and fear washed over her in dark, heavy waves. Her tears left warm, slick tracks on her cheeks. Her nose got stuffy, but no matter how hard she sniffed, the feeling wouldn't go away. A salty, choking sensation clogged her throat as she cried.

She never heard the footsteps on the stairs until a voice spoke suddenly behind her.

"What's the matter, Mom?"

Angie let out a squeal of surprise as she sat up and spun around to see JJ standing in the bedroom doorway. He had a bewildered expression on his face and looked at her as though he didn't quite dare come any further into the room.

"You okay?"

Forgetting for a moment that she was holding the revolver

in her hand, Angie sniffed and, wiping her eyes with her free hand, forced a smile as she nodded to him.

"Yeah ... I'm okay," she said, although she didn't think her voice sounded like she was at all okay.

"What are you doing home from school so early?" she asked when she realized that it was still not even one-thirty.

"Half-day today, remember?" JJ said with a lopsided grin. "Teachers' workshop or something."

"Oh, yeah ... right," Angie replied, nodding. "Were you home earlier? When I got home, the front door was unlocked."

Still smiling thinly, JJ shook his head.

"I was over at Sammy's," he replied. "I just came home to get my glove and heard you in here. Sammy and me were gonna go play ball with some of the guys."

"Sammy and I," she said, correcting him.

"Whatever," JJ snapped. They looked at each other for a lengthening moment, then JJ said, "Umm ... Mom ... Why do you have a gun?"

Angie could hear that his voice was close to breaking, and she instantly realized his concern that she might actually have been sitting here contemplating suicide.

"Oh, this? It was your father's," she said softly, looking at the gun in her hand and turning it over. She shook her head, and more tears rolled down her cheeks. She sniffed loudly and rubbed her nose.

"So what are you doing with it?" JJ asked, still sounding nervous.

"Nothing ... nothing at all," Angie said in a paper-thin voice. "I was just ... when I got home, I had a funny feeling that ... that something had happened, and I wanted to check and make sure nobody had ... found this. That's all."

"Oh," JJ said, not looking entirely convinced.

"As a matter of fact," Angie continued, "I was thinking about getting rid of it, maybe turning it in at the police station. You know I don't like guns in the house."

"How come?" JJ asked. "You never know when you might need one ... for protection or whatever."

His question sounded almost casual, but there was a tight

edge in his voice that Angie didn't like. She bit down her lower lip and shook her head firmly.

"Because I don't *like* guns. Period. I *never* have, even when your father was alive. I realize that he needed them to do his job, but I . . ." She sighed and shook her head as though totally bewildered. "I don't know," she finished lamely.

"Can I have it?" JJ asked.

The question and his tone of voice surprised Angie so much that, at first, she wasn't sure she had heard him correctly.

"What?" She frowned as she placed the gun on her desk and turned in her chair to look directly at him. JJ shrugged nervously and shifted from one foot to the other.

"I just thought . . . you know, that if you didn't want to keep it, that I could have it. I think I'm old enough to take care of a gun."

"A BB gun, maybe," Angie said, feeling a sudden flash of fear for her son. "but not a gun like this. This is a .38 caliber. It's designed specifically to *kill* people."

She knew from the police report that John's killer had used a .38 on him. The memory of the horror she had experienced that night outside *Le Bistro* last winter made her shudder. The cold hollowness of panic and loss that she felt was like a bottomless pit opening up in the center of her stomach.

"Don't be ridiculous!" she said sharply. "You certainly don't need to have anything like *this!*"

"But it was Dad's," JJ said, his voice so high-pitched and pleading it irritated Angie all the more. "Did you ever think that he might *want* me to have it?"

"Maybe once you're an adult," Angie said, "but certainly not *now!* You're too young to know how to handle something like this. It's dangerous."

"If it's so dangerous, why do you still have it?" JJ asked, nailing her with a hard look.

Angie stared back at her son for a long time but didn't say anything because she had no idea what to say. The truth was, she had no idea why she kept it. If the revolver represented something about John to her, it was symbolic of everything that she had hated about him or, at least, hated about his job.

Maybe she kept it because it was what her husband had lived and died by, and she felt subconsciously that, if she held on to it, then maybe she could control the grief and anger she felt about his untimely death.

"I . . . I really don't know," Angie finally said, shaking her head and looking away from JJ. Tears burned her eyes, blurring her vision as she looked out the bedroom window over the backyard. The beautiful spring afternoon contrasted dramatically with what she was feeling. She knew, no matter how much she wished that things could be otherwise, they weren't. And worst of all was that, in so many ways, she could see those same strands of violence and impatience getting stronger, day by day, in her son. She had vowed to do anything and everything to stop them now before they destroyed JJ, just as they had destroyed her husband.

"Well, *I* don't want you to get rid of it," JJ said with a commanding edge in his voice that Angie couldn't help but notice. "Even if *you* don't want it for protection or whatever, I want you to keep it so I can have it when I'm older."

"We'll see about that," Angie whispered softly.

Still looking away from him, she closed her eyes tightly as though saying a prayer.

"We'll see about that . . ."

"So what did you finally decide?" JJ asked Angie the next morning as soon as he came downstairs into the kitchen for breakfast. He was already dressed for school and had his backpack dangling from one hand, dragging across the floor.

"Decide about what?"

Angie cast a furtive glance over at Brandy. Her first and only thought was that JJ was going to start pushing her again about letting him have his father's revolver, so she was surprised when he said, "About me getting a dog."

"A dog?" Angie echoed, letting the idea register slowly.

"Yeah, a dog," JJ said quickly. "Remember our deal? I agreed to move here only on condition that I could get a dog."

Angie grunted as she leaned back against the counter and rested her chin in her hand.

"Now that Blackie's—" JJ's voice caught and broke off, and he couldn't continue until he cleared his throat. "—that Blackie's dead, I really want to go and pick out a dog. You said I could."

"Yeah, but are you sure you're ready for that?" Angie said. "I mean, having a dog's a lot of responsibility, you know."

"I know," JJ snapped, shaking his head impatiently.

Angie nodded slowly, but she was barely paying attention to what he was saying because she was thinking about how a dog might provide almost as much protection as a gun—maybe even better because a dog would provide an early warning if a prowler ever came around.

"I'll have to think about it," Angie said, turning her back to him and busying herself with running the cold water to start a pot of coffee.

"That's what you've been saying for months. I'll *never* get one if all you ever do is *think* about it!"

"And you think talking to me like that is going to get you what you want?" Angie glanced at him over her shoulder.

"Yeah. Cut your whining, for crying out loud," Brandy piped in, looking up from her breakfast for the first time and nailing him with an angry scowl. "You sound like an imbecile."

"I'm not whining," JJ shouted, his face flushing as he clenched his fists. "And you keep out of this! I wasn't talking to you!"

Before Brandy could respond, he wheeled around and punched her hard on the arm, just below her shoulder. Brandy let out a yelp, then pulled back and, moving fast, lunged at JJ. She gave him an even harder punch on the back as he turned away, trying to duck. The impact made a hollow *thump* sound as JJ cried out.

"That's *enough!*" Angie shouted. "Both of you cut that out this *instant,* or we'll *never* get a dog!"

"That wouldn't bother *me,*" Brandy said, making a sassy face at JJ, who stood there rubbing his shoulder and seething with rage. "Dogs are smelly and full of fleas, anyway."

"Just like you!" JJ said.

"I said cut it out. Now!"

Angie took a threatening step forward. She seldom—if ever—punished him physically, but she was feeling particularly edgy this morning and knew that it wouldn't take much before she lashed out at either one of them.

"She started it," JJ whined, moving a few steps away from his mother.

"Yeah, right," Brandy said looking at her mother with a wiseguy smirk. "I started it by hitting him back first."

"It's none of your damned business, anyway," JJ shouted at her. "Mom. You promised I could get a dog, and I think you ought to keep that promise."

"Hold on a second. I didn't *promise* anyth—"

"Yes you did!" JJ slammed his clenched fist on the kitchen table hard enough to make the silverware and dishes rattle. "See? I *knew* it! I *knew* you'd end up doing something like this!" His face flushed bright red; his body was shaking as he turned and yelled at his mother. "You're nothing but a lousy liar!"

"You can't talk to me like that," Angie said. Her first impulse was to do something she had never done to him before—spank him. Instead, she walked over to him and took hold of his shoulders with both hands. When she tried to draw him close for a hug, he pulled away from her violently.

"You can't lie to me!" he shouted.

"Better watch it, Mom," Brandy said, her voice still high and mocking. "You don't want the little baby to start crying because he doesn't get his way, do you?"

"Why don't you clear your place and get ready so you won't miss the school bus," Angie said to Brandy, barely glancing at her over her shoulder. Looking JJ squarely in the eyes, she tightened her grip on his shoulders so he couldn't pull away from her. "I didn't say we'd *never* get a dog, okay? I just said I'm not sure right *now* is a good time to do it."

"Why not? Why can't we at least go and check 'em out?" JJ's lower lip was pale and quivering, but he obviously was not going to give his sister or mother the satisfaction of seeing him cry.

"Because you know and I know that as soon as you see one, you're going to have your heart set on getting it, and you'll be begging me to bring it home today."

"What's wrong with that?" JJ asked, shrugging and pulling away from her.

Angie didn't have a comeback because the truth was, she couldn't see any reason not to get a dog. Spring was probably the best time of year to get a new dog because it could spend a lot of time outside. And a dog would be a good thing to have around, especially if she was going to get rid of John's revolver.

"Let me think about it today while you're at school, all right?" she said. "Tomorrow's Saturday. Maybe we'll drive out to the animal shelter in Greene and see what they've got."

"Why not after school today?" JJ asked.

"Maybe . . . maybe," Angie said, shaking her head. "I just said that I wanted to *think* about it."

"Promise?" JJ asked, his eyes brightening as he looked at her eagerly.

"Yeah," Angie said, smiling as she nodded. "I promise."

She stuck out her hand and took JJ's hand to shake firmly.

"It's a deal, then," JJ said, beaming a smile at her.

She pulled him close and gave him a big hug and was glad that this time he didn't resist her.

"Oh, so now the baby's happy because he's going to get his way, huh?" Brandy said from the sink where she was rinsing off her breakfast plate.

"Screw you," JJ said.

"Watch your mouth, JJ, or we won't go *anywhere!*"

"She started it again! She's always picking on me!"

"Do not."

"Do too!"

"Stop it right now! I mean it!" Angie shouted, looking back and forth between them and wagging her forefinger. "I wish you two would stop arguing like this all the time."

Brandy started to say something, but then both she and JJ fell silent. Angie could tell just by looking at them that they were ready to go at it again as soon as one of them even looked at the other wrong.

"Brandy, your bus will be here in a minute or two," Angie said, "and JJ, you should be heading over to pick up Sammy in a couple of minutes. I don't want either one of you to be late for school."

"Okay, Mom," JJ said. He grabbed his backpack loaded with books and started to walk away, but before he left the kitchen, he looked back at his mother and said, "Just remember. You promised." The last thing he did before he left was stick his tongue out at Brandy.

JJ let out a whoop of joy when he got home from school that afternoon and, without even having to mention it, his mother told him to put his backpack up in his bedroom and hurry up so they could go out to the animal shelter and get back in time for her to make supper.

He couldn't believe that she was actually following through on what she had promised. As he hurried about getting ready to go, he couldn't help but wonder if there was a catch.

"Can Sammy come?" he asked as they walked out to the car, which was parked in the driveway by the front door.

When his mother started to say something, he was sure she was going to say *no,* but she surprised him again by saying, "Sure. I don't see why not . . . as long as his mother says it's okay."

They drove over to the Hardings, and a few minutes later the three of them were on their way to the Animal Refuge League shelter out on Route 202, in Greene.

"Now I don't want you pestering me when we get there, understand?" his mother said as she drove. "Even if you see a dog that you *really* love, I want to take our time and think about it. Choosing a pet isn't something you hurry."

"I know, I know," JJ said, but he was hardly listening because he was determined they would come home with a dog *today.*

Sammy commented several times about how lucky JJ was

to be getting a dog. His mother, he said, wouldn't let him have one because, she said, dogs were smelly and messy, and that you could always tell if someone owned a dog as soon as you stepped into their house because of the "doggie" smell.

Listening to Sammy made JJ think about Blackie. He almost said something about how it was too bad that the black dog had died, but he didn't. Whenever he thought about how horribly Blackie's face and body had been beaten, a strong surge of fear and nausea churned in the pit of his stomach. He and Sammy had talked about Blackie's death and whether or not they thought the man who had played baseball with them could have done it, but they couldn't decide. The man had seemed much too nice ever to do something terrible like that!

But JJ quickly forgot about Blackie, and he could hardly contain his excitement when they pulled into the parking lot in front of a small, gray shingled building. Through the two wide picture windows on either side of the red door, he could see lines of cages containing cats and dogs.

"Now remember what I told you," his mother cautioned him as they got out of the car and walked up to the door. A chorus of barking and a powerful animal smell greeted them when they opened the door and entered. JJ felt a twinge of embarrassment when his mother sniffed the air and whispered to Sammy, "I know *exactly* what your mother means."

A thin, white-haired man who introduced himself as Mr. Foster greeted them and asked if they were looking for anything in particular. He had a thick Maine accent that JJ found kind of funny. After JJ explained that they were just out looking for a dog, preferably a puppy or young dog that they could raise, they spent the next fifteen minutes or so looking at the assortment of dogs.

For the longest time, JJ didn't see any dog that he really liked. There was a cocker spaniel that he kind of liked, but his mother immediately said no, insisting that cocker spaniels shed too much hair. Finally, in the last cage at the back of the room, JJ saw a dog he immediately liked—a young, rail-thin German shepherd with large, brown eyes and thick, padded paws. The dog was wedged into a corner of the cage with one paw lying over its muzzle, like he was trying to hide. He had a sad, wet look in his eyes, but he jumped up and started wagging his tail as soon as JJ knelt in front of the cage and whistled.

"I want him," JJ said to his mother as he pointed at the forlorn-looking dog.

"That there's a nice, friendly little pup," Mr. Foster said. "Come to us just yesterday from a family out in Wayne who found him wandering around. Since they already had a dog and couldn't find anyone else who wanted 'im, they brung him to us."

"Has he had all his shots and everything?" Angie asked, frowning.

The man nodded.

"Whatever dog you choose, I'll give you a complete record of all the shots he's had from us and when he'll need 'em again. This particular puppy is still a little too young to be fixed, but since he's a male, at least you won't have to worry 'bout finding a litter of puppies on the kitchen floor sometime next week."

JJ saw his mother roll her eyes around as if that was the last thing she'd want to deal with.

"Well," she said, followed by a deep sigh. "We're not really in any big hurry. JJ, why don't we keep—"

"I *really* want this one, Mom," JJ said quickly, before she could raise her objection. When he stuck his fingers between the metal bars, the German shepherd immediately came up to him and started lapping his hand so eagerly it tickled. The dog's tail was beating back and forth so fast it was almost a blur.

"JJ," Angie said, her voice low and patient, "we agreed before we came here that we weren't going to make any snap decisions."

"I know, Mom, but . . . just *look* at him!"

As soon as JJ pulled his hand out of the cage, the dog sat back on his haunches and let out a high-pitched yip. The instant JJ put his hand between the bars again, the dog jumped up, placed his front paws on the bars, and started licking it again.

All the while, his tail was wagging back and forth so rapidly it almost knocked him off balance.

"How can you resist, Mom?"

"This *is* a very nice dog," Mr. Foster said looking at Angie. "He has a very nice temperament. He'd be great with kids."

"How big will he get?" Angie asked, squinting as she looked more closely at the dog. JJ could tell that she was taking this seriously.

"He's been malnourished," Mr. Foster said, "so even with a steady diet he may not reach his full weight potential, but I'd guess he'll still grow to be a fairly sizable dog."

"Look how big his paws are," JJ said eagerly. "Maybe I'll call him *Bear.*"

"He looks more like a wolf to me," Sammy offered.

JJ could tell by the way Sammy was staring at the dog that he was wishing there was some way he could convince his mother to change her mind about dogs.

But JJ couldn't worry about that.

Right now, his only problem was getting his mother to agree that they could take *this* dog home today.

"I don't think you have to decide on a name right away," his mother said. "We haven't even made up our minds if this is the one we want."

"*I* have," JJ said. "And you said it'd be *my* dog."

Bouncing up and down on his toes like he had to go the bathroom real bad, JJ grabbed his mother's arm and gave it a quick tug.

"I don't know," she said softly, frowning as she shook her head.

JJ wanted to push her a little more, but he knew it was time to back off when he saw her squinting and running her teeth back and forth over her lower lip. She always did that whenever she was starting to change her mind about something. Her resolve was starting to waver.

"I *promise* I'll take good care of him, Mom," he said. "I'll do *everything!*"

His mother didn't say anything for a long time, and in that time JJ thought that his heart was going to stop beating. The only sound in the room was the ear-piercing chorus of barking from the other dogs. Finally, his mother straightened her shoulders. Shaking her head as though she knew she'd regret it, she said, "Well . . . I guess a promise is a promise."

"It sure is," JJ said, nodding eagerly.

"I'm serious about this, though," his mother said, pointing at him as though scolding him. "You're going to do *all* the work. If this dog pees or poops on the floor, you're the one who's going to clean it up. And it's going to be up to *you* to feed him and make sure he doesn't chew things up and destroy half the house."

"I will. I *promise* I will," JJ said eagerly.

"Well . . . okay then," his mother said reluctantly.

JJ let out a whoop that drowned out the other sounds in the room, then turned to Sammy and slapped him a high five.

"There must be some paperwork or something for me to fill out," Angie said to Mr. Foster, but JJ ignored all of that as he worked to open the cage door and take his new dog out so he could hug him. The dog scrambled into his arms and started licking his face like he was a prime cut of sirloin.

On the drive home, all three of them kept tossing out suggestions for names. Finally, after careful deliberation, JJ settled on Sammy's suggestion, and named the dog *Wolfgang* because he thought he really did look like a wolf. Later that night as he was settling down to sleep, JJ admitted to his mother that he decided to use that name because he felt sorry that Sammy wasn't able to have a dog.

Maybe this will be the end of it!

That thought kept running through Angie's mind as she stood on tiptoes and shined her flashlight into the narrow, dusty space between the top blocks of the stone foundation and the thick, rough-cut floor joists that supported the first floor. She strained to see as far back as she could, but the darkness swallowed her light.

It was Saturday morning. Brandy was still asleep, and JJ and Sammy were in the backyard, playing with Wolfgang. Angie had picked this spot in the cellar underneath the living room floor because it was in the darkest corner, the furthest away from the stairs, and behind the large, rusted bulk of the furnace, as far away as she could get from the dull glow of the light bulbs strung along the ceiling beams. There were three narrow windows on either wall of the cellar that looked out on the front and back yards, but they were so thick with dirt and grime that very little daylight filtered through, even on a sunny day like today.

Thick clots of black cobwebs hung down from the joists and floorboards. Afraid of touching a spider or maybe something worse, Angie wore a work glove on one hand as she felt as far back as the outside wall. The area was much deeper than it appeared from the cellar floor. She figured that—for now, anyway—this was about the best hiding place she could find for John's revolver.

Her stomach was tensed, and her body trembled as she turned and walked over to the workbench where she had left the gun and picked it up. She had already checked it several times to make sure there were no bullets in the chamber. She had decided to keep the remaining ammunition separate from the gun, so it was still locked up in her bottom desk drawer. If JJ or anyone else poking around down here ever found the revolver, they still wouldn't be able to load and shoot it.

Of course, the easiest thing would have been for her to do exactly what Ellen Harding had suggested and turn the gun over to the police; but that seemed like too permanent a solution. She still couldn't bring herself to consider actually getting rid of John's gun. Once it was safely hidden down here, she could decide later what—if anything—more to do about it.

The damp gloom of the cellar gave her a bone-deep chill as she walked over to the place she had chosen and reached up into the dark space again. She wanted to make sure the gun wouldn't fall behind the stone wall. Once she was satisfied, she wrapped the gun in the old hand towel and slid it up onto the stone edge of foundation.

"Rest in peace," she whispered, pushing it back as far as it would go.

When she was done, she stepped back and brushed her hands on her jeans. She knew that she should feel better about this than she did, but at least she had done *something*. She spent the next several minutes moving around the cellar, keeping the beam of her flashlight trained on the spot where the gun was to make sure that she couldn't see it from any location. Even after she was satisfied that she couldn't see it, she considered placing some wood or a couple of bricks in front of it just to make sure. Finally she decided that would probably only draw attention to the location and left it as it was.

"Maybe that's an end to it," she whispered as she walked up the cellar stairs, back into the kitchen.

Before turning out the cellar lights, she hesitated and looked back down the narrow stairway. A wave of sadness swept over her like the dark current of a river. As she closed and locked the cellar door, she told herself just to forget all about it. As far as she was concerned, John's revolver could stay down there until it rusted away into a useless piece of metal. She'd be happy if she never saw it or even thought about it ever again.

Angie had herself pretty much convinced that she was feeling good about her decision, but worry still gnawed at her mind. She jumped when the telephone rang but walked quickly over to the counter and picked it up.

"Hello?"

"Mrs. Ross," said a deep, male voice.

Angie didn't recognize the voice and was instantly on her guard.

"Yes," she said, casting a glance out the window to make sure JJ and Sammy were still out there. She saw them, tugging on a stick that Wolfgang had clamped between his jaws.

"This is Fred Doyle, JJ's Little League coach."

"Uh-huh," Angie replied noncommitally.

Her gaze went a little unfocused as she remembered the mutilated remains of the black dog on the playing field and JJ, questioning whether or not the man he and Sammy had met out there could have done such a thing to Blackie.

Was this the same man?

"I was just calling the players to let them know we're going to have a practice this afternoon at the field behind the elementary school. I know it's kind of short notice, but do you think John would be able to make it?"

"JJ," Angie said softly, hearing the catch in her voice. "Everyone calls him JJ."

"Sorry . . . Yeah, I can see that right here on his registration sheet. Do you think JJ will be able to come?"

"I—I'm not sure," Angie said shakily. "I'll have to ask him when he gets home."

She wanted desperately to ask this man if he was the one who had been out there with JJ and Sammy the other day but didn't know how to broach the subject without sounding too suspicious.

"It'd be great if he could be there around one o'clock. Of course, he should bring his glove."

"Sure. I'll tell him."

"It's no problem if he can't make it. It's an informal practice. I just thought, since it's such a nice day and all, I'd get together as many boys I could."

"Tell me, is Sammy Harding on your team?" Angie asked.

"He sure is," the coach replied. "He was on my team last year. He's quite the little player."

A feeling of apprehension passed like a dark wind through Angie. She didn't know why, but she was having trouble believing that this man was who he said he was. When she closed her eyes, all she could picture was the battered, bloody face of the black dog.

She jumped when the back door slammed open and JJ and Sammy ran into the kitchen with Wolfgang barking and nipping at their heels. They were laughing about something, but Angie signaled for them to be quiet.

"Like I said," she said, cupping her over the phone to cut down the sound of the puppy barking, "I'll ask him when he gets back."

"Thanks," the man said.

There was a soft click, and the line went dead. Angie still felt tense as she replaced the phone on its base.

"Who was that?" JJ asked, kneeling beside Wolfgang who had his face in his water bowl and was noisily slurping a drink. Water splashed all over the newspaper under the bowl.

"Your Little League coach," Angie said. "There's practice this afternoon, over behind the school."

"Cool," JJ said as he opened the refrigerator and pulled out a jug of orange juice. He raised the bottle to Sammy, who nodded that he'd like some. JJ handed the jug to Sammy, then looked over at his mother and suddenly froze.

"I just hope it's not that same guy," he said with a tremor in his voice as he cast a nervous glance over at Sammy.

"His name's Fred Doyle," Angie said.

"Oh, Mr. Doyle? He's cool!" Sammy said, watching as JJ got a couple of glasses from the cupboard and set them up on the counter. "He was my coach last year. I was hoping I'd be on his team again."

"He's not the same man who was out there the other day, is he?" Angie asked, unable to hide the nervous edge in her voice. Sammy shook his head while watching eagerly as JJ poured him some juice.

"Oh, no way. Mr. Doyle's really cool."

"Well," Angie said, telling herself to relax, "if it's all the same to you guys, I think I'll go along with you just to be sure."

Both boys glanced at her with questioning looks, but JJ didn't protest. They gulped down their drinks, then put their glasses into the sink.

"Sammy. If you want, why don't you call your mom and ask if it's all right for you to have lunch here," Angie said. "We can drive over to the field together after."

"Sure thing, Mrs. Ross," Sammy said. "I'll have to go home and get my glove, though."

"Sure."

"Com'on," JJ said, turning to Sammy. "You can call from my room. I want to show you how far I've gotten in that game."

The house filled with the sound of running feet as they scampered upstairs. For a long time, Angie just stood there staring blankly ahead as though she had no idea what to do next. Finally, she set to work making sandwiches for the boys.

Working didn't make her feel any better, though. She had hoped that getting rid of John's gun would eliminate the strange, nervous feeling she had, but it was just as strong.

She couldn't identify what was bothering her, but she knew that she'd feel at least a little bit better once she met JJ's baseball coach and made sure everything there was okay.

If that's what was bothering her, then fine.

If it was something else . . . then she'd just have to figure out what it was and take care of it.

Chapter 21
Car Problems

"Want me to check your oil?" Greg asked after springing the catch on the gas pump trigger so it would fill automatically, and he wouldn't have to stand there holding it. He resisted the impulse to reach down and grab his crotch.

Yeah, sweetheart, he thought with a twisted grin. *I wouldn't mind checking your oil, all right!*

Angela Ross barely looked at him through the open car window before nodding her agreement. As Greg walked around to the front of the car, he heard the release for the hood pop. He was whistling tunelessly as he raised the hood and propped it open with the metal support arm.

After glancing at the engine, he pulled out the oil dip stick, wiped it clean on the greasy rag he took from the back pocket of his coveralls, then pushed the stick back in to get an accurate reading. Holding the stick up high, he saw that the oil was a little dirty, but the level was fine. As he slid the dip stick back into the hole, though, he leaned forward and reached with his other hand underneath the distributor cap. With a quick flick of his hand he pulled on one of the wires.

"Your oil's fine," he called out as he came back to the

driver's window, wiping his hands on the rag. Angela nodded
but still didn't look directly at him.

Don't you even KNOW who I am?

He wanted to grab her by the shoulders and shout it into her
face.

Can't you just FEEL what I wanna do to you?

He leaned close to the window and inhaled deeply, enjoying
the flowery smell of her perfume that wafted out of the car.
He remembered that same smell on her bed sheets and couldn't
help but feel the stirrings of an erection.

"You know what though?" he said, adopting a serious tone.
"Some of the wires in your distributor cap look a little loose
and frayed. You been having any trouble starting your car in
the morning?"

Angela looked straight at him and shook her head.

"No. I just had a tune up a month or so ago, and nobody
mentioned that."

Greg shrugged as if it was entirely out of his control before
going back to the front of the car and lowering the hood. He
enjoyed seeing her startled reaction when he let go of the hood,
and it slammed shut. He was still whistling to himself as he
walked over to the pump, topped off the gas tank, and replaced
the nozzle. He felt as though he was smiling like the village
idiot when he came back to her window.

"That'll be fifteen dollars even," he said flatly.

He shifted from one foot to the other as he waited for her
to take a twenty dollar bill from her wallet and hand it to him.
Greg peeled a five dollar bill off the roll of bills he kept in his
pocket and handed it to her.

She nodded her thanks but didn't look at him again as she
started up the car. Before she drove away he caught her attention
and said, "You know, you might want to keep an eye on that
distributor cap. You never know when they're gonna go on
you."

"Yeah, I'll do that. Thanks," she said, but Greg knew as
she shifted into gear and pulled away from the pumps that she
would forget all about it. Like most women, she probably had
no idea what preventive maintenance was. He leaned one elbow

on the pump and watched as she drove down the road, heading
back to Bolton.

It wasn't until her car had disappeared around the corner
that he got an idea of what he could do next.

Greg got off work at the gas station a little after eleven
o'clock that night. After stopping off at a corner store to pick
up a six pack of beer and an Italian sandwich, he drove out to
Taylor Hill Road, where he parked his car on a dirt turnoff in
the woods a half mile or so past Angela's house.

For the next hour or so, he slouched in the front seat and
ate his sandwich while sucking down four of the beers. The
first couple of beers were cold and tasted just fine, but by the
time he got to the fourth one, they were so warm he didn't
enjoy them quite as much. Whenever he burped, his mouth
filled with the aftertaste of onions.

The night was dark, and the woods were filled with the high
buzzing sound of insects. Closing his eyes, he tried to enjoy
the sound. He had heard that people actually found this sound
soothing, but it wasn't long before it got on his nerves. He
looked up at the bright wash of stars that sparkled in the sky
above the dark line of trees. The view made him feel cold in
spite of the warm night.

Satisfied that he had a pretty good buzz on, but not enough
so he couldn't function properly, he got out and locked the car.
Keeping to the side of the road, ready to duck into the woods
if a car drove by, he started down the road to Angela's house.
As soon as he could see the house through the trees, he stepped
into the woods, thinking it would be safest to approach the
house from the rear.

The underbrush was dense, and the going was tough. It
wasn't long before Greg was seething with anger. He muttered
a swear whenever an unseen branch slapped him in the face
or he tripped over something on the ground, a root or branch.

Keeping to the shadows of the woods that edged the backyard, Greg circled around the house to make sure there was no
activity inside. The back of the house glowed silvery-blue in

the moonlight. It looked creepy, and if he hadn't known better, he might have thought it was haunted. Dark and dangerous thoughts filled his mind as he imagined Angela Ross and her children asleep inside the house . . . and what he could do to them.

What he *should* do, right now, he thought, was break into the house and take care of all three of them!

He hadn't brought his baseball bat with him. After killing that black dog, the bat had been so stained with blood and fur that he had thrown it into the river near his hotel. He hadn't had a chance yet to buy a new one.

But he didn't need a weapon.

He could easily grab a knife from the kitchen.

Before he broke into the house, though, he thought he should locate the telephone wire and disconnect that, first, and he would make sure to have all possible escape routes blocked before he let anyone in the house know he was there.

Maybe it was more trouble than it was worth, at least tonight, to try to do all of that in the dark.

Maybe he should just do what he had come here to do and see what happened.

There was always tomorrow.

He waited in the woods out behind the garage for a long time, all the while watching the house for any signs of activity. Once he was positive it was safe, he broke cover and, crouching low, ran across the lawn to the back of the garage.

He was panting heavily as he pressed himself against the garage wall. Every breath burned his lungs, and his heart was thumping so heavily in his chest it almost hurt. Clinging to the deep shadows, he crept around to the front of the building, all the while poised and tense, ready to respond if anything happened.

"All right," he whispered when he came around the front of the garage and saw that Angela had left the car parked in the driveway. "You're making this too easy for me."

Greg wondered how Angela dared leave her car out like this, but then he remembered that this wasn't the city. People did things differently here in the country.

Keeping the car between himself and the house, he darted from the shadow of the garage to the side of the car. He swore when he tried the passenger's door and found that it was locked. If the driver's door was also locked, then he'd either have to forget about his plan tonight or think of something else.

His heart was racing fast, and his legs ached as he skittered around to the driver's door. His hand was trembling as he reached up for the handle. Feeling tense and filled with anticipation, he grabbed the latch and squeezed it.

The door didn't resist at all. Greg let out a breath he hadn't even realized he was holding when the door popped opened.

He got ready, knowing that, as soon as the door opened all the way, the dome light would come on. He mentally counted to three, then swung the door open and jumped into the driver's seat. The light stung his eyes, but everything was plunged back into darkness when he pulled the door shut behind him.

It took a while for his eyes to adjust to the darkness again, but after a minute or two, he reached down below the dashboard until he found the hood latch and pulled it. The front hood made a loud *clang* sound and popped up when the catch released.

This was going a lot better than he could have hoped.

For a few seconds more, Greg sat there in the darkness, thinking about his next move. He knew that he would have to shut the car door tightly when he got out. Angela would no doubt notice it if the door was ajar in the morning, but he didn't want to make any more sounds that might alert anyone inside the house. He certainly didn't want her to be suspicious of anything, at least not until she tried to start the car in the morning.

"Fuck it," he whispered as he opened the door and tumbled out onto the driveway. Maybe he'd had one too many beers, he thought. The dull glow of the dome light hurt his eyes again, and he eased the door shut just enough so it winked off, then leaned his weight against it to shut it tightly.

Moving as quickly and as quietly as he could, he went around to the front of the car and raised the hood. He felt underneath the distributor until he found the wire he wanted and pulled it.

Just to be on the safe side, he also loosened a few of the spark plug covers.

Satisfied that Angela's car wouldn't start for her in the morning, he eased the hood down, leaning his weight against it until it clicked shut. He was just about to leave when a dog started barking.

"Shit," Greg muttered, looking around and trying to get a direction on the sound.

The barking sounded muffled and seemed to be coming from several directions at once. For a fleeting instant, Greg imagined that it was the black dog he had killed the other day out behind the school. After a moment, though, he realized that the sound was coming from inside Angela's house.

"When did they get a fucking dog?" he whispered.

Sweat broke out across his forehead. He tripped and almost fell a dozen times as he ran into the dark woods behind the garage. The barking sound from the house continued unabated as Greg withdrew deeper into the woods. Once he was far enough away, he stopped and looked back at the house. A light had come on in one of the upstairs windows. As he crouched in the darkness and watched, he saw another light come on downstairs and then the silhouette of someone—it looked like it was the boy—came to the back door. The outside porch light winked on, flooding the yard with a bright white glare.

Greg wanted to get up and run, but was afraid that any motion or sound might draw attention to himself. He crouched and watched as the back door swung open, and the boy stepped out onto the porch. A little dog—it looked like nothing more than a puppy—zipped out between the boy's legs and started running around the yard, all the while barking and sniffing the ground.

"What is it, Wolfie? Huh, boy?" the boy said. His voice was faint with distance, but it seemed close enough to make Greg nervous. If that dog caught his scent and followed after him, there would be problems he wasn't sure he wanted to deal with right now.

"What do you smell, boy? What is it?" the boy called out as he watched the dog from the porch. The puppy's head was low as he ran around the perimeter of the yard, still sniffing and yelping.

Keep the fuck away from me or you're dead meat, Greg thought, but he didn't dare move a muscle, even to grab a tree branch or something to use to protect himself. He wished he'd brought his baseball bat with him. Then he could take care of that mongrel *and* the boy, if he had to!

"What was it, a raccoon or something?" the boy called out.

Greg was relieved to see the dog run back onto the porch. The boy knelt down and scruffed him behind the ears.

"That's a good boy," he said, his voice carrying faintly to Greg where he crouched in the darkness. After another few seconds, the boy opened the door and went back inside. Greg still didn't move for several minutes, not until after he saw the last light upstairs wink off.

When he stood up and stretched, the blood rushed from his head, and bright spots of light spun across his vision. He felt shaken as he made his way through the trees and back to the road. He kept glancing over his shoulder, expecting to see a police car coming, responding to a call from Angela, but the road was deserted.

Greg didn't feel better until he was in his car and driving back to his hotel. Only then did he remember that he had done what he'd set out to do. If things worked out the way he hoped, a tow truck would be dragging Angela Ross' car into the station sometime tomorrow. He cracked the flip top on a warm beer and drank it as he drove up Route 202, and by the time he pulled into the hotel parking lot, he was feeling good about what he had accomplished tonight . . . *Damned* good!

"I'll bet it was Evan," Brandy said the next morning as she and her mother were sitting at the kitchen table.

"Why would Evan be out here that time of night?" her mother asked, looking at her with one eyebrow raised.

Nibbling at her lower lip, Brandy glanced downward and shrugged. A surge of nervousness ran through her, and she had to look away from her mother.

"Brandy . . . ?"

"We were—"

Brandy's voice caught in her throat, and she had to take a sip of orange juice before she could continue. All the while, her mother was looking at her with that intense look she got whenever she was trying to pry something out of her.

"The other day . . . at school . . . we had . . . kind of an argument."

"An argument . . . ? About what?"

Brandy bit her lower lip, shook her head, and shrugged again. "Just about . . . stuff."

"And are you going to tell me what this *stuff* is?" her mother asked, pressing.

Brandy closed her eyes and ran her hand across her forehead as she considered for a moment. Finally she looked her mother straight in the eyes and said, "It's not important. Honest, Mom."

"Are you sure? I mean, I don't want any trouble. If you think he might be prowling around outside our house late at night, maybe I should talk to him or his parents or maybe the police about it."

"We don't *know* it was him," Brandy said sharply. "I just thought . . . you know, that he might have come over and wanted to . . . talk to me."

"Are you sure that's all he would have wanted? . . . To *talk?*"

"Mom," Brandy said, unable to keep the whining tone out of her voice. "You can trust me, okay?"

For a long, uncomfortable moment, her mother regarded her with a cold look in her eyes. Finally, she nodded and said, "I hope I can. I just hope you've got the good sense to be careful."

"Don't worry, Mom. Besides, it probably wasn't even him. Like JJ said, Wolfgang probably just heard a raccoon or skunk banging around in the trash or something."

"Umm . . . Probably," Angie said, but Brandy could tell that she wasn't convinced.

Glancing up at the wall clock, Brandy said, "Well, I don't want to miss the bus," and got up from the table. As she hurried out of the kitchen, she could feel her mother's gaze, burning like a laser into her back. She told herself that she would have to settle things with Evan once and for all. Either they were going to be going steady on *her* terms, or else she wanted a clean break.

The next morning, Greg had to mask a smile when the truck from Bailey's Towing pulled into the station with Angela Ross' white Subaru in tow. Angela, looking small and pale, was in the cab with the driver. The backup warning buzzer started beeping as the driver—Greg had seen him around town but didn't know his name—started backing up to one of the open garage bay doors.

"What seems to be the problem?" Greg called out to the driver once he was out of the truck cab and working to release the hoist.

"Looks to me like someone frigged with the wiring," the truck driver said. "Some wires're pulled out of the distributor."

"Yeah, I noticed that just yesterday when she was in here for a fill up," Greg said.

He smiled and nodded to Angela as she got out of the truck and walked over toward them.

"It looked to me like they might just be plumb worn out."

"Could be, I s'poze," the truck driver said with a casual shrug. This wasn't his problem. He hit the winch release, and the car started rolling backward as the flat bed tilted up. Greg and Angela watched as he removed the chains, threw them into the back of the truck and, with a curt nod, got back into the cab and drove away.

Greg wiped his forehead with one hand and turned to Angela.

"I don't know as I can get to it 'till later today," he said as they started over to the office. He opened the door and held it for her. She wrinkled her nose as she entered and saw how messy the office was.

"Depending on what parts it might need," Greg went on, "I can't say for sure when I'll be able to get it done."

Angela was silent for a moment, thinking; then she shrugged

and, looking at her car through the grime-streaked window, said, "The work's got to be done. I really don't have a choice. I didn't have anything important planned for today, anyway."

Greg nodded as he took the car keys from her. He noticed that she was savvy enough to give him only the car key, and not leave the house keys or anything else on the ring. He took a yellow tag and ring from the box behind the counter and wrote her license plate number on it.

"I'll need your name and a phone number where I can reach you during the days," he said, not looking up at her. He gripped the pen tightly, poised and ready to write.

Angela gave him her name and phone number, and Greg dutifully wrote it down even though long ago he had looked up her number and memorized it.

"S'there anyone you can call for a ride home?" he asked as he hung the key on one of the hooks behind the desk. Angela pursed her lips and shook her head.

"I called my brother from the house, but he said he couldn't get away form work for an hour or so."

Greg's back stiffen when she said that. He hadn't known that she had a brother or any other relative living locally, but it made sense. Why else would she choose to move from New York to a dipshit little town like Bolton?

"Where's that?" Greg asked, thinking he'd better know everything he could learn about this brother of hers, just in case he ever ran into him. It wouldn't hurt to check him out and make sure he wasn't going to be a problem.

"Where's what?" Angela asked, looking at him confused.

"Your brother," Greg replied, hoping to hide his obvious interest. "Where's your brother work?"

"Oh, he teaches history at the regional high school," Angela said with a half-smile.

"Well, since he can't come by and pick you up, I guess I could give you a ride home . . . unless you don't mind waiting." Greg was trying hard to keep the excited edge out of his voice.

Angela considered his offer for a second or two, then nodded slightly and, her smile widening, said, "Yeah, I'd really appreciate it."

"No problem-o," Greg said, waving a hand. He came around the counter and opened the door for her, and they walked back outside. Angela seemed relieved to be out of the office. Greg didn't blame her, although over the last few days, he'd gotten used to the smell.

Larry, the owner, had taken the day off to go fishing, so Greg told the pimple-faced teenager whose name was Billy Davis that he was in charge of the station until he got back.

Angela seemed a bit nervous, tentative as she walked with him over to his car, which was parked beside the building. Greg couldn't help but smile to himself as he thought that, if she only knew what he intended to do to her eventually, she would have every reason to be nervous.

And maybe *today* was the day!

He opened the passenger's door for her and watched as she slid onto the seat. He liked the way she moved, and felt his erection hardening.

"Make sure you buckle up," he said once he was behind the steering wheel. "With that new seat belt law, the cops can fine me up to a hundred buck if you don't it."

Angela stretched the belt across her chest and clicked it. He couldn't help but notice the way the belt ran between her breasts, emphasizing their size. He grinned at her as he started up the car and pulled out of the station lot, stepping on the accelerator hard enough to make the tires chirp on the asphalt.

As he drove, heading back to Bolton, Greg felt almost dizzy with elation. He couldn't help but feel as though this was all a dream, and that he would wake up soon. He inhaled sharply, trying to convince himself he was awake.

"That's a nice perfume you're wearing," he said, glancing over at her.

"Oh, thank you," Angela said, looking a little flustered by his compliment. She seemed to be making a point of keeping her gaze fixed on the road ahead.

As they drove through downtown Bolton, Greg slowed down when he saw the Dunkin' Donuts on the corner of Main and Mill Street.

"Feel like having a coffee and donut?" he asked brightly. "My treat."

Angela looked at him curiously and then, biting her lower lip, shook her head sharply and said, "Uh—no thanks."

A sudden jolt of anger shot through Greg. His first impulse was to ask her if she thought she was just a little too good to be seen around town with *just* a car mechanic, but he knew that he couldn't let his feelings show and shrugged it off.

"Just askin'," he said, trying his best to sound casual.

Once they were through town, Greg took the turn onto Pine Street, which led to Taylor Hill Road. Angela suddenly shifted forward in her seat.

"How'd you know to turn there?" she asked.

Greg could hear the trepidation in her voice but, with a casual shrug, said, "I'm just driving. I figured you'd tell me when to turn."

Out of the corner of his eye, he caught her looking at him suspiciously. Hoping to put her fears to rest, he let a thin smile spread across his face. After a moment, he looked over at her.

"The fact of the matter is, yesterday, after you came by the station, my boss, Larry, said something about how he thought you lived out this way."

"Is that so?" Angela said. She obviously didn't like being the subject of conversation with people she didn't know.

"Uh-huh, and I can see why." Greg glanced from one side of the road to the other at the trees and scattered houses and farms. "It's really nice country out here, ain't it?"

Angela still seemed poised and tense. She nodded her head but said nothing.

"I can see why you'd want to live out here. I'll bet you really appreciate the peace and quiet."

Angela still said nothing, but Greg kept right on talking.

"Now take me, for example. I live right smack dab in the middle of Augusta. Talk about noise."

"You don't sound like you're from around here originally, though," Angela said. "Your accent's pretty New York."

Greg thought he detected a funny glint in her eye, as if she didn't trust him in the least.

"I'm originally from Brooklyn," Greg said, but he let it drop at that, not wanting to say any more about himself than he had to.

As they were approaching her house, Greg reminded himself not to start slowing down until she said something. When he saw her house up ahead, he tensed and felt a thin sheen of sweat break out across his forehead. Angela still didn't say anything.

Okay, Greg thought, smirking to himself. *You want to play games? We'll play games.*

Pressing down a little harder on the accelerator, he sped right past the turn to her driveway without even a sidelong glance. He didn't react until Angela suddenly jerked forward in her seat. He glanced over at her as if there was something wrong, and again caught a glimpse of the way the cross strap of the seat belt angled between her breasts. They looked so round and tempting beneath the thin blouse she was wearing.

"Damnit, we missed it," Angela said. She put her arm on the back of the seat and looked over her shoulder out the rear window. "That's my house back there. Sorry. I must have spaced out for a second."

Absolutely convinced that she was suspicious of him, Greg smiled tightly but said nothing as he pulled over to the side of the road and stopped. The gravel crunched beneath the tires. Looking ahead and behind, he didn't see any other cars around. Through the open widow, he could hear the high, buzzing of insects. The sound drilled his nerves, making him feel tense.

For just an instant, he considered doing her right here, right now. His vision clouded with a thin red haze, and he thought that he could hear faint voices whispering inside his head, urging him on. He quickly let the sudden impulse pass and did a sharp U-turn, forcing a smile as he drove back down the road.

Maybe he'd pushed a little too far when he'd asked her to go out for coffee with him, he thought. Or maybe he'd blown it by driving out on Taylor Hill Road without asking for directions.

Whatever the case, it sure seemed as though she had purposely not told him that her house was coming up just to see his reaction. He cautioned himself that he would have to watch himself very closely with her. One little slip, and he could blow the whole thing.

"The yellow house on the right?" he asked as he slowed for the turn into the driveway.

Angela nodded tightly, and Greg turned in. Even before he pulled to a stop by the front door, he saw that she had her seat belt unhooked and her right hand on the door handle. He wanted to say something to pacify her but couldn't think of anything other than, "Nice place. I've noticed it before."

She looked at him strangely, making him think that even as casual a comment as that made her suspicious of him. Prickly heat rushed up his back.

"On my days off, I like to drive around the area, looking at houses I know I'll never be able to afford," he said lamely.

"Thanks for the ride," Angela said, obviously wanting to end any further conversation. She opened the door and put one foot out onto the driveway, looking like she was ready to run if she had to.

"You'll give me a call when my car's ready?" she asked.

"Sure thing," Greg said, nodding. He didn't want to say anything else that might give himself away.

"Thanks again," Angela said as she stepped out of the car and swung the door shut. Greg waved back to her and, shifting into gear, pulled around to the road entrance. He tooted his horn and waved as he glanced in his rearview mirror, but he didn't see her. She had already gone inside the house. He imagined her, peeking out the window, watching him as he drove away.

On the drive back to the gas station, Greg was at first furious with himself for how things had turned out. He kept telling himself that what he should do right now is drive back to her house and go in there and take care of her.

But he knew he couldn't do that.

The kid back at the station knew that he'd driven out here with her. If she turned up dead later today, Greg was sure that he'd be the first and probably only suspect. He also realized that it wouldn't be anywhere near as easy to disappear in Maine as it had been in Brooklyn or Manhattan.

The more he thought about it, though, the more he had to admit that he rather enjoyed what Angela Ross had done today.

She was no fool, that was for sure!

And he told himself that he was going to enjoy playing a little game of cat and mouse with her before he finally did what he'd come to Maine to do. After all, he still had the whole summer to get ready for his move to Florida.

What else was he going to do to kill time?

Chapter 22
Checking Out

As she went through the day, Angie felt uncomfortable about some of the thoughts she was having about the man who had given her a ride home earlier that morning. For one thing, it was only after he had dropped her off and driven away that she realized he had never even told her his name.

She didn't like that.

Usually, only people who were hiding something didn't tell you their name.

In fact, there wasn't very much about him that she liked. She didn't like the way he kept sneaking sly glances at her that he obviously thought she didn't notice. And she didn't like the way he talked to her. Even when he was saying the most mundane, innocuous thing, he seemed to load his expression with veiled innuendo that Angie couldn't help but see as sexual.

She kept telling herself that she was being ridiculous, that the man had simply been doing her a favor, offering her a ride home. He didn't have to take time off from work to do that.

Maybe, she thought, she was merely overreacting because she had lived for so many years with John that his suspicion and subtle paranoia had worn off onto her. Cops certainly had enemies, and as a group, cops seemed to be suspicious of *everyone* else. Over the years, John had taught her—perhaps all too well—to be wary and watchful at all times.

The more she thought about it, the more she realized that there had been nothing *wrong* about that man today.

Not really.

In fact, beneath the grease on his clothes and face, Angie had to admit that she found him rather handsome, in a plain sort of way. He had short, dark hair and dark, liquid eyes. He certainly seemed pleasant and polite enough, but she couldn't shake the feeling that he was hiding something from her ... either hiding something ... or else pretending.

He certainly didn't look or act like a "typical" grease monkey, whatever that was. Time and again throughout the day, Angie found herself thinking that he really did seem harmless enough. Maybe she should have accepted his invitation to go out for coffee and donuts. What would it have hurt?

Still, the uneasy feeling she had didn't go away all day. Even late that afternoon, after the kids had come home from school and gone off with friends—Brandy with Evan, and JJ to Little League practice with Sammy—Angie couldn't stop thinking about the man from the gas station.

What the hell is it about him? she kept wondering.

Could it be that, beneath it all, she was attracted to him?

That struck her as almost silly, but she had to admit that it had been a long time since she had been with a man. She still missed her husband terribly. Many nights, she cried herself to sleep. But maybe the problem was something as basic as her own physical needs for love ...

For *sex!*

After all, this man was the only person she'd met since moving to Maine who'd shown even the slightest bit of interest in her. It wasn't like she was looking for any romantic involvements, but she hadn't noticed anyone who sparked an interest in her, either. The grief she still felt over John's death was too sharp.

But then again ...

As evening fell and thin fingers of deep purple clouds streaked like claw marks across the western sky, Angie was working silently in the kitchen, preparing supper. The family generally had supper at six-thirty every evening. She kept glancing at the clock, wondering if Brandy and JJ would be home on time. The uneasiness and strange sense of disorientation she'd been experiencing all day grew steadily stronger as the sky darkened. In spite of the warm breeze blowing in through the open kitchen window, she shivered whenever she looked out at the backyard.

What if something's happened to one of them? she thought, as she tried to penetrate the dense shadows gathering beneath the trees.

The gray glow of dusk filled the kitchen like a wash of ink as she walked out into the hallway to the front door, turning on the lights as she went. When she opened the front door and looked outside, her heart went suddenly cold in her chest.

There was a car parked up on the road in front of the house!

"What the—?" she murmured, leaning against the edge of the door.

She glanced nervously around, remembering how she had felt the other day when she'd been absolutely convinced someone who didn't belong here had been in the house. She felt the same way now.

The only sound she could hear was the whispering rush of her pulse in her ears as she eased the door shut until there was nothing more than a narrow crack through which she peered outside.

The stone wall in front of the house blocked her view of most of the car. In the gathering gloom, all she could see was the roof and a bit of the rear side panel. In the twilight, the car's windows looked like polished black marble. Whoever it was out there, he didn't have his headlights on. All Angie could tell for certain was that the car was light-colored and that the engine was running.

She felt a thrill of fear when she realized it looked quite a bit like the car she had ridden home in this morning.

The coldness clutching in her chest grew steadily stronger and began radiating down her arms as she considered that, while the man from the gas station had certainly seemed nice enough this morning, he very well could have been hiding something from her.

Tension mounted inside her as she listened to the low, steady rumble of the car's engine. Standing on tiptoes, she strained to see if the driver was sitting behind the wheel, or if he might have gotten out, but she couldn't see into the car.

"Jesus," she whispered as she looked around the yard, trying to see if anyone was lurking nearby. She didn't see any hint of motion in the shadows, but that didn't alleviate her fear. The disquieting sense of unease grew even stronger, bordering on panic. She wanted simply to close and lock the door and get back to making supper, but she didn't dare look away from the idling car. She wouldn't feel safe until her children were home.

For a moment, she considered walking out there, bold as could be, and confronting whomever it was. She even considered going down into the cellar and getting John's revolver from where she had hidden it before going outside. Or maybe she could call Rob and have him swing by the house just to check it out.

No, she told herself. *It's probably one of Brandy's friends . . . or maybe someone who's lost or broken down.*

But she didn't quite believe herself. The sense of menace was almost palpable. She had no idea what to do, but after a few tense minutes that seemed much longer, the decision was taken out of her hands. The car's engine revved up, and the car pulled away slowly, leaving behind a cloud of exhaust that slowly dissolved into the gathering darkness.

As the car drove away, still without its headlights on, Angie flung the door open and rushed out onto the front lawn but was unable to get a good enough look at it, much less see the driver. The brakes lights flickered once as the car crested the hill and then disappeared, heading down Taylor Hill Road, away from town.

For the next minute or so, Angie stood there in the front yard, panting heavily with her hands braced on her knees as she looked down the road where the car had gone.

Forget about it, she told herself; but even much later, long after the kids had gotten home, and they were all sitting down to supper, Angie couldn't shake the feeling that whoever it had been in the car, they'd been watching the house . . . watching her! After thinking about it through supper, she decided not to mention it to the kids. She saw no sense in getting them worried, too.

Before she went to bed that night, she made sure that both doors, front and back, were locked.

"Keep an ear open tonight, okay Wolfie?" she whispered to Wolfgang before she went upstairs to bed.

The dog was sleeping so soundly on the rug by the back door that his ears didn't even twitch at the sound of her voice.

"Sheesh, some watchdog," Angie muttered as she went upstairs. She put on her nightgown, washed up, and got into bed; but as she lay there in the darkness, trying to drift off to sleep, dark, unsettling thoughts filled her mind. A hard knot of tension formed in her stomach and wouldn't go away. She couldn't help but think that, if there *was* someone prowling around her house, it very well *could* be that man from the gas station.

Late that night, Angie had a disturbing dream that involved several people, none of whom she recognized, entering her room and speaking with her. When she awoke in the morning, she couldn't remember any of the details of the dream except one. All of the people who had visited her room had been wrapped in wide strips of dark linen. It was only in the morning that Angie realized they had looked like funeral shrouds.

After breakfast, Angie called Rob and practically demanded that he take time off from work so he could drive her out to the Larry Lee's Mobile station to pick up her car. She didn't tell Rob why, but she wanted to make sure that someone was with her because she was feeling so nervous about seeing that man again. When they pulled into the station, she felt only a slight measure of relief when she saw that the man was busy pumping gas into a battered, rusted pickup truck. An old man wearing a tattered white T-shirt and several day's beard stubble sat behind the wheel, smoking a hand-rolled cigarette. The station attendant smiled and waved to Angie when she got out of Rob's car, but she barely acknowledged his greeting as she strode into the office.

"Good morning, Larry," she greeted the man who was sitting at the desk, eating a cream-filled donut. "You called and said my car was ready?"

She only knew Larry's name from the oil-stained patch above the breast pocket of his stained work shirt.

"The Subaru, right?" Larry said, stuffing the remains of the donut into his mouth and wiping his hands on his pants legs as he turned around and fished the work order from the wire basket on the desk. The bulge of his belly seemed to get in his way as he hoisted himself to his feet and leaned forward.

Angie smiled and nodded, then cast a nervous glance out the window at the other man who—thankfully—was still busy with the customer at the pumps.

"Wasn't too bad, as it turns out," Larry said. "Just a couple of parts and an hour and a half labor."

Larry tried to smooth out the wrinkled work sheet with the heel of his hand but managed only to smudge some of the writing before he showed the bill to Angie. The price was a lot higher than she'd expected, but she didn't say anything as she took her checkbook from her purse and flipped it open.

"Make that payable directly to Larry Lee, if you don't mind," the man behind the counter said.

Angie nodded and quickly wrote the check.

"Did you do the work yourself?" Angie asked as she handed the check over to Larry. "Or did your helper do it?"

Larry squinted as he scanned the check, then nodded and pulled the hand crank of the antique cash register. The machine made a loud *ca-chang* sound that startled Angie, and Larry slipped the check under the cash drawer.

"Nope. Greg worked on it, mostly," Larry said, and then slammed the drawer shut, hard. It made another, louder noise.

"Greg?"

"Yeah. Greg Newman. New fella who works for me." Larry nodded to the window. "Just moved here a couple of weeks ago. Says he's from down 'round New York City.'' Larry looked at her with dull eyes. "Say, you're from down 'round there, too, ain't yah?"

Angie's shoulders tensed as she nodded slowly and said, "Yeah, well, sort of. Bedford Heights. It's just outside the city."

She could barely repress a shudder as she glanced out the window again at the man working the pumps. The pickup truck had pulled away, and he was busy stocking the wire rack with cans of oil, but Angie had the distinct feeling that, until just a second ago, he'd been watching her. The hairs at the nape of her neck stirred.

"Do you know where in New York he's from?" Angie asked, hearing the tightness in her voice.

Larry shrugged, obviously not really picking up on the tension she felt.

"I dunno," he said as if it didn't matter. "Brooklyn, I think he might've said. I can't rightly recall."

He looked up at the ceiling and scratched the side of his flabby neck, leaving faint pink lines on the flesh. Then he turned and grabbed a set of keys with a dangling yellow tag from the peg board on the wall and handed them to Angie. She ripped the yellow tag off and, smiling, said "Thanks," before walking out of the office. It was a relief just to go outside and get some fresh air.

"You all set, then?" Rob called to her. He was leaning his elbow out the open window of his car, looking anxious to get going.

Angie smiled and waved to him before opening the car door and slipping onto the front seat. She slid the keys into the ignition and cranked it, relieved to hear the engine start right up. Only then did she realize that she had been expecting her car not to start, as if that man at the pumps—Greg Newman—was setting a trap for her. She waved again to her brother, who waited until she pulled out into the road before following after her.

As she drove away, Angie glanced at the rearview mirror and saw the man at the pumps, standing with his hands on his hips and watching after her. His figure receded quickly in the mirror, but just before she lost sight of him as the car went around the bend in the road, she was positive she saw him raise his hand and wave to her.

The Bolton police station was small but it smelled exactly like every other police station Angie had ever visited. The predominant smell was a powerful, pungent aroma of floor wax, and the floor—a pattern of brown and black linoleum tiles—gleamed brightly with reflected light. Beneath the industrial wax smell was a subtle, more curious mixture of old coffee, sweat, and—even in these days of no smoking in public buildings—lingering cigarette smoke.

Besides size, the only difference between this station and John's precinct house in New York City was that there were fewer people waiting in the lobby to see someone. In fact, there was only one person here: a young man with long, stringy hair and a sallow complexion was sitting on the worn wooden bench underneath a bulletin board littered with public service announcements and yellowing FBI wanted posters.

Angie felt a slippery coil of nervousness in the pit of her stomach as she walked up to the main desk. Her shoes squeaked with loud *chirps* on the linoleum. She smiled at the dispatcher, an elderly woman with a long, braid of brown hair hanging down her back and thick glasses that distorted her round, blue eyes.

"Good morning," Angie said, smiling thinly as she folded her hands and leaned her elbows on the chest high counter.

"Morning," the woman said, looking at Angie with a polite but distant smile. "How can I help you?"

For a second or two, Angie was stumped because she wasn't quite sure what to say. From years of living with John, she was used to dealing with cops, but she realized that she didn't even have the name of someone to ask to see.

"I—ah, I'd like to talk to someone," Angie said tightly. "A detective, maybe."

"I think Detective Murray's free," the dispatcher said. "Can I tell him who's here?"

"Angie . . . Angela Ross."

"Just a minute, Ms. Ross," the dispatcher said. She turned and picked up the phone, pressed a number on the switchboard, and said something that Angie didn't catch into the receiver, then nodded and hung up. She pressed a button on the side of her desk, and a loud buzzing noise sounded from the door to the right of the desk.

"He can see you right now. Third door on the right," the dispatcher said disinterestedly, and then looked away.

Angie felt a sharp undercurrent of trepidation as she opened the door and entered the wide, dimly-lit corridor. When the door swung shut behind her, she heard the heavy lock click. Resisting the sensation of being trapped, she started down the hallway. Before she got to the third door on the right, she saw it swing open. Dusty light spilled across the floor as a stocky, rather good-looking man with short hair stuck his head out and acknowledged her.

"Angela Ross?" he said, stepping back so Angie could enter the room.

"Angie," she said, shaking hands with him.

Before she said anything more, the detective waved her to a chair beside his desk. She sat down stiffly and folded her hands in her lap.

"I'm Pete Murray," the detective said as he walked behind his desk and sat down heavily. The chair creaked beneath his weight. "What can I do for you?"

Shoulders stiff, Angie shifted uncomfortably in her chair as she considered what to say next. The truth was, she wasn't quite sure where or how to begin, and she was felling suddenly foolish that she had decided to come by the police station in the first place.

"Well, you see, I moved to Bolton recently with my two children," she began. Noticing that she was twisting her hands in her lap, she commanded herself to stop it. "My brother is Robert Morgan."

"Oh, sure. I know Rob. My son had him for American History last year. Good man. Excellent teacher."

Angie accepted the compliment with a curt nod.

"This isn't about Rob," she said. "You see, last winter back in New York, my husband was murdered."

It surprised her that she said those words without choking or instantly breaking down. She guessed it might be because she was in police station where talk about life and death always seemed more detached.

"I'm sorry to hear that," Murray, his eyes taking on a soft, sympathetic cast that seemed genuine. "Did they arrest the person who did it?"

Biting down on her lower lip, Angie shook her head tightly and stared down at the floor, needing a moment to collect her thoughts.

"He—umm . . . No. They didn't catch him," she said hesitantly. "My husband was a detective, in Manhattan, for the last twenty years. The investigating detective thinks it must have been someone related to a case he'd worked on, but—" She looked up and shrugged helplessly. "The last time I talked to him, he didn't have any leads."

"Too bad," Murray said, gritting his teeth as he shook his head. For several seconds, he regarded Angie in silence. Finally, he cleared his throat and said, "Is this what you wanted to see me about?"

"Not really," Angie said, shaking her head again. "There's something else. You see, ever since we moved here . . . We have a house out on the Taylor Hill Road."

"Umm, there are some nice houses out there."

"Well, for the last few—I don't know, maybe couple of weeks or so, I think there's been someone prowling around outside our house at night."

Murray's chair creaked loudly as he leaned forward, his expression deepening.

"Have you seen anyone?" he asked sharply.

Angie shook her head.

"Not really, but the other night, our dog started barking like crazy and wanted to go outside. Then, the next morning, I think someone had tampered with the wiring in my car because it wouldn't start.''

"What was wrong with it?"

Angie shrugged. "Some wires got pulled out. I had to have it towed, but it's fixed now.''

"Uh-huh,'' Murray said, still frowning as he nodded. "Well, I'd say it's a good thing you have a dog.''

"Yeah, well—that's another thing.''

Relaxing a bit, Angie leaned back in the chair and told Murray about what had happened to the black Labrador out at the baseball field. Murray listened without responding until she was finished, but she could tell by his expression that he didn't see any immediate connection between this and anything else.

"The thing that's got me kind of worried is—'' She squared her shoulders and took a deep breath. "I know this is going to sound really silly, but there's a man who works at the Mobil station on Route 202—''

"Larry Lee's place?'' Murray said.

Angie nodded.

"Yeah, well he has a man working for him who—I don't know how put it, but I kind of wonder if it might be him.''

"You mean who's prowling around your house.''

Angie nodded.

"What makes you think that? Has he said or done anything directly to you?'' Murray asked.

Again, Angie shook her head.

"Not really,'' she said. "He gave me a ride home yesterday, after they towed my car to the station. But—no, he's never said or done anything . . . offensive.'' She sighed and shook her head. "It's just that I—I don't really know what it is. I almost think I recognize him from somewhere, but I can't place him. When I went to pick up my car today, Larry told me that this guy was from New York City.''

"What's his name?'' Murray asked, looking more concerned as he opened a small notebook and took a pen from his shirt pocket.

"Greg Newman.''

A slight chill raced through her the instant she said the name out loud. She wondered if it was because Greg had made her feel so nervous, or if it was because she had found his subtle but obvious interest in her vaguely appealing.

"And *do* you recognize him?" Murray asked. "I mean, New York City's a big place, and I'll admit the odds are pretty slim, but maybe you've seen him there sometime."

"I doubt it," Angie said.

Murray stroked his chin as he sagged back in his chair and started tapping the pen on the blotter on his desk.

"I don't know the man," he said. "I've seen him there and may have spoken to him once or twice, but I've never seen him around town. I can run a check on him if you'd like."

Still feeling as though she was being ridiculous, Angie considered his suggestion for a moment, then nodded.

"I don't want to cause any trouble for him, you understand," she said softly. "Like I said, he hasn't done anything overt. It's just that there . . . there's something about him."

"Your 'blue sense'," Murray said with a wry smile.

"My what?"

"Blue sense. It's an expression cops use that means their intuition. You know, the feeling you get about someone for no obvious reason. Maybe a bit of it rubbed off on you from your husband."

Angie smiled thinly.

"Well, living with a cop isn't the easiest thing in the world."

"I think my wife would agree with you on that one," Murray said, chuckling as he shifted in his seat. "Look, I can't make any promises, but I'll run his name through the computer and see what comes up. If nothing else, it might help to put your mind at ease."

"If it's not a—"

"It's no problem," Murray said. "It's the least I can do for someone whose husband was on the Job."

"I—I'd appreciate it," Angie said, fighting back the feeling that she may have overstepped a line here and was possibly getting a man she didn't even know into trouble.

"I'll ask the fellas out on patrol to make a few more swings out your way and keep their eyes open," Murray said, standing

up and extending his hand to Angie so they could shake. His
grip was warm and strong, and Angie felt a wave of relief shift
through her for the brief moment they held hands.

"Thanks," she said softly before turning to leave.

"Just doing my job," Murray said as he walked her over to
the door.

As Angie was leaving, he said to her, "Stop by or call any
time. Oh, and give my regards to your brother when you see
him, okay?"

"I'll do that," Angie said with a smile. "Thanks."

She left the office, closing the door quietly behind her, and
walked down the hallway and through the door into the lobby.
The long-haired man was no longer on the bench. She smiled
and waved to the dispatcher on her way out the front door, but
the woman barely acknowledged her.

As she got into her car, started it up, and drove away, Angie
couldn't help but wonder if she had made a mistake giving Greg
Newman's name to Detective Murray. Chances were Greg was
a harmless enough guy who was just trying to make a living and
who had been polite enough to offer her a ride home yesterday. So
what if he might have found her attractive? The truth was, she
didn't mind thinking that men might still find her attractive.
Although she couldn't quite deal with the idea yet, she knew
that—eventually—she was going to want to meet other men.
Rob had already dropped a few hints that he knew an eligible
bachelor or two. No one would ever take John's place, and she
seriously doubted that she would ever want to remarry, but you
never could tell who might come along . . .

She couldn't deny that she felt a strong measure of relief,
just knowing that Murray was aware of her concerns, and that
the night patrolmen would be keeping an eye on her house
from now on. Whether it was Greg Newman or someone else—
if it was *anyone*—maybe now she would feel a little more
secure in her own home.

It was late afternoon, and the baseball field was alive with
noisy chatter from both players and parents as the first Little

League game of the season got under way. JJ felt a flutter of nervousness as he ran onto the field and took his position at first base. He repeatedly punched his fist into the pocket of his baseball glove and tried to focus his attention on Sammy, who was throwing a few warm up pitches to the catcher.

"All right! Play ball!" the umpire called out as he adjusted his face mask and stepped behind the catcher at home plate.

A skinny kid that JJ didn't recognize from school stepped up to bat first. As much as he tried to concentrate on the game, JJ couldn't stop his gaze from drifting over to the woods that fringed the ball field. The sun was already lowering in the sky. A hazy yellow light filtered through the trees, making it difficult for him to see any details. Long, dark shadows stretched like groping fingers from the woods across the field.

What if—right now—someone's hiding out there . . . watching me? JJ wondered.

A shiver rippled like a stream of ice water down his back.

"Come on, now! Strike him out, Sammy-boy!" JJ shouted, trying to focus on the game, but he couldn't stop thinking about what had happened to Blackie out here.

He wasn't sure what bothered him more—wondering if that man who had played ball with them that day was the one who had beaten Blackie to death might still be lurking in the woods, watching him; or thinking that the ghost of Frank Sheldon, the kid Sammy had told him had committed suicide in the woods behind the school, might still be haunting the dense shadows beneath the trees.

Or maybe Blackie's ghost is out there, JJ thought with a bone-deep shudder.

His vision clouded over, and tears welled up in his eyes as he thought about the black Labrador. Of course, JJ loved his new puppy, Wolfgang, but he couldn't stop missing Blackie and thinking that, if only his mother had let him bring the dog home when he had asked her, he might still be alive.

Lost in thought, JJ kept scanning the darkening border of the woods, his eyes jumping from one shifting shadow to another. No matter how hard he tried, he couldn't shake the unnerving feeling that *someone* was hiding there, watching him.

JJ gasped and sudden stiffened when he saw—or *thought* he saw—a huge, dark shape that looked an awful lot like a person shift from behind one tree trunk to another. His teeth clenched together, and dry a rawness gripped his throat as he stared into the shadows, trying to see better.

A sudden, loud *crack* sound snapped him back to attention.

He looked toward home plate just in time to see the baseball bounce off the grass and head straight at him. He cried out as he ducked more out of reflex than anything else, and held his glove up in front of his face for protection. He was only distantly aware that he stopped the ball when he felt it drill with a sharp sting into the palm of his hand.

"First base! Go to first base!" his coach shouted, his voice rising about the sudden cheering of the crowd, but JJ was too stunned to move. His eyes widened with gradually mounting terror as he looked over to the woods again, convinced that he had seen a human-shaped shadow shift in the darkness under the trees.

Cold, clutching fear gripped JJ as he looked around slowly, still wondering what he was supposed to do. Everyone was yelling at him, but none of it made sense. Things seemed to be happening in slow-motion. He saw the kid toss the bat aside and start running full tilt down the first base line. His coach was off the bench now, moving toward him, all the while waving his arms wildly and shouting at him to *run*.

The problem was, nothing made any sense to JJ. The whole world had turned into a chaotic blur of color and noise.

"Tag him! *Tag him!*" his coach yelled.

"Run to first base, JJ! Run!"

That sounded like Sammy, but by now all of the players and parents were shouting. By the time JJ realized what he was supposed to do, it was too late. He made an awkward lunge for first base, but before he got there, the runner stepped on the bag, raising a little puff of yellow dust. A chorus of hoots and jeers rose from his teammates as JJ turned and feebly tossed the ball back Sammy on the pitcher's mound.

"Smooth move, X-Lax," Sammy said, scowling.

"Sorry," JJ said with a shrug.

Glancing over at his coach, JJ shook his head and shrugged helplessly.

"That's all right, JJ," Coach Doyle shouted. "Just stay awake out there. Remember what I said about focus."

JJ nodded and, gritting his teeth, got into ready position leaning forward with his hands on his knees. The next player hit a double that, because of an error by the player in right field, drove in one run, but Sammy struck out the next three batters in a row. JJ was feeling miserable as he trotted back to the bench with his teammates. Coach Doyle came up to him and patted him on the shoulder.

"Shake it off, son," the coach said mildly. "Just first game jitters. That's all it is. We held 'em to one, and that's what counts."

JJ nodded sullenly as he sat down on the bench, his head hanging low. He felt terribly uncomfortable with his back to the woods, but he tried hard not to think about how he could almost *feel* someone's steady gaze boring into the back of his head.

He cringed inwardly, wishing that he dared to turn around and look to see who it might be, but he didn't have the courage. He didn't know which would be worse . . . actually seeing that man or the ghost of that kid who had hanged himself . . . or *not* seeing anything, but still *knowing* that somewhere in the deepening shadows, unblinking eyes were watching every move he made.

Chapter 23

Invitation

Two days after Angie spoke with Detective Murray, he called to tell her that—at least according to the interstate computer system—Greg Newman didn't have a police record. Not even any unpaid parking tickets. Although this didn't prove anything one way or another, he told her, usually someone who might pose a threat had *some* kind of history of trouble with the law. He suggested that, if she didn't like the guy, it might be a good idea for her patronize some other gas station and let it be. He also reminded her that, if she ever saw or heard anyone sneaking around her house, she could call him, day or night.

On Friday afternoon, the last week of May, Angie was driving east on Route 202, heading to Augusta to do some shopping. Although the day had started out sunny and warm, it had clouded up and been raining steadily since noontime. Because the road had warmed up earlier in the morning, wisps of steam rose phantom like from the cooling asphalt that glistened like dark seal skin.

Angie tensed when she saw a solitary figure walking along the side of the road. It was a man, she could see that much even from far away. The figure was hunched over, walking against the rain.

Her first impulse was to speed past him without even looking because she *never* picked up hitchhikers; but as she got closer, she realized that it was Greg Newman, huddled inside the hood of his raincoat, looking pathetic in the downpour as he turned to face her oncoming car and stick out his thumb.

"Oh, shit," Angie muttered, cringing a little as she approached him.

She wanted to drive by as if she hadn't even noticed him, but she was certain that he would recognize her car, so she slowed down and pulled to a stop a hundred or so feet ahead of him. Slipping the car into *reverse,* she backed up to meet him as he made a dash for the car.

Leaning across the seat, Angie unlocked the passenger's door.

"Whew! Thanks for stopping," Greg said, shaking his head and huffing as he dropped onto the seat and closed the door, cutting off the rain-laden gust of wind.

"Nice day . . . if you're a duck," Angie said, thinking immediately how stupid she must sound.

"Oh. Hey. It's you. I didn't even recognize your car," Greg said, smiling as he wiped his face with the flat of his hand.

Angie laughed tightly, finding it hard to maintain direct eye contact with him.

"I generally don't pick up hitchhikers," she said, "but I figured—you know, it was the least I could do to return the favor when you drove me home the other day."

"I appreciate it," Greg said.

His face was dripping water, and his eyes had a strange twinkle as he looked at her. Angie had the momentary feeling that—somehow—he had known she was going to be driving by and had planned this, but—of course—that was ridiculous.

"Where's your car?" she asked as she shifted into gear and drove off.

The wipers swept steadily back and forth, but the rain was coming down so hard, even at full speed they had trouble clearing the windshield.

"I—ah, had a little problem with the carburetor," Greg said, sniffing as he wiped his nose. "You didn't see it parked on the side of the road?"

Angie shook her head and glanced into the rearview. She hadn't seen an abandoned car, and she was pretty sure she would have noticed one if it had been Greg's.

They drove for a while in silence, the only sound the steady slapping of the windshield wipers and the humming of the defroster. Angie took the time to reevaluate her feelings about Greg. For some reason, he didn't seem quite as threatening today. In fact, he struck her as quite pathetic. He looked pale and miserable, almost drowned from the weather.

"So, are you on your way home?" she asked.

Greg grunted and shook his head. Droplets of rainwater dripped onto his jacket.

"Yeah," he said, "but you don't have to go out of your way for me. If you're heading into Augusta, you can drop me off anyplace downtown. I'll catch a bus back to the hotel."

"I don't mind driving you there. Where is it?"

Angie surprised even herself by her forwardness. She noticed when Greg looked at her that he still had that funny gleam in his eye and hoped that he wasn't thinking she was coming on to him. But the truth was, in a strange way, she *did* find him at least a bit attractive.

"It's over on Canal Street," Greg said.

Angie bit her lower lip and nodded. "You know," she said, "we've never been formally introduced. My name's Angie Ross."

She held her hand out to him. When he took it and shook it, she noticed how strong and cold his grip was. It felt funny to be touching a man's hand. It seemed to be more than just a greeting.

"Angie," Greg said, letting a smile play across his face as he shifted around and glanced into the back seat. "That's a beautiful name. My name's Greg . . . Greg Newman,"

"Pleased to meet you, Greg," Angie said, smiling wider. "I want to thank you again for all the help you gave me with my car."

"Hey, it was nothing. Just doing my job," Greg replied, waving his hand dismissively.

"Well, I certainly appreciated it," Angie said. "My car's running better than it has in a long time."

A nervous tension filled Angie because she wasn't quite sure what to say next. From talking to Larry, she knew that Greg had moved to Maine from New York City, but she wasn't sure she wanted to delve into that. She kept sneaking glances at him, trying to figure out why he looked so familiar; but no matter how hard she tried, she still couldn't place him.

They drove a while in silence. Angie noticed that Greg kept glancing over his shoulder into the back seat, almost as if he was expecting to see someone sitting there. She glanced into her rearview mirror but didn't see any other cars following them.

They made small talk until they drove into Augusta. Greg directed her through the rotary, then down Water Street and over to Canal Street. The streets, at least in this part of the city, looked desolate. None of the businesses seemed to be thriving. The buildings and storefronts looked shabby and rundown. Many of them had whitewashed windows and boards nailed across the doors. Certainly this was nothing like New York City, but it surprised Angie to find this kind of drab bleakness in Maine. She had assumed that the whole state was as rural and pleasant as Bolton. This section of Augusta, at least, looked almost "innercity."

"Have you been living here long?" Angie asked.

"In Maine?" Greg said. He smacked his lips and stroked his chin as he shook his head. "Not really. I move around a lot."

"Oh? Where are you from . . . originally, I mean."

She sensed that she might be pressing him a little too hard on this point, but she wanted to hear his answer, if only to see if it matched what Larry had told her.

"I was living in Brooklyn for the last couple of years," Greg said.

"Really," Angie said, nodding. She almost told him that she was from New York, too, but caught herself and let it drop.

"Before that—"

Greg shrugged, then glanced over his shoulder into the back seat again. There was tightness in his expression that bothered Angie.

"Before that, I lived in Oregon, Florida, and California for a while."

Angie was driving slowly down the street when Greg indicated a building up ahead on the right. A peeling, white sign with black scroll lettering announced the KENNEBEC HOTEL.

"You can drop me off on the corner there," he said, pointing to an empty parking spot near the door.

Angie detected a tightness in his voice, but when she pulled up to the curb and looked at him, he was smiling broadly.

"Well, here we are," she said. She sat back with both hands on the steering wheel and looked at him.

"Thanks," Greg said. He reached for the door handle, then paused and turned back to her.

"You know—" he said, but then cut himself off.

In the awkward silence that followed, Angie told herself to let it drop. She could guess what he had been about to say, and she wasn't sure she wanted to hear it.

Not yet, anyway.

She was trying to convince herself that she didn't find him attractive in any way, but she couldn't deny that there was *something* about him, a familiarity that appealed to her. She wished she could put her finger on what it was. Nibbling on her lower lip, she stared straight ahead at the windshield wipers, slapping back and forth.

"Thanks for the lift," Greg said.

Once again, he reached for the door handle and hesitated. Finally, he cleared his throat and, leaning closer to her, said, "You know . . . I was just wondering."

Angie wanted to say something but couldn't.

"It's just . . ." Greg's voice trailed away as he shook his head and ran his fingers through his still-damp hair. "I was wondering if you'd like to come up to my room for a drink."

Well, there it is, Angie thought. A ripple of excitement ran through her. Her first impulse was to say *no* because the truth was, she really wasn't looking for any kind of involvement with *anyone.* Even though the immediate grief of John's death was passing, she missed him terribly and still couldn't imagine ever replacing him. She was forty-two years old and had pretty much decided that she'd be content simply to raise her children, start her teaching job in the fall, and leave it at that.

But her second impulse was to say *yes.*

She couldn't deny that there was something about Greg Newman that she found powerfully attractive. There was a roughness about him, but below that she could detect a sensitivity that was appealing. She knew it might simply be because she hadn't been with a man since her husband's death, but it seemed more than that. In a vague, inexplicable way, she felt almost as though she and Greg Newman were linked somehow. If she believed in reincarnation, she might even have said that they had known each other—maybe even have been lovers— in a previous lifetime.

Greg shifted nervously in his seat and looked at her with an eagerness in his expression that simultaneously attracted and disturbed her.

"Look, if I'm out of line here—you know, like, if you're married or something, just say so."

Greg was speaking so softly Angie could barely hear him above the steady patter of the rain on the car roof. Biting her lower lip, she shook her head and said, "No, it's not that. It's just that I . . ."

Her voice trailed away, and a sharp jab of grief hit her when she pictured John the night of the shooting—the pale look of shock and surprise on his face . . . and the blood. There seemed to be blood everywhere. The mere memory of the wrenching panic she had experienced that night was almost as strong and real now as it had been that night. She wanted desperately to tell Greg about it, to explain why she didn't think it was such a good idea for her to accept his invitation, but she had no idea where to begin.

"I . . . I just can't right now," she finally said, hearing the rawness of emotion in her voice. She was shaking inside and knew that she was close to tears.

"Hey, I understand," Greg said softly. He started to reach out to touch her, then drew his hand back. "I mean—" He sniffed with laughter and shook his head. "Who the hell am I, right? We meet once or twice at the gas station where I work, and then, out of the blue, I'm hitting on you. I'm sorry. That isn't at all what I—"

"No, don't be sorry," Angie said softly. "It's not that at all. Really. It's just that I . . . I'm not ready to . . ." She took a deep breath and let it out in a gasp. "My husband died last winter."

There! She'd said it!

"Oh, Jesus. I'm sorry to hear that," Greg said.

Angie swallowed with difficulty. "I appreciate the offer," she said. "I really do, but I have to be back home before three o'clock."

"I understand," Greg said with a sympathetic nod. "Maybe some other time, then."

"Yeah . . . Maybe."

The instant he opened his door, a cold rush of wind and rain entered the car, chilling Angie. She wanted to try to explain herself better, but she watched silently as he got out of the car. Pulling his hood over his head, he hunched his shoulders and started up to the dark entrance of the hotel. Angie waited until he was on the stairs before she honked the horn. When he turned and looked back at her, she waved, then opened her door.

"What the heck?" she called out as she pulled the keys from the ignition.

The rain was cold and stinging in her face as she dashed over to the protection of the doorway. A slow, sly smile spread across Greg's face as he reached to open the door for her.

"What's one little drink, huh?" Angie said.

Greg was so furious at himself for blowing another chance that he almost couldn't believe his luck when he saw Angela get out of the car and call to him. He watched her like she was a ghost or an illusion as she ran over to him, shielding her face from the rain with her hand.

"What's one little drink, huh?" she said.

He liked the eagerness he saw in her eyes, and when he thought about what he wanted to do to her—what he *ought* to do to her right now!—he felt himself getting an erection.

"Yeah," he said, still playing the meek role she seemed to respond to. "I figured . . . you know, that it'd just give us a chance to get to know each other."

Greg's insides felt all tight and tingly as he opened the hotel door for her, and they entered the dimly lit lobby. He had never liked the smell of the hotel. There always seemed to be a faint smell of cheap wine and urine in the air, as if some of the seedier tenants brought the stench of the gutter inside with them. He started to apologize for it but stopped himself.

They crossed the lobby and rode the small, rattling elevator up to the fourth floor where they got out. As they walked down the hall, Greg's hands were trembling as he fished in his pants pocket for his keys.

"Don't expect too much," he said, smiling thinly as he fitted the key into the lock and turned it. He opened the door, then stood back so Angela could enter first.

Are you really going to do it? a voice whispered inside his head.

The voice sounded close and so real that he glanced over his shoulder to see if someone else was standing nearby.

"Sorry 'bout the mess," he said as he shut the door behind him. Not wanting to make her any more nervous than she might already be, he made a point of not locking the door or hooking the security chain.

Greg walked over to the bed and quickly kicked aside a pile of dirty clothes that was on the floor. The wastebasket was overflowing with the litter of takeout food and empty beer cans. Once again, he started to apologize but didn't. Instead, he slid the wastebasket between the bed and the wall so she wouldn't have to look at it.

"It's not much," he said, looking around and rubbing his hands together, "but—you know, it'll do . . . for now."

He could tell that Angela wanted to say something, but all she did was look around and nod solemnly. He noticed that she opened her raincoat but didn't take it off as she sat down on the only chair in the room.

Greg went into the bathroom and returned with a clean towel, which he offered to her.

"No thanks. I'm not all that wet," she said, waving him off. Greg used it to dry his face and hair, then tossed it onto the floor beside the bed.

"I—ah, I don't have any wine or anything," Greg said, indicating the array of bottles and beer cans on top of the rickety bureau. "Just some beer and a little whiskey." He held up the nearly empty bottle of whiskey and inspected it.

"Do you have any ginger ale?" Angela asked. "A little whiskey and ginger would be fine."

Greg was still trembling terribly inside with excitement. He couldn't believe that Angela Ross was really here in his hotel room, and he kept thinking that he was going to wake up soon and realize it was all a dream.

He walked into the bathroom again, took the glass from the sink, and hurriedly rinsed it out under the cold water. Smiling, he walked back into the room and looked at Angela.

You know, when it comes right down to it, you don't really have the balls to do it, do you?

The voice was faint inside his head. Greg was still convinced that there must be someone else in the room with them. His eyes widened as he looked around, but he didn't see anybody. Even with the window shades up, the overcast daylight made the room look small and gloomy. A dull, gray light—like the light in his dreams—filtered into the room, taking the hard edges off everything except his raging nerves.

He excused himself for a moment and went down the hall to the soda machine to get a can of ginger ale. When he got back to the room, he mixed Angela's drink using the bureau top as a bar. After handing her the drink, he cracked open a can of warm beer from himself and, wincing, took a sip.

Angie was still sitting in the chair, so Greg sat on the edge of the bed, leaning forward and resting his elbows on his knees. He was so tense his grip dented the flimsy beer can.

"So," he said, still aware of the tightness inside himself. "Tell me a little bit about yourself."

He took another gulp of beer, hoping it would help him calm down, but he could tell that it was going to take a lot more— and maybe stronger—drink to do that. He still was having trouble believing that Angela Ross was really here in his room.

Angela shifted slightly in the chair, then took a tiny sip of her drink. Greg could tell by the way she wrinkled her nose that she wasn't used to drinking whiskey, even when it was cut with something as sticky sweet as ginger ale. He guessed that she was more of a wine or maybe a scotch drinker.

"There's not much to tell, really," she said.

Greg noticed the way her eyes fluttered when she spoke, and he could tell by her posture that she was holding back on him. The bedsprings squeaked as he reclined on the bed, resting on one elbow. He shifted his leg around so his erection wouldn't be too obvious.

He told himself that this was going to be *fun!* He should enjoy every second of it, wondering how long it would take him to break her down. He could do it easily, he thought, if he could get her to talk about what had happened to her husband.

"How long have you lived in Maine?" he asked innocently.

Angela took another dainty sip and shrugged as she placed the drink down on the table beside her.

"I—we just moved here this spring . . . in April. In fact—" She laughed and shook her head. "It was during a blizzard. Can you believe that it actually was *snowing* in April?"

"I remember that storm," Greg said, nodding. He was hoping that he could keep her doing most of the talking, but after a moment, an uncomfortable silence descended on the room.

"You see," Angela finally said, "after my husband died last winter—"

"How did that happen?" Greg asked, softening his eyes as he shifted forward. On some level, he wished that he could tell her—right now—that *he* was the one who pulled the trigger. Imagine her reaction to that!

Angela bit down on her lower lip and glanced at the floor. "I'd just as soon not talk about it, if you don't mind."

Her voice was close to breaking, and Greg smiled to himself, realizing how close she was to crying. He knew he couldn't allow what he was thinking to show, so he looked away and took another sip of warm as piss beer.

"I can understand how you feel," he said with feigned sympathy. "My mother died this past winter, too."

"Oh, I'm sorry," Angela said, looking at him with a pained expression. She seemed about to say something more but didn't. Her eyes were shimmering as they filled with tears.

Once again, an uncomfortable silence filled the darkened room. Greg was distantly aware of the steady sound of rain, washing against the grimy window, but below that, he could also hear . . . something else.

At first, he thought it might be a radio or TV on in another room; but the more he focused on it, the more he realized that it sounded like those same voices he heard every night when he was trying to fall asleep. They were whispering something, but he couldn't make out what it was.

"You said 'we.' Do you have any kids?" Greg asked, hoping if nothing else to block out the faint voices. Although he couldn't understand anything they were saying, their tone was agitated and seemed to be growing steadily louder.

Angela nodded. "A son and a daughter. Brandy and John . . . JJ. Both teenagers." She rolled her eyes as though exasperated, and Greg nodded his understanding.

"But you know what?" Angela said. She picked up her drink again but didn't take another sip before placing it back down on the table beside her. She looked evenly at Greg. "I have to ask you something. I hope you won't be offended or anything."

"Sure . . . Go ahead," Greg said, instantly dreading what she might ask. He hoped his voice sounded casual enough. He was fairly certain that Angela didn't recognize him from that night last winter out in front of *Le Bistro*. Obviously, she wouldn't have come up to his room alone like this if she had. But Greg was filled with a sudden apprehension that she was going to confront him about something he didn't want to talk about.

That would, of course, be foolish on her part because, if it came right down to it, he could take care of her easily, right here and now if he had to. But unless she forced it, he was thinking that he wouldn't kill her today. Not in his hotel room. It would be too much of a problem disposing of the body. He felt confident that no one who might recognize her later on had seen them arrive here together, but he didn't dare take a chance like that. Besides, he was more and more convinced that he was going to wait if only so he could include Angela's son and daughter in his revenge.

It made sense to make a clean sweep while he was at it.

He certainly didn't want to leave any potential witnesses behind *this* time.

"One day last week," Angela said haltingly. "There was a car parked out in front of my house. Right around sunset. I was just wondering if that might have been you."

Greg couldn't help but laugh and shake his head, and had to remind himself that she was pretty sharp. She didn't seem to miss a thing; he would have to watch himself around her.

"Yeah," he said, making himself sound slightly embarrassed as he glanced at the floor. "It was me."

"What were you doing out there?" Angela asked a little more edgily when he didn't offer anything more. Greg shrugged and scratched behind his ear. Shifting his gaze back to her, he saw that she was smiling tightly.

Did she think it was funny that she'd caught him like this?

A surge of rage flared up inside him, but he quickly quelled it.

"I . . . I drove out to see you," he said meekly. "That day you dropped your car off at the station, after I got out from work, on my way home, I decided to drive by your house because I—" He laughed again, hoping to God that she was buying this act. "I wanted to ask you out for a drink then." He gave her a lopsided smile. "But I guess I chickened out."

"Oh, really," Angela said, covering her smile with one hand.

He could still see the amusement in her eyes, and that irritated him all the more.

Greg couldn't tell if she was laughing at him or with him, but he knew that she'd better be careful. He looked at her earnestly and shrugged.

"Look, Angela—"

"Please. Call me Angie."

"Okay, Angie. Look, I'd be lying to you if I said I wasn't— you know, attracted to you."

He could tell that she was responding to his shy, sensitive act, so—as much as it went against what he was really feeling— he decided to play it a little longer. It was rather amusing to consider that he might actually seduce her before he killed her and her children. That sure as hell would put an edge on things that he hadn't anticipated. The prospect was intriguing.

"I don't want you to get the wrong idea about me or anything," he went on, making himself sound more nervous than he felt. "I mean, just because I work as a car mechanic and all, that doesn't mean I'm just some sexist jerk who . . . you know, who's looking to get laid, if you'll pardon the expression."

Angela didn't say anything, but Greg was happy to see that her response wasn't to laugh at him, and it wasn't to get up and walk out of the room. He was pretty sure that he had her in his power now.

She was hooked. All he had to do now was reel her in.

Wanting to stay in complete control of the situation, Greg glanced at his wristwatch and said, "Whoa, look at the time. You said you had to be home by three o'clock, right?"

Angie frowned and nodded, then stood up slowly.

"Yeah, I do," she said in a halting voice.

Greg noticed that, other than those first two tiny sips, she hadn't touched her drink, but that didn't matter; he'd finish it off after she left. He couldn't let good booze go to waste.

"What is it, one of those talk shows you like to watch or something?" he asked with a soft chuckle.

Angie smiled and shook her head.

"No. I just like to be there when the kids get home from school."

"I understand completely," Greg said just as a small voice in the back of his head whispered, *And some day . . . some day real soon now, honey, I'm gonna be there with you when they get home!* It took a great effort not to say that out loud.

They left the room together. He walked her down the hall to the elevator, but she told him there was no need for him to get wet again walking her out to her car. They said an awkward goodbye after the elevator had rattled to a stop, and the door slid opened.

"So," Greg said, hearing the tightness in his voice, "I guess I'll see you around."

He wanted to ask if he could call her, but he knew that would be pushing too hard. She was smart . . . and cagey. He'd have to play her loosely, but for now he was content. She wasn't going to slip away from him again.

"Yeah, I guess so," she said, hesitating for a moment before stepping into the elevator. There was an awkward moment when he thought he should try to kiss her, but he let that pass. He waved to her as the door clattered shut. The last view he had of her was of her eyes, looking at him through the narrowing slit of the elevator doors. They were bright and sparkling, but was it with interest or fear?

For a few seconds, he stood there and watched as the numbered lights indicating the floor level flashed. When the *L* for lobby lit up, he went back into his room and walked over to the window. Pressing his face against the cool, slick glass, he looked out at her car parked along the curb. A fiery rage gripped him as he watched her unlock the car door and then get inside.

"Yeah, you bitch," he whispered. His breath fogged the glass, distorting his view of her. Now that there was a little distant between them, he realized that he could allow the anger he felt for her fully blossom.

"You're gonna die . . . real slow," he whispered. He clenched both fists so tightly at his sides his wrists and forearms throbbed painfully.

He watched the cloud of exhaust that shot out of the tailpipe when she started up the engine and listened to the low, steady rumble of her car through the window. Her left blinker light started flashing, and then she pulled out onto the street and drove away. The last he saw of her was a flicker of taillights as she slowed for the turn back onto Water Street.

Greg lost all sense of the time as he stared out at the rain-washed street. The rain splattering on the glass inches from his face lulled him into a hazy mental zone.

Groaning softly, he closed his eyes and listened to the voices inside his head, teasing and taunting him like a chorus that swelled louder until—finally—he realized that he recognized some of them.

He could hear the flat, demanding tones of his mother . . . and the rough, commanding voice of his father. And there were other voices . . . voices he thought he recognized but which he couldn't quite place.

They were all telling him one thing.

They were saying that he was worthless and foolish, that he was a weakling and a coward for not taking care of Angela Ross when he had the chance.

Rage, thick and salty, boiled up inside him.

With a low, wavering moan, Greg turned away from the window and walked over to the table where Angela had been sitting. He picked up her drink and swallowed it in three, greedy gulps. When he looked around the room, everything seemed oddly distorted. The shadowy walls pitched inward at odd angles that frightened him. The dingy ceiling rippled as though it were made of some half-solid substance that was sliding steadily downward, crushing him. The floor pitched from side to side like a ship being tossed about by an angry sea. Everywhere he turned, he saw indistinct shapes that shifted in and out of focus whenever he tried to look at them directly.

Panic as cold and sharp as a stainless steel razor blade cut through him when he realized that the room was closing in on him. The air felt suddenly too thin to breathe. No matter how hard he tried, he couldn't get enough into his lungs. The pressure of being watched by unseen eyes squeezed him. Taking hold of his oil-stained work shirt with both hands, he let out a ragged cry, threw his head back, and ripped his shirt open.

"Fuck!" he wailed.

Leaning forward and moaning, he punched the sides of his head repeatedly with both fists as hard as he could. The voices became a roaring rush of sound that ripped like a hurricane through his mind.

He staggered over to the bed, reached under it, and came up with the new baseball bat he'd bought the day before to replace the one he'd thrown away. Gripping the handle so tightly his hands went numb, he spun around and swung as hard as he could at the wall beside the bed. When he connected, a shivering shock as powerful as any electrical shock he'd ever experienced traveled up his arms to his neck and shoulders. Chunks of plaster and dust rained down onto the floor.

"Fuck! ... Fuck! ... Fuck!" Greg wailed as he turned around quickly and smashed the bat against the bureau, hitting it hard enough to cave in its side and almost knock it over.

He pivoted on one foot. A dull, thundering sound filled his head, and he imagined for a moment that Angela Ross was still sitting in the chair. Snorting wildly, he took a vicious swipe at the chair. The impact splintered the chair back and knocked it over. Jagged chunks of wood scattered across the floor with a loud clatter.

Greg was so lost in the release of his pent-up anger and frustration, he smashed and banged anything and everything within reach. After a while he realized that he wasn't the only one making a sound. He could hear someone banging on his door.

"Hey in there!" an angry voice shouted.

All Greg knew was that it was a man's voice. He guessed it was either another tenant or that fat slob of a hotel manager.

"What the fuck's going on in there, asshole?"

Greg stared at the door, panting heavily, his mouth hanging open. He wiped the saliva from his mouth and tried to answer, but rage choked him. Bellowing like an enraged bull, he brandished the baseball bat over his head and charged the door, slamming into it so hard the top wooden panel splintered. Through the gap, he saw a face, peering in at him.

"I'm callin' the cops right now!" the man on the other side of the door shouted. His face was beet red with anger. "You're outta here, fella! You can't go trashing the place like this."

"*Fuck you!*" Greg wailed, and he cocked the baseball bat back and took another savage swing at the door, widening the hole.

The man's face disappeared, and even through the storm of his anger, Greg knew that he had gone to call the police.

Trembling violently, Greg stalked over to the bureau, grabbed what few clothes he had there, and stuffed them into his suitcase. Then he scooped up the pile of dirty laundry and shoved that into the suitcase. He had some trouble closing the latch, but he finally got it shut. After grabbing his raincoat and the last two cans of beer, which had fallen onto the floor, he flung the door open and ran out into the hall. He was panting raggedly and still maintained a tight grip on the baseball bat as he looked up and down the hall.

The elevator was in use. For all he knew, it could be the police, already responding to the manager's call that a tenant was going berserk in his room.

A sharp pain jabbed like a knife under Greg's ribs as he dashed to the stairwell and ran down the four flights to the street level. He barely noticed that he set off a fire alarm when he slammed open the back door that led onto a narrow alley. Clutching his few belongings tightly, he ran down the alleyway, then up the street just as a police cruiser with its lights flashing and siren wailing pulled up in front of the hotel.

It wasn't long before the cold rain soaked Greg to the skin, but it wasn't until much later, when he was walking in the cold blast of rain looking for someplace to spend the night, that he calmed down enough to realize what he had done.

Shivering in the chill, Greg huddled into his still damp raincoat in a narrow doorway. Then, gripping his suitcase in one hand, and the last of his six pack of beer and his baseball bat in the other hand, he started down the street.

Chapter 24
Giving In

The rain ended late Friday night, and Saturday morning dawned warm and bright. After breakfast, Angie stood at the front door, watching as JJ and Sammy took off on their bikes. They were headed over to the playing field behind the school where their Little League team had a game at ten o'clock. They said they wanted to get there early to warm up.

"I'll be there for the game," Angie called after them, but the boys didn't hear her. At least, they didn't respond. The last she saw of them was two figures, pedalling furiously down the road.

Angie still felt uncomfortable about what had happened to that black Labrador. Because the dog had been a stray, the police hadn't put much effort into finding out who had done it. Still, it bothered Angie that *someone* in this town could do such a terrible thing to a poor, defenseless animal. She knew there would be plenty of parents at the game, but she wanted to be there all the same.

First, though, she had a few errands to run in town. She asked Brandy if she would mind cleaning up the breakfast dishes. Brandy set to work, complaining that she had plans of her own, to meet Evan and two other friends and drive down to Portland for the day.

"I hope you'll be home before dark," Angie said.

Standing at the sink rinsing dishes, Brandy shrugged casually and said, "I'm not sure. I'll call you if I'm not going to be home for supper."

Telling herself that she should be satisfied with even that much, Angie left.

One thing she needed to do was get gas for the car, but for some reason—after spending time with Greg Newman yesterday—she didn't feel like going to the Mobile station. Instead, she drove out of town in the other direction and went to the Sunoco on Route 132, heading toward Sabattus.

As she drove, she tried to sort out what she thought about Greg, but she didn't make much progress. He was certainly handsome, and he had seemed pleasant enough yesterday; but the more she thought about him, the more she sensed that just beneath his mild demeanor was . . . something else. Something that, at least on a subconscious level, might not be so nice. She kept reminding herself that she couldn't judge him too harshly simply because he might be uneducated and was working at a menial job. Still, there was *something* about him that bothered her. She was so distracted, thinking about Greg, that she found it difficult to focus on what she was doing.

After getting the gas, she drove back to Bolton and stopped by the hardware store to pick up a new sprayer for the kitchen sink, and the post office to mail some bills and buy a roll of stamps. She went into a mild panic when she noticed that it was already ten o'clock. It was time for the game.

A coil of nervousness slithered through her as she drove the short distance from downtown to the elementary school. The parking lot was surprisingly full of cars as she parked and walked out to the field.

As she was walking across the field, she saw that the game was already underway. JJ and Sammy's team was at bat, and Angie was happy to see that JJ was still on the bench. Unless he had already struck out, she hadn't missed his turn at bat.

Smiling and nodding to a few of the parents, Angie took up a position behind the chest-high link fence that ran parallel to the third base line. A young couple had spread out a multicolored blanket, and their toddler was rolling around on the grass while they watched the game.

Sammy was in the on-deck circle, and after the batter in front of him struck out, he took his place at the plate. The first three pitches were high and outside, but he swung and missed on the next two, so the count was three and two.

"Come on, Sammy! Nail it!" Angie called out.

Sammy looked over at her and smiled, but on the next pitch he swung and missed. His face was bright red as he threw the bat and kicked at the dirt before walking back to the bench and sitting down.

The next batter hit a single, and Angie's heart went into her throat when she saw JJ pick up a bat and walk to the on-deck circle.

"Come on. Get a hit," Angie called out, even though she didn't know the boy at bat. He missed on the first two swings, but on the third pitch, he connected. Everyone cheered as the ball arced across the vault of blue sky. The left fielder ran hard to get under it, but he missed.

"Run!" *Run!*" Angie shouted, caught up in the excitement.

The runner on first base made it to third, and the batter had a standing double before the cut-off player tossed the ball to the pitcher.

"Let's go, JJ!" Angie shouted as her son walked up to the plate. Feeling as if she needed an explanation, she glanced at the couple with the toddler and said, "That's my son at bat." They nodded.

JJ dug in his heels and cocked the bat back, his elbow raised high. Leaning forward, he stared at the pitcher.

The first pitch was high and outside, but JJ stretched for it and caught a piece of it, sending it foul. Angie squealed and, clenching her fists, stood tensed and waiting as the pitcher wound up again.

The next pitch was a fast ball, right down the middle. JJ grunted out loud as he swung the bat around and connected. The ball went flying high over the center fielder's head, and JJ started running for all he was worth toward first base. Angie could see that the player didn't have a chance of catching the

ball, but he ran after it, scooped it up, and threw it to shortstop.
JJ ran to second base as the runner who had been on third
scored, and the other runner made it safely to third base.

"Yeah! Way to go!" Angie shouted, happy and relieved
that JJ hadn't struck out his first time at bat. A good confidence
builder. When he looked over at her, she was expecting to see
him smiling, so she was surprised when she saw his expression.
His face looked several shades paler than normal, and his mouth
was set in a narrow line.

Angie was tempted to call out and ask him what was the
matter. He should be happy that he'd driven in a run, but he
looked so tense that her concern for him rose sharply.

After a moment or two, Angie realized that he wasn't even
looking at her. His gaze was fixed on something behind her.
A chill slithered up her back as she turned around slowly and
looked.

The fringe of woods that lined the playing field was a riot
of green, but she could see someone—a person—standing deep
in the shadows. Angie glanced back at JJ to confirm that this
was what—or who—he was looking at. When she looked back
at the person in the woods, he stepped forward into the sunlight.

Oh, Jesus!

A jolt of panic hit her the instant she recognized Greg Newman. She smiled thinly and started to wave, but then realized
that he wasn't looking at her. Staring ahead at JJ, Greg let a
wide grin spread across his face as he gave him a quick thumbs
up.

How the hell does he know JJ? Angie wondered.

The panic inside her spiked even higher. A numbing chill
gripped her stomach. Looking back to JJ, she saw that he was
purposely avoiding looking over in her direction.

And he knows him! she thought.

After a moment, it dawned on her. Greg must be the guy he
and Sammy met out here the other day.

"Oh, Jesus," she whispered, and the couple on the blanket
looked at her curiously.

What if he's the guy who beat Blackie to death?

Waves of nausea swept through her. She wanted to turn and

look at Greg again, but something warned her that, if he hadn't noticed her yet, she shouldn't bring attention to herself. Cringing inwardly, she gripped the chain link fence for support and focused on the game, but all the while, she could feel his gaze drilling into the back of her head.

Angie's heart was thumping fast. A thin sheen of sweat broke out over her body. As the next batter stepped up to the plate, Angie wanted to call out to JJ to cheer him on, but she didn't dare make a sound. Her throat closed off. She could feel Greg's presence like a dark, threatening storm cloud behind her. She was afraid she would faint if he came over and started talking to her.

Go away! Jesus, just go away! she thought, wishing to God that she dared turn and confront him directly. If he really was the man who had been out here that afternoon, then the slight stirring of doubt she'd had about Greg was accurate.

He might even be dangerous!

She tried to convince herself that maybe it was all innocent . . . a coincidence, or that maybe Greg had noticed her before she had noticed him. Maybe he had tried to get to know JJ as a way of getting to her. But even if that was the case, it still didn't explain what had happened to that black Labrador. If Greg was responsible for that dog's death, then maybe he wasn't what he seemed.

The muscles in Angie's neck and shoulders bunched up with tension as she stood there, trying to find the courage to confront Greg. She knew that's what she should do. If he was following her and her family around, stalking them, he might be a real threat. She had no way of knowing if he'd been following Brandy around, too?

The next batter struck out, and the teams changed sides. JJ looked stiff as he trotted back to the bench and grabbed his glove to take his position at first base.

"Maybe next time you'll score a run," Angie called out to him, but her voice sounded thin and tight.

A hot, hard lump formed in her throat when, finally, she started to turn around slowly. Her eyes widened with surprise when she saw that Greg was nowhere in sight.

Where'd he go? she wondered, her eyes darting back and forth as she searched the shadows beneath the trees. She couldn't rid herself of the unnerving feeling that—maybe—Greg had never even been there. He had appeared and then disappeared so suddenly and silently, fading away like a shadow, that she was left with the impression that it hadn't really happened.

She could almost convince herself of that if it hadn't been for JJ's reaction.

He had seen him, too. He'd been looking in the same direction, and he had most definitely looked scared by what he had seen.

Angie was anxious to walk over and ask him what he had seen, but she knew that she couldn't until the game was over. As the game progressed, she tried to absorb herself in the excitement—especially when, the next time at bat, JJ's team scored four runs—but the feeling that she was being watched wouldn't go away. The more she thought about it, the more she was convinced that Greg Newman was a danger to her and her family. Detective Murray had told her that he hadn't found anything on Greg, but that didn't mean he couldn't be trouble.

For whatever reasons, he might have fixated on her and her family. As soon as the game was over, Angie was determined that she was going to take JJ home and call the police. The least she could do is ask Detective Murray to talk to Greg and try to find out exactly what he was up to. She also mentally vowed that, if she ever saw Greg Newman near one of her children, she would call the cops and have him arrested.

"It's not as bad as you think," JJ said.

He was scowling as he got into the car and sat down with his arms folded across his chest. They had put his bike in the back of the car but, because there wasn't enough room for Sammy' bike as well, Sammy had ridden home alone. JJ had protested, saying that he wasn't going to ditch his friend, but Angie insisted that he ride home with her.

"I'm not saying that it's bad," Angie said. She was trying

to stay calm, but an edge of panic kept creeping into her voice. "I'm just saying that this guy gives me the creeps."

JJ grimaced as he shook his head. All around them, parents and players were getting into their cars and driving off. JJ's team had ended up losing the game, so the team wasn't going out for ice cream, as the coach had promised.

"I don't know *who* it was I saw, all right?" he said. "I was just—" He cut himself off sharply. Angie shifted in her seat and looked straight at him, but he seemed to be trying his best to ignore her.

"You just *what?*" she said softly.

"Nothing," JJ said, not making eye contact with her. He stared blankly at the people leaving the parking lot.

"You're not telling me everything," Angie said, making an effort not to yell at him. She could tell that he was scared, and she didn't want to make it any worse, but she *had* to know.

"It's nothing . . . really," JJ said. "I just . . . The other day, I got a little freaked out."

"Freaked out about what?" Angie asked.

She knew it sounded like she was grilling him, but she couldn't help it. Seeing Greg today had given her the creeps. Because he had appeared and then disappeared so suddenly and silently, she still had a vague sense that maybe he hadn't even been there, that she had imagined seeing him there, but that was impossible.

She wasn't seeing things.

He'd been there, and JJ had seen him and reacted to it.

"Just . . . some stuff," JJ finally said, still not looking directly at her.

Angie reached over and placed her hand on his shoulder, but JJ flinched and pulled away from her. She reminded herself that he was growing up, that he wasn't her little boy anymore. It was obvious that whatever was bothering him was something he was determined to deal with on his own.

"He hasn't . . . done anything to you, has he?" Angie asked, her voice tight and trembling.

JJ took a shuddering breath and shook his head firmly, but he still didn't make eye contact with her.

"It's nothing like that, okay? I'm not a fag . . . like Uncle Rob!"

A hot surge of anger made Angie's face flush. On reflex, she almost slapped JJ across the face, but she checked herself and, in as firm and steady a voice as she could manage, said, "I don't *ever* want to hear you refer to your uncle like that again, do you understand me?"

"Well he is," JJ said.

"I mean it, JJ!"

Scowling, JJ sat back and nodded his agreement, but Angie could tell by his sullen silence that he was trying hard not to listen to her.

"Just because your uncle has a different kind of lifestyle, that doesn't make him any less of a person."

"I know, I know," JJ said impatiently.

Tears suddenly welled up in Angie's eyes when she thought how, now that John was dead, her brother Rob and her kids were all she had left of her family. She knew how important that was, and she wished she could make JJ see it, but at his age, it's hard to see beyond your own immediate concerns..

"Look, honey," she said softly. "I'm just saying that, if there's something you want to tell me about that man who was at the game today, I'll listen. I'm here for you. You know you can count on me, right?"

JJ didn't answer.

"I said *right?*"

"Yeah . . . Right," JJ said, sounding as if he didn't believe it in the least.

"Now, was that the same man you and Sammy saw out here the day Blackie was killed?"

"I . . . I didn't see anyone," JJ said, shrugging as though totally helpless. His voice almost broke, and tears formed in his eyes, making them glisten. She knew that he was lying to her, but she was stumped as to how to pry the truth out of him. Sighing with exasperation, she looked around the parking lot, which was now almost completely deserted except for them.

"You know who I mean," she said evenly, "and I want you

to tell me if you *ever* see him around again or anywhere near the house, do you understand?''

"Get off my case, will you, Mom?'' JJ snapped.

When he turned and looked at her, his eyes were glowing with the same barely repressed anger Angie had seen so many times before in her husband's eyes. Nausea filled her.

"No I *won't* get off your case!'' she said, struggling to keep from crying. ''Whether you like it or not, I'm still going to protect you. You got that?''

"You don't have to *protect* me. I can take care of myself,'' JJ said, but his fragile tone of voice contradicted him. Angie's first impulse was to lean over and hug him, but she held back, not wanting to embarrass him further.

"Look, honey—'' she said. She was trying to stay in control, but she felt so alone and helpless. There was so much she wanted to say to him, but she had no idea how to begin. ''I'm just saying that I saw someone here today . . . someone that I met the other day and who . . . it kind of bothers me, okay? I'm just asking you to be careful.''

"I *will*,'' JJ said, sounding totally exasperated as he shook his head. ''Can we go home now? I promised Sammy I'd hang our with him this afternoon.''

"Sure,'' Angie said as she started the car. ''I just want you to remember what I said, okay?''

JJ didn't respond, and all Angie could do was hope that he was listening to her. Her hands felt clammy on the steering wheel, and as she drove away form the school, she kept glancing at the rearview mirror, expecting to see Greg Newman standing off in the distance, watching them.

The moon cast long, frosty shadows across the backyard as Greg, basketball bat in hand, crouched beside the garage and looked up at Angie's house. No lights were on inside, and he was just getting ready to break into house when a car pulled into the driveway. He quickly ducked behind the building, staying out of the wash of headlights. Once the car stopped and the headlights went off, he cautiously peeked around the corner to see who it was. At first, all he knew was that it wasn't Angie's car.

Maybe it's her brother, Greg thought, squeezing the grip of the baseball bat. He'd asked around town and learned that Angela's brother's name was Robert, and that he lived with his "friend" Craig. Greg knew what *that* meant!

He watched as both car doors opened, and two people—a boy and a girl—got out. When they swung the doors shut, the sound was as loud as two gunshots going off in the still night.

"—to the movies in Augusta," the girl was saying as she came around the side of the car. "I'll bet they won't be back until ten o'clock at the soonest."

Her voice filled the night, sounding much closer to Greg that she was. Greg had never heard Brandy speak before, but he knew this had to be Angela's daughter. The guy had to be her boyfriend because, as soon as they came together, they hugged and started toward the house.

"We can't go inside," Brandy said, halting at the foot of the stairs. "Another one of my mom's stupid rules. She says I can't have anyone in the house when she's not home."

"Oh," the boy said, sounding a bit mystified.

Greg watched their silhouettes shift against the brighter background of the house as they embraced and kissed. Sensing subtle motion behind him, he turned and scanned the backyard but didn't see anything. The buzzing sound of insects in the darkness was almost deafening.

"We can go out back and sit, can't we?" the boy asked.

Greg couldn't help but snicker to himself. He could hear the sexual tension in the boy's voice and knew exactly what was on his mind.

Crouching low so they wouldn't see him, he watched as Brandy and her boyfriend walked over to the lawn furniture in the middle of the lawn. The wash of moonlight made them look almost ghostly, but Greg could see clearly enough what was going on. He smiled and shook his head when the boy sat down on one of the chaise lounges and Brandy straddled him.

Greg felt the stirrings of an erection as he watched the boy and girl hug and kiss, more passionately now. This was turning out better than he could have planned. They were locked in a heated embrace that seemed to last for a very long time, but suddenly Brandy pulled back.

"No," she said, her voice ringing out clearly in the night, instantly breaking the mood.

"What?" the boy said, sounding wounded.

Greg knew exactly what had happened. The boy had probably tried to cop a little feel, and Brandy wasn't going to give him any, at least not yet.

Yeah, maybe you're nothing but a little cock teaser. Is that it? Greg thought. He let go of the bat with one hand and reached down and started massaging his crotch.

"I *told* you," Brandy said, her voice so low Greg could barely hear her. "I don't want you to . . . do that."

"Aww, come on," the boy said with near desperation in his voice. He reached up and tried to hug Brandy again, but she pulled away from him and stood up. Moving quickly, she went over and sat down in one of the other chairs.

"What's the matter with you, anyway?" the boy said.

I know what's the matter with you! Greg thought. *You've got a serious case of blue balls.*

"I just wish you'd get it through your head that I don't want to go that far," Brandy said softly. "Not until I'm ready."

"How about if I'm ready even if you're not?" the boy pleaded.

"That's not good enough," Brandy replied.

"Are you telling me, on a romantic, moonlit night like this, that you don't want a little cuddling?"

The boy got up from his chair and walked over to stand behind her. He massaged her shoulders for a little while, then leaned down and kissed her upturned face. In the glow of the moonlight, Greg could see the boy's hands were on her shoulders, but it wasn't long before they started sliding down to her breasts.

"What *you* want is a little more than cuddling," Brandy said in a throaty whisper. By the sound of her voice, Greg guessed that she really wanted it too, and was just playing hard to get. She'd be giving it up to him any second now. He kept

up a steady, rhythmic pressure on his crotch as he watched
them and imagined that the boy was about to nail her. Wouldn't
that be fun to watch?

"I . . . I just don't want to hurry things, that's all," Brandy
said as she reached up and pulled him closer.

"It's not hurrying things," the boy said. "Not if you love
someone."

His hands ran down the length of her arms and then up. Greg
almost laughed out loud when he saw the boy grab the bottom
of Brandy's blouse and start tugging it up. Her skin and her
exposed bra glowed pale white in the moonlight.

"Please . . . don't," Brandy said, but there was little convic-
tion in her voice.

"I just love you so much," the boy whispered heatedly, and
his hands were all over her breasts, rubbing and squeezing.
Brandy moaned softly, offering no resistance when the boy
slipped the edge of her bra up, exposing her breasts to the
moonlight. Greg stared in total fascination at her breasts and
increased the pace of his rubbing on his crotch.

Moving clumsily, the boy kept kissing Brandy as he walked
around in front of her and then, kneeling on the ground, pulled
her down on top of him. Their sighs and moans filled the night
as the boy rolled over on top of her and, within seconds, had
her blouse and bra off. It didn't take him long to start working
to unbutton her jeans and get them off.

Greg chuckled as he watched them. The boy worked with a
furious, almost desperate passion while Brandy just lay there,
barely moving, as if she were surrendering against her will.
Greg had no idea if she liked it or not, but he knew that he
sure as hell was enjoying the show.

Suddenly a low, moaning sound from out of the woods filled
the night.

"What the hell is *that?*" Brandy cried out as she sat up and
covered her chest with her arms.

Greg looked around furtively as a wave of chills washed
through him. The sound—a low, wavering howl—rose and fell
in the night. It seemed to be coming from the woods behind
the house, but Greg couldn't get a definite fix on it.

"Something's out there," Brandy said, her voice tight with tension.

"Naw. It's nothing to worry about. Just a coyote or something," the boy said, waving his hand dismissively.

"A coyote?" Brandy said edgily.

"It's nothing. Honest," the boy said as he eased back down onto the ground and tried to drag Brandy down with him. She resisted, still scanning the dark fringe of woods.

"Come on," he said, the desperate pleading returning to his voice.

After looking all around, Brandy finally settled back down onto the ground, but Greg could tell by the way she sat that she wasn't relaxed. The boy didn't seem to mind, and after meeting with a little more resistance, he finally wiggled her jeans and panties off. For a long time, he clung to Brandy, hugging her tightly and kissing her while he ran his hands all up and down her body. Greg could imagine that Brandy's eyes were wide open with mounting terror as she imagined what might be out there in the woods.

If you only knew, he thought, trying to forget how much the sound had unnerved him as well.

Sitting up for a moment, the boy peeled his T-shirt off over his head. Brandy lay on the ground, staring up at him. Her naked body was luminous in the moonlight. Greg stared, fascinated, at the rounded, white swell of her breasts. The boy stood up and was just starting to take his pants off when the sound of an approaching car drew their attention. Suddenly the bright glare of headlights washed across the garage and swept the backyard. Greg ducked out of sight as a car pulled into the driveway.

"Oh, shit! My mother!" Brandy said as she leaped to her feet and hurriedly began to dress.

"I thought you said she wouldn't be home until ten," the boy said, scrambling to pull his pants back up and put his shirt on. Greg smiled, hearing the raw edge of sexual frustration in his voice.

Brandy made nervous whimpering sounds as she dressed. The car pulled to a stop in front of the garage beside the boyfriend's car, and the engine cut off. The car doors opened then slammed shut.

"How'd you like the movie?"

Angie's voice carried clearly in the night. Greg looked over and saw that the boy was finished dressing, but Brandy was still struggling to get her blouse tucked in.

"'S okay," JJ said, walking around the car. "Thanks for taking us."

Greg smiled grimly, remembering the sheer panic he had seen on JJ's face this morning when he had walked out of the woods. Tightening his grip on the baseball bat, he thought about how wonderful it had felt last week, when he had beat the shit out of that dog that had been pestering him. He imagined now that the satisfaction would be even greater if—right now!—he used the bat on JJ and the rest of his family!

"I wonder where Brandy and Evan are," Angie said, looking around as she walked up the porch steps to the back door. "The lights aren't on. I hope they're not—"

"Hi, Mom," Brandy called out cheerily as she and the boy walked out from the darkness in the backyard.

Peeking around the corner of the garage, Greg watched them.

"What are you doing out there?" Angie said sharply.

"Just taking a little moonlight walk," Brandy replied.

Greg had to chuckle at the fake innocence in Brandy's voice. He wished he could tell Angela right now that her daughter and boyfriend had been seconds away from fucking like rabbits out there on the back lawn.

"I thought you were going to a concert in Portland," Angie said. She was at the back door now. Greg could hear the jangle her keys made as she unlocked the door.

If you're gonna do it, now's the time, he told himself, but as soon as Angela opened the back door, something small and dark darted outside. It was the dog, and it immediately began yipping and running around the yard.

"Fuck," Greg muttered and started backing away from the garage into the woods. He watched over his shoulder as Angela, Brandy and the boyfriend went into the house, but JJ stayed outside with the dog.

Keeping to the dark shadows, Greg moved away from the house as quietly as he could, but he stepped on a fallen branch that snapped loudly in the still night. The dog instantly froze and stared in his direction. Then he started barking, deeper now, as he ran toward where Greg was hiding.

"Wolfie!" JJ shouted, but the dog ignored him as he darted into the woods, yipping loudly.

Greg tensed, filled with rage. The last thing he needed was this little shit giving him away. He turned and started running, but he could hear the angry growl coming up fast behind him.

"All right, you little fucker," Greg muttered softly as he turned and tightened his grip on the bat. "You wanna play?"

He took a solid stance and waited until the dog was right in front of him, and then he swung.

"Go fetch," he said with a savage grunt. He smiled when he felt the impact at the same time as he heard a loud cracking of bones. The dog let out a sharp, pained howl and then flopped to the ground. Without waiting to see what would happen next, Greg took off into the woods, sure that the pained sounds the dog was making would mask any noise he made as he thrashed through the underbrush.

"Wolfie! . . . *Wolfie!*"

JJ's panicky voice echoed in the night, but it was almost lost beneath the frantic howling of the dog.

Once he was safely deep in the woods, Greg turned and looked back. Through the dense foliage, he saw JJ running toward the wounded animal.

"Mom! Hey, *Mom!*" he called out, his voice breaking with panic. "Mom! Wolfie's been hurt!"

Ducking low into the brush, Greg saw the back porch light come and then Angela and the others raced outside.

"He's really hurt, Mom," JJ wailed when Angela came over to where he was kneeling over the dog. Brandy and her boyfriend stood a few steps behind. "Look at his leg, Mom. He can't even get up!"

"Don't worry, honey. We'll take care of him," Angela said in a reassuring voice. "Did you see what happened?"

"No," JJ said, his voice cracking. "He just ran off into the

woods and then he started howling. He must've fallen down
and broken his leg or something.''

''We heard what we sounded like a coyote in the woods a
little earlier,'' Brandy offered. Even as far away from them as
he was, Greg could hear the nervous edge in her voice.

''A coyote wouldn't do something like this,'' her boyfriend
said. ''If they'd gotten into a fight, Wolfie'd be all chewed
up.''

''Help me get him into the house,'' Angie said as she slid
her hands under the dog and, with JJ's and the boyfriend's
help, lifted the dog.

Greg chuckled softly to himself as he watched from the dark
woods. They moved slowly as they carried the dog back to the
house and then went inside. When the backyard light winked
out, the darkness seemed much deeper. Greg waited for his
eyes to adjust to the darkness again. He was just about to leave
when he noticed something on the lawn, over by the chairs
where Brandy and her boyfriend had been earlier. Suddenly
curious, he moved closer to get a better look. His eyes still
hadn't fully adjusted to the darkness, but he saw a small, pale
object that glowed bone-white in the moonlight.

Greg halted at the edge of the woods and looked at the house.
The kitchen light was still on. Through the curtained window,
he could see Angela and the boy, obviously tending the injured
dog. Sucking in a sharp breath and moving fast, he ran out
onto the lawn to see what had caught his attention. When he
got up to it and saw what it was, he let out a short burst of
laughter.

''Jesus Christ! Well I'll be!'' he whispered as he bent down
and scooped up the pair of sheer, white panties. Raising them
to his face, he closed his eyes and inhaled deeply, reveling in
the moist, womanly smell.

After casting one last glance at the house, Greg tucked the
panties into his back pocket and took off into the woods. His
car was still broken down, so he'd had to walk out here after
work. He still didn't have a place to stay, but he figured he'd
go back to Larry's garage and work on his car. Then maybe
he'd try to find a motel where he could stay for the next night

or two. Even if it was a little more expensive than the room
he'd had at the Kennebec Hotel, he wanted someplace closer
to Bolton. He figured he wouldn't be hanging around town for
more than another day or two, anyway.

Chapter 25
Healing

"Don't you worry, JJ. Your dog's going to be just fine," Betsy Zsiga, the veterinarian at the Augusta Animal Hospital, said.

It was obvious to Angie that this woman completely understood JJ's concern for his pet and wanted to put his mind at ease, but tears spilled from JJ's eyes as soon as he saw Wolfgang lying on the operating table with the heavy cast on his right front leg, all the way up to his chest.

The puppy, usually so full of energy, whimpered softly as he rolled his head around and looked at JJ with a distant, glaze clouding his usually bright eyes.

"How long's he gonna have to wear that?" JJ asked, his voice tight and threatening to break. He sniffed and wiped his eyes with the back of his hands as he looked back and forth between his mother and the veterinarian.

The fear that Angie saw in her son's eyes cut her to the core. All she could think was that, after losing his father so recently, the fear of losing something else that he loved so much must be threatening JJ more deeply than he might be able to handle right now.

"We'll have to leave the cast on for at least six weeks,

maybe as long as two months," Dr. Zsiga said, making direct eye contact with JJ and smiling sympathetically. "With a puppy as healthy and active as Wolfgang, it may be more on the six weeks side. The x-ray showed a clean break that I expect will heal quite fast." She placed her hand on JJ's shoulder. "We'll just have to wait and see."

Glancing at Angie and looking mildly perplexed, she said, "You say you don't know how this happened?"

Biting her lower lip, Angie shook her head.

"All we know for sure is that he ran off into the woods barking like crazy about something, and then he started howling," Angie replied. A wave of pity swept over her as she looked down at the dog. "Could he have done this just by falling down or tripping over something?"

"I supposed so," Betsy replied, "but by the way this break looks, at least in x-ray, I'd say it's more consistent with an injury like, for instance, if he got hit by a car or something."

Angie shrugged, but before she could say anything, JJ said, "Can he still—like, do stuff? He looks so out of it. He's gonna get better, isn't he?"

"I gave him a tranquilizer and a general sedative before I set the broken bone," Betsy said. Angie admired the way she maintained such a soft, sympathetic tone, yet still sounded completely professional. "He'll no doubt lay low for the rest of the day to sleep it off, but I guarantee he'll be back to his usual self by tomorrow morning."

"Except he won't be able to run," JJ said softly.

"Oh, he'll try to run, all right," Betsy said with a pleasant laugh. She turned to Angie. "I'll give you some mild sedatives to mix into his food for the next few days, just until he learns his limits with that cast on his leg. Some antibiotics, too." Turning back to JJ, she added, "The important thing is that you can't let the cast get wet, and that you keep an eye out for any swelling. He's growing so fast, we want to make sure the cast doesn't get too tight on his leg."

JJ nodded his understanding, but all Angie was thinking was that she would also have to keep a close eye on JJ.

"How can we tell if the cast's too tight?" JJ asked.

"Watch for any swelling, both above and below the edge of the cast," Betsy said. "And you should probably bring him into the office once a week, just so I can check him over. That won't be too much of a problem, would it?"

"Not at all," Angie said.

Turning back to JJ, Betsy said, "So, JJ, I guess you're gonna have your hands full keeping ole' Wolfgang as calm as possible for the next few days, okay? That's not going to be the easiest thing in the world with a puppy."

JJ tried to smile but he still looked tense and grim as he nodded curtly, then glanced at his mother. Angie could see in his eyes that he was still worried sick that Wolfgang wasn't going to get better. Several times on the drive into Augusta this morning, he had said that he was afraid Wolfie would never be able to walk again. Angie knew that question was still burning in her son's mind, but that he didn't quite dare ask it, so she decided to ask it for him directly, just to put his mind at ease.

"Once he heals, though, he's going to be able to walk and run normally, isn't he?"

Betsy let fly a loud burst of laughter as she reached down and scruffed Wolfgang's neck. The dog's head lolled lazily back and forth. He stuck his tongue out and tried to lick her hand.

"I guarantee that a month or two from now, you won't be able to keep up with him."

JJ smiled wanly, but Angie could still see the dark worry in his expression. After Angie paid the bill and got the sedatives from Betsy, together they wheeled Wolfgang outside and got him settled into the back seat of the car. JJ sat in back with him and didn't say much for most of the drive to Bolton. He just sat there with Wolfgang's head in his lap and stared at him all the while caressing the bog's head.

"You're gonna be just fine, fella . . . You're gonna be just fine," he kept saying until it became almost a mantra.

As she drove down Route 202, Angie felt hopeful that Wolfgang would be fine, but a sudden cold dread filled her gut when she saw the sign for Larry Lee's Mobile station up ahead.

Glancing automatically at the gas gauge, she saw the needle was already on *E* and realized that she had been so concerned about getting Wolfgang to the vet's this morning that she hadn't thought to make sure the car had enough gas.

"Damn," she whispered, realizing that she would have to stop here and get a fill-up.

The knot in her stomach got steadily tighter when she wondered if Greg would be on duty this morning. That fear blossomed into near panic when she slowed down for the turn into the station and saw his car parked off to one side of the garage. The garage doors were opened, and there was a car in both bays.

Angie's nerves zinged when she drove over the rubber tube that snaked across the lot, setting off a warning bell that clanged inside the garage. The pressure building up inside her head decreased only slightly when the pimple-faced teenage boy sauntered out of the office and headed over to her.

"What'll it be?" he asked.

"Fill it up with regular, please," Angie said, having a bit of trouble controlling the tremor in her voice

As the boy set to work, she glanced around the station, looking for any sign of Greg. She didn't see him, but someone was working one of the cars in the garage. She could hear a loud clanging sound followed by a string of curses that sure *sounded* like Greg.

Praying that he wouldn't look out and see her, she cringed down in her seat, positive that she would faint if Greg came out and talked to her. After what had happened yesterday out at the baseball field, she was sure that she never wanted to see him again. It irritated her that she had entertained even the slightest bit of interest in him.

A twinge of curiosity ran through her when she looked over at Greg's car again and noticed something hanging from the mirror in the front window. It took her a moment or two to realize what the object was. When she did, a hot surge of anger rushed across her face. A pair of women's panties was hanging from his rearview mirror the way some kids hang the tassel from their high school or college graduation caps.

"You sleazy son of a bitch," Angie whispered, forgetting for a moment that JJ was in the back seat.

"Huh?" JJ asked.

Angie glanced at him into the rearview; he was looking at her with a perplexed expression.

"Oh . . . no . . . nothing," she said, shaking her head quickly. "I was just . . ." Her voice trailed away as she looked over at Greg's car again just to make sure that it was what she *thought* it was hanging from the mirror.

There was no doubt.

He had looped a pair of sheer white panties over the mirror so they hung from the leg holes.

The attendant startled Angie when he came up to her window and said, "That'll be nineteen dollars and fifty cents."

Angie's hand was shaking as she handed him her credit card and waited while he went back into the office to fill out the charge slip. Her throat went suddenly dry, and a razor-edged shiver ran through her when she saw motion in the dark depths of the garage bay. She wanted to turn away, pretending that she didn't see him, but Greg stepped out in to the sunlight, smiling broadly.

"Well hello, there," he called out, waving a greasy hand holding a wrench in her direction.

Angie smiled thinly and looked at him but only nodded slightly. She was aware that JJ had shifted around and was looking over at Greg.

Please don't come over here! she thought desperately.

Her body was tingling with expectation when the teenager walked back to her car and handed her the credit card. She made an indistinguishable scrawl on the bottom of the slip. Her hand shook when she tore off the customer's copy and handed the signed copy and pen back to the boy. Her heart was beating so fast she was afraid she was going to faint as she started up the car and shifted into gear.

As she pulled away from the gas pumps, she stepped down a little too hard on the accelerator. The tires spun on the asphalt with a loud chirp as the car lurched forward. Glancing over her shoulder as she drove away, she saw Greg was standing in the garage doorway, the wide grin still on his face as he watched her leave.

He knows how nervous he makes me, and he's enjoying it, she thought, narrowing her eyes and wishing she had never met or spoken to him.

"Was that him?" Angie asked tightly, casting a fearful glance at JJ in the rearview mirror.

"Who?" JJ asked. He sounded all innocence, but she thought she detected a slight flutter in his voice.

"That man back there!" she yelled, unable to keep the edge of fear out of her voice. "That man in the garage! Is he the same one who was out at the baseball field the day that stray dog was killed?"

Jesus, Angie thought, feeling suddenly cold. *What if Greg was responsible for what happened to Wolfgang, too?*

Reflected in the rearview mirror, JJ's face looked pale and tight with worry. Angie thought—she hoped—that it was still because he was so upset about what had happened to Wolfgang, but she would never be sure unless he talked to her. She felt suddenly angry at both herself and JJ for letting the lines of communication between them go down.

"I have to know," she said, making an effort to keep her voice low and steady. "Have you ever seen that man before?"

For the longest time, JJ was silent. Angie kept glancing back and forth between the road ahead and her son's reflection in the mirror.

"I . . . I'm not really sure," he finally said with a quick shake of his head. "He might have been, but I . . . ."

"Jesus," Angie whispered to herself.

Glancing at her own reflection in the rearview mirror, she shivered when she saw the haunted, hunted look in her own eyes. She was suddenly, absolutely convinced that Greg was the one, that for whatever reason, he was stalking her and her family and that he was enjoying it!

When the telephone rang at nine-thirty that night, Angie was alone in the family room, watching a Barbara Walters special.

JJ was in his bedroom playing *Mirage,* the new computer game he'd borrowed from Sammy, and Brandy had gone out to the movies with Evan.

Fearful that this might be Greg, calling to taunt her, her first impulse was not to answer it. She got up from the couch and walked into the kitchen where she waited for the answering machine to click on. After the fourth ring, her taped message played, followed by a loud *beep.* Then a man's voice began to speak.

"Hey, why the heck aren't you home by now?"

Angie immediately recognized her brother's voice and let out a sigh of relief as she picked up the receiver.

"Wait, wait. I'm here," she said, pushing the *off* button on the answering machine.

"Screening your calls, huh? What's the matter, haven't you been paying your bills?" Rob chuckled softly.

"No, I was . . . in the bathroom," Angie said, quickly thinking of a lie. "JJ's upstairs, but I guess he didn't hear it. What's up?"

"Just calling to ask you something," Rob said, but Angie was hardly paying attention to him because she was wondering if she should tell Rob her concerns about Greg Newman. Was she being foolish, or was he really a danger to them? Earlier today, after she and JJ had gotten home from the veterinarian's office, she had called Detective Murray at the police station and left a message, but—so far, anyway—he hadn't returned her call.

"You know, the forecast is calling for it to be sunny and warm right through the weekend," Rob said cheerily. "Craig and I have a little camp on Benton Pond, just outside of Clinton."

"There's a Clinton, Maine?" Angie said, feeling a prickly rush up the back of her neck. "We lived on Clinton Street in Bedford Heights."

"I know," Rob said with a tight laugh. "Matter of fact, that's why I looked for property out there, because of the connection with the name. It's just outside of Winslow. Anyway, we were thinking about going there this weekend and opening the place up. I was wondering if you and the kids would like to come along.''

''Oh, gee . . . I don't know.'' Angie said, still feeling distracted. ''It sounds like fun, but—''

''There's some great fishing. I'll bet JJ's never been fishing,'' Rob said, pushing her a little.

''He went a couple of times with John,'' Angie replied, ''but—no, he hasn't been that much.''

''Don't you think all of you would appreciate a chance to get away for a few days?''

''Yeah . . . Sure, but I—''

''Oh, come *on,* Sis! This isn't like you!'' Rob said. There was just a hint of concern coloring his voice. ''You've always been the one who's up and at 'em, all fired up to go.''

''Yeah, but . . . you know, wouldn't you and Craig like some time alone? I mean, having kids around can get pretty active.''

''You don't think I know that?'' Rob said. He sounded almost offended, but Angie knew that he wasn't . . . not really.'' It's a great place to get away. Nice and quiet. Right there on the lake. The nearest neighbor is, like, almost a mile down the road, and this time of year, there won't be many boats on the lake—if any. Come on, Ange. You'll *love* it.''

''Oh, I know I would.''

Angie shivered as she shifted her gaze to the window above the kitchen sink that looked out over the backyard. For an instant, she could imagine Greg Newman out there, lurking in the darkness, watching her through the lighted window. She felt suddenly exposed, vulnerable.

''Let me talk it over with the kids,'' she said, fighting the tightness in her voice, ''I ll get back to you tomorrow afternoon.''

''There's no real hurry,'' Rob said, ''just so long as I know before the weekend so we can plan food and where people are going to sleep and all.''

''How about this,'' Angie said, stepping away from the open window. ''Why don't you just plan food and whatever you need for you and Craig. If we're coming, we'll bring our own stuff . . . Maybe even a few treats.''

"Sounds like a plan to me," Rob said. "You know, I'm looking forward to it because it'll be a good chance for us to sit and talk. We haven't done that in a long time."

"I know," Angie said. "Not since the—"

Her voice cut off sharply when she remembered how Rob had come down and stayed with her for John's funeral.

"Thank for the invite," she said. "I'll give you a buzz tomorrow."

"S'long."

As she hung up the phone, Angie was thinking that she and Rob had a good chance to talk anytime they wanted, now that they lived so close, but still, maybe out of habit, they seemed not to get together often. She wished she had brought up the subject that was most on her mind—Greg Newman—but she couldn't stop wondering how much of it might be her imagination.

She hoped she never found out.

After drawing the shade over the kitchen sink window she walked back into the family room. By the time she was settled on the couch, Barbara Walters was talking to Jim Carrey. She had no interest in what he had to say, so she switched off the TV and just sat there, listening to the silent house.

The windows behind her were open, allowing a soft breeze to blow in, carrying with it a fresh, woodsy smell. She leaned back and closed her eyes, telling herself to relax, but the coiling tension inside her wouldn't let go. She considered making a cup of herbal tea, maybe Sleepy Time, but even that seemed like too much of a chore. She'd be content just to sit here and appreciate the peace and quiet.

"I'm depressed," she whispered to herself, hearing the low rasp of her voice, an intrusion on the silence.

It made sense, of course.

She didn't think she would ever get over the grief of losing John . . . not fully. The guilt she felt because she had been so close to telling him she was leaving him only made her feel worse. She knew this was something she was going to have to carry for the rest of her life. She regretted that the police—at least as far as she knew—hadn't caught the person who had shot John. If they had, she might feel as though there was at least *some* element of closure to the whole thing.

She certainly still missed John, especially on nights like this when everything was so quiet. But she knew that she was also missing his help in raising Brandy and JJ. They weren't getting any easier as they grew older. The truth was, JJ was much harder to handle now than he had been even a year ago. Angie knew that it was preadolescence as much as his own grief over losing his father. As for Brandy—for all she knew, her daughter was off with her boyfriend, smoking pot and drinking and screwing. At moments of weakness like this, Angie questioned whether or not she had the stamina for the job of raising kids alone.

"Of *course* I do," she whispered.

She shifted her eyes around the room, looking for something to anchor her gaze. What she ended up focusing on was the framed photograph of John on the mantel. It had been taken the day he graduated from the police academy, so he was wearing his dress uniform. Tears stung her eyes, as she thought how young and vital he looked, so full of hope and promise.

"And where did it all go" Angie asked herself, shivering and hugging herself because she knew all too well the answer to the question of where John's life had led.

And what about mine? she wondered as the deep chill inside her got stronger.

Where is my life taking me?

What will be my end?

Fighting back a rush of tears, she stood up and walked back into the kitchen. She glanced at the clock and saw that it was a little past ten o'clock. Brandy should be getting home any time now.

Covering her mouth with one hand and biting down on the knuckle, Angie looked over at Wolfgang, who was asleep by the back door. He looked so pitiful and small with the huge cast on his leg. Already it was scuffed and brown. The sedative she had mixed into his food had knocked him out cold.

"Good boy, Wolfie," she whispered, but the dog didn't even stir.

Still feeling sad and wistful, Angie walked into the hallway and then up the stairs to get ready for bed. It was still a little too early to start worrying about Brandy, but she decided that she would wait up—as she always did—until her daughter got home safely. As wearing as it seemed at times, it was all part of the job.

As she passed JJ's bedroom, she paused at his door when she heard a faint sound from inside the room. Stepping close to the door, she cocked an ear and listened until the sound came more clearly.

It was a low, watery sniffing sound.

JJ was crying.

Angie's first response was to knock on the door and ask him what was the matter, but she hesitated, thinking that—maybe at twelve years old—JJ didn't want his mother to catch him crying like this.

For almost a full minute, Angie just stood there in the hallway and listened.

The crying sound was low and muffled. She could clearly imagine JJ lying on his bed, his face buried in his pillow so no one else—his mother, especially!—would hear him.

Angie wanted to continue down the hall to her own bedroom and get her nightgown on, but she couldn't resist the impulse to open the door. The doorknob felt slick in her hand as she grasped and turned it.

JJ's bedroom was dark and, just as she had guessed, he was face down on the bed. The hall light shining into his room cut a lemon-yellow wedge across him and his bed.

"JJ . . . Honey?" Angie called out as she took a hesitant step into the room. She wasn't sure if he knew that she was there. It still wasn't too late. She knew she could leave now and let him deal with whatever was upsetting him on his own, but her maternal instincts were too strong.

With a few, quick steps, she came over to the bed and sat down on the edge. Her weight on the bed made the mattress sag, but still JJ didn't stir. If she hadn't heard him crying and if she couldn't see him breathing, she might have panicked. She could tell that he was purposely avoiding her.

"Hey, champ," she said, reaching out and shaking him gently by the shoulder.

JJ rolled over and looked up at her but said nothing. His face was streaked with tears that made his skin glisten in the dim light.

"You can talk to me about it, whatever it is, if you want," Angie whispered, leaning close and wiping his cheek with the tips of her fingers.

JJ opened his mouth and started to say something, but no sound came out except for a low groan that seemed to originate in the pit of his stomach. He sniffed loudly and twisted his head away from her, facing the wall as though embarrassed that she had caught him crying.

"Hey. Come on, honey," Angie whispered. "It's all right. Tell me what's bothering you." She paused and took a deep breath. "No matter what it is, it helps to talk about it, you know?"

JJ sniffed again, louder, and wiped his face on his pillow before turning to face her again. His mouth worked as though he was dying to say something, but still no sound came out.

"Is it about Wolfie?" Angie asked, smiling reassuringly. "You know, I just checked him, and he's sleeping like a log. That's the best thing for him, you know."

"No," JJ said, his voice high and strangled. "It's not about Wolfie."

"What is it then?" she asked.

She placed a hand lightly on his shoulder, feeling how thin and frail it was as she tried to pull him to her. He jerked away from her, and she let her hand drop to the mattress.

Facing the wall, JJ tried once more to say something, but his voice twisted off before he could get more than the first word out.

"I—"

Then fresh tears flowed, and he pulled the sheet up and covered his face.

"It's . . . about Dad, isn't it?" Angie said softly.

"Kind of," JJ said from behind his hands. His voice was

so distorted that Angie wasn't sure at first what he had said; but on a deep level, it gradually registered.

"I know, hon," she whispered, pulling him close to her. "I know . . ."

JJ sat up suddenly and, moaning softly, buried his face into the crook of her neck.

"I . . . I really miss him . . . all time," JJ said, his voice hitching as he talked against his mother's shoulder.

"I do, too, honey," Angie said, rubbing his back.

She knew that JJ could probably never be able to conceive just how true that was. As rocky as their marriage may have been over the last few years, as close as she had been to be actually leaving him, she missed John terribly.

"That day . . . out at the ball field . . . I was hoping that . . . that man . . . I was . . . was thinking that . . . he could . . . you know, like, replace Dad, you know?"

His voice was broken by painful gasps. Angie could feel him shudder in her embrace. Her body stiffened when she realized who JJ was talking about. A sinking sensation hit her stomach, and she was afraid for a moment that she was going to pass out. The darkness of the room pressed in on her with an cold, unrelenting pressure.

"Do you mean the man who was out at the gas station today?" Angie asked, surprised that she could speak at all.

She felt JJ nod against her shoulder. Needle-sharp spikes of panic shot through her as she closed her eyes and hugged her son tightly as she stared into the swelling darkness behind her eyelids. Before long, the image of Greg Newman formed in her mind, his face floating in the darkness starkly underlit by vibrating colors that shifted subtlety through the spectrum. She heard a low whimpering sound, and it took a moment for her to realize that she was crying.

"It's all right, JJ . . . It's all right," she whispered as tears streamed from her eyes. She clung to him as much as he seemed to be clinging to her.

"Everything's gonna be all right . . . I promise . . ."

"Is it really?" JJ asked.

His voice seemed to come from an impossible distance.

Angie knew that she couldn't honestly answer his question. She had no idea whether or not things were going to be all right. Right now, all she was certain of was that John's death—John's *murder!*—had cast a terrible shadow over her children's lives as well as her own, and there seemed to be no escape from it.

Even if she went off for the weekend with her brother and his lover to their camp on the lake, she wouldn't be able to truly escape because it would follow her there.

Her grief and misery would go everywhere she went. They would haunt her for the rest of her life.

Angie lost track of the time as she and JJ sat there hugging each other and crying together in a way that they had never cried before, even when he was a little boy. Only vaguely did she realize that *this* and *only* this—crying together—was what might heal them . . .

If not now . . . maybe eventually.

Chapter 26
Taking Off

JJ was boiling mad when his mother woke him up early on Saturday morning. He'd been counting on sleeping late, like he did most weekends, but that—obviously—wasn't going to happen today.

"Come on, JJ!" she shouted from the foot of the stairs, her voice echoing shrilly in the stairwell. "Uncle Rob will be here in less than an hour! We've got to get a move on!"

JJ rolled over and looked at his bedroom clock. Seeing that it was only a little after seven o'clock, he grumbled something that wasn't even close to the English language.

His mother paused, but only for a moment. "I want you out of bed right *now!*"

"Jesus Christ," JJ whispered, cupping his hands over his ears and grinding his teeth together.

"You have to eat breakfast, get dressed, and pack whatever you want to bring for the weekend," his mother yelled. "And make sure you pack a sweatshirt or two. Rob says this time of year it can still get pretty cold there at night. Oh, and bring your sleeping bag. We're still not sure where everyone's going to sleep. I think you and Evan might have to sleep in a tent outside, if there's not enough room in the camp."

"Evan's coming, too?" JJ asked.

He had heard Brandy begging her mother last night to allow her boyfriend to come along and was surprised that she had agreed.

"Yes. Evan's coming." his mother said simply.

"Well, there's no way I'm sleeping outside in a tent," JJ grumbled as he pulled the blankets over his head and squeezed his eyes tightly shut. Patterns of light swirled like pinwheels behind his closed eyelids.

"You'll sleep wherever there's room for you to sleep," his mother replied firmly. "Now get your butt moving!"

"All right . . . all right. I'm coming." JJ scowled deeply and pressed his head back against the pillow. He'd been hoping he could drag this out a little longer, but he could tell that his mother was going to keep calling him every couple of minutes. Just after seven thirty, after she had called to him at least a half dozen more times, he finally threw the covers aside. He stood up so fast the blood drained from his head, making him feel momentarily dizzy.

"I'll be right down," he shouted angrily.

Even though the day was warm, almost muggy, he shivered as he looked around his bedroom. The sunlight pouring in through the windows hurt his eyes. A cold sinking sensation filled his stomach as he contemplated what lay ahead of him for the next two days.

No, he told himself, *only for the next day and a half!* He'd made his mother promise they'd come back early Sunday afternoon, and he intended to hold her to that.

Any way he looked at it, though, he wasn't looking forward to this little family trip at all. Earlier in the week, he had pushed his mother a little—but not *too* hard—about letting him stay home alone for the weekend, or maybe with Sammy's family, but she wouldn't even discuss it. Brandy had asked the same thing a day or so earlier and gotten the same result. JJ was sure that his mother didn't relish the idea of leaving Brandy with an opportunity to be home alone . . . all weekend . . . unsupervised . . . with her boyfriend.

Walking over to his desk, JJ emptied the books out of his

backpack, then got two pairs of socks, some underwear, a couple of clean T-shirts, an extra pair of jeans, a pair of shorts, and his Portland Sea Dogs sweatshirt, and stuffed them into the bag without folding them. Next he got his toothbrush and the tube of toothpaste from the upstairs bathroom and tucked them into the front compartment. He was reading an Arthur C. Clarke novel, was about halfway through it, so he jammed that in with his toothbrush, figuring he'd be bored out of his mind and would have *plenty* of time to read.

"JJ? . . . Get down here *now!*" his mother called.

"Yeah, just a minute!" he replied with an edge in his voice. "I'm packing, if you don't mind!"

"Oh, that's right. Uncle Rob says the fishing's really good there, so you might want to bring your fishing pole."

"I'm not sure where it is," JJ replied, glancing around the room. He checked inside his closer but didn't see it there.

"I though I saw it down in the cellar with your tackle box," his mother said, her voice sounding further away. JJ guessed she was in the kitchen, probably preparing his breakfast.

He quickly shucked off his pajamas, stuffed them under his pillow, smoothed out the blankets, then pulled on a clean T-shirt and jeans he'd worn for the last couple of days. His fingers were shaking as he buttoned and zipped his pants. After sitting on the edge of his bed and pulling on a pair of socks, he left his room and went downstairs.

He'd guessed right. His mother was at the stove, frying eggs and bacon. Two pieces of toast had already popped.

"This'll be ready for you in just a sec," his mother said, barely glancing at him over her shoulder.

"I'm gonna look for my fishing stuff," JJ said as he started for the cellar door. He thought his voice sounded a little strained, but his mother seemed not to notice.

Casting a cautious glance over his shoulder, he unlocked the door, flipped the light switch, and started down the stairs. The light on the stairway wasn't very bright. Wolfgang struggled up from the rug where he'd been sleeping and hobbled over to the head of the stairs, then stood there, wagging his tail as he watched.

The gnawing hollow in JJ's stomach got steadily worse as he entered the cool, dank cellar. The musty smell of the air almost made him gag. The light bulbs on the ceiling didn't seem to be nearly strong enough to push the darkness all the way back. In the corners of his vision, JJ saw thin, gray shadows shift across the cement floor. They seemed to reach out to him.

He immediately saw his fishing pole right where his mother had said it would be, propped up against the old workbench over by the bulkhead door, but he didn't walk straight over to it. Instead, he walked to the darkest corner of the cellar behind the furnace. His body was wire-tight with tension as he looked up at the cobwebbed ceiling.

"Is it down there?" his mother called out.

The suddenness of her voice startled JJ, making him jump. His voice was so tight it almost broke when he shouted back to her, "I'm still looking."

Sweat broke out across his forehead as he walked over to the spot that he and Sammy had found a few weeks ago when they'd been playing down here. Standing on tiptoes, he reached one hand up into the gap between the top of the stone wall and the floor joists and felt around. For a fleeting instant, he was afraid that the bundle had been moved, but then his fingers brushed against the coarse material of the hand towel. A teasing shock went through him.

"Come on. Your breakfast's ready *now*. We'll look for that stuff later," his mother shouted.

JJ's throat was too dry for him to answer. A small shower of grit and dirt sprinkled down on him as he grasped the bundle and pulled it down. It was surprisingly heavy for its size. His legs felt all rubbery and weak at the knees as he opened the bundle just enough to make sure the revolver was still wrapped inside.

"Uh, yeah . . . Got it," he said, not even sure if his mother could hear him.

JJ's eyes were wide and staring as he looked around the cellar, not quite sure what to do next. Finally, with no better plan, he shoved the towel and revolver down into the front of his pants and smoothed his T-shirt over it, hoping to hide it.

The package bulged out noticeably, but as he went over to the workbench and picked up his fishing rod and the red, rusted tackle box, he was already calculating how he'd get the gun back upstairs to his bedroom without his mother noticing it.

His stomach felt as loose as jelly as he started up the stairs. He was tensed and ready to pull the gun out and drop it the instant it looked as though his mother saw that he was trying to sneak something. He hesitated at the top of the stairs only long enough to snap off the cellar lights. Then, telling himself to look cool, he stepped into the kitchen, angling his body away from his mother. He leaned the fishing pole against the wall by the door and, gripping the tackle box tightly with both hands, pressed it against his stomach, hoping that it would hide the thick bulge underneath his shirt. "Sit down. It's all ready," his mother said pleasantly, indicating with a quick nod of her head the plate of food on the table.

"Just a second," JJ said shakily. "I—there's stuff up in my room I wanna get, first."

Moving so fast that he thought his mother couldn't help but get suspicious, he hurried out of the kitchen and up was stairs, back to his bedroom. He'd broken a sweat and was breathing so hard his throat hurt as he eased the door shut behind him.

"Jesus," he whispered.

The excitement was almost unbearable as he walked over to his bed and pulled the package out from under his shirt. His hands were trembling uncontrollably as he opened the package and gripped the revolver.

The gun felt good in his hand as he raised it as though aiming to shoot.

"Come *on,* JJ!"

His mother's voice jangled his nerves like a buzz saw, making him almost drop the gun.

"Your breakfast is getting cold!"

JJ wondered how it was possible that his mother *hadn't* noticed how funny he was acting. After kicking the discarded towel under the bed, he opened his backpack and jammed the gun down as far as he could underneath the tangle of clean clothes. He worried that it might get some oil or grease on his clothes, but it was too late for that.

He quickly zipped the backpack shut when he heard footsteps on the stairs. Before he could put the bag down, there came a rapid knocking at his door.

"Yeah?" he said, turning around and looking furtively at the door as his mother opened it.

"JJ, don't ruin this weekend for me, all right? I can't stand it when you drag your feet like this," his mother said, looking at him with pleading with her eyes.

JJ stood stiffly in the middle of the floor. He could feel how pale his face must look as he faced her and forced a thin smile.

"Are you feeling all right?" she asked, her brow creasing with concern.

"Yeah . . . Sure," JJ said. He was trying to sound causal, but his voice kept catching and sounding much too high, even to him.

"Well then . . . ?" his mother said, eying him suspiciously. "Why don't you came downstairs and eat? You can finish packing while I clean up the kitchen and get everything else we're taking ready. I'm going to need help packing the car, too."

"Can't Brandy do that?" JJ said.

She turned and left without a word, and JJ followed her down the stairs. He couldn't stop wondering how he was going to get some of the bullets he knew she had hidden in the bottom drawer of her desk. He'd figure out a way because, once they got to lake, he was planning on taking off for a while and doing a little shooting.

Greg wasn't due at work until noon, so the first thing he did that Saturday morning was drive out by Angela's house to see what—if anything—was going on.

He'd spent the last two nights at Lakeview Motel, in Greene, but because he wasn't sure if he was going to be staying there another night, he paid his bill and threw his suitcase into the back seat of his car. Before driving off, he checked to make sure his baseball bat was where he had left it, underneath the front seat. After eating a huge breakfast at the *Railroad Cafe,* a nice enough place just down the road from the motel, he drove the short distance to Bolton.

He realized how lucky he was as soon as he drove past Angela's house and saw what was going on there. Because he didn't want to slow down and draw attention to himself, he only caught a quick glimpse, but it was enough. Angela was leaning into the back of her car, placing a suitcase beside several bags of groceries. Brandy was just exiting the house with a suitcase in one hand and a rolled up sleeping bag in the other. Her boyfriend was a few paces behind, his arms loaded as well.

"What the hell?" Greg muttered, scratching his chin as he drove past.

He glanced into the review mirror but couldn't see much else, so he drove a short way out on Taylor Hill Road and then pulled over to the side of the road. His bladder was aching from all the coffee he'd drunk at breakfast, so he turned the car off, got out, and relieved himself behind a stand of pine trees. Satisfied, he got back into the car and sat there drumming his fingers on the steering wheel, lost in thought.

He knew that he had to find out exactly what was going on. He was pretty sure it wasn't anything as serious as the family moving away, but still, he had to know where Angela was going. This might finally be the opportunity he was looking for to get rid of her and be done with it. After her visit to his hotel room, he'd started losing interest in the cat and mouse game he'd been playing with her. The time had come to kill her and the kids, and get his ass down to Miami or wherever the hell he ended up.

The window on the driver's side was open, and through it he could hear the piercing chatter of morning birds singing. God, how that sound got on his nerves! The day was heating up fast, and insects buzzed in the tall grass by the roadside. As he mulled over what he should do next, a sheen of sweat broke out over her face. He licked his upper lip, tasting the salt.

"What the fuck . . . What the fuck," he whispered. He

glanced now and then at his reflection in the rearview mirror, surprised by how glassy and distant his gaze looked to him. For a dizzying moment, he had the distinct impression that his face had melted away, and that he was looking at someone else's reflection. Leaning close enough to the mirror to fog the glass with his breath, he smiled at himself, but his smile quickly froze when, faintly, just at the edge of hearing, he heard a paper-thin voice whisper his name.

"Shit," he muttered. He wanted to turn and look into the back seat but was unable to tear his gaze from his reflection in the mirror. When he spoke, he noticed that his voice had an odd quality to it that sounded foreign, almost as if someone else had spoken through him.

He sensed something—a pale, gray motion—shifting behind him in the back seat, but no matter how hard he strained to see what it was in the mirror, he saw nothing.

Time seemed to have stopped as he stared into his own eyes, seeing the rest of his face peripherally as it shifted, seemingly changed shape. At times, he thought he almost recognized the person his face resembled, but before he caught who it was, his features would shift again and subtly alter to someone else. Very faintly, he could hear several voices, whispering to him. They seemed to be calling his name and telling him something, but no matter how hard he focused on them, he couldn't make out what it was.

He snapped out of his reverie when a truck hauling a small camper sped by. The sudden concussion hit his car like a huge fist, shaking it as it blew a cloud of grit and dust through the window.

Choking and swearing under his breath, Greg raised his middle finger and jabbed it at the rapidly receding truck and camper. A second later, before he could do anything else, another car sped past. Greg froze, instantly recognizing Angela Ross' white Subaru. He wasn't sure, but it looked like there were four people in the car—Angela, Brandy, JJ and, no doubt, the boyfriend.

"What the fuck?"

He reached for the key in the ignition and twisted it so fast

his hand slipped, and he skinned his knuckles on the steering
column. The car started up instantly, but already Angela's car
was out of sight, having crested the hill up ahead. Greg sucked
in sharp breath, his throat painfully dry from tension as he
shifted into gear and took off. His rear tires squealed in the
dirt, shooting gravel out behind him in a dusty fantail.

It didn't take Greg long to catch up with Angela's car. She
wasn't driving nearly as fast as it had seemed while he was
standing still along the roadside. Once he had her back in sight,
he didn't want Angela to see his car. She had ridden in it and
no doubt could recognize it.

Angela drove east on Route 202 until she got to Augusta
where she turned onto the Interstate, heading north. The first
road sign Greg saw indicated that Waterville and Bangor were
straight ahead. He had no idea what those towns or cities were
except that he had heard someplace that the famous horror
writer, Stephan King, lived in Bangor. Greg couldn't imagine
why someone as rich as that would actually *choose* to live in
a dipshit state like Maine.

The drive took much longer than Greg had anticipated, but
he should have guessed it because he had seen Angela and her
daughter packing as though going away for at least an overnight,
if not longer. Probably a weekend jaunt, he guessed. They
couldn't be going very far because Angela would have to be
back home by Sunday evening so the kids could go to school
on Monday.

After driving for almost an hour, Greg began to worry that
he might run out of gas. His fuel gauge was reading less than
a quarter of a tank. He had no idea how he could stop for gas
and not lose track of Angela. After a while, he realized that
she was travelling with the truck and camper. He noticed that
she sped up whenever the truck sped up, and slowed down
whenever it slowed down, always keeping it a few car lengths
ahead of her. The little caravan exited the Turnpike in Waterville and started east on Route 104. Greg swore to himself
when he saw Angela signal for a turn into a gas station.

Greg's face was bathed with sweat as he pulled over to side
of the road and watched them. He saw JJ get out and run into

store while Angela got out of the car and went over to the truck where a tall, rather plump man wearing a bright green polo shirt and tan chinos was pumping gas. Greg figured this was either Angela's brother or else her new love interest. The way they talked to each other, keeping a respectable distance, finally convinced him that they weren't lovers, not that it mattered.

He left his engine running, raising his concern that he was going to run out of gas, but he knew that he couldn't possibly pull into the station and fill up while they were there . . . and if he waited until they were gone, he was sure to lose them.

A sudden, almost blinding rage took hold of him, but he knew that there was nothing he could do about it. He would simply have to follow them as far as he could and hope that he wouldn't have to turn back if he got too low on gas. The last thing he wanted was to be stranded somewhere out in the middle of nowhere.

While he was waiting for Angela and the truck to leave the gas station, a police cruiser drove by in the opposite direction. The patrolman slowed down enough to eye Greg but, thinking fast, Greg pulled the road map down from where he kept it tucked under the visor and held it up, pretending to be studying it while surreptitiously watched the cruiser pass by. He let out a long sigh when the cop kept on going and disappeared around the corner.

Greg watched as JJ got back into the car, and Angela and the driver from the truck started out again. He had a momentary fear that they were going to double back and head in the opposite direction, but they turned right onto Route 104 and kept driving east. After waiting for the flow of traffic to pass, Greg pulled out onto the road and followed them, dropping a few cars behind them.

They passed through downtown Waterville, a run-down little place that Greg thought looked surprisingly busy. After crossing the river into Winslow, they turned left onto Route 100.

By now, Greg was seriously concerned that he was going to run out of gas. He kept looking from the road to the gas needle, now just touching the last notch before *E*. He looked longingly at the Sunoco station they passed just outside of a

little town named Benton. Then Angela and the truck and
camper turned left onto an unmarked road.

This can't be very far from where they're going, Greg thought
eagerly, but he knew that he was going to have give up following
them after another mile or two if he was going to get back
without walking. He heaved a sigh of relief when he saw the
car and truck slowing for a right hand turn onto a dirt road
marked by a weathered, wooden sigh that read: BENTON SHORE
DRIVE. Greg watched them pull into the road, raising a cloud
of yellow dust in their wake. Satisfied that he would now be
able to find them easily enough, he did a quick U-turn and
headed back to the gas station he'd seen in Benton. Just as the
gas station came into sight, his car sputtered and bucked. He
shifted into neutral and coasted up to the pumps. A tall, beefy
man with black hair and grease smudges on his face and hands
sauntered over to greet him.

"You running on fumes or what, mister?" the man said,
smiling wide enough to show that he was missing several front
teeth.

"Looks like I just made it," Greg said, exaggeratedly wiping
his forehead with the back of his hand. "Let's fill 'er up, why
don't you?"

As the station attendant set to work, Greg eased back in his
car seat and closed his eyes. When he inhaled deeply, the thick
gas fumes stung his nose, but he hardly noticed. He was content
with the prospects. When the attendant finished pumping the
gas, Greg paid him in cash.

"Say," he said as he took the change from the attendant
and folded it into his wallet. " 'S there a good restaurant around
here?"

The attendant stroked his chin as he considered for a moment,
looking like someone who didn't have anywhere near all of
his lights on upstairs.

"Nothin' much 'round here," the man said, his Maine accent
so thick Greg half-suspected he put on just for the tourists.
"Over to Winslow, though, there's a nice little place called
Perry's Pizza. Might wanna try that. Right on Main Street.
Can't miss it."

"Thanks" Greg said as he started up the car and drove off.

Heading down the road, Greg laughed out loud, happy now because he knew that he had plenty of time . . . all the time he would need to get something to eat and then, with a full belly and a full tank of gas, he would drive back out to *Benton Shore Drive* and have a look around. It wouldn't be too tough to find Angela Ross and her family.

"This is . . . absolutely unbelievable," Angie murmured to herself as she walked down to the shore and looked out over the lake. The sun was high and warm in her face, and the wind-ruffled water glittered like hammered foil. The distant shoreline was almost lost in a blue heat haze.

When she closed her eyes, the darkness behind her eyelids vibrated with bright red flashes of light. The strong breeze blowing in off the water carried with it a fresh, wet smell that mixed with the thick, resinous scent of hot pine. In the distance, she heard the faint warble of a loon.

"The property faces west," Rob said as he came up behind her and placed a hand gently on her shoulder. "We get some dynamite sunsets, especially in the fall."

"You told me about this place so many times," Angie said, "but I never *imagined* that it was *this* nice."

A wistful smile tugged at the corners of her mouth as she hooked an arm around her brother's waist and pulled him close as she surveyed the wide expanse of water.

Out behind the camp, Craig was backing the truck and camper around, positioning it so the camper's front faced the water.

"Well, inside the camp's not much to look at," Rob said, "but we figure, over the next couple of years, if we pick away at it, we'll have it all fixed up by the time we retire."

"Is that your plan? To retire out here?" Angie asked, tilting her head back and inhaling noisily. She couldn't help but feel a stirring of envy, even though she knew that, with the benefits and insurance money she'd gotten after John's death, she could easily afford a summer place on a lake . . . if that's what she wanted. She had decided to save the money to pay for the kids' college . . .

Until now, anyway.

At this moment, she was thinking that lake front property didn't seem like such a bad idea.

"Why don't we get all our stuff unloaded and set up now, so we can enjoy the afternoon and evening?" Rob said.

Without waiting for her answer, he turned and walked away, but Angie couldn't stop looking around at her surroundings. The worry and tension seemed to be melting away inside her like a snow bank in August. Only after she heard JJ start complaining to Brandy that he didn't want to carry *all* the heavy stuff did she snap out of it.

The plan was for Angie and Brandy to share the double bed in the small upstairs bedroom. Rob and Craig were going to sleep in a camper but, because it still might be too cold at night to sleep outside, JJ and Evan had a choice of either settling in the camper with the two men or sleeping on the couch and floor in the living room. JJ's expression revealed that he wasn't too pleased with either choice, but he didn't complain much as he lugged his backpack and sleeping bag into the house and dropped them in the living room beside the couch.

Inside, as Rob had said, the camp wasn't quite as nice as Angie had imagined it would be, but it wasn't too bad, either. After a winter of being shut up, there was a stale quality to the air that chocked her. The first thing Rob did was unlock the shutters, and throw open the windows downstairs and up so the lake breeze could blow in. A winter's worth of dust swirled in the air, but with sunlight streaming across the floor, it wasn't long before the place seemed a lot more inviting. Angie tried to ignore the dead, dried-up spiders and bugs that littered the windowsills, thinking that she'd get Brandy to vacuum them up later.

After Rob and Craig got the power switched on and made sure the refrigerator was running, Angie started unloading the bags of groceries she and Rob had each brought. It took her a while to figure out where everything went, but she made out all right while Rob and Craig busied themselves under the camp, getting the water pump hooked up and running.

Angie knew that she would have to keep her eye on Brandy and Evan all weekend. All they seemed to want to do was sit around, holding hands and kissing. Finally, after some convincing, the two of them pitched in and helped her while JJ went outside to get Wolfgang settled. Only after she got Rob's approval had Angie allowed JJ to bring his dog along, rather than leave him at Sammy's for the weekend. JJ said that he was going to take a walk down the road to check the area out after he made sure Wolfgang was all set.

"That's all right, isn't it?" Angie asked Rob, a little fearful because JJ didn't know his way around.

"The nearest camp's a mile or so down the road, but there's probably nobody up here yet," Rob said. "He can't get lost as long as he stays on the road."

"You hear that?" Angie asked, but JJ was already out the door, letting it slam shut behind him.

For the next couple of hours, everyone including Brandy and Evan worked hard getting things set up. Angie enjoyed the work, feeling that it was the least she could do to help Rob who had been so supportive to her after John died. Once the water pump was running and they at least had cold running water, Angie set to work washing the accumulated dust off the dishes and glasses they'd be using. Then she set to work washing the counter tops and floor while Brandy dusted and Evan ran the vacuum through the downstairs.

Angie screamed when she slid open one of the counter drawers and found a mess of chewed-up newspaper, cloth, and pink insulation. Brandy, Evan, and Rob all came running to see what was wrong.

"Ahh, it's nothing but a squirrel's nest," Evan said, laughing as he poked the pile with his index finger.

"Probably a red squirrel," Rob added. "The problem with those little bastards is they get in between the walls and chew the crap out of your wiring, too."

Thankfully, the nest was no longer occupied, but Angie wasn't taking any chances. She pulled on a pair of rubber

gloves before scooping the nest into a trash bag. She made sure
to use full strength Lysol when she washed and rinsed the
drawer.

As the afternoon gradually passed and shadows lengthened
across the floor, Angie was beginning to feel right at home
here. Once the kitchen was cleaned to her satisfaction, she went
outside and checked to make sure Wolfgang was all set and to
look for JJ. He had tied the dog's run to a tree near the camper,
but he was nowhere in sight.

She called for him a few times as she walked down to the
narrow strip of beach but got no answer.

Little waves lapped at the smooth rocks that lined the water's
edge, making a soothing sound. She closed her eyes and leaned
her head back, imagining that all of the anxiety and tension
she'd been feeling for the last several weeks and months were
sloughing away. The only edge she felt was when she thought
about how much John would have liked it out here, but then
she remembered how much John hadn't really liked her brother.
Although he had never come right out and said so, she was
sure it was because he felt uncomfortable about Rob's gayness.
A lingering twist of sadness filled her when she thought about
the missed opportunities John and Rob had to become genuine
friends, and not just family.

"A penny for your thoughts," Rob said as he walked up
behind her.

Angie turned and smiled at him. He had a bottle of beer in
one hand—Sam Adam's Lager—and was grinning as he placed
a hand on her shoulder and started out over the water with her.

"Just thinking," she said with a faint trace of wistfulness
in her voice. "About how lucky you and Craig are."

"Don't you know you're not supposed to *think* when you're
in a place like this?" Rob said. His voice sounded dreamy and
far away.

Angie snickered and nodded.

"The whole rest of the world and all its problems seem to
be a thousand miles away, don't they?" Rob said.

"I don't know," Angie said. "I can't think."

Rob offered Angie a sip of beer, but she refused. He shrugged as he raised the bottle to his mouth and drank.

"At least a thousand miles away," she said, glorying in the feeling of the warm sun on her face. Her voice wasn't much more than a murmur that even she almost couldn't hear above the sound of the wind high overhead in the pines and the water, lapping gently at the rocky shore.

"A thousand miles away . . ."

Chapter 27
Surprise

Cutting through the dense blackness of the forest, the distant campfire was a flickering orange beacon that teased and danced in the night. Fainter still, a single light shone in the cabin's downstairs windows. As he crept closer, moving through the underbrush as quietly as possible, Greg could hear the blazing fire crackling and popping. Sparks spun skywards, fiery corkscrews against the night sky before they winked out of existence.

Greg cursed under his breath every time he stepped on a twig or branch. The dry snap of wood sounded as loud as a gunshot in the darkness, but he was sure that none of the people huddled around the campfire could hear whatever noise he might make. They were all too busy laughing and talking, their voices echoing hollowly in the night.

In one hand, Greg gripped his baseball bat, but he couldn't stop thinking that, being out in the middle of nowhere like this, maybe he should have brought a knife or a gun. Having been born and raised in the city, he had no idea what dangerous animals might be lurking about. For all he knew, right now a bear or a wolf, unseen in the night, could be sneaking up on him from behind.

As he got closer, Greg saw—just as he had suspected—that Angela, her son, Brandy, and her boyfriend, and two other men, neither of whom he recognized, were sitting on logs that had been arranged in a horseshoe-shape around the campfire. One of them must be the brother who had driven Angela out to the garage the other day, but at this distance Greg couldn't tell which one it was. Brandy was sitting on the sand, her knees to her chest, her head leaning back in her boyfriend's lap. Greg felt the stirring of an erection when he remembered watching those two going at it out behind the house.

The two older men were drinking beer from the bottle. Angela had a glass of red wine. Brandy and her boyfriend were each holding a can of Coke, but they seemed much more intent on kissing and touching each other. JJ sat off to one side, alone and stone-faced as he stared into the fire and poked it with a long stick. Even at this distance, Greg could see that the boy was bored out of his mind.

Well, we'll see what we can do to generate a little excitement around here for you, Greg thought, sniffing with laughter.

He started to move a little closer but suddenly stopped when he saw something else beside the campfire. At first glance, he thought the large, dark object at JJ's feet was a jacket or sweater somebody had dropped. After a moment, he realized that it was a dog.

"Shit!" Greg whispered, clutching the baseball bat all the tighter.

In the glow of the fire, he could see something large and white on the dog's front leg, and he chuckled to himself when he realized it was a plaster cast and that he must have broken the dog's leg the other night when he wailed it with the bat.

"Goddamned good thing, too," Greg whispered, crouching low behind a bush and slapping the bat into the palm of his hand. He was confident that no one could see him beyond the bright ring of firelight. The real problem was, now that he had found them, he wasn't quite sure what to do next.

Obviously, it would be ridiculous to charge in there and attack all of them at once. Three or four against one weren't the kind of odds he favored, and he had no idea what kind of

fight Angela might put up. Probably a pretty good one, if her
children were threatened.

No, he was going to have to wait for a better opportunity to
strike . . . sometime when they weren't all together.

But while he knew that he had to be cautious, he also was
convinced that he had to do *something* to them—to *all* of them
while they were isolated out here in the wilderness. It would
probably be a few days, minimum, before anyone even noticed
they were missing, maybe a few more days before anyone
found them out here. That would give him plenty of time to
get out of Maine and down to Florida or wherever he was going
to go.

As darkness settled over the land, The temperature steadily
dropped. Greg was shivering wildly, his teeth chattering as he
watched them gathered around the warm blaze. The raucous
sound of their laughter especially grated on his nerves, and
watching the two men drinking beer gave him a powerful thirst.

He glanced at the luminous dial of his wristwatch and saw
that it was already well past ten o'clock. Hopefully they would
be going to bed so he could figure out where he was going to
spend the night. His car was parked off the road a mile or more
down the road, and it looked as if he was going to be freezing
his ass off in the back seat tonight.

"You'll pay for that, too, bitch," he whispered, glaring at
Angela and clutching the handle of the baseball bat so tightly
his hands and wrists began to throb. A gauzy-red haze shifted
across his vision.

He jumped and couldn't help but let out a shout when a loud
ruffling sound suddenly filled the night close behind him. In a
flash, the dog by the campfire struggled to his feet and started
barking.

"Hey! Easy there, Wolfie!" the boy shouted as he grabbed
the dog's collar and held him back so he wouldn't try to run
off into the woods. Because of the cast on his leg, the dog
wasn't able to move as quickly as he had the other night, but
he kept barking, drowning out most of the voices around the
fire.

Winding tension filled Greg as he stared into the swelling

darkness behind him. He had no idea what that sound might have been or where it had to come from. Greg cringed, realizing that it was almost directly over his head. Braced for an attack, he looked up at the trees. They stood out in dizzying perspective against the star-filled sky.

"What *is* that?" Angela asked. Greg could barely hear her above the dog barking and the loud *whooshing* sound that filled his ears.

"Just an owl," one of the men said, his voice carrying clearly in the night. Greg turned and saw him staring into the darkness beyond the fire, almost exactly at the spot where he was crouching. A hard lump formed in his throat as he wondered if the man was going to enter the woods.

"Yeah, it's probably that barn owl that nests in the barn at the old Foster place," the other man said, shielding his eyes with his hands and scanning the dark forest. He turned to Angela and added, "We hear that one a lot, especially this time of year, for some reason."

"Cool," JJ said, but he didn't look into the darkness for very long. Still holding the dog's collar, he sat down on the log and resumed jabbing the burning logs with his stick. The dog lay down in the sand, but he was still alert, his ears erect and listening.

Greg crouched low and watched them, poised and ready to fight if he had to.

"Well, I guess I'll tuck in," Angela said, now that the conversation had died down. "You really tuckered me out, working me so hard today."

She stood up and yawned as she stretched her arms above her head. Greg liked the way the firelight underlit her breasts.

"I really appreciate all the help, Sis," one of the men said, standing up and coming over to give her a firm hug and a quick kiss on the cheek.

"Yeah, I'm kinda tried, too," JJ said. "Uncle Rob, is it all right if Wolfie sleeps in the living room with me?"

"JJ," Angela said, giving him a scowling look.

The man who had called Angela "Sis" looked at JJ and, nodding, said, "I don't have any problem with that."

"Thanks," JJ said, and he turned and started walking toward the camp, moving slowly so the dog could hobble along beside him. Over his shoulder, he called out, "G' night everybody."

"I think you'd better come along, too," Angela said, indicating with a wave of her hand that she wanted Brandy to come with her and JJ. Brandy frowned as she looked at her mother but made no move to stand.

"Evan and I want to stay out a little longer," she said.

Greg smiled to himself, hearing the almost desperate pleading in her voice. From what he had seen the other night he had a pretty good idea what they wanted to do.

"Brandy," Angela said, sounding impatient as she folded her arms across her chest. "We had a deal about this."

Reluctantly, Brandy and Evan stood up. Holding hands and leaning their heads close together, they started toward the camp as well.

After Angela and the kids went inside, Greg tensed, wondering if this might be the moment he'd been waiting for. He watched a light come on in the upstairs window, and saw two silhouettes—Angela's and Brandy's—moving back and forth across that drawn bedroom shade.

Only the two men remained outside. Greg felt a strong impulse to make a move on them now, but he stayed where he was and watched as they sat back down on one of the logs close to the fire. He felt a sudden rush of nausea sweep through him when one of the men leaned close to the other and placed his arm around the man's shoulders. His stomach tightened when he saw the men turn to face each other and then embrace and kiss.

"Oh, Jesus," Greg whispered, shaking his head in amazement and disgust. He stood up slowly from his hiding place and started walking away. There was no way he was going to stick around to see what happened next. He moved off into the woods, figuring he'd go back to his car and catch whatever sleep he could, then come back out here first thing in the morning to see what might develop. When he paused and glanced quickly back toward the campfire, he saw that one of the men was kneeling down on the ground in front of other with his hands on other's hips.

The night wind moaned softly, gusting hard enough every now and then to make the car bounce. Throughout the long night, Greg, who was lying on the back seat, found himself staring wide-eyed up at the too-close ceiling of the car. He was never sure when—or if—he fell asleep. It didn't take long for the cold to penetrate the car. With only a thin blanket to cover him, he was shivering uncontrollably. The chattering sound of his teeth was enough to keep him awake all night, but there was something else that held sleep at bay.

The voices.

For the longest time, Greg listened to them without being consciously aware of doing so. They were so faint that he easily confused them with the sound of his own voice inside his head. As the night wore on, though, the voices took on distinctive tones and personalities, and at some ill-defined point, Greg realized that he was listening to muted conversations.

Once he was aware of the voices, he tried to make out what they were saying, but they seemed to be speaking in a foreign language or something. He heard tone and inflection in each voice, but what they said didn't make sense. Every now and then he caught a word or phrase—words like *death* and *punishment* and *waiting for you* were repeated many times—but no matter how hard he tried, he couldn't put them together into anything meaningful.

"Shut up! Just shut up and leave me the fuck alone!" Greg whispered angrily into the darkness, but the voices continued to whisper as though they weren't even aware of his presence. Time and again, he would cry out and sit bolt upright and look around. Faint moonlight edged the trees and narrow dirt road with silver. Long, black shadows, like ink stains, reached across the ground, and the wind moaned softly.

Shivering in the dark, he wondered where these voices were coming from. He kept trying to convince himself that they were all in his head, that they were nothing more than products of his overactive imagination; but they all sounded so clear and distinct he couldn't shake the feeling that unseen people were hovering behind him, fading in and out of sight whenever he turned and tried to see them.

"Fuck you! Fuck you all!" Greg growled, squeezing his hands tightly into fists and smacking them against the car seat. *"Just leave me the fuck alone!"*

But the voices didn't stop. Throughout the night, they continued to mutter and buzz around him. Only when the first traces of dawn lit the eastern sky with hazy light did they finally cease, and Greg drifted off into sleep for a few minutes. Even then, he was aware of the voices and couldn't stop listening to the slow, receding echoes as they gradually faded away.

"But you *promised* we'd leave *early* today," JJ said. He was aware of the whining in his voice, but he didn't care. All he could think was that he wanted to get back home and do something *he* wanted to do instead of hanging around here with a bunch of adults and Brandy and Evan.

"I know I promised," Angie said, leaning close and taking hold of him by both shoulders, "but Uncle Rob really wants to take you out fishing today."

JJ didn't like the way his mother was looking at him, as though she was counting on him to do what she was asking—for her, if not himself.

"I don't even *like* fishing," JJ said, even though that wasn't entirely true. He and his dad had gone fishing a couple of times when he was younger, and they'd had a lot of fun together. This was different, though. One reason was because he didn't like the way his uncle seemed to be trying so hard to take his father's place. It made him feel awkward and uncomfortable, especially knowing that his uncle was gay. JJ knew that he couldn't tell anyone—not even his mother—how much he still missed his father.

"Uncle Rob got up really early this morning and busted his butt, getting the motor and boat ready," she said, looking at him earnestly.

JJ frowned and blinked his eyes rapidly, fighting back the rush of tears he felt just thinking about his father.

"I know," he said. "I heard him banging around so much he woke me up."

"Look, if you do this for me, as favor, I'll make it up to you, I promise," Angie said. "I've got a picnic lunch made for you, and while you're out, Brandy, Evan and I will pack up all our stuff."

JJ stiffened at that suggestion, knowing that his father's revolver was hidden in his back pack. He hadn't had a chance to go off yesterday and try shooting it, and he'd hoped to do that today. He would have if his mother hadn't started pushing him so hard to go fishing. What if she noticed that his back was unusually heavy? What if she checked into it and found the gun? At the very least he'd be grounded for rest of his life.

He tried to communicate with his expression how miserable just the thought of this fishing expedition was making him, but it wasn't working. His mother had made her mind.

"I'll ask Rob to make sure to have you back so we can leave by two o'clock, okay?" she said, smiling thinly. "That'll still get you home with plenty of time to hang out with Sammy before supper."

"Come *on,* Mom," JJ said, giving her a pained look as he shook his head. He could see that no amount of pleading was going to work.

"This *really* means a lot to me," his mother said, staring at him with a beseeching expression in her eyes.

Unable to see any way around it, JJ finally nodded and said, "Yeah . . . well . . . okay, I guess."

He was still concerned that she might find the gun, but there was nothing he could do about it now. He didn't have time to get it from his backpack and hide it.

Moving slowly, he went out to the car, opened the back, and took out his fishing rod and tackle box. Uncle Rob had said something earlier about already having gotten some bait, so JJ walked down to the beach where the small boat was pulled up onto the sand. His uncle was busily loading the boat with his own fishing equipment and other supplies, including a couple of bright orange life jackets.

"All right," Uncle Rob said, rubbing his hands together vigorously. "All set to go?"

JJ nodded glumly, then cast a glance over his shoulder. His mother was watching them from the kitchen window. When she smiled and waved, JJ felt like sticking his tongue out at her, but he didn't. He waited until Rob had pushed the boat out into the water, than clambered aboard, getting his feet wet in the process. The boat rocked from side to side as Rob got in and walked to the back of the boat and pushed the motor down. After squeezing the rubber fuel bulb, he started tugging on the Evinrude's cord.

The engine didn't start with the first few pulls, and JJ stared hoping that the trip was going to have to be called off, but on the tenth or so try, the engine chugged to life. It sputtered and shot a blue haze of smoke out across the water.

"There we go." Uncle Rob said as he grabbed the handle and steered the boat around. The wake spread out across the water, a widening black, razor-edged line.

"That isn't gonna conk out on us after we're out in the middle of the lake, is it?" JJ asked with a thin smile.

Rob shook his head but said nothing. Slanting his hat so the brim shaded his eyes, he opened the throttle. The boat took off fast enough to knock JJ back on his seat.

"I figure we'll head out to the sandbar over by Horse Island," Rob said, shouting to be heard above the steady buzzing of the motor. That didn't mean a damned thing to JJ. He was just along for the ride, so he sat back and stared out at the fast moving shoreline. As far as he was concerned, this morning couldn't pass by fast enough.

The dog heard him coming and reacted, but Greg came around the side of the trailer and attacked him so quickly the dog got out only one short, sharp bark. Greg swung the baseball bat at the German shepherd's face but missed and hit the ground hard enough to send a vibrating hum up the length of his arms.

The tip of the bat dug up a clot of dirt that rattled like birdshot against the metal side of the camper. Hampered by the leg cast, the dog whimpered as he scrambled under the camper. Greg stepped forward to finish him off, but just then the camper door slammed open.

"Who the hell are you?" shouted the man who appeared in the doorway, blinking in the sudden bright sunlight. He was wearing plaid shorts and a dingy, white T-shirt. His hair was rumpled from sleep.

On pure reflex, Greg wheeled around and swung the bat at the man, connecting a solid hit on the side of his head. The man looked surprised as he staggered forward. His knees buckled, and then he dropped down, landing in an awkward sitting position on the top step. Greg lunged forward and caught him before he pitched forward and fell onto the ground.

"Goddamned dick-smoker," Greg muttered as thrust the man back inside the camper, then climbed the few steps and entered. The curtains hadn't been drawn yet. Dull, yellow light filled the camper with an eerie glow.

Grabbing the unconscious man under the armpits, Greg dragged him the short distance into the tiny kitchen and propped him up against the refrigerator. The blow had caught the man just behind the right ear and ripped open his scalp. A thick wash of blood as bright as rubies was streaming from the open wound. In contrast with the blood, the man's skin looked as white as bone.

Greg could see that the man wasn't dead. Not yet, anyway. Taking the roll of duct tape he had brought along for just this purpose, Greg pulled off a long strip and, turning the man around so he could bring his hands behind his back, wrapped several loops around the man's wrists. Then he tore off another strip and smoothed it across the man's mouth.

"I guess you won't be sucking anyone's dick with *that* on your mouth, huh?" Greg asked, chuckling as he leaned closed to the man's face.

The man opened his eyes and looked up at Greg with a dull, unfocused stare. He tried to say something, but the tape muffled whatever it was.

Greg stood back and silently regarded him for a moment, his upper lip curled in disgust. Then he shook his head as though thoroughly disgusted.

"Man, the things I saw you two doing last night . . ." He clicked his tongue like a school teacher, scolding a child. "And right out in the open, where innocent children could see you!"

The man's eyes rolled around in his head, and he made no effort to respond. Greg could see the silent pleading in his eyes, and that made him feel good . . . better than he had felt in a *long* time.

"Don't you have *any* shame?"

The man struggled to focus on him, and that made Greg feel a charge of nervousness. He didn't like the way the man's eyes glowed in the dim light of the camper. It reminded him of the eyes he had seen so many times late at night in his bedroom.

"Don't you worry," Greg said with a thin smirk. "I ain't gonna kill you . . . Not just yet, anyway. Then again . . ."

He gripped the base ball bat tightly, choking up on the handle like he was going to make a bunt. With a short, quick chop, he hit the man squarely on the side of the head. The impact made a loud *clunk* sound as it knocked him back against the refrigerator. The man's eyes rolled back, and he slumped down, his head lolling to one side. A thick string of bloody snot ran from his nose onto his chest.

Getting down on his hands and knees, Greg brought his face up close to the unconscious man's ear and whispered harshly, "But don't you be going anywhere. I'll be back for you. We'll have a little more fun, okay?"

Before he left the trailer, Greg pulled off another long strip of duct tape and bound the man's ankles, on the off chance he regained consciousness and thought he'd try to play the hero.

Straightening up, Greg studied the man for a moment, satisfied with his work so far. The man's breathing was deep and regular as though he were asleep. He would have looked absolutely peaceful if it weren't for the blood streaming across his chin and soaking into his T-shirt.

If the rest of the family was going to be this easy, Greg thought, then he'd be finished and out of here well before noon.

Of course, he had a couple of ideas of what he could do to—
and with—Angela Ross and her daughter before he killed them.
That all depended on how it played out. One thing for sure,
though, was that he wanted to tell Angela just before she died
that *he* was the one who had killed her husband. He couldn't
wait to see her reaction when he told her *that!*

"Did you hear that?" Angie asked.

"Hear what?" Brandy glanced over her shoulder at her
mother and gave her a quick shrug. "I didn't hear anything."

They were both in the kitchen, cleaning up the breakfast
dishes, Angie washing and Brandy drying and putting things
back into the cupboard. Evan, still looking half-asleep even
after a hearty breakfast, was slouched on the couch in the living
room, idly flipping through a thirty year old issue of *National
Geographic*.

"I thought I heard Wolfgang bark," Angie said, frowning.
Learning over the kitchen sink, she looked out the window.
The side yard and what she could see of the beach out front
were deserted, but she had a funny feeling that something was
wrong. The shadows under the trees looked suddenly threatening. She had made sure JJ fed Wolfgang before he left to go
fishing, so she knew the dog couldn't be hungry. She glanced
at the clock above the stove and saw that it was a little before
nine o'clock.

"It's too early for JJ and Uncle Rob to be back . . . unless
something's happened."

A nameless worry filled her.

"I didn't hear anything," Brandy repeated, shaking her head.
There was a loud clatter as she put the frying pan she'd just
dried into the cupboard with the other posts and pans.

A subtle sense of panic was gathering strength inside Angie
as she walked to the back door and opened it. When she stepped
outside onto the landing, she let out a small grunt of surprise
when she saw a man walking toward her from the camper. She
knew right away that it wasn't Craig, but in he surprise, it took
her a heart-stopping moment to recognize him.

When she did, she couldn't believe what she was seeing.

"Greg? . . . Jesus, is that you?"

Her knees went suddenly weak, and the blood drained from her head, making her dizzy.

Greg smiled at her as he moved quickly to the back steps. Angie saw that he was holding something behind his back, but she wasn't sure what it was. After a moment, she realized that there was something on Greg's face that looked like a splash of blood.

"Surprised to see me?" Greg asked, smiling wickedly as he looked up at her.

The sunlight fell on his face, and she could see clearly that it *was* blood on his face. He brought what he was holding around from behind his back and she saw a baseball bat with a bright red smear on the tip. Her first thought was that Greg had done something to Wolfgang.

Too late, she read the dangerous gleam in his eyes and reacted. She turned and tried to get back inside the camp to lock him out, but he leaped onto the steps and grabbed the thin edge of the door. He snarled as he yanked it open so hard the top hinge ripped out of the jamb with a splintering sound. The door slammed back against the house and hanged down at an odd angle. From somewhere inside the house, Angie heard Brandy scream.

"Hey, what's the matter?" Greg said, leering wickedly at her. His face was flushed, and his mouth was twisted into a horrible grin that exposed his wide, flat teeth. His hand shot out as fast as a striking rattlesnake and grabbed Angie by the wrist in a painfully tight grip.

"Ain't you even happy to see me?"

Chapter 28

Showdown

Greg was so excited that, no matter where he looked as he entered the small camp and locked the storm door behind him, his vision shimmered with a dull, red haze. He tried to take everything in quickly, but his brain seemed to be moving at a different pace. Not really slower—or faster. He wasn't sure what was different, but everything anyone said or did seemed to be happening in sludgy slow motion. His senses were honed and primed, ready to react to anything.

Angela had said something to him as she retreated into the kitchen, but he hadn't caught it. Now she was cowering against the far wall beside the refrigerator, her hands clapped across her mouth, her eyes wide open and staring at him as though in absolute disbelief. She seemed to be trying to say something, but her voice was muffled behind her hands and kept choking off. Brandy and her boyfriend were huddled together in the living room, their arms locked around each other.

"You know," Greg said, drawling his voice as he stepped forward and smiled wickedly at Angela, "I have to admit that I'm kinda surprised it turned out this way. Aren't you?" He clicked his tongue and shook his head as he glanced from one to another. He was filled with an unaccountable sensation of well-being, of power and control. "And look here." He snorted through his nose. "It's the little love birds." Turning back to Angela, he said, "Now you tell me . . . Ain't they just the cutest little couple you've ever seen?"

Angela didn't say a word. For a tension-filled moment, Greg felt his gaze locked with hers and was suddenly quite positive that she could see right through him, that his confidence was a masquerade.

"Oh, you should have seen them the other night," he said softly, struggling to maintain control until his momentary feeling of vulnerability passed. He laughed out loud when he saw Brandy's face go pale as she turned to her mother. "Out behind the house . . . Remember, Brandy? Let me tell you, they were going at it hot and heavy." He whistle and, smiling, shook his head.

"What do you want from us?" Angela said sharply.

Greg found it amusing the way her voice sounded so constricted and unnatural. He could tell that she was trying hard to put up a brave front for her daughter and the boy, but she was failing miserably.

"What do *I* want?" he said, tightening his grip on the bat and raising it as he took another step closer to her. "What I *want*—what I've wanted all along—is *you!*"

He tossed his head back and laughed as though this was the joke of the year. He laughed so hard his stomach began to ache, and tiny white pinpricks of light spun across the red haze of his vision.

"You still don't get it, do you?" He sighed and shook his head as though deeply saddened. "You just don't fucking get it!"

Angela started to answer him, but the only sound she could make was a strangled grunt.

Greg narrowed his eyes and took a deep, calming breath. For a flickering instant, he thought he could hear those other voices, like someone had left the TV or radio on upstairs. He shivered, remembering the voices he had heard in the car last night and what they had said.

Easy now, he cautioned himself.

He took another, deeper breath, commanding himself to calm down. This was the moment for which he'd been waiting for so long. He wanted to do everything right so he could enjoy every second of it.

"I've already taken care of what's-his-name—the fag-boy out in the trailer," he said, pointing at the back door with the tip of his bloody baseball bat.

"You mean Craig," Angela said in a shattered voice.

"Yeah. Whatever. And now . . ." He gave a helpless shrug. "Now it's your turn."

"Why are you—? What the hell are you talking about?" Angela said. Her fists were clenched, and her body was so tense she was visibly trembling. Greg knew that she wasn't going to do anything. He had seen her reactions that night last winter, outside *Le Bistro.* He knew that she didn't have the guts. What she apparently still did not realize was that he knew exactly how frightened she was, and that she was frozen by her panic.

When Greg took another few steps forward, out of the corner of his eye, he saw Brandy's boyfriend make his move. Ducking his head low, he charged at Greg like a football player making a tackle, but Greg was so jazzed up he reacted with lightning speed.

Bracing his feet in a wide stance, he gripped the baseball bat with both hands and spun around, timing his swing just right. As soon as the boy was within striking distance, he hit him with every ounce of strength he could muster.

The wooden bat made a loud *clunk* sound when it caught the boy on the side of the face, just above his chin, hitting with so much force the boy's head snapped back with a loud, satisfying *snap.* Either the boy's jaw or neck was broken. The momentum of the attack carried the boy forward a few steps, but his legs quickly gave out on him, and he landed hard on the floor, sprawled at Greg's feet.

"Idiot," Greg said, sneering as he looked down at the fallen boy. He hawkered deep in his chest and spit at the boy. The red haze intensified, obscuring Greg's vision as a dull sound like paper, ripping, filled his head.

Blood was gushing from the boy's smashed mouth and nose, pooling on the worn linoleum. The boy's body twitched once, violently, so Greg cocked back and delivered another vicious blow, chopping downward like he was splitting wood. The bat caught the back of the boy's head with so much force his skull caved in with a splintering sound. Blood and tiny bits of bone and lumpy gray matter seeped out from the long indentation.

Brandy collapsed to the floor and let out a piercing screech so shrill it hurt Greg's ears.

"Shut your fucking mouth right now," he said, his voice low and controlled as he raised the bat and took a threatening step closer to her.

Brandy clapped her hands over her mouth and cringed away, her eyes brimming with tears as she gazed back and forth between her mother and the crumpled form on the floor. After a few seconds, the boy's body stopped twitching and lay perfectly still with no sign of breathing.

"You know, that's the gooddamned problem," Greg said as he knelt down beside the boy and inspected him. "Everybody wants to be a fucking hero. Don't they know that's how you end up getting hurt?"

He rolled Evan onto his side and saw the horrible mess that was the boy's face. Points of broken teeth protruded from his shredded, bloody lower lip. His jaw had been knocked so much out of line it gave his face a comical, lopsided look. His eyes were wide open in an expression of permanent surprise. The left eye had popped out of his head from the impact.

Dead eyes, Greg thought with a wild shudder, and he remembered again the people he imagined were watching him unseen from the darkness.

"He shouldn't have ought to done that," Greg said simply shaking his head as he flicked his gaze back and forth between Angla and her daughter.

"Jesus Christ! You're insane!" Angela said in a harsh whisper as she shifted across the floor, closer to her daughter. She stopped suddenly when Greg glared a warning at her.

"Gee, do you really think so?" he said, followed by another boisterous laugh.

Even though he figured it wasn't really necessary, he tore off a few strips of duct tape and bound the boy's arm and legs. For good measure, he also slapped a piece of tape across the boy's mouth, but it didn't stick very well because of all the blood. Greg was positive the boy was dead, but he figured, even if he wasn't now, he sure as shit *would* be before the day was over.

"Now then" Greg said, straightening up slowly. He held the roll of duct tape in one hand, the baseball bat in the other as he moved closer to Angela. "You're both gonna cooperate with me and be nice and quiet, right?"

"Why should we?" Brandy wailed, her voice cracking with tortured emotion. Tears coursed from her eyes. *"You're just gonna kill all of us, anyway!"*

Greg could see that she was hysterical, and he knew that could be dangerous—not for any threat she might pose to him, but because Angela might finally find the courage to resist if she realized just how much danger they were in. He was tempted to tell the girl the truth—that, of *course* he intended to kill her along with her mother, her brother, and her faggot uncle—but he decided not to just yet. He was having too much fun watching her lose control like this. It was difficult to look away from her staring, terror-filled eyes.

"Oh, I have other plans for you, little girl," he said, leering at her. "And maybe—just maybe I'll let your mother watch us. Would you like that?"

"Fuck you," Angela snarled.

"What, you don't think that be fun?" Greg said, glaring at her. Her face had gone sheet white, and her body was trembling horribly.

'I know *I* sure enjoyed the little show they put on out in the backyard the other night. You remember that night, don't you, Angela? The same night that stupid little dog of yours got his leg broken."

"You . . ."

"And—yes, to answer one more question I just know you're dying to ask, I also killed that fucking black dog. I have to tell you, I enjoy the hell out of it."

Greg narrowed his eyes as the hazy memory of that day came back to him. He remembered something about a voice then, urging him to kill the boys, and how convinced he had been that the dog was communicating with him telepathically. Obviously, that hadn't been the case. He could see that clearly now, but the impulse to kill Angela and her daughter was as strong if someone was prodding him on.

"What can I say?" Greg asked with a casual shrug. "I don't like dogs." he sniffed with laughter as he looked over at Brandy, who was staring at him with a vacant, glassy distance in her eyes. He could tell that she was already halfway around the bend, and he was hoping that he could drive her all the way over the edge before he finally finished her off.

"And now *you!*" Greg snapped, turning back to Angela and pointing at her with the bat. "Turn around and put your hands behind your back."

"Don't do it, Mom!" Brandy wailed, her voice choking with tears as she crawled over to the boy and tugged at his lifeless body. The shattered bones of his skull made a loud crinkling sound as his head rolled from side to side. Greg stared at the bloody, hairy mess that was the back of his head, and the sight made him smile.

"No! . . . No! Oh, Jesus . . . No!" Brandy cried. Her voice warbled higher and higher as she stared fearfully over her shoulder at her mother. Moaning softly, she sat back on her heels and rocked back and forth. All the while her body trembled uncontrollably.

"He's . . . dead! . . . Jesus! Oh my God, he's dead! . . . He's dead! . . ."

Angela's eyes shimmered with sympathy as she watched her daughter's outpouring of grief, but she said nothing.

"I mean it, Angela," Greg said, his voice low and seething with barely pent-up rage. "Put your hands behind your back right *now,* or else she dies!"

"He's gonna kill us anyway, Mom!" Brandy wailed, but her voice was muffled behind her hands as she slumped forward and pressed her face against her boyfriend's back.

With a look of resignation in her eyes, Angela turned and

placed her hands behind her back, crosssing her wrists. Greg quickly tore off a strip of tape and wound it around several times, pulling it so tight Angela let out a sharp yelp of pain.

"Oh, I'm so sorry," he said, his voice almost cooing. "Did I hurt you?"

He grabbed her by the shoulder and spun her around so fast she lost her balance and almost fell. When they were looking at each other face to face, Greg came up so close to her he could feel her warm breath on his skin.

"You wanna know what?" he said softly. "She's one hundred percent right. I *am* gonna kill you . . . *all* of you. And do you want me to tell you why?"

Before he could say anything else, Angela made a low rumbling sound deep in her throat and spit into his face. Greg chuckled as he steeped back and wiped his face and then eagerly licked her spit from his fingers.

"Umm-ummm, good," he said, chucking. "So, Angela Ross finally gets up enough courage to fight back, is that it? Well darling, it's too little, too late . . . a *lot* too late!"

And with that, he turned to face Brandy.

"Now you come here," he said in a savage growl as he reached for his belt. "I have a little something for you!"

"How come you didn't wear a hat?" Uncle Rob said, shouting to be heard above the sound of the engine. "I thought all you kids wore hats these days."

Rob's eyes were shaded by the white beach hat he was wearing. JJ thought it made him look like a complete dork, but with the sun beating down on him, it didn't seem like such a bad thing now. He shrugged and, for a moment or two, didn't reply.

"I just didn't think of it, I guess," he said, so softly he wasn't sure his uncle heard him.

That was a lie. His mother had reminded him several times to take a hat, but he had purposely left it behind, hoping that not having one might shorten the time they were out. After less than two hours on the water, he had asked his uncle to bring him back to the camp.

The only sound on the lake was the high buzzing sound of the Evinrude as the little boat cut across the glassy surface, leaving a widening black V in its wake. The sun in front of them made the water sparkle so bright it brought tears to JJ's eyes.

They hadn't had much luck fishing. JJ had caught only one fish—a little sunfish which he unhooked and released. His uncle caught a tangle of underwater weeds and had been forced to cut his line and lose one of his favorite lures.

"I'm surprised they're not biting today," Rob said, scratching his head as he surveyed the lake. "You know, there's an inlet across the lake we might give a try."

JJ scratched his neck as though actually considering the suggestion, then shook his head and said, "I guess not. I'd just as soon pack it in for today."

"You're the boss," Uncle Rob said, and he opened the motor up wide.

JJ was surprised that he didn't recognize the camp until they were close to it, but it was with a great sense of relief that he heard his uncle cut the engine, letting the boat drift to the shore. The hull made a soft scraping sound as it ran up onto the sand. JJ got his sneakers wet again when he climbed ashore, but even as he grabbed his fishing equipment and was heading for dry land, instead of feeling relief, he instantly sensed that something was wrong.

Where's Wolfgang, he thought with a sudden jolt of concern.

He looked back at his uncle, who was tying off the boat. His first impulse was to run out back to make sure Wolfgang was all right, but he felt as though he ought to wait and make sure to thank his uncle, first. His shoulders bunched up as he placed his rod and tackle box on the ground. Turning toward the camp, he cupped his hands to his mouth and called out, "Hey, Wolfie!"

When he didn't receive an answering bark, the current of worry inside him grew stronger.

"Wolfie!" he shouted, louder. His voice echoed back from

the surrounding woods but was answered only by the distant
song of a bird. Without a word to his uncle, he ran toward the
camper where he'd left Wolfgang tied up. The yard was so
quiet he thought for a moment that his mother and the others
may have left, but his mother's car and truck were still parked
out front.

Something's happened, he thought. A tingle of apprehension
ran through him when he came around back and saw that
Wolfgang wasn't there. The rope he'd been tied to snaked
across the ground and disappeared under the trailer.

JJ's first thought was that his dog had gotten loose and run
off while he was gone. Maybe his mother and his uncle's friend
were off looking for him. Even so, where were Brandy and
Evan? They probably wouldn't have gone looking for Wolfgang
and would have taken this opportunity to have some time alone.

Putting his fingers to his lips, JJ whistled a quick, shrill blast,
but other than the dying echo, no reply came from the woods.

"Somethin' the matter?"

JJ jumped and cried out when Uncle Rob spoke so suddenly
behind him. He wheeled around and looked at him, trying
desperately to mask the depth of his worry.

"I'm not sure," he said, hearing the low tremor in his voice.
"It looks like no one's here."

"Did you check in the camp?"

When they both saw the screen door hanging from one hinge,
Rob stiffened. "Shit . . . something's happened," he muttered.

They were both silent as they scanned the backyard and
woods, trying to figure out what to do next.

"Maybe they left a note inside," Uncle Rob said, starting
for the steps. He tried to open the storm door, but the doorknob
wouldn't turn.

"Damn. It's locked," he muttered. He reached into his pants
pocket and took out a ring of keys, selected one, and fit it into
the lock. JJ almost couldn't bear the suspense as he watched
his uncle unlock the door and push it open slowly. Sticking
his head into the camp, Rob cupped his hands to his mouth
and called out, "Hello? Anyone here?"

There was no answer. Looking past his uncle, JJ could see

something—a dark form—lying on the floor. His first thought
was that it was Wolfgang.

"There's a cellular phone in the camper," Uncle Rob said
his shoulder. "Better go get it just in case—"

Before he could finish his statement, a dark rush of motion
came at him from around the corner. JJ didn't see clearly what
was happening, but he heard his uncle cry out when someone—
a man—hit him with something. Rob staggered back, tripping
over his own feet and almost knocking JJ over as he staggered
outside. His hands covered his face, and as he turned around
and started to fall, JJ saw blood seeping from between his
fingers.

Uncle Rob tried to say something, but it was lost in a watery
gargle behind his hands. Immobilized by shock, JJ stared at
their attacker, his heart stopping cold in his chest. It took him
a moment to recognize the man standing in the doorway with
a bloody baseball bat in his hand.

"Hello, JJ."

". . . no . . . no . . ." JJ whispered in a tiny voice that wasn't
much more than a gasp.

"Remember me?" the man said, smiling wickedly as he
stepped outside. His face was slick with sweat. It looked greasy
in the direct sunlight. When JJ didn't respond, Greg snorted
with laughter.

"You know, I've been getting a little impatient, waiting for
you to come back. Come inside with me. There's something I
want to show you." He waved his hand, signalling like he was
a friend, inviting JJ in for a treat.

Numb with shock, JJ didn't think to resist or run. He just
stood there unmoving until the man stepped forward and
grabbed him by the arm.

"Hurry up," Greg said, pulling him up the steps to the
landing. With a rough shove, he pushed JJ into the camp kitchen
so hard he tripped and almost fell. The air was cool inside the
camp, and a terrible chill gripped JJ as the man guided him
into the living room.

The window shades were drawn, and the room was lost in
shadows, so it took a while before JJ's eyes adjusted to the

gloom. After a few breathless seconds, the scene registered, and he saw that his mother was sitting on the couch. Her eyes were open and staring, but they didn't blink as tears rolled like quicksilver down her cheeks. For a paralyzing instant, JJ thought she was dead, but after a moment he saw her shift her gaze around slowly to him. Her eyes were dull with hopelessness. She was sitting in an odd way, and JJ realized that her hands were bound behind her back.

Beside her at the other end of the couch sat Evan. His head was thrown back, and his wide open eyes stared blankly at the ceiling. The side of his face as well as his throat and chest were crusted with drying blood that had soaked his shirt all the way down to his waist. It took JJ a stunned moment to realize that Evan was dead. Just like when he had looked at his father lying in his coffin, JJ couldn't stop the impression that Evan was still breathing. Propped up in the easy chair by the window was another body—his uncle's friend, Craig. He, too, was obviously dead. Someone had arranged him so his head tilted forward and his eyes stared sightlessly across the room at the people on the couch.

Brandy was in the center of the living room, stripped naked and lying bound across a wooden chair with her hands and feet wrapped with duct tape. He head was hanging down so her hair covered her face, but JJ knew she was still alive because her ribs were moving as she took shuddering gulps of breath. A faint whimpering sound was coming from her. In the dimly lit room, his sister's skin looked pale white except for her butt which was marked by numerous bright red welts.

"I was just waiting for the rest of my audience to come," the man said smoothly, smiling at JJ. "Why don't you have a seat?"

He shook the baseball bat at JJ, who cowered away from him.

"Oh, but first, I need to take care of something," Greg said. "Turn around and put your hands behind your back."

The man's voice was harsh with command, and JJ, functioning on automatic, started to do what he was told without resistance. It was only when he looked at his mother again and saw the futility in her eyes that he reacted without thinking. Spinning around quickly on the ball of his foot, he clenched his fist and swung blindly at the man. It was sheer luck that he connected with the side of Greg's face, just above the eye.

The blow was solid enough to stagger Greg as searing pain shot through JJ's hand. It hurt so much he was sure he had broken some fingers, but he didn't have time to notice as Greg lunged forward, jabbing him in the chest with the tip of the bat. The impact sent JJ flying backwards, his arms pinwheeling wildly as he tried to maintain his balance. He hit the floor hard, landing in a heap at his mother's feet.

"You little cock-sucker!" the man shouted. "You're gonna be sorry you did that," Greg shouted, his eyes flaring as he stepped forward and brandished the bat. JJ quickly scrambled out of the way, cowering behind the arm of the couch.

"You ain't gonna get away with shit like that," the man said, drawing back and panting hard as he wiped the sweat from his face with the flat of his hand. Then he gingerly touched the side of his forehead where JJ had punched him.

"*You're* the cock-sucker!" JJ shouted, but he reminded cowering on the floor out of the man's reach.

The man raised the bat and scowled at him, but before he stepped forward, something outside banged against the side of the camp. JJ watched the man glance over his shoulder, his upper lip curling into a thin sneer.

"Speaking of cock-suckers," he said, "I'd better check on your faggot uncle. Gotta make sure he's down for the count. Or maybe that was your fucking dog, huh? Christ! How many times do I have to whack him?"

"Screw you!" JJ shouted, trembling with rage. A tidal wave of blinding grief washed over him, blanking his mind. Only after Greg had disappeared into the kitchen did JJ realize that his backpack was pressing into his side.

"Yeah," he muttered.

His hands trembled uncontrollably as he unzipped the bag. Cringing, he listened as Greg opened the back door and went outside. He plunged his hand into the bag, feeling around until he found the revolver he'd hidden there. He hadn't grabbed it before he heard Greg slam the door shut and start back into the living room.

"Well, I guess that cock-sucker's stone cold, too," Greg said, laughing wickedly as he looked over at JJ and his mother. He had a sick smirk on his face as he walked over to Brandy and lovingly caressed her bare backsides with one hand.

"Umm . . . Nice white meat," he said, chuckling softly. He leaned down and, sticking his nose to Brandy's backsides, inhaled deeply. "Oh, yeah. Smells like fish, but tastes like chicken." Straightening up, he turned to look at JJ and his mother. "You know," he said, "I just can't understand how any man—any *real* man, anyway—can resist a piece of something like *this!*"

When he said the last word, he slapped Brandy on the butt, making her cry out and jerk violently. Her hands and legs were tied down securely, so she couldn't move very far.

"I probably ought to get you tied up before I finish with her, don't you think?" he said as he hooked on thumb over his belt, pulling the front of his pants down enough so JJ could see the curly hair on his bare belly.

"Fuck you, asshole," JJ said heatedly, and with that he gripped the cold handle of his father's revolver and pulled it out of the bag. He was shaking uncontrollably as he aimed it at Greg.

It seemed to take Greg moment to realize what was happening, but when he saw the gun, he leaned back and let fly a burst of laughter.

"Ohh," he said, snorting loudly, "so you've got a gun, do you? Do you even know how to use it?"

JJ's vision blurred with tears as he aimed as well as he could at Greg's chest.

"I'm *so-o-o* scared," Greg said, chuckling. He held out his hand and flapped it. "Look at me shake!"

"You killed him, didn't you?" JJ said, his voice tight and close to breaking on nearly every word.

"Who? You mean that dog . . . or your father?" Greg snorted and spit in JJ's direction. The glob of spit hit the floor a few feet in front of him.

"My father—"

JJ's voice chocked off sharply.

"That's right," Greg said, narrowing his eyes. "I already explained the whole thing to your mother, here. I did in your old man."

In the dark room, Greg's face seemed to be floating, disembodied, reminding JJ of one of the tricks the Cheshire Cat played on Alice.

"Go ahead. Do it," whispered a soft, scratchy voice. JJ thought it sounded like it came from behind him and wasn't sure if he had heard it correctly or not. He glanced at his mother, telling himself she had spoken, but she was leaning her head back as though drained of all strength and watching him with a glassy-eyed stare.

Suddenly, all around him, JJ heard faint rustling sounds and saw fleeting hints of motion in the shadows. A small corner of his mind told him that he was imagining things, that his eyes and ears were playing tricks on him in the dim light; but no matter where he looked, faint, ink-wash shadows shifted as though several nearly transparent people were standing around then in the living room.

"Do it!" another voice whispered, louder and more demanding, and this was followed by several more voices, all of them muttering just at the threshold of hearing.

Stark, stinging terror gripped JJ as he glanced at his mother, convinced that she had to be the one who had spoken, but she was sitting absolutely still . . . silent.

"Go ahead," Greg said, his voice high and taunting. "Pull the trigger. What's the matter, are you a pussy?"

He was hunched over, gripping the baseball bat in one hand and staring at JJ with an insane gleam lighting his eyes. Shadows swirled around him, at times obscuring his face, but he seemed not to notice.

"I knew it!" he said. "Just like your mother and your faggot uncle and even this dipshit here—" He jabbed the bat toward Evan's silent form on the couch. "Like *all* the rest of them, you don't have the fucking balls to do it, do you? *Do you?*"

"*Go on, do it!*"

"Pull the trigger!"

"Now!"

"Shoot him!"

"Yes, do it now!"

"We want him!"

The chorus of voices rose higher even as JJ was trying to convince himself that it had to be his mother or Brandy, or maybe the two dead men, Evan and Craig, shouting at him.

The gun felt suddenly heavy and cold in his hand. JJ felt his aim waver, and he was afraid that he wouldn't have the strength to hold it up much longer. The tension was vibrating through his fingers and arm like an electrical shock.

"Shoot him!"

"Do it now!"

"Send him to us!"

JJ looked beyond the wavering tip of the revolver and saw Greg's face looming closer. The man's eyes blazed, and his grin crazy spread from ear to ear, exposing wide, flat teeth. Behind him, JJ could see other faces materializing out of the shadows drifting like smoke in the darkness of the room.

"There, you see?" Greg said, his voice a teasing singsong as he held his empty hand out to JJ. "You don't dare to do it, so come on. Give me the gun.

Closing his eyes and keeping them tightly shut, JJ pushed himself as far away from Greg as he could get while simultaneously squeezing the trigger. The gun kicked back hard in his hands, once . . . then twice.

He heard the sharp reports follows by a shrill cry, but he didn't dare open his eyes to see what had happened. After the first two shots rang out, he heard the hammer click several times as it fell on empty cylinders. He couldn't stop pulling the trigger as he was swept backwards in a dark, dizzying rush.

At last, he couldn't hold the gun any longer. He was falling, spinning, being sucked backwards and downwards into a swirling tornado that howled all around him. From the center of this churning darkness, he heard something else—voices, rising in a chorus of shrieks and howls. For an instant, JJ thought they sounded like souls, crying out in agony and pain, but after a timeless moment he realized that they were laughing and cackling with glee.

"Yes! . . . Yes!" one voice shrilled.

"We've been waiting!" said another.

"Waiting so long . . ." said a third.

And then numerous other voices joined in, some male, some female, crying out in unison, "And now . . . he's OURS!"

Chapter 29
The Tunnel

Greg heard the first shot clearly and, through the red haze that clouded his vision, he saw Angela jerk violently to one side as she cried out. Before he could begin to figure out what had happened, another shot rang out, and his vision instantly went black.

He didn't feel any pain—not at first, anyway—just a violent tug on his left shoulder, as if someone had grabbed him from behind and was trying to turn him around. An instant later, the pain began, flaming hot and freezing cold at the same instant. It was centered in his chest and radiated outward in strong pulses.

He was tumbling backwards through darkness, spinning in crazy free fall with no sense of direction. The rushing sound of the wind, piping low, pulled at him like invisible, grasping hands. Deep inside, he could feel a surging heat that—somehow—he knew was his pulse, but the cold that gripped him was spreading through him quickly.

Greg tried desperately to understand what had happened, but he couldn't. When he tried to take a breath, a loud wheezing sound louder than the wind filled his ears. Panic as clean as chrome seized him when he realized that his lungs weren't filling with air the way they should.

I've been shot!

The thought filled him with a cold, dark dread.

Jesus, that's it! I'm dying!

Fear clutched him as he looked around, surprised to see that the camp's living room had disappeared. In its place was a dense, impenetrable wall of darkness.

The sensation of falling, of floating inside a long, narrow tunnel intensified. Darkness surged like the ocean as it closed over him, crushing him. Greg flailed his arms and legs, but he soon realized that the motion was futile. Through his steadily rising terror, he could see, up ahead, a faint, pulsing white light drawing rapidly closer.

He could feel himself being drawn inexorably to the light. At first he willed himself to resist it, but he quickly gave up the effort. It was much easier to allow himself to move toward it.

The light at the end of the tunnel spiralled and twisted like the glowing inside of a tornado's funnel, growing steadily brighter the closer he got. He wanted to scream, but with no air in his lungs, he had no idea how to make a sound. For all he knew, he could be screaming as loud as he could, and the sound was lost inside the howling wind.

He had no idea when he first noticed them, but at some indeterminate point he became aware of hazy figures, floating around him in the shadowy darkness. He sensed hands, hooked into claws, reaching out, groping for him. He could feel more than see hate-filled eyes, watching him, tearing into him. Gradually he became aware of voices and the words they were saying.

"We've waited so long . . . so long . . ."

The words reverberated in the darkness, simultaneously inside and outside his head.

"At last!"

"Finally . . . You're ours!"

Greg opened his mouth and tried to scream, but he had no sensation of air entering his lungs.

What's happening to me?

He concentrated, trying to focus on the pulse of life in his body, but he felt none. The light loomed steadily closer, burning white-hot, glaring so brightly it stung his eyes. He had never experienced light like this before—so pure, so radiant.

But as he stared into the light, shifting shapes got between him and it, obscuring its glare. When the shadows were directly in front of him, he could see that they were people . . . men and women, floating, drifting like seaweed in surging ocean currents. Their hands waved gently, beckoning to him . . . reaching for him . . . and their eyes glowed with cold, baleful fire.

Through the chaos of his fear, Greg tried to tell himself not to panic, that if in fact he was dying—if he was already dead, then he should just . . . surrender.

Surrender . . .

But when the dark shapes floated closer and grabbed at him, even the slightest, grazing touch of their hands sent indescribable pain ripping through him.

"No! . . . Please! . . . Leave me alone!" he whimpered, his voice so feeble he could hardly hear it himself.

The rushing sound of the wind rose louder, whistling shrilly, and below that sound, a chorus of voices called out to him.

"We've been waiting . . . so long for you . . . so . . . long . . ."

Greg tried to dodge to one side to avoid the shape that was grasping at him, but when he turned around, another figure lunged at him with hands raised, fingers hooked like a hawk's claws.

"No! . . . *No!*" he cried, swinging his arms and trying to bat them away, but the shapes loomed all the closer, engulfing him. Through the frenzy of his panic, Greg tried to count them, but their bodies and voices all blended together in the blazing white light, then emerged again, fluttering around him with sweeping, dizzying motion. He was lost in a dizzying sweep of vertigo. A face suddenly materialized out of the haze directly in front of him.

"*No! Not you! It can't be!*" he screamed, but his voice was whisked away by the wind. He was staring into the face of a young Korean man—the man he had beaten to death last winter in the convenience store on Forty-Seventh Street. The man's eyes gazed blankly at him as thick streams of blood ran from the gaping wound that ripped open his scalp.

"I've been waiting for you," the Korean man said, his voice edged with malicious glee.

Other faces resolved from the darkness—faces Greg immediately recognized. The two policemen he had attacked and killed that night . . . the old woman in the heavy coat . . . the wino he had given the baseball bat to . . . the valet . . . and John Ross, his chest blow apart, exposing shredded flesh and splinters of bone . . . and—worst of all—his mother, her pale, tired eyes burning into him like a laser beam.

"Why did you do it?" one of the cops asked, his mouth dripping with blood.

"I didn't deserve to die."

"I wanted to live, and you killed me."

"No . . . No, I didn't," Greg said feebly, but his voice was drowned out as other voices wailed accusingly from the surrounding darkness, and skeletal hands slashed and tore at him. Greg had the frightening sensation that his body—or whatever was left of him—was no more substantial that old, rotten cloth, and that these figures were shredding it, tearing him apart.

"We've been waiting for you," whispered a voice which Greg recognized as his mother's but tried to deny. Her tired, wrinkled face billowed like a wind-blown bed sheet in the darkness in front of him. Her tongue, blue and swollen, hung from the corner of her month like a swollen slug.

"I—I didn't hurt you . . . I *never* hurt you!" Greg screamed, waving his arms in a desperate attempt to fend them off.

"Oh, yes you did!" his mother said. "You killed me!"

"And you killed me. You killed all of us!" said the ghastly figure of John Ross, his voice echoing with a wavering hollowness that blended into the shrieking wind. Ross' face was pale and skeletal, his eyes dark and burning with fierce hatred. The unblinking stare cut through Greg like a heated blade. He ducked to one side when Ross reached for him and found himself facing other figures that grabbed at him.

"You killed us all," said one of the cops, his voice thick and resonant. "You killed us . . . and now *we* have *you!*"

"You're ours now," hissed another.

"We've waited long enough."

The shrill voices rose higher until their words merged into a screaming cacophony of insane laughter.

Greg thrashed about wildly, trying to get away from them, but no matter where he turned, horribly underlit faces darted at him, and hands lashed at his face with stinging slashes.

The white light was intensifying steadily, throbbing heavily. Grey could feel himself being drawn into it, and in the core of his being, he knew that only after he entered that light would his true torment begin. Then these beings, all of these people who blamed him for their deaths, would tear his soul apart in eternal torment.

"No! . . . *No!* . . . I don't want to *die!*"

"None of us wanted to die," answered John Ross' voice, rising clearly above the howls and shrieks.

"You can't do this to me! *You can't!*"

"Oh, but we can . . . and we will! . . . We can wait here forever if we have to . . . but eventually, you'll be ours!"

With a great effort of will, Greg forced himself to move away from the white light. He stared falling, tumbling head over heels into the cold darkness behind him. The wind roared around him, and the white light rapidly receded into the distance so fast it left behind a hollow concussion in the air.

"Come back," screamed a voice laced with desperation.

"You're ours," wailed another, faint with distance.

But Grey was flying rapidly away from them, and soon the white light was nothing more than a tiny dot in an immense, dark void.

"We'll be waiting . . ."

". . . waiting . . ."

". . . for you . . ."

The voices carried to him, echoing with an odd reverberation from out of the darkness, then vanished just as the dot of white light winked out of existence. The pure, black density of night closed around him.

Greg grunted viciously, the sound loud and harsh in his ears when he hit the floor, hard. For a timeless moment, his mind was a chaos of confused images and thoughts that filled him with terror. When he opened his eyes and saw someone—a woman—leaning over him, staring into his face, he began to scream and wasn't able to stop.

The pain in Angie's leg was as sharp and clean as a bee sting, but much more intense. She couldn't remember hearing the shot that had hit her, but a spilt second later, she turned and saw JJ, aiming a gun at Greg Newman. She instantly recognized her husband's service revolver.

"Do it!" she yelled, only distantly aware the blazing pain in her leg. *"Shoot him! . . . Shoot him now!"*

"But Mom . . . ?" he said.

Angie saw the fear etched on JJ's face. The expression reminded her of how he had looked the instant she had told him that his father had been shot and killed. It tore her heart to see her son in such agony, but she knew that their only hope was for him to shoot Greg now!

"Do it!" she screamed, but her voice was masked by a second explosion.

Angie heard this one clearly, and she watched with horrified fascination as the impact of the bullet knocked Greg back a few steps. He gazed at JJ with a stunned expression of surprise.

"You . . . little . . . prick," Greg muttered, then he dropped the baseball bat and clapped both hands across his chest. A think wash of blood ran in bright ribbons between his fingers. When he tried to speak again, his voice was nothing but a watery wheeze.

For a paralyzed second or two, Greg remained on his feet. Then his legs went all goofy on him, and he staggered backwards a few steps before falling to the floor.

"Yes!" Angie shouted. Ignoring the pain that wracked her body, she flopped onto the couch and turned her bound hands toward JJ. "Hurry! Get me loose"

"What—? How?" JJ said, looking absolutely amazed by what he had just done. He couldn't stop staring at the fallen man.

"Jesus, JJ! He was going to kill us all! Now cut me loose!"

Angie said while twisting her hands frantically back and forth, trying to get free. The duct tape binding her wrists was twisted and wouldn't give.

"In the kitchen . . . Get a knife!"

Lying on her side on the couch with her face almost in Evan's lap, Angie watched as JJ walked slowly, like an automaton, into the kitchen. She heard the loud clatter as he drew open one of the drawers.

"Hurry!" she shouted, glancing at Brandy, horrified to see that she was either dead or unconscious. Her naked form looked pitifully small slumped across the chair.

It seemed like hours before JJ returned with a steak knife. His body was trembling as he knelt by the couch and set to work, sawing at the tape. He inadvertently sliced into Angie's wrists, but she was so swept up by her own fear for her daughter's safety that she barely noticed the pain.

Her leg was another matter. As she lay there, waiting for her son to release her, she realized that JJ's first shot had gone wild and hit her in the leg just above the kneecap. Right now the wound didn't hurt. It just felt cold and numb, as though she'd been given a shot of Novacaine. But when she looked down and saw the bloody mess through the hole in her jeans, she knew that it was serious. Splinters of bone were sticking up through the shredded flesh.

But it wasn't going to stop her from helping her children, she thought in a sudden rush of panic. JJ was all right. Greg hadn't had time to hurt him, but she feared what Brandy had suffered might prove to be too much to bear.

Angie let out a loud cry of relief when she felt her hands suddenly free. She tried to get up and go over to Brandy, but her wounded leg gave out on her, and she sprawled onto the floor. Heedless of the pain, she started crawling over to her daughter.

"Brandy . . . Jesus God, *Brandy!* Can you hear me?" she said, her voice wracked with sobs. She grabbed her daughter's face and turned it so she could see into her eyes, all the while praying to see some indication of life.

Brandy's expression was impassive. Her eyes were closed.

her mouth slack. After what seemed like forever, almost imperceptibly, her eyelids fluttered.

"Oh, baby," Angie sobbed, hugging and kissing her. "Please, baby. Everything's okay . . . You're gonna be all right . . . Everything's gonna be all right . . ."

"Evan," Brandy whispered, her voice so weak it sounded like a dying breath.

A cold jolt of grief shot through Angie. She knew that she couldn't let Brandy know what had happened to Evan . . . Not yet.

"JJ," Angie said sharply, looking at him over her shoulder. "Give me the knife . . . and get a blanket to cover her."

JJ just stood there by the couch, staring at his mother as though he had no idea what she had just said. His face had gone sheet white, and his gaze was focused on some distant point.

"Come on, pull it together, JJ," Angie said firmly. "I need you *now!*"

Like someone waking up from a deep sleep, JJ shook his head and focused on his mother. The distant glaze was still in his eyes, but he seemed to have finally grasped what she had said. Moving much too slowly, he walked over to the couch and picked up the blanket that was draped over the back. When he pulled it out from under Evan's head, Evan slumped forward. A thin wash of blood was leaking out from underneath the duck tape across his mouth, staining his chin and shirt front. JJ wanted to tear the tape off Evan's mouth, but he was afraid to touch him.

"Here," he said numbly as he handed the blanket and the knife to his mother. Then, without another word, he dropped down heavily on the floor beside her and leaned against the couch edge.

Angie was concerned about him, too, but right now all she could think was that she had to help Brandy. She was alive, at least, but she kept making a low, moaning sound deep in her chest like a sleeper who was having a terrible nightmare and couldn't wake up.

"Take it easy, Bran. Just take it easy," Angie cooed as she

carefully sliced through the duct tape that bound her daughter's wrists and legs to the chair legs. When she was finally free, Brandy rolled over and slumped like a rag doll into Angie's arms. Angie covered her with the blanket, then sat there for a long time just rubbing her daughter's face and staring at her closed eyelids.

"Is he . . . Do you think he's . . . dead?" JJ asked. His voice seemed to come from an impossible distance. Angie turned to look at him and, smiling thinly, said, "I certainly hope so." She glanced at Greg and saw that his body was still twitching like a dog, asleep on the floor and dreaming.

"Mom? . . . Oh, *Mom!*" Brandy said, sobbing so loudly she sounded like she hadn't had anything to drink for days.

"I'm right here, honey," Angie said. "Just take it easy. I'm right here."

The longer Angie sat there on the floor, the more her leg began to hurt. She shifted around so she could look at the wound and was shocked to see how bad it was. A large flap of flesh was hanging down to one side, looking like a thin cut of beef. Blood was seeping form the wound, staining her pant leg all the way to her ankle.

"We've got to get help," Angie said softly to JJ over her shoulder.

Rage and fear gripped her when she looked at Greg and saw his body twitching, like a sleeper having a bad dream. His lips were peeled back in a wide grimace that exposed his wide, flat teeth. He looked like someone who had been frozen in the moment of letting loose a heartrending scream.

"JJ!" Angie said in a whisper. She could herself weakening from the pain and shock. "We need to get help. You have to do something."

JJ didn't move. He just sat there on the floor, staring at her, his mouth hanging open. He was still holding the gun in his right hand. Raising it slowly and looking at it like he had no idea what it was, he whispered softly, "I . . . I just killed him . . ."

"Yes, you did," Angie said, wanting to shout but not finding the strength. "And now you have to pull it together and help us!"

JJ shook his head slowly from side as he rubbed his eyes. When he spoke, his voice was flat, toneless.

"There's a . . . Uncle Rob said there was a cellular phone in the . . . in the camper."

"Go get it! Get it and call the police. Hurry!"

At last, her voice seemed to get through to him. He dropped the gun onto the floor, stood up slowly, and walked to the back door. Angie jumped when she heard the door slam shut behind him.

Moving slowly, Angie shifted Brandy off her lap and lowered her gently to the floor. With the knife still clutched in her right hand, she crawled across the floor to Greg, who lay motionless on his back. Coming up close to him, Angie took several raspy breaths as she studied him, trying to determine if he was alive or dead. His eyes started twitching and shifting spastically beneath his eyelids.

"You lousy *bastard!*" Angie murmured as rage boiled up inside her. She could feel the strength seeping out of her, but she wanted to make sure—she *had* to make sure. If Greg was going to die, she wanted the last thing he ever heard to be her cursing him.

"I hope you rot in hell, you piece of human shit!" she said in a raw, scratchy voice.

Angie jumped when Greg's body suddenly stiffened, and his eyes snapped open. For a timeless, frozen instant, their gazes met; then Greg thrust his head violently back and started to scream.

"They're waiting for me!"

His voice twisted up so high it almost broke, but he kept on yelling.

"Jesus God Help me! Help me! They're all there! All of them! And they're waiting for me!"

His voice choked off with a strangled gasp, but his eyes were still wide open and staring into Angie's eyes. Gripping the handle of the knife tightly with both hands, Angie raised it high above her head and then, with a savage grunt, brought it down toward his chest with all her might.

"They can *have* you!" she screamed, and that was the last thing she heard before she slipped into the blessed relief of unconsciousness.

Epilogue
Year's End

It was the last week of November. The sky was shifting with low, fast-moving clouds that were the color of stove soot, and a needle-fine rain was falling as Angie pulled into the Riverside Cemetery and parked her car along the side of the narrow paved road. The windshield wipers slapped noisily back and forth. For a long time, that was the only sound in the car.

"Do you want us to wait here?" Angie finally asked, glancing at Brandy in the rearview mirror.

Brandy looked much thinner than she ever had. Her face was pale and drawn. Even after all these months, her eyes still held the same frightened, haunted look Angie had first seen in them that horrible day at her brother's camp last spring, when Brandy had realized that Evan really was dead.

JJ was sitting in the back seat next to Brandy. Like her, he had been seeing a therapist twice a week since May, but he didn't look anywhere near as shell-shocked as his sister. Angie attributed it to the resilience of his youth that he had rebounded so well from the terrible experience of shooting and killing a person. Between them sat Wolfgang, breathing heavily with his tongue lolling out. The cast had been removed from his leg months ago, and he was growing fast.

In the front seat next to Angie sat Rob. He still bore a long, pink scar down the side of his face from where Greg had clubbed him with the baseball bat. Ever since the death of his lover, Rob had become much quieter and introspective. Angie didn't like this change in her brother. She prayed every night that he would eventually get back to his old self, but she wasn't convinced that was possible after everything they had been through.

"You can come . . . if you want to," Brandy said, her voice flat and not much more than a whisper.

Angie turned off the engine. Before opening the door, she zipped her raincoat all the way up and pulled the hood over her head. Even the slight motion of swinging her legs out the car door hurt terribly. She sucked her breath in sharply and grimaced, telling herself not to let the pain show. The gunshot wound to her leg had long since healed, and she'd completed several months of physical therapy, but her legs felt shaky as she stood up and leaned on her cane for support.

"I'll wait here, if you don't mind," JJ said. "I don't feel like getting all wet."

Angie felt a faint spark of hope when she saw Brandy glare angrily at her brother, looking like she wanted to slug him for saying something like that. Maybe . . . just maybe things were slowly getting back to normal, she thought with a bittersweet tug at her heart.

The drizzle was steady. This late in the fall, the leaves had long since been stripped from the trees. The bare branches looked like tangles of nerves against the gray tissue of the sky.

Huddling close, the three of them—Brandy, Angie, and Rob—started slowly across the yellowing grass. For some reason, Angie remembered that winter day so long ago when the three of them had first checked out their house on Taylor Hill Road. Tears filled her eyes as she glanced at her daughter. Brandy was clutching a small bouquet of red flowers in one hand. Her face was almost lost inside the shadowing hood of her raincoat. Angie limped along beside her. With every other step, the tip of her cane sank into the rain-soaked earth and pulled out with a loud sucking sound.

Nobody said a word. There was nothing to say . . . nothing that hadn't already been said hundreds of times before.

The wind sighed in fitful gusts through the tree branches. Bursts of rain washed the rows of gravestones, making the polished pink and gray granite blocks glisten like quicksilver. It didn't take long for the chill to reach through Angie's raincoat and make her shiver. Her eyes were stinging, but she told herself it was from the rain, not from crying. It had been almost a year now since John had died, and in that time, she had cried too many times for too many people . . . for both the dead— John, Craig, and Evan; and for the survivors—herself, her brother, and her children. All of them had suffered—were *still* suffering—because of one man—Greg Newman.

Angie and Rob stopped a short distance from the grave and let Brandy walk up to it to lean her flowers against the rain-slick stone. The birth and death dates were half-obscured by the flowers, but Angie could clearly read the freshly carved name: EVAN MCDOWELL.

Sobbing deeply, Brandy dropped to her knees, heedless of the wet ground. Folding her hands in her lap, she slumped forward. Her shoulders shook uncontrollably as she bowed her head. Other than the gentle hiss of rain on the grass, the sound of her sobbing was the only sound.

For a long time, they waited in silence, as they had done so many times over the past several months. Finally, Brandy stood up, wiped at the wet spots on her knees, and turned to face her mother and uncle.

"Thanks for coming," she said, her voice breaking with strained emotion.

Angie nodded but said nothing. There was nothing to say . . . nothing she *could* say.

Together, they turned and, supporting each other, walked slowly back to the car. Angie held Brandy's hand tightly, and Rob had his arm around Angie's waist.

Seeing her daughter shattered like this filled Angie's heart with a cold, lonely ache. She knew that there was little if anything she could say or do to help Brandy, other than to support her and show how much she loved her. That was the key—to let her know that she loved her more than anything in the world, and that she understood the depth of her grief . . . perhaps better than Brandy realized.

But Angie also recognized how important it was for Brandy to find expression for her grief. All she hoped to accomplish by bringing her out here like this was that—eventually—it would help her cope with and get past the loss she was feeling so deeply. Angie suspected that a lot more than Evan's death was bothering her. This most recent loss had opened Brandy's still unhealed wounds of losing her father. Angie was seriously concerned that her daughter would carry deep psychological scars for the rest of her life.

As they walked back to the car, Angie couldn't help but think of another grave on a low, forested hill in Ashland Cemetery, in Bedford Heights, New York. That grave stood lonely and unattended except for the three times last summer when she had driven down to New York to place a fresh bouquet on it. All three times, she had remained at John's grave, lost in her grief until the sun went down, and the cemetery gates were closed and locked.

"Thanks . . . I really appreciate it, Mom," Brandy said before ducking into the back seat. She closed the door and turned to look out the side window. JJ said nothing.

Angie nodded silently, but before she got into the car, she glanced over the car roof at her brother.

"I'll be right back," she said in a dry, hoarse voice.

Rob started to say something, then caught himself and nodded to her before getting back into the car.

Angie's teeth were chattering as she started up the road until she came to a bend by a stand of maple trees. Rain and tears were running down her face as she looked out across the silent rows of tombstones. Fitful gusts of wind plastered wet leaves against the gravestone and whipped the bare branches overhead.

She had been here before, so she knew exactly where to go.

Against her will—or in spite of it—she took a deep breath and started across the soggy ground to the small, plain marker that read GREG NEWMAN. As she drew closer to it, a cold, unrelenting pressure clutched her heart.

There were no flowers on this grave, and while that should have made her happy, a terrible wave of sadness washed over her. Tension twisted like a ball of thin wire in her chest when she glanced over her shoulder, back at her family in the distance, waiting for her in the car. It took immense effort, but she turned and looked at the tombstone again.

"You rotten bastard," she whispered.

The steam of her breath in the cold air was quickly swept away by the wind. The stinging in her eyes got steadily worse as she focused on the name so intently her vision began to blur.

"If only . . . If only you knew—"

Her voice caught with a sharp jab. Shaking her head and gritting her teeth, she tried to control the sudden flood of emotion that swept through her. She shuddered when she tried to imagine all the people she had loved—her husband and her parents most of all—their bodies cold and alone in that silent, impenetrable darkness of the grave. Sorrow cut through her, making her feel suddenly weak and defeated and so alone.

"If only you realized the . . . the misery you caused us," she whispered.

A sudden gust of wind blew cold rain into her face, and she wiped it and her tears away with the back of her hand.

"But I promise you one thing," she said, her voice hitching on nearly every word. "No, two things . . . First, I promise that I will never come out here to your grave again."

She tried to take another deep breath, but the feeling that her chest was restricted by thick iron bands wouldn't go away.

"And second, I promise that—that I will never, *never* forgive you for what you did to us—to *all* of us!"

She cleared her throat roughly, then spat onto the headstone, watching as the rain washed away the thin glob of spittle. Squaring her shoulders, she turned and walked away, heading back to her family and the life that she knew they would—somehow—have to make for themselves. She was trembling as she got into the car, having to move slowly because of the stiffness in her leg. It always seemed worse in bad weather.

"You okay, Mom?" Brandy asked softly from the back seat.

The sound of her voice nearly broke Angie's heart.

"Yeah, hon . . . I'm okay," she said throatily. "I love you, honey."

"Love you too, Mom."

She reached into the back seat and took hold of Brandy's hand, giving it a tight, almost desperate squeeze. Something that bothered her was acknowledging that she and her family still had that single ingredient that was the one thing Greg Newman had been missing from his life.

Love.

Not having that, she thought, was what had turned him into the monster he had become.

A wave of dizziness swept over her as she started up the car and drove away from the cemetery. She sniffed and rubbed her eyes, but there was no stopping the flood of tears. Worst of all was knowing, deep in her heart, that she was crying as much for Greg Newman as she was for herself.

"Even the wicked get worse than they deserve."
—W. Cather

**ORDINARY LIVES DESTROYED BY EXTRAORDINARY HORROR.
FACTS MORE DANGEROUS THAN FICTION.
CAPTURE A PINNACLE TRUE CRIME . . . IF YOU DARE.**

LITTLE GIRL LOST (593, $4.99)
By Joan Merriam

When Anna Brackett, an elderly woman living alone, allowed two teenage girls into her home, she never realized that a brutal death awaited her. Within an hour, Mrs. Brackett would be savagely stabbed twenty-eight times. Her executioners were Shirley Katherine Wolf, 14, and Cindy Lee Collier, 15. *Little Girl Lost* examines how two adolescents were driven through neglect and sexual abuse to commit the ultimate crime.

HUSH, LITTLE BABY (541, $4.99)
By Jim Carrier

Darci Kayleen Pierce seemed to be the kind of woman you stand next to in the grocery store. However, Darci was obsessed with the need to be a mother. She desperately wanted a baby—any baby. On a summer day, Darci kidnapped a nine-month pregnant woman, strangled her, and performed a makeshift Cesarean section with a car key. In this arresting account, readers will learn how Pierce's tortured fantasy of motherhood spiralled into a bloody reality.

IN A FATHER'S RAGE (547, $4.99)
By Raymond Van Over

Dr. Kanneth Z. Taylor promised his third wife Teresa that he would mend his drug-addictive, violent ways. His vow didn't last. He nearly beat his bride to death on their honeymoon. This nuptial nightmare worsened until Taylor killed Teresa after allegedly catching her sexually abusing their infant son. Claiming to have been driven beyond a father's rage, Taylor was still found guilty of first degree murder. This gripping page-turner reveals how a marriage made in heaven can become a living hell.

I KNOW MY FIRST NAME IS STEVEN (563, $4.99)
By Mike Echols

A TV movie was based on this terrifying tale of abduction, child molesting, and brainwashing. Yet, a ray of hope shines through this evil swamp for Steven Stayner escaped from his captor and testified against the socially disturbed Kenneth Eugene Parnell. For seven years, Steven was shuttled across California under the assumed name of "Dennis Parnell." Despite the humiliations and degradations, Steven never lost sight of his origins or his courage.

RITES OF BURIAL (611, $4.99)
By Tom Jackman and Troy Cole

Many pundits believe that the atrocious murders and dismemberments performed by Robert Berdella may have inspired Jeffrey Dahmer. Berdella stalked and savagely tortured young men; sadistically photographing their suffering and ritualistically preserving totems from their deaths. Upon his arrest, police uncovered human skulls, envelopes of teeth, and a partially decomposed human head. This shocking expose is written by two men who worked daily on this case.

Available wherever paperbacks are sold, or order direct from the Publisher. Send cover price plus 50¢ per copy for mailing and handling to Penguin USA, P.O. Box 999, c/o Dept. 17109, Bergenfield, NJ 07621. Residents of New York and Tennessee must include sales tax. DO NOT SEND CASH.